Where I Stand

M.J. Piazza

DEDICATION

To everyone who's made it to adulthood without going on a date. Accept my long-distance high-five and know you're in good company.

CONTENTS

While I stare in hope at the ocean,
My gaze set on water and stone,
I see naught but waves set in motion,
No person, for I am alone.

Speak, flaming sunset! O, what have you seen?
What visions to you have been shown?
Tell me the fate of the one who has been,
The person who left me alone.

Nothing tonight meets my vision,
The wind and the rain walk me home.
Tomorrow I'll repeat my mission,
With hope that I won't be alone.

ONE

"What are you doing here, old man?"

Lukas McCamden met the sailor's gaze calmly. The pier rocked beneath them, the wind trying to push them into the choppy waters below. The steady rain danced on the ocean, sending dimples running across the crest of every wave. The noise was amplified as a gust of wind blew the raindrops diagonally.

"I'm here to meet the ship," Lukas said.

"How'd you know we was coming?"

Lukas was steady. "I've my ways. I'd like to speak wi' Sigmund."

The sailor snorted. "Get off the pier, and he'll meet you. We've got enough landlubbers about. You're insufferable."

Lukas returned the sailor's sentiments. The pier creaked beneath his boots as he made his way back to dry land, cautious not to slip on the rain-dampened wood. The rain had soaked through his cowl, scapular, and tunic; even his undershift stuck to his wet shoulders. The wind set a sharp ache in every bone he'd ever fractured. He wished for his cloak.

The ship was finally secured against the pier, and Lukas watched a young man as he ran, blond head ducked to the rain, towards dry land. He stumbled on the slick wood but caught

1

himself before he fell. He brushed hair out of his eyes with his left hand, a hand fashioned from wood.

"Sigmund!"

The young man's head jerked up. "Lukas!" he exclaimed, running up to him and shaking his hand. "You'll not believe all the Lord's done in Hrafney!"

"The missionary trip went well, I take it?" Lukas asked.

"The chief himself was converted," Sigmund said. "Seventy-eight salvations in total."

"Seventy-eight?" Lukas repeated. Sigmund nodded, shivering as the wind blew through his slight frame, and Lukas wished again for his cloak. "God be praised, that's good news! Now suppose we get out of the weather."

Sigmund led him down the wood-paved street, every bit as slippery as the pier. He went not to his father's house—after abandoning his pagan faith and marrying against his father's wishes, he was no longer welcome there—but to the tailor's small, well-kept home near the center of town. "Of course. Remind me, though, I've got to tell you about a Scottish captain I met. He said he was a friend of Alynn's father."

Lukas glanced at Sigmund. He obviously didn't know the magnitude of what he'd just said. He was glad instead to be on dry ground, anxious to see his wife and son for the first time in five weeks. "A Scotsman?" Lukas repeated.

"Judging by his accent, which doesn't mean much. But he mentioned Alynn by name. Seemed rather concerned about the matter." Sigmund once again ducked his head to the wind and quickened his pace. "Hrafney is sending a young man to study for the pastorate. I assumed you wouldn't mind training him."

"Not at all. I'll be glad to meet him. What's his name?"

"They haven't decided who they're sending. It's either going to be the chief's cousin or future brother-in-law." Sigmund nearly ran the last four steps to the tailor's house and rushed inside. Lukas heard the glad cries that only arise when a traveler is welcomed home—the shouting of names and the clapping of hands, the tears of a young wife who had never been apart from her husband before. The excited squeals of eight-month-old Matthew as he greeted his father. It overpowered the din of the rain and the occasional clap of thunder.

And Lukas stayed outside, recalling the tales he'd been told of a Scottish sea captain, a friend of Alynn's father.

"Alynn! Come inside, child! You're crazy!"

A sixteen-year-old girl spun circles in the midsummer afternoon's rain. "Mum, can't you see the rainbow?" she asked, laughing as the raindrops tickled her neck. "'Tis out above the ocean! I wonder who's to find the pot of gold!"

The girl's mother, Caitriona, sighed helplessly from the doorway of St. Anne's Monastery. "You'll catch yer death of cold. Come inside."

Alynn filled her chest with fresh, damp air. "'Tis rain worse than this I've been out in, and I don't think I've died yet," she said. Laughing, she flew through the yard and took her mother's hand. "Come see the rainbow!"

"What—Lynder—"

"Come on!"

Clutching her skirts, Caitriona ran into the yard with her head ducked against the rain. Alynn smiled. She knew that her mother, somewhere deep within her, had a free spirit. It shone through her shamrock-green eyes and her smile as she looked up at the heavens.

Suddenly, Alynn slipped on a patch of mud. Her shoulder blade hit something wooden, and she landed hard. She looked up—she was sprawled in the vegetable garden, propped up against the pea trellis. Helpless with laughter, Alynn glanced up at Caitriona to find her laughing, too.

"Not the peas again, Lynder!" she exclaimed before tripping over a tussock and landing in a puddle. She looked at her ruined dress, then at Alynn, and laughed even harder.

Alynn beamed. She gazed at the heavens to see the rainbow,

glowing like a smile from God. Truly, He was smiling—restoring in a moment of time the years that had been stolen from her childhood. Even Caitriona, her dripping golden hair hanging nearly to her knees, had returned as the mother Alynn remembered.

Caitriona helped Alynn to her feet and pulled her into a hug, whispering a "thank you" as she fingered Alynn's strawberry-blonde tresses. Alynn smiled.

"I missed you, Mum."

"Beautiful girl, I missed you, too."

Even though it had been over two years since she and Caitriona had been reunited, there were times when Alynn still couldn't believe it. The moments were rare when Caitriona was exactly as she had been before the Vikings took her, but when she was, Alynn was eight years old again.

Caitriona gave her a squeeze, then took her hand and led her back to the monastery. "Let's get you dried off."

She led her through an arched doorway, then the kitchen that was designed to feed a hundred monks. Alynn passed rows of unlit cooking fires on her way to the hearth. She spun before the fireplace, letting her blue dress drip-dry on the stone floor.

Caitriona snatched a rag and made Alynn stand on it. "Don't slip," she said. "Did you finish lengthening yer Sabbath dress?"

"Almost."

Caitriona sighed, toweling her hair dry. "Child...."

"I've my plain dress."

"It needs mended."

"'Tis still a dress."

Caitriona handed Alynn her towel. "Hurry and change, then put some bread in the oven. I've half a day's worth of carding to do."

The back door opened, and hurried footsteps sounded throughout the building. Alynn smiled as a brown-clad monk rounded the corner, praying under his breath and forgetting to shut the door. "Good evening, Lukas," Caitriona said.

The monk pushed back the hood of his cowl to reveal a halo of cropped white hair. "Evening," he murmured, hurrying past with hardly more than a glance. He and his Latin musings disappeared up the stairwell.

"You don't have time for a hug?" Alynn called up after him. "Lukas?"

"Don't pester him, Lynder, his mind's on the things of God," Caitriona said. "Knowing him, he's probably half-starved, too. Change yer clothes, will you? You'll catch cold."

Alynn stared up at the stairwell. She couldn't remember all the times she'd watched Lukas's mind drift back to earth after a round of silent prayers. It was as if life sprang back into his clear blue eyes, a silent gleam hiding in their depths. When she couldn't pry a smile out of them, something was wrong.

It was nearly an hour before footsteps once again sounded down the stairs, but this time, they were unrushed and placid. Lukas peered at the boiling salt cod, stole a leaf from the watercress salad, and left to draw some water from the well. "Everything smells delicious," he said.

"Thank you." Alynn tried to fish the cod out of the kettle, but she splashed boiling water on the plain oat-colored dress she'd ripped during sword fighting practice earlier that day. She prayed Lukas wouldn't notice her leg peeping from the rip in the skirt.

"I'll get that," Caitriona said, taking the platter out of Alynn's hands. "Sit down before he comes back."

Alynn hid in a chair just as the back door opened and shut. She took the opportunity to heap her plate with *skyr*—a Norse cheese so soft it was eaten with a spoon. Lukas sat down and helped himself to the watercress.

"How was yer day, Lukas?" Alynn asked.

"Not bad," he said, which was the highest he spoke of anything. "Sigmund's returned from his missionary trip."

"He has?" Caitriona snatched a serving spoon from the cupboard. "How did it go?"

Lukas gave a halfway twitch of a smile, but he meant it with his eyes and his heart. "He said it was very much a success." He took Alynn's hand, waited for Caitriona to sit, and took hers. "Lord, we thank Ye fer this day, and the chance to spend it wi' friends and family. We thank Ye fer the miracles Ye wrought wi' Sigmund on Hrafney, and I pray that many others would come to see Yer light."

Alynn and Caitriona repeated the rest of the prayer with him— "Bless us, O Lord, and these, Yer gifts, we are about to receive, from Yer bounty, through Christ our Lord. Amen."

For a while, no one spoke. Caitriona's food was too delicious for that.

Finally, Alynn glanced up at Lukas. She couldn't tell if he was staring at her or past her, but she could see his mind working. "Alright, Lukas. What's on yer mind?" she asked.

Lukas half-smiled and took another bite of cod. "Sigmund had some wonderful stories to tell from Hrafney. Seventy-eight souls were brought to the saving knowledge of Christ. He even translated the epistle to the Romans into Norse fer them, and he's working on the Gospel of Matthew." Excitement shone from Lukas like light from a candle. "The Lord's doing a wonderful work there, just as He is here."

Caitriona smiled. "That's grand."

"Who's their pastor?" Alynn asked.

"They're sending a young man to study fer the pastorate," Lukas said. "He should be here afore the summer's out. But afore I forget, Alynn, Sigmund met someone who might be of interest to ye."

Alynn lowered her spoon. Lukas was staring at her with a solemn gaze that she couldn't help but return. Gravity settled in the air around them.

"Who was it?" she asked.

"The Scottish captain of a cargo ship," Lukas said, glancing at Caitriona to include her in their discussion. "He and Sigmund struck up a conversation, and the captain asked if he knew of a girl who was fifteen, perchance sixteen, and had fallen off a ship in the area two Septembers ago."

6

Alynn blanched. *She* had fallen off a ship two Septembers ago. She could still hear her little brother crying her name as she tripped over the ship's edge. She remembered the shock of the water, the pain of the cold that nearly killed her. Her father's hand reaching vainly for hers as it disappeared under the waves, never to rise again. She blinked and forced her memories aside. "The Scotsman—who is he? What's his name?"

"Tamlane McMahon, captain of the *Darting Swallow*."

Alynn let her spoon clatter onto her plate. "Tamlane McMahon," she repeated. "*Captain* Tamlane McMahon? Are you certain?"

"Aye, I'm certain."

Alynn drew in a shaking breath. The world was spinning.

"And his ship—the—" Caitriona drew a breath, as if she was afraid to speak what was on everyone's mind. "It survived the storm? And the passengers?"

"The ship's fine. Where its passengers are, I'm not sure, but Sigmund saw the *Darting Swallow* wi' his own eyes."

Caitriona blinked. "So if Tamlane...and the ship survived, then...Tarin...och, praise God!" She flew from her chair and rushed headlong out the back door.

Lukas stood. "Caitriona—!"

"I'm going to find my son!"

The door slammed shut, and it barely moved Alynn from her stupor. Tarin. Sweet, quiet, curious Tarin—he'd be ten now. How long had they been apart? And him alive all this time? Where was he? Was he safe? Was he warm and fed and loved, taken in by a church or a kind family? Oh, she hoped so! She prayed so!

She could do better than pray. She could find him.

Lukas set his hand over hers. "Are ye alright, my dear?"

Excitement grew within her, and she grinned. "Tarin's alive," she breathed before running after Caitriona.

Alynn was met with cold rain, as well as her mother on a high-strung horse. The saddle's girth was twisted and two holes too loose, and the seal-brown bay was making every effort to inform her oblivious rider.

Alynn grabbed the reins. "Mum, we ought to talk things out first!"

"What's there to talk about?" Caitriona demanded. She grasped the saddle as the mare reared, nearly throwing Alynn off her feet. "Yer brother's out there—"

"I know he is. Five minutes, Mum. We'll make a plan, we'll—"

"Leif will get us a ship," Caitriona insisted. "Do you remember where Captain McMahon was headed?"

"I don't!"

"Just get it as close as you can, Lynder. We'll find him, I promise."

Alynn closed her eyes. *It sounded like skyr,* she said to herself. *Skare...Skey....*"Skerray! Mum, 'tis Skerray! He's in Skerray!"

Caitriona spurred the mare on, ripping the reins out of Alynn's hands as she set off at a gallop toward the village on the northern shore.

And she had taken Alynn's horse.

Alynn stamped her foot before running into the stone-and-wood stable. Why, *why* did she have to be the adult in this situation? She ignored the cackling of chickens and bleating of sheep on her way to Lukas's stallion, Honor. She threw a blanket on Honor's snow-white back, then followed it with a saddle. As she tightened the girth, the stable door opened, and Lukas stepped in.

Alynn looked up at him, grabbing a bridle from its hook on the wall. "Are you coming with?" she asked.

Lukas met her gaze. "To the village?"

Alynn nodded.

"Not at this hour." Lukas shut the door and took off his hood. "I doubt ye'll be coming back until morning."

"Probably not. Do you want to come with us to Scotland? You'd love Tarin—you love everyone, but he's special—and I know you don't like being left alone—"

"Calm down, Alynn," Lukas said. The sound of his voice, with his Highland brogue and his comforting tone, brought almost as much sanity into the situation as the words he spoke. "Don't give a thought to me, I'll take care of myself fer as long as it takes to find him. Just worry about helping yer mother. I was wondering if ye'd like to finish eating afore ye leave."

Alynn smiled, putting the bridle over Honor's head. "Thank you, Lukas, but I'm too excited. Faith, I wish Mum wouldn't run off like that...."

"Does yer brother take after her?"

"Hardly." Alynn turned, as if Lukas could see the lump in her throat. "He was—curious, sweet as honey, built like a freckled, redheaded fence rail. I always imagined that he'd grow up to be—quite a bit like you, actually. But—with hair."

Lukas and Tarin didn't look a thing alike, Alynn realized. Lukas had no freckles, his hair had probably never been red, and he tanned every summer from working in the fields. But he still half-smiled at the comparison. "I'll take most of that as a compliment," he said.

Alynn smiled, kissed him goodbye, and disappeared on Honor's back into the darkening forest.

Just as the sun's dying afterglow disappeared into the clouded dark of night, Alynn and Honor cantered into a small Norse village. Alynn realized how tired she was. Summer days were long, sometimes with eighteen chore-filled hours of daylight. She yawned as she followed the wood-paved main road to a large longhouse in the center of town. Alynn tethered Honor to a hitching-post and knocked.

No one answered. Alynn could hear her mother's voice and the crisp Norse accent that belonged to her uncle Leif, but she couldn't make out what they were saying. She knocked louder.

"...stay awake, son, we need your help," Leif's voice was saying as the hired girl opened the door. Alynn hugged her quickly, and Leif finally caught eye of the visitor. "Alynn!" he boomed, finding a tired smile within him. "Come inside, have a seat! Try to keep Drostan awake while you're at it."

Alynn hugged Leif and glanced at his seventeen-year-old son, Drostan. He was sitting on the edge of a sleeping bench, leaning against a column that supported the roof, idly moving the pieces to a board game. *Tafl*, he'd said she could call it, since its true name of *hnefatafl* was too large of a mouthful for her. His hair looked like a rat had tried to nest in it.

Alynn smiled. "Hard day?"

Moving his head half an inch in her direction, Drostan shoved the game board aside so she could sit next to him. "Felling trees and carting timber, all day," he groaned, his eyes glassy with sleep. "What have you been doing since I last saw you this afternoon?"

"I found out my brother's alive." Alynn slipped her fingers under Drostan's warm hand, realizing how cold her own was.

"Good Lord, your hands are like ice!" Drostan exclaimed.

"I know. The wind doesn't realize 'tis June."

A bit of life came into Drostan's eyes, and he took a sheepskin from the bed behind them. He draped it around Alynn. His arm rested on her thin shoulder, his leather vambrace cool as she leaned against it.

"Thank you," she said.

"For goodness' sake, ye're sittin' too close together," Caitriona scolded. She pulled Alynn two feet away from Drostan and wrapped the sheepskin tighter around her. "Try to stay awake. Ye can poke each other if ye start to nod off."

"Aye, Mum," both Alynn and Drostan said.

"Now, for the last time, Drostan, do you have a ship we could use?"

"We're working on one right now—lovely Karve, if you can wait a week to use her," Drostan said, brushing his red hair from his eyes. "We just sold our last Longship. It would be fastest. You could make the trip in a lifeboat if the currents were right."

"When are we leaving?" Alynn asked.

"We're not sure at the moment," Caitriona said. "The winds are contrary, or some such nonsense—"

"The winds are perfect if you're traveling to Iceland," Leif interrupted.

"What about rowing?" Alynn asked.

"If you feel like taking five days instead of two to get to Scotland, then I suppose it's doable," Drostan said. He stabbed Alynn with his index finger.

"What?"

"Your mother said I could poke you."

Alynn shoved his shoulder. "Save it for mornin'. I'm knackered."

Caitriona studied the flames of the fireplace. "Are there men who would row for money?" she asked. "It isn't gold, but—Rowan would want me to—" She tugged at a goldtone ring that was reluctant to come off her left hand. Voice trembling, she asked, "How much is this worth?"

"Mistress, don't do anything daft—that you'll regret, I mean," the hired girl interjected. She blushed and bowed her head. "My apologies."

"Not at all. You're right, Valdis," Leif said, fingering the simple ring on his own hand. "Not your wedding band, Caitriona. I wouldn't give mine up, either, not for the world, and certainly not to save a few days' waiting time. The winds will change soon enough. I promise. And I'll pay the sailors."

"You're a good man, Leif."

Leif chuckled. "It's what brothers do—at least in a functional family. Valdis, you had a normal family once, didn't you?"

The hired girl's blonde head dipped again. "Depends on what you'd call normal, sir."

Leif laughed. "You couldn't find a man to row anyway, not with Althing coming up. We're hosting this year."

Caitriona muttered something under her breath—whether it was a prayer or a profanity Alynn couldn't tell, but the latter was unlikely. She kicked at the rushes that covered the dirt floor, then took a breath and collected herself. "Can we plan on leavin' the moment Althing ends?"

"As soon as possible. I promise."

"Perfect. Now give me somethin' to do before I go mad with worry."

"I might have you stay here for the week, act as hostess if you're willing," Leif said. "And say a prayer. Neither Drostan nor I are officially going to be the chief of this island until one of us sacrifices to Odin—unless something changes. And blast it, we need something to change."

"We'll be prayin'," Caitriona promised.

"Isn't Althing rather powerful for a meetin' of tribes?" Alynn asked.

"It's a parliament, not just a meeting, so it demands power," Leif said. "I'm surprised they haven't killed us for converting to Christianity."

"They wouldn't have done anything after the Battle of Faith," Drostan insisted. "Alynn would have disbanded Althing singlehandedly."

Alynn blushed. She considered punching Drostan's shoulder, but finally decided to lean against him and close her eyes. "You'd have helped me, just as you did on the battlefield," she said.

"You don't need help," Drostan insisted. "You're a berserker, for Thor's sake. Or do Irish girls tend to fight fiercer than Norse madmen?"

"Drostan, don't even *think* that she's a berserker, and Alynn, sit up," Caitriona ordered. Alynn sighed and straightened, but not without a caustic glance at her mother. Caitriona returned it.

"Master Leif, will you be needing anything else this evening?" Valdis asked. She was combing her hair that barely passed her shoulders—hardly longer than Leif's or Drostan's.

"No, thank you. Go on to bed," Leif said. "Cait, we can think more in the morning. I'm exhausted."

Caitriona laughed. "I can't believe I'm still standin' up. Where can I sleep?"

Leif gestured to the wide benches that lined either side of

the longhouse. "Pick a bed, any bed. Or the closet, whichever you prefer."

"I've always hated that closet."

Drostan nodded towards the bedcloset—a section of bench with walls around it, making it darker and warmer and much cozier than the rest of the beds in the longhouse. "Do you want the closet, Alynn, or would you rather I take it?"

"I'll take it. It doesn't bother me."

"Don't forget to lock the latch," Caitriona cautioned.

Drostan snatched a few sheepskins and a blanket and tossed them into the closet. "Have a good night, milady."

After glancing up to see his smile, Alynn returned the gentle embrace he offered. She buried her face in his tunic. Drostan pressed her head against his chest, and she could hear his heartbeat. He smelled of wood and sea and hard work, stained with a medley of scents from the midsummer forest. She smiled.

Thank You, Lord, for Drostan.

He kissed her forehead before leaving for the bed he shared with his father. "I'll see you tomorrow, then," he said, raking his hand through his hair and making it even wilder than before.

Alynn smiled. "Goodnight, love."

Alynn crawled awkwardly into the bedcloset and rearranged the sheepskins before she shut and latched the door. In the complete absence of light, the only sounds those of her family readying for bed, Alynn found a call to pray.

"Be with Tarin, Lord, if he's not with You and Father already," she murmured before drifting to sleep. "And if he is...please tell him I said hello."

TWO

Alynn was awakened by the smell of griddle cakes and the sound of voices drifting through the cracks in the closet wall. "Don't worry, Valdis, 'tis a life's worth of practice you need to get it right," Caitriona was saying. "Use more sour milk. It makes everything better, and use more lard to grease the pan."

Valdis's voice came from the fireplace—so near to the door that Alynn was afraid she'd hit her with the door if she tried to open it. "So, do you use half sour, half sweet, or—"

"You don't—not quite. Use two parts fresh milk, one part sour, and throw in some buttermilk if you have any," Caitriona corrected.

Alynn pulled her dress on over her undershift, then groped around for the latch. She heard Drostan's voice ask, "How many ways are there to drink milk?"

"Twenty, at least."

Alynn's hand found the latch, and she tumbled out the bedcloset door and onto the dirt floor. Even Valdis laughed at her.

"Are you alright, Alynn?" Caitriona asked, hiding her smile behind one hand and helping her up with the other. Alynn glared at Drostan, who was doubled over with laughter, and nodded.

"I'm grand," she said. "What can I do to help with breakfast?"

Laughing, Caitriona hugged Alynn. "Set the table, if you've a mind to. Try to stay out of trouble, dear heart. You'll be the death of me someday."

"Please stop saying that," Alynn said. "I don't want it to come true."

Caitriona smiled and picked up a bowl of batter. "Sure, it won't. Wash this, will you?"

"I will, Mum—oh, blast it! Today's washin' day, isn't it?"

"All day, Mistress," Valdis agreed, flipping a griddle cake. "If you're staying, perchance you could lend me a hand."

Alynn sighed, taking four plates from the cupboard and placing them on the table Leif had brought down from the rafters. "I'd love to, Valdis, but 'tis my own washin' I have to do, and I won't be staying for breakfast."

"Aye, you will be," Caitriona insisted.

Alynn grabbed a wedge of cheese from the pantry and took a bite. "Don't worry, I'll eat."

"Off so soon?" Drostan asked. "Yesterday, you mentioned wanting extra sword fighting practice."

Alynn shoved her foot into a boot. "I don't have time today. Knowin' Mum, we'll be back soon. Where's Uncle Leif?"

Drostan shrugged. "Getting water."

Alynn kissed Drostan's cheek. "Tell him I said goodbye." She roughly donned her second boot as she hopped to a door at the east wall of the longhouse.

The door opened into the stable, and Alynn was quickly greeted by whinnies and clucks and bleats. She quickly found her mare, a white star on her forehead and gentle freedom in her eyes.

"I missed you," the mare seemed to say.

Alynn stroked the mare's soft nose and kissed it before putting a bridle over her head. "I know, Humility. I missed you, too. 'Tis a long day we have, so let's get started. Did Mum bring yer saddlebags?"

The mare snorted, as if to ask, "Do I go *anywhere* without my saddlebags?"

Alynn smiled. She set the saddle on Humility's back, then reached into the saddlebag that was always tied to it. Her fingers brushed against a burlap sack that was full of oats, and she added her piece of cheese to a pile of small wedges that were tied up in a handkerchief.

Just as Alynn pulled the last strap on Humility's bridle, the stable door creaked open. Drostan came in, raking his fingers through his hair and deciding it looked good enough. As far as Alynn was concerned, it did—flames of bright ginger red that nearly hid his eyes and brushed against his shoulders. "I hoped you'd be staying longer," he said. "I was looking forward to spending the morning with you."

Alynn smiled. "I wish I could stay, but the clothes won't wash themselves."

Drostan took Humility's reins from Alynn and tied them around a post. "You can stay for a proper breakfast," he insisted.

"I got cheese."

"Cheese is not a meal. I've seen typhoid survivors that aren't as thin as you are. Come inside for some griddle cakes."

"I'm grand. You, on the other hand, have circles under yer eyes, which either means you didn't sleep well or you're fallin' sick."

Drostan wasn't sick; Alynn could tell that much by looking at him. But he sighed, and his shoulders drooped, which meant he was thinking of going back to sleep. "Are all girls like this, or—"

"What's wrong, love?"

"Nothing. I just had a bad dream."

"About what?"

"Althing."

Alynn wrapped her arms around Drostan's chest, and she could hear his heart racing. "Drostan, 'tis only a—"

"No, no, it's not," Drostan insisted. "It's not 'only'

anything. Remember Gythia, the tribe we drove off the island so we could live here? Their chief is going to be here. The chief of Eitravik is coming, and they hate us for being Christians. Half of Darsidia is going to be here, and they hate everyone in general. And Father wants me to conduct part of the opening ceremony! I can't talk in front of people!"

Alynn took Drostan's sweating hands in hers and began to work the stress out of them, running his strong fingers through her own. "You'll be a grand public speaker. When the time comes, you'll be a grand chief. I know you will."

Drostan broke away and paced a few steps. "I wish it were as simple as that...I'd decide what I wanted to be, and I *would* be....I hate myself fer getting so worked up about it. It shouldn't be this big of a deal."

He sat on a hay bale, and Alynn sat next to him. "Drostan, you'll be alright," she promised. "You need to pray. You need to take authority over the enemy! 'Tis Satan who's tryin' to make you afraid. You can't let him."

"What do I say?"

Alynn smiled. "You know how you talk to God like He's right in the room with you? Talk to Satan the same way. Tell him to leave you alone and not come back. Mean it when you say it. Pray in Jesus' name. Try it!"

Drostan crossed his arms. "Satan, go back to hell, stop bothering me, and take this fear with you! In Jesus' name, amen!"

Alynn smiled. "Amen."

"Thank you, Lynder." His hand was steady as it slid next to hers, his fingers gently caressing her work-worn palm. "Now, would you mind giving me a hand with my speech?"

"I'd love to."

Drostan grinned, pulling a piece of paper out of his pocket and handing it to Alynn. He leapt onto a milking stool and gave an over-exaggerated bow. "On behalf of the Tribe of Diaparn," he began, "I welcome you to the...thirty-fifth or thirty-sixth?"

Alynn unfolded the paper to see a written copy of Drostan's speech. "Thirty-sixth, and you forgot to name the island. You're fine. Keep going."

Drostan stood a bit more rigidly on the stool. "On behalf of the Tribe of Diaparn *of St. Anne's Cleft,* I welcome you to the thirty-sixth annual meeting of Althing. We...I ask...hang it all, I've forgotten."

Alynn made up some exaggerated hand signals to go with her next words. "For *decades,* The *Seven* Tribes of *Orkney*...." she encouraged.

Drostan balanced carefully on one foot. "On behalf of the Tribe of Diaparn, I wel—blast it. *On-behalf-of-the-Tribe-of-Diaparn-of-St.-Anne's-Cleft* I welcome you to the thirty-sixth annual meeting of Althing! For decades, the Seven Tribes of Orkney have...Alynn, is it 'met' or 'convened'?"

"Em, 'met.'"

"In which case, we've met peaceably, with honest hearts and open minds to discuss matters...matters of...."

"Justice."

"To discuss matters of justice and inter-tribal interest. It is my prayer that this week's meeting may proceed in...justice? Respect?"

"Peace and honor."

"This week's meeting may proceed in peace and honor, as have many before it, and that all argu—*disputes*—may reach a reasonable and respectable end. And to...don't tell me—ask, request....And to invoke the blessings of God on this meeting, I ask the priest to lead us in prayer." Drostan bowed again, a bit more subdued this time, and leapt off his milking stood.

Alynn applauded. "You did wonderfully, Drostan. You just need to memorize it a wee bit more—"

"I've been working on it for five days."

"Memorization takes *time,* don't worry about it," Alynn said. "You're going to do wonderfully."

Drostan smiled. "Could you do me a favor, Lynder, and be there when I give the speech? Somewhere in front, if you can manage, where I can see you."

"I'll be there, I promise."

"Thank you." Drostan's arms slipped around her, fingers brushing through her waves and curls of rose gold. Alynn smiled. Drostan's hugs were like a warm bath on a cold day, or a bowl of soup on an empty stomach—warm and comforting. She felt like she belonged there.

Suddenly, Alynn felt something soft on her face. She opened her eyes to see Humility nudging them apart, snorting impatiently. "Can we please go now?" she seemed to be asking.

Drostan laughed as deeply as the bell at the monastery. He squeezed Alynn once more and kissed her forehead. "I'll see you tomorrow," he said. "Godspeed."

The door nearly fell off its hinges as Alynn rapped on the door, and she made a mental note to bring nails on her next visit.

The house reminded Alynn of the many she'd lived in back in Ireland—always the ones with the cheapest rent and the draftiest walls. Weeds cropped around the door, as had many generations of weeds before them that had been fattened for the soup pot. Patches of sod had blown off the roof, and the walls were less wattle than daub.

Alynn heard approaching footsteps and shook herself. Quickly, she laid the sack of oats and the parcel of cheeses by the door and left.

Just as she was out of sight, the door creaked open, and Alynn turned to see the face of a nine-year-old girl. Her hair was the color of jute; her dress was threadbare and patched. Even from a distance, Alynn could see her eyes light up as she picked up the parcel of food. "Eyvind, our Guardian Angel's back!" she cried.

As always, the eldest child came out to search for her— eleven-year-old Eyvind. His gaze scanned the entire street, and

Alynn ducked behind the corner of the building. "Did you see anyone?" he asked.

"No."

For a moment, all was silent again. Finally, Eyvind shouted to the wind, "Thank you, Guardian Angel!" Alynn heard the door creak closed, and the joyous shouts of children as they ate their morning meal.

They deserved it—seven children, all cousins, who had lost their fathers when they had tried to raid the monastery. They weren't the only ones killed, but their deaths had the worst effects. The shock waves were still ripping out, even now that Eyvind was old enough to help his aunt and mother put food on the table. For where the other widows had brothers, nephews, and in-laws to help them, this family had no one.

Alynn swallowed the lump in her throat as she turned to leave.

The wooden pavement creaked beneath her feet, and she led Humility quickly. Shame gnawed at her soul. She should have done more. She should have given more, found a way to be of more help. She'd ruined the lives of seven innocent children, given them over to the hunger that she knew all too well, and she was powerless to do anything about it.

But she felt her stomach pinch with hunger, remembered that she'd given them all the food she'd see until seven that evening, and convinced herself that she couldn't have done anything more.

Perhaps she could convince her mother to help her do more. She remembered the gift her neighbors had given her once—a pot of stew and three loaves of bread. It had fed her and Tarin for three days, and maybe it was time for Alynn to return that gift. She still remembered the evening they'd spent together, even though she had been Eyvind's age when it happened. She could smell the stew's tantalizing odor, hear the laughter of the neighbor children and the songs her father played on his timpan. Alynn began to sing them as she led Humility down the street.

Dance by the River Shannon, my love,
Dance on the glistening streams.
Dance in the moonlight silent, my love,
Dance your way into my dreams.

And, without realizing it, she walked up to another door and rapped on it.

A squall rang out, and Alynn took one step backward.

"Maggie, it's hurting me!"

"If ye don't want it to hurt ye, don't pull on its tail, ye nitwit!"

The door opened, and Alynn was met with a toddler's deafening cry and a wave of water.

Dripping wet, Alynn forced a smile onto her face. She glanced at the girl who had opened the door and the now-empty bucket in her hand. "That's not a chamber pot, is it?" she asked.

"Alynn, what are ye doing here?" the girl exclaimed. She hugged Alynn like a too-tight corset. "Next time the monastery has kittens, please don't give us any. Slodi's evil enough without a henchman."

Alynn could feel her circulation being cut off. "Maggie—"

"Sorry." The girl stepped back, tucking a renegade curl behind her ear. "Anyway, what are ye doing here so early?"

"Mum's going to Scotland, and we're tryin' to get a ship."

"What's in Scotland?"

"My wee brother, perchance."

Maggie gasped, squeezing Alynn again. "Och, that's wonderful! Are ye bringing him here to live at the monastery? Is he Olvir's age or a bit aulder?"

"Maggie, I can't breathe—"

"When are ye leaving?"

"I don't know anything right now." Alynn wrung water out of her dress. "Please tell me this is dishwater."

"Aye, it is. Don't worry."

Alynn sighed with relief. "You're from Scotland. What do you remember about it?"

"I was five when we left, so not much. Mum could tell ye more." Maggie grabbed Alynn's wrist and pulled her through the door, shutting it behind them. "Mum, what can ye tell Alynn about Scotland?"

Maggie's mother, Nora McKenzie, had just finished putting the last of the dishes in the cupboard. "Don't leave without trying their food," she advised. "They serve haggis in heaven, I'm sure. And don't forget yer cloak and hood. It's a wee bit chilly, rains a lot, especially inland. What do ye need to know fer?"

Before Alynn could answer, a four-year-old boy ran up to her and hugged her leg, tears in his eyes. "Alynn, the cat bit me."

"Sure, and what did you do to it first?" Alynn asked. She lifted the boy into her arms and looked at his bleeding hand. "Did you pull its tail?"

The boy nodded.

"Slodi, you can't do that to cats. They don't like it," Alynn admonished. "How'd you like it if someone pulled yer hair, hmm? Go wash yer hand." The boy squirmed out of Alynn's arms and ran to the bucket of water near the back door.

The sight of him made Alynn's heart hurt, wishing Tarin was safe in her arms. "We probably won't be leavin' until after Althing, but Tarin's there, or at least we all hope he is, and I miss him—I'm worried for him—"

"Listen to me, lassie," Nora said, setting a hand on Alynn's arm. "The Lord looks after His own. Don't ye waste a worried thought on yer brother."

"Thank you, Miss Nora." Alynn hugged her and Maggie. "I have to go and wash clothes. I'll see ye at Mass tomorrow."

Maggie sighed. "Please don't leave me alone wi' Slodi...."

"You'll be fine, don't worry."

Maggie looked up at Alynn and forced a smile, a dimple in each freckled cheek. "I hope ye find yer brother, Alynn. I'll be praying for ye."

"Aye, we both will," Nora agreed.

Alynn slipped out the door with simple "Thanks," but she couldn't have meant it more.

"Lord, help Mum not to get her hopes up," Alynn prayed for the hundredth time as Humility slowed to a stop in the monastery's yard. Mud squished beneath her boots as they hit the ground, and Humility's coat was damp with sweat as she stroked it. "And if Tarin is alive, please help us find him without too much of a fuss. Help him be alright."

Alynn moved quickly as she unsaddled Humility, wiping off her lather and running a currycomb through her silky coat. "Wash the clothes, weed the garden, card some wool and sweep the kitchen," Alynn muttered to herself. She glanced around the stable and realized that it needed to be mucked. "And clean the stable before Lukas gets around to it."

A shrill squeal interrupted Alynn's thoughts, and she glanced at Humility's yearling filly, Patience. Patience looked more like a deer than a horse, and she was about as flighty as one. Lukas was having a hard time training her and forever contemplated selling her. But Alynn had promised her help.

Quickly and gently, she slipped a bridle over Patience's head and led her out into the yard. They walked together for a while, then Alynn stopped and Patience tried to keep walking. Alynn braced her arm for the inevitable jerk, tried to keep her balance, praised Patience when she listened and scolded her when she didn't, and repeated the process all the way through the yard.

After the third stop, Patience stamped her foot, and Alynn knew that her temperament was wearing thin. She pranced on her lead rope as she led her back to the stable. "Stop that," Alynn chided. "Can you be calm for once?"

Patience sneezed, as if to say, "No."

"You," Alynn said, putting Patience in her stall and grabbing a carrot from a nearby bin, "are the most stubborn eejit, man or beast, I've ever met." Patience refused the carrot

Alynn offered her, and Humility reached over from her stall to eat it instead.

Alynn glared at her mare before turning to leave.

"Lukas?" she shouted as she ran inside, shutting the cupboard door on her way towards the stairwell. "I'm home."

Alynn scanned the chapel as she passed the railing and, seeing no one, peeked through Lukas's half-open door. He was writing at his desk, intent on his work. Alynn knocked quickly. "Lukas, could I have yer laundry?"

Lukas jumped, but looked up with a half-smile. "I'm glad ye're back, Alynn," he said, standing up so that Alynn could hug him gently. Since she'd met him, he'd gained just enough weight to cover the gnarls in his ribs left over from fractures that had never knit right. She was still careful not to cause him any more pain than he already dealt with.

"I'm glad I'm back, too, may I have yer laundry?" she asked again.

"Stay a while," Lukas encouraged. "Do ye know when ye're leaving fer Scotland yet?"

Alynn shook her head. "It won't be until after Althing. Asides, the winds have to change."

"I understand. The wind is stubborn." Lukas leaned against his desk, a smile in his eyes. "I am looking forward to Althing, though. The trials by combat, the crowds, the food. And the shopping. I'd always get notebooks and wine fer Eucharist." He smiled when he saw Alynn's confused look. "It's held on St. Anne's Cleft every seventh year, and I used to sneak in. It did me good to be around people."

"I didn't know that," Alynn said. "Dirty clothes. Please."

Lukas took Alynn's chin in one hand and looked into her eyes. "Alynn, what's wrong?"

"Nothin'."

"Nothing. Aye, I'll believe that." Lukas's fingers began toying with Alynn's hair. She normally enjoyed it, but today, her eyes rolled in protest. She had work to do.

"I'd just like to get the washin' done before the rain starts up again."

"Come, now. Ye're worried about Tarin. What do we do wi' worry?"

"I've already said a dozen prayers this mornin'. It hasn't helped."

"Then talk to me."

Alynn took a breath. "You never had siblings, Lukas. You don't know what 'tis like to miss someone with everythin' you've got in you. I want him back, and come hell or high water, I'll get him back. And at the same time, I'm afraid. Suppose he's dead? Suppose he's sick? Suppose he's moved from Skerray and we'll be on another wild goose chase to find him? I'd rather not spend any more of my life wanderin' town to town, tryin' to find someone who might not be alive anyway. And faith, I hope Mum doesn't lose her head over all this."

Lukas waited to make sure Alynn had finished talking, then opened his arms to her. She was quick to accept his offer of a hug. "I know what it is to miss a loved one," he said. "And if ye love Tarin half as much as I love ye, I know ye can't stand being apart from him. But when ye first came here, ye put yer brother in God's hands. And, fer the time being, that's where he needs to stay."

"Thank you."

"Any time, my dear." Lukas kissed the top of Alynn's head before taking off his cowl and apron-like scapular. "You needn't wash the braies, I've only worn them once this week."

Sighing, Alynn took a pair of loose shorts from a drawer in Lukas's desk. She hadn't washed them last week, and it wasn't as if a dunk in the washtub would hurt them. By the time she'd collected the laundry from her own cell and Caitriona's, Lukas's tunic and undershift were piled outside his door.

Alynn rapped on the doorframe. "Socks too, Lukas."

Two socks flew out the door, propelled by Latin mutterings. Alynn could never tell if he was praying, swearing, or talking to himself.

"Thank you."

Although she felt better about Tarin after talking to Lukas, Alynn was still upset with herself. Didn't growing up mean being able to solve her own problems? She scowled as she drew water, and it started to rain just as she had filled the washtub.

Halfheartedly, Alynn began scrubbing mud and sweat and food wiped on sleeves. Her knuckles grated across the washboard, but she pretended not to notice. Why did she run to Lukas every time she had a problem? He had plenty of his own problems, but he never burdened her with them. Why couldn't she be more like him?

Alynn glared at her reflection in the washbasin and punched it. Then, scraping her knuckles raw on the washboard, she turned back to her work. Focusing on tasks to keep her mind off things. Just like her father had done

Alynn.

The voice was quiet and compassionate, easy to miss and hard to concentrate on at times. But it was beautiful, and Alynn would never grow tired of hearing it.

"I'm listenin', Lord."

Don't talk about My daughter like that.

Alynn took a deep breath. Worrying was normal. Needing help was normal. She was only sixteen, she was only human, and if Lukas could confess to making a mistake every now and again, so could she.

"Thank You."

Saying prayers, and even having them said over you, was one thing, Alynn realized. But taking the time to listen as God responded was another thing altogether, and it was this oft-forgotten part of prayer that could bring peace to even the darkest of circumstances.

When she scraped her hand again, Alynn decided that the clothes were clean enough. She wrung out the clothes and folded them over her arm. There was a clothesline set up in one of the spare bedrooms where everything would dry faster.

Lukas helped Alynn set the clothes out to dry, then they began chapel. Refusing to keep all eight Divine Offices as prescribed by the Rule of St. Benedict, Lukas instead held three simple prayer services. Alynn never bothered attending Prime or Vespers, but noon usually found her in the chapel, listening to Lukas read Psalms aloud. Sometimes, she would be invited to read something. Today, as usual, she simply joined in singing the hymns with him.

Kyrie Eleison—Lord, have mercy. *Christus Eleison*—Christ, have mercy. Mercy on Tarin. Mercy on the quest to find him.

"Is it alright if I check my trap line?" Lukas asked after thirty minutes had flown by.

"Do what you need to," Alynn said. "You needn't ask me."

"I'll need to use Humility."

"Take her. She's yer horse."

"I'm certain that, if ye asked her, she'd say otherwise. And ye're alright here alone?"

Alynn smiled. "Don't give a thought to me. I'll take care of myself."

Lukas ruffled Alynn's hair and hugged her on his way out the door. "Och, dear child. Be safe."

"I'll do my best."

She followed Lukas outside and, as soon as he left, began to muck the horses' stalls. She hated carting loads of manure in the rain, but Lukas had a small handsled that made the job much easier. And it was one less thing Lukas had to worry about.

When she came outside with a full cart, she was surprised to see a wet white horse and his rider cantering towards her. It was a while before Alynn recognized the rider.

"Mum?"

Caitriona's dress stuck to her skin, and her hair was full of twigs and leaves. She looked like a woodland nymph coming home from playing in the waterfalls.

"And *what* were you doing at the McKenzie's house this mornin'?" Caitriona demanded, sliding off Honor's back.

"Sayin' hello to Maggie," Alynn said. "What took you so long at the village? 'Tis past noon!"

"I wasn't about to start off down a deerpath during a thunderstorm," Caitriona said. "It was bad enough as it was. Humility would have spooked. Why'd you run off in such a hurry?"

"One of us had to do the laundry."

"There's more important things than clean clothes," Caitriona said, taking off her hood. Sodden snarls of blonde hair had escaped her kerchief and stuck to her forehead. "Why didn't you stay longer? Help persuade some sailors to take us before Althing? There's a chance we could get back before it starts."

"Althing's a big deal, Mum."

Caitriona's voice grew shriller. "A bigger deal than findin' yer brother?"

"To most people. No one's going to help us anyway. There's not a use in askin'."

"'Tis because you've never asked them that they won't help. Faith, Lynder, aren't you worried about Tarin?"

"I raised him for longer than you did! Of course I'm worried about him!" Caitriona blinked, and Alynn felt a prick in her heart. "I didn't mean it that way, Mum. But you'll drive yerself mad thinkin' about somethin' you can't change. Ask how I know. Tarin's alright. You need to let it go for the moment."

"He is my son, and I will never let him go." With flaming eyes, Caitriona yanked Honor's reins and led him into the stable. Alynn kicked at the handcart and left it for Lukas to take care of. Cleaning the stables was his job, anyway.

She felt a bit of remorse for getting her mother so worked up, but a few deep breaths put her at ease. The next few days would be normal. Then a week of Althing, and the moment the vendors started packing up their wares, Alynn and Caitriona would be on their way to find Tarin, who was hopefully healthy, happy, and waiting for them in Skerray.

After all, God *had* been looking after him since two Septembers ago. Surely He wouldn't mind watching one of His favorite children for two more weeks.

June 8, A.D. 966—

The fact that blessings are so often intermingled with hardships shall never cease to amaze me. Sigmund has returned from his missionary journey, and his tales of its success are unparalleled. But he also brought with him the fact that an old friend of Alynn's father is looking for her, and that her brother Tarin may still be alive. While I rejoice with Alynn and Caitriona, I also worry, for I wonder if Tamlane McMahon intends to take them away from me.

I have resigned myself to the fact that someday, Alynn will be lost. I have enjoyed the short yet wonderful assignment of being her guardian. I wish nothing but bliss upon her and the family that she will one day have, the family that will draw her heart farther and farther away from the monastery. I fear that she will forget the days we spent together, healing and growing, learning and teaching.

And yet I know my place, and that place is somewhere in a corner while the McNeils take center stage. I am content in my corner while Caitriona and Alynn fuss over Tarin, preparing for a hopefully-short trip to Skerray to retrieve him, and yet I can't help but look wistfully at them. Their heads are in the clouds, too busy thinking and praying and worrying about their journey to even greet me in the hallways. Alynn seems in a daze, as if she hasn't fully realized the magnitude of Sigmund's words. I pray for her—there is something deeper, less easily healed than simple shock, in her spirit. It resembles a form of unbelief.

I remember Caitriona's actions when she was first reunited with Alynn. I remember the care she took of her, the nights she spent simply staring at her as she slept, the tears and prayers poured out for her. I wonder if she will react the same when she sees Tarin again. The two have not met in seven years; he will have no memory of her, just as I have no memory of my natural parents. Or is there some divine spark of recognition between blood relatives? I am a fool for asking; I shall never know.

Alynn has yet to leave and I miss her. I pray that she will return quickly and permanently. Even last night, as she and Caitriona were in the village discussing their voyage, I was distraught. The monastery seemed so quiet, so dark, so devoid of human life, as if it would swallow me. I have forgotten that God hears my prayers for companionship; I have forgotten how to be lonely and sane at the same time.

—L. McCamden

THREE

I've had this dream before. I remember the meadow, the brilliant green of the grass, the perfect oval of trees around me. When I see the angel, I remember her, too. All the same, she astounds me. She's nobler than any queen, more beautiful than any painting. Her wings have the grace of a butterfly and the strength of an eagle.

And, just like last time, Tarin is sleeping, his head on the angel's lap. I don't hate myself for speaking this time. "Give me Tarin back."

"I am watching him," the angel says. "You needn't fear for him."

"I need him."

"He is safe," the angel promises. "He is safe in the hands of God."

"I need him!"

I take one step towards him, but the angel holds out her hand, and something stops me. I'm paralyzed, held back by some invisible cord. I fight and I close my eyes to throw myself into the fighting. He's right there, Tarin is, right in front of me, and I can't take five steps to get to him. I can't even reach out a hand to him.

The angel stands; she's taller than any human and twice as intimidating. "Ask for him."

"I'll get him myself!" I snap. I fight until I'm breathless, knowing that the cords will break and I'll be free to run to Tarin, pick him up in my arms and carry him home with me. But the cords never break, I never move, and I fall exhausted to the ground.

Grass tickles the back of my neck. I can't do it. Tarin's right there. If

31

I turned my head, I'd be able to see him, but I can't have him. "I can't do it," I tell the angel. "I can't find Tarin. Please. Please help me."

A hand touches me, and I look up to see Tarin, precious, perfect. "I know you always do things on your own," he says, "but you need to let God help you this time. You need to trust that He'll take care of you. And me."

"But what if—"

"Don't worry. He helped you fight off the Norsemen, right? He'll help us find each other." He kisses my cheek and smiles, then goes back to the angel. I sit up in time to see them disappear before dreamless sleep comes over me.

Alynn didn't have time to remember her dream the next morning, much less divine its meaning. She was up with the summer's early dawn, helping Lukas and Caitriona make the final preparations for Mass. The bread for Eucharist was placed in baskets, Lukas found some elderberry cordial to replace the wine they didn't have, and the last of the sewing was put away. St. Anne's Monastery looked like the church it was supposed to, rather than the home Alynn had come to know it as.

Just as Lukas left to feed the horses, Maggie McKenzie and her two hyper half-brothers stormed through the back door, all of them talking and shouting and barking orders at once. Maggie's voice rose above the clamor: "Slodi, will ye get *off* yer brother—Olvir, that bread is for Eucharist! You just ate breakfast, for shame!"

"There's bread?" Slodi asked. He made a beeline for the basket, but Maggie slapped his hands away from it.

"Ye twits, will ye stop it?" Maggie snapped. "Alynn, I'm sorry, hello, how are ye?"

"I'm grand," Alynn smiled. She broke a piece of the Eucharist bannock, split it, and gave it to the younger children. "No more, now, do ye hear me? Would you like a bit, Maggie?

Are you alright?"

Maggie sighed. "Aye, goodness…my mind's spinning. I had to share a horse with Slodi, and he elbowed me about a hundred times because he wanted to go faster. Then Olvir fell off his horse, Slodi wandered off while Mum was trying to patch him up, and it took Drostan's help to get everyone going again!"

Alynn's eyes let up. "Drostan came with you?" she asked.

"Aye. He's helping Mum put up our horses."

Alynn smiled, not quite at Maggie, and quickly went out the back door. She scanned the yard. Drostan was in the paddock, filling the water trough for the four horses gathered around it. He caught Alynn's eye and smiled.

"Good morning, milady!" Drostan grinned. He leapt over the paddock fence and gave her a quick kiss on the cheek.

"Good morning, sir," Alynn smiled, hugging him. "I heard you were a hero for the McKenzies earlier."

"Not a hero so much as any man with morals," Drostan said. "Has Aunt Cait calmed down any?"

"Calmed down? Have you known Mum to be calm about anythin' she's set her mind to?"

"At least tell me she's sleeping. She'll make herself sick worrying so."

Alynn smiled. "She fell asleep on her knees last night, prayin' for Tarin and our trip and God knows what else. I should probably be more worried about her than I am."

"No, love, you can't worry. Not about her, or Tarin, or anything." Drostan took Alynn's hand and pulled her closer so that their shoulders touched. "Between me and God, we'll get everything worked out."

"Thank you."

Drostan smiled, leaning closer to Alynn and kissing her cheek ever so gently. His eyelashes tickled her face. She smiled, and when she opened her eyes, she saw Lukas glaring quietly at them. "We're being watched," she whispered.

"I don't care."

"I wouldn't either, except that 'tis Lukas."

With one last kiss on the cheek, Drostan stepped aside and waved at Lukas. "Good morning, sir!" he called. "Lovely day!"

"Aye."

Although Alynn and Drostan had been courting for a year and a half, Lukas still didn't know what to think about them together. He probably didn't know what to think about romance in general, having been raised since infancy surrounded by monks and chastity and virgin saints. He hadn't even read Song of Solomon all the way through.

"There should be a rule," Lukas muttered as he escorted Alynn and Drostan back to the monastery, "against courting on Sabbath."

"You could always renounce your vow of chastity," Drostan suggested. "Find yourself a girl, get married like Elder Steingrim did a while back. You won't feel so alone that way."

"That sort of love isn't fer me, lad."

"You need to at least find a friend," Alynn said. "One good friend, like Mum has Nora and I have Maggie. Someone close to yer age."

"Everyone my age is either dead or not dying fast enough."

With a chuckle, Drostan opened the door, but he took Alynn aside as soon as they were inside. "Could you—will you—Lynder...meet me tomorrow, would you? After dinner?"

"Normal place?"

"Aye—thank you, love." Hurriedly, he kissed her forehead, and Alynn caught the slightest glimpse of his flushed face as he left. What had gotten into him? Was he embarrassed or frightened or angry?

She tried to follow him, but she was met by a cacophony of music, voices, and caterwauling. Caitriona and Nora McKenzie were warming up their voices and instruments in the chapel. Slodi and Olvir had found Cara the cat, and Alynn had heard babies at their baptism make less noise. Maggie had surrendered, sitting at the kitchen table and wishing she was invisible. Lukas looked at the fiasco waiting to happen, sighed, and called, "Children!"

The boys dropped the cat they were fighting over and ran towards him. "Pastor Lukas!" they exclaimed. Slodi jumped on him, Olvir hugged him, and even Maggie looked up and smiled.

"I'm sorry they're acting up," she said. "Can we put them in that room where ye keep yer swords and tell them to fight each other?"

"Can we?" Olvir asked.

Lukas half-smiled. "Nay, we keep that room locked."

Alynn crossed her arms. "Olvir, Slodi, outside. Run around the monastery five times. Both of ye."

Maggie squeezed Alynn gratefully as the boys ran out the back door. "Och, thank ye, Alynn," she sighed. "*Please* tell me I can sit next to ye today. I can't stand another two hours of being poked in the arm."

"Of course," Alynn promised.

Olvir's blond head popped through the back door. "Alynn, do we have to run through the graveyard?" he asked. "Slodi's scared of ghosts."

"Tell him that ghosts only eat naughty children," Maggie said.

"Don't do that," Alynn sighed. "Tell him that ghosts don't come out until after dark, and if he's still frightened, just run around it."

Maggie grinned as the door shut, but it didn't stay shut for long. Alynn immediately recognized two arguing voices as Erik and Ulfrik Havardson, fifteen-year-old twins that hardly looked related.

Erik sauntered into the kitchen, his blond hair perfect and his eyes haughty. Ulfrik was right on his heels, yelling something in Norse than Alynn was glad she couldn't understand.

"Shut up, please," Erik said, smiling at Maggie and bowing gallantly. "Good morning, milady!"

"Hello, Maggie," Ulfrik added before turning to yell again

at his brother.

Alynn smiled. "Ulfrik, can you be a bit quieter, please?"

Ulfrik looked at her. His eyes melted her heart in some sweet way, like Tarin's always had. His eyes were too round, his nose hardly had a bridge at all, and he'd been introduced to Alynn as a simple-minded boy. Simple-minded or not, Ulfrik was a dear.

"Hello, Alynn," he said.

"Hello, Ulfrik," Maggie smiled, just as enamored by Ulfrik's childlike spirit as Alynn was. She shot Erik an evil glare rather than speak to him.

"What are you doing at Mass so early?" Erik asked, standing uncomfortably close to Maggie. "Showing your dedication to the Lord, are you?"

Maggie rolled her eyes. "Come off it, you twit. You know better than anyone that my mother helps with worship."

"You needn't be so modest," Erik said. "You could have come later, by yourself. If I didn't play the *bodhran*, I'd be inclined to escort you."

"Speaking of worship, sir, I believe you're late for practice and ought to sod off to the sanctuary."

"She doesn't like you, Erik," Ulfrik said.

"Shut up!" Erik demanded. He half-thumped, half-punched Ulfrik in the back so hard he nearly fell over.

"Stop it, both of ye," Alynn ordered. "Ye should be ashamed of yerselves, fightin' in the Lord's house! Erik, apologize to yer brother."

"Sorry, Ulfrik," Erik said, clearly for the sake of appeasing Alynn. He sauntered into the sanctuary, tapping his circular drum with a bleached chicken bone, and Alynn breathed a sigh of relief.

Ulfrik scowled for a moment, but suddenly, his face lightened. "Is Jesus going to make Erik friendly someday?"

Alynn smiled. "I'm sure He will."

"That's good. Come on, Maggie. Let's go sit next to each other."

Alynn knew there was something she should be doing. More people would be arriving soon, and she glanced around the kitchen to see everything put away. She double-checked the communion bread, put more wood in the fireplace, and realized she wasn't wearing her Sabbath dress.

"I should have noticed sooner," Alynn muttered to herself as she scurried upstairs. "Of all the gomeys in the world, you can't even pick the right clothes...as if it matters. Shut yer gob, Lynder!"

"Alynn, what's going on?" Caitriona called from the chapel. Alynn glanced over the railing to see her mother, Erik with his *bodhran* drum, and Nora McKenzie with her lyre. Caitriona had several dresses from her days as a chief's wife, and today she was arrayed in a gown of stunning deep green.

"I'm just changin' clothes," Alynn said.

"Come spend time wi' Maggie, won't ye?" Nora asked. Her brogue was every bit as Scottish as Lukas's, maybe even thicker. "The lass doesn't give a fiddler's fart what she looks like."

"I haven't time!"

Alynn threw on her Sabbath dress—a pink gown with hanging sleeves, the skirt lengthened with a strip of white. It was plain enough, but two steps up from her simple blue work dress and forest-green frock. Alynn ran her fingers through her hair, heard feet climbing up the stairs, and ran to greet whoever was looking for her.

She hardly made it past her doorway before she tripped on her newly-lengthened hem, falling hard and bashing her face into the railing that separated the hallway from the chapel below.

Worship practice ended abruptly, with Nora laughing and Caitriona's flute hitting a high note as she inhaled sharply. "Are you alright, Alynn?" she called. "What happened?"

"I made my blasted skirt too long," Alynn muttered, rubbing her nose. "I'm grand." She looked down to see Caitriona worried, Nora trying not to laugh, and Erik struck with an incurable paroxysm of laughter. Standing up, Alynn noticed blood on her hand and put it back on her nose.

She looked at the stairway to see a seven-year-old girl staring at her, brown eyes wide. "Did you hurt yourself?" the girl asked, shrinking back into the stairwell.

"I'm fine, Kyrri, but can I borrow your handkerchief?" Alynn asked. She held her nose as she spoke, and the girl smiled before fishing a handkerchief out of her pocket. "Thanks."

"You sound funny."

"I know that." Alynn pressed the handkerchief to her nose and looked at Kyrri. "What do you need? Is yer Uncle Sigmund here?"

"He is. He wants to talk to you, and I wanted to know if I could help with anything."

Alynn smiled, wiped her hand before ruffling Kyrri's dirty blonde hair, and left to find Sigmund. "Thank you, my heart. I'm fine, so you can go play with your friends if you'd like."

Kyrri smiled and ran ahead of Alynn down the stairs.

Alynn made her way carefully, determined not to trip on her hem again. She sat at the kitchen table and leaned forward, still pinching her nose and clutching Kyrri's bloody handkerchief with warm, sticky fingers. Alynn had helped Tarin stop a nosebleed countless times before, but she'd never had one herself.

Footsteps approached her, but Alynn didn't risk looking up. She heard the tinkling of buckles as leather straps were undone, and suddenly, a wooden forearm was thrust into her field of vision. "Need a hand?"

"Sigmund!"

Sigmund laughed, and a baby's happy squeal let Alynn know that little Matthew was there, laughing at his father's joke. "Really, though. What happened?"

"I made my skirt too long and tripped over it. Nothing I haven't done before. You're doing well?"

"Never better. It's so good to be home." Alynn glanced

sideways to see Sigmund pull up a chair, sit beside her, and reattach his prosthetic. "And Matthew's grown so much. He's crawling now."

"Och, sweet thing!" A blood clot dripped onto the handkerchief, and Alynn pinched her nose with a bit more force.

"Aye, we're so proud of him. How are things here?"

"We're grand. You think I have questions, don't you?"

"I'll save you the trouble of asking them. The man I met on Hrafney was undoubtedly—"

"I heard a bang," Drostan's voice interrupted. Alynn glanced up to see him hand her a bouquet of white flowers. "And I thought that this was in order."

She smiled, but she stopped short of using the leaves to stop the bleeding. "Look again," she said.

Drostan took the flowers back. "Isn't it…och, why do they have to look so much alike?"

"You got her hemlock instead of bloodwort?" Sigmund asked.

"Aye, I'm sorry—"

"You were in a hurry, love, 'tis alright." Alynn wiped her nose and was glad to see that the bleeding had stopped of its own accord. "I don't need bloodwort, anyway."

Drostan quickly strode to the front door, tossed the flowers into the yard, and wiped his hands on his tunic as he returned. "Thank God you noticed that."

"It would have been fine anyway," Sigmund said, checking Matthew's chubby hands to make sure he hadn't grabbed any leaves by accident. "Hemlock won't hurt you unless you eat it."

"I've gotten rashes from pickin' it out of the herb garden," Alynn said. "And there was a story back in Limerick of a cow that grazed on Devil's Bread—that's what we called it in Ireland—a whole family died from drinkin' its milk." Drostan shivered, and Alynn smiled comfortingly. "Don't worry, love. It's a simple mistake. Now, Sigmund, how'd you meet Captain McMahon?"

Sigmund smiled. "I met him about a week before my return to St. Anne's Cleft. He was with a merchant. It didn't leave him much time to spare, but I saw him talk to several people before he was directed to me. Once we shook hands, discussed the weather and all, he asked me if I knew a girl of fifteen, maybe sixteen, who'd fallen off a ship in the area. When I asked him if the name Alynn McNeil meant anything to him, he nearly fell over." Sigmund looked at Alynn and found her entranced. "He asked if you were well, said that he'd given you up for lost, but he made a promise to your brother. It was the only reason he was asking for you."

Alynn blinked. "So...so Tarin's alive?"

"That's what I get out of it. Then he said, just before he was called away, 'Tell her to stay where she is. As soon as I'm able, I'll fetch her and bring her home.'"

Alynn's breath caught in her chest, and a tear slipped down her face as she hugged Sigmund. "Thank you," she whispered. "Thank you so much."

Drostan's hand rested on her shoulder. "I'm glad for you, Alynn," he said. His voice was soft; she knew he meant it. "How about you let go before Brynnhilde comes in?"

"Sorry." Alynn stood up, wiped her eyes, and smiled at Drostan. "Tarin's alive."

Drostan drew Alynn into his arms. For a moment, Tarin was so real to her—she could almost feel the softness of his hair, see his freckles and hear the beating of his little heart. She smiled and let tears slip silently down her face.

Sigmund set Matthew on the floor and produced a carved wooden horse from his pocket to keep him occupied. "What town is Tarin in?"

"Skerray," Alynn said.

"Skerray...Skerray. Drostan, where is that?"

Drostan thought. "I'll need a map. I think it's nigh Eilean Nan Ron, which...shouldn't make it too far from Port Ellyn."

"But it's a port town?" Sigmund asked.

"I think so. Is that a problem?"

"I—when—em—someone—och, blast it—"

Alynn froze and stared at him. He'd grown out of his stuttering; he only reverted to it when something was wrong. "What is it?" she breathed.

"You can't panic."

"Tell me what's wrong."

"I—I saw another ship come in," he said. "A Darsidian ship. Their crops failed last autumn, and this autumn doesn't look much better for them. So they need an alternative source of income. Half their tribe is making their way across the Scottish coast, and they aren't coming home until their ships are nigh sinking with goods." He took a breath. "The one I saw was a slave ship."

Alynn's stomach twisted. "Did they take Tarin?"

"Nay. There were no boys under twelve. The captain said they'd come from Portnancom, they're making their way east."

Alynn felt a change come over her. No longer was she afraid; she was seething with anger, fists clenched, heart beating like a war drum. "I swear, if they lay hand on him—"

"Calm down," Drostan said. "Lynder, Skerray is a small town. They might not bother raiding it."

"Not bother! They raided Limerick City, they raided Shanagolden, they raided Ennis. They raided Fletcher's Point twice, and it didn't even have a decent church. I'm finding Tarin before they do."

"Lynder—"

"Don't try to stop me."

"Look at me, love. Calm down."

Alynn forced herself to take a deep breath. Being a berserker was helpful in battle, but if there was no real danger, it often did more harm than good. She wanted to laugh at herself; she'd never gone berserk from simply hearing about a threat before.

Tarin's fine for now, she told herself. *We've got time, the Darsidians aren't hurrying, we'll get there before they do, we'll get Tarin. We'll get Tarin.*

"How long before they get there?" she demanded. Now that her anger was gone, she was free to worry and fret until Tarin was safe in her arms.

"It depends on the winds and weather," Drostan said. "Also on the towns' defenses. It could be two weeks, could be a month. I'll check my map and see if we can't estimate a deadline."

"But we've two weeks?"

"Probably three," Sigmund said. "They'll need to stop every few towns for water, and if I know Darsidia, more mead than is good for them. The hangovers at least should slow them down."

Alynn shuddered at the thought of a drunken Viking grabbing Tarin's arm and dragging him, kicking and squalling, to a boat full of fellow slaves. Would they hit him? Bind his wrists too tightly? Would they refuse him food and water, or make him row until he was too sore to move?

"Can ye pray for him?" she asked. "Please?"

"Of course," said Sigmund, scooping Matthew off the floor with remarkable dexterity considering his wooden arm. "Now, I'm off to save some seats. Best of luck finding your brother, Alynn."

"Thank you."

Gently, Drostan set his hand on Alynn's shoulder. "We'll get there afore they do," he promised. "Do you want to pray about it now?"

"Please."

Drostan led her into the chapel and, not wanting to disturb the worship leaders, sat with Alynn in the back row and began to pray. He asked for God's protection on Tarin, for safe travels to and from Scotland, for good winds and smooth seas. And with everything within her, Alynn agreed.

They stopped praying when worship practice was over. Peace had settled upon Alynn; she smiled and embraced Drostan. "Thank you."

"You *did* clean the blood off your hands before you rubbed

them all over my tunic, didn't you?"

Alynn gasped and jumped back. "I hope I did...."

"Lynder—"

"Just let me see yer back...you're good. Don't worry. Did I get any on my dress?"

Drostan scanned her head to toe and smiled. "You look lovely. And nay, your dress is clean."

Alynn smiled gratefully and took Kyrri's handkerchief outside. She had just enough time to wash it before people started coming for Mass.

The next half hour was a flurry of greeting people and engaging in small talk, of making sure no one ate the communion bread and everyone felt welcomed. The three people Alynn could never seem to talk with, though, were Maggie, Erik, and Ulfrik.

Maggie by herself was a joy to spend time with, but when she was flanked by two boys who clung to her like cat claws on a shepherd's-knit quilt, she tended to shut down. Ulfrik was never one for much conversation, and Erik was insufferable. When they were together, all hell broke loose.

Alynn saw the three of them together, Maggie cornered between them and the kitchen table. She tried to eavesdrop on their conversation, rescue Maggie if things were out of hand, but she tripped once again on the hem of her dress and found herself on the floor.

Ulfrik began to laugh, Erik guffawed, and even Maggie was giggling. "You make a lovely rug, milady!" Erik exclaimed.

Alynn scowled as she picked herself up. "I'm sure you'd make a decent one as well."

Erik opened his mouth, but Maggie drove her pointy elbow into his ribs before anything could come out of it. "Ye're already in a hole, I suggest ye put down yer shovel."

Erik's face betrayed nothing except his anger. He grumbled at Maggie in Norse. Ulfrik grabbed Maggie and thrust her out of harm's way just as Erik jammed his own elbow into the unfortunate soul to his left, not really caring who it was. Ulfrik gave an angry cry and struck his brother.

"Lads, either take it outside or save it until ye're home," Alynn scolded. "Church isn't a place to be fightin'."

Erik sniffed. "You're worse than my mother."

"Erik, be nice," Ulfrik demanded. He smiled at Maggie—a childlike smile with one tooth missing—and took her hand. "I saw a comfrey flower outside. Can I show you?"

"You can certainly show me."

Alynn couldn't help but smile as the two sidestepped the crowds and made their way out the back door. "They're adorable together," she accidentally said aloud.

Erik scowled. "Come off it," he ordered.

"Shut yer gob," Alynn snapped. "She'd like you better if you respected her."

"Aye, I'll be sure to lay my cloak over the next puddle she walks over," Erik retorted.

Rather than smacking him like she wanted to, Alynn left to find Lukas. He was visiting with a family in the kitchen, trying to speak Norse but getting it mixed up with the four other languages he knew.

"And the *gratia Dei*—*Syngnómi, ti chári tou Theoú*—" Sighing, Lukas turned to Alynn and gratefully returned to Gaelic. "Do us a favor and ring the bell fer service, Alynn. I give up."

"Do you need Leif to translate the sermon?" Alynn asked, knowing that Lukas always tried to preach in Norse.

"I'll be alright. Thank ye, though."

"You're doing better thank you think," Alynn promised, remembering to pick up her skirts as she left.

The ladder to the belfry was nearly hidden in the upstairs hallways, tucked neatly behind the stairwell. Alynn only stepped on her skirts twice as she scaled it. As she stepped into the circular belfry, she was met by an arctic wind that whistled through the delicate stone arches. She tried not to shiver as she untied the pull rope and yanked on it.

Dong-dong, dong-dong, dong-dong!

The noise was deafening, yet sweet and deep and

melodious. Alynn's arms fell into a rhythm with the swinging of the bell. Her spirit soared as the wind whipped through her hair.

Dong-dong, dong-dong, dong-dong!

And as the bell rang, she forgot Erik, she forgot the cold, she forgot her nosebleed and even her quest to find Tarin. She felt free.

FOUR

"Isn't it a beautiful day?" Alynn asked, skipping alongside Lukas and letting the tempestuous winds play with her hair. She could almost feel the sunshine seep through the clouds and warm her heart.

Lukas half-smiled as he watched Alynn's free spirit. "Lovely weather," he said. "Enjoy it while ye can."

Alynn laughed, letting the wind snatch her spirit and spin her in circles. "Would it be too foolish for me to wear my Sabbath dress to meet Drostan, or should I just have Mum fix my hair?"

"I think yer hair is beautiful just as it is," Lukas said. "As fer yer dress—ye realize a four hundred and fifty-year-old book dictates what I wear. Ye should probably ask yer mother."

"I know, but Mum's got her head in the clouds, and I'm needin' an opinion I can trust." Alynn's spinning ceased, and she looked at Lukas with a light in her eyes. "Maybe I could borrow one of Mum's dresses."

"Pin up the hem. Ye'll trip over it otherwise."

Alynn smiled, and she was almost too giddy to notice as Caitriona rode Honor into the yard. Honor was panting, and Caitriona's face was drawn and pale.

"Mum, 'tis alright," Alynn said as soon as she dismounted. "Captain McMahon's going to bring him here."

"I know." Caitriona's voice was thin. "Tamlane's a busy man, it's summer, he's probably got a dozen ports to visit before he comes this way again. I can't stand being away from Tarin for much longer, especially with the Darsidians on the warpath. I'd think that at least Leif would understand, but with Althing coming up, he won't get us a ship."

Caitriona leaned wearily against Honor's neck, and Alynn felt a pang of concern. "Are you alright, Mum?"

Caitriona managed a smile. "I'm fine, dear heart. I'm just tired. Could you put the horse up for me?" She handed the reins to Alynn before she could answer. "Thanks."

"Not a bother," Alynn said. Her dress and her hair were forgotten as she put Honor in his stall. She couldn't remember the last time she'd seen Caitriona that tired.

She wished Drostan was there. He knew how to handle a lot of situations; he knew how to laugh, and how to smile in a way that warmed the hearts and raised the spirits of everyone around him. And if he drew her into his arms, and stroked her hair with gentle fingers, not even the end of the world could frighten her.

Alynn smiled and danced back to the monastery to make the evening meal.

She was still caught up her in her thoughts as she mixed dough for bannocks. Drostan didn't often ask to meet her someplace—especially this late at night. Maybe they would watch the sun set together. Maybe they would dance, or laugh and talk together. Or, best of all, they might simply sit and enjoy each other's company. Alynn smiled, imagined Drostan's arm around her, his gentle hand resting over hers and....

Alynn shook herself. She had a meal to make.

She quickly finished making the bannock dough and loaded it on the spider-legged skillet. When she tried to put the pan in the fireplace to bake, her hand grazed the hot embers. She jumped, banging her hand on the soup kettle that hung over the fireplace.

Alynn drew a sharp breath, said nothing, and quickly left to get ready for her evening with Drostan.

A year ago, Drostan had given her a sword belt, complete with a lovely birchwood sheath that he'd covered with carvings of flowers and vines. She strapped it around her waist, then turned her attention to her hair. She combed out her strawberry-blonde kinks and waves and curls until it shimmered, then styled it fifteen different ways. Could she braid it? Put it up? Put half of it up? Tie a knot at the base of her head, like so many of the Norse women did? Alynn knew the bannocks would be done cooking before long, she in desperation, she knocked on Caitriona's door.

The door opened half an inch. "What are you needin', Alynn?" Caitriona asked.

"Mum, can you do my hair?"

"Yer *hair*, child?"

"I'm meetin' Drostan this evening."

Caitriona sighed, opening the door the rest of the way. "Sit down. I'll see what I can do."

Alynn sat at Caitriona's desk, smiling as her mother braided small sections of her hair away from her face and brought them together in the back. In an effort to sit still, she began idly glancing through a notebook. It was full of the poems that Caitriona had written—beautiful poems that weren't done justice by the ungainly penmanship they were written in. While most of Caitriona's poems dealt with the love of God or the beauty of nature, towards the end of the book, they turned more personal.

"You miss Tarin fierce much, don't you?" Alynn asked.

"I can't see why you don't," Caitriona put in "What are you gawkin' at?"

Alynn let Caitriona see the cover of the notebook before realizing it was a simple, leather-bound notebook, exactly like the dozens Lukas had copied Scriptures into. "'Tis a pure beautiful poem...but 'tis so...sad." Alynn began to read the poem. "'Like a knife upon my heart, I wish we weren't apart...a bite out of my soul'—"

"'I feel out of control,' Lynder, put that down," Caitriona ordered. She snatched the notebook from Alynn's hands and set it on the desk. "You left the bannocks bakin', did you?"

"I did."

Quickly, Caitriona finished braiding the two sections of hair together. "Go check on it."

Alynn hugged her mother on her way out the door. "I will, Mum. Thanks for doing my hair."

When Alynn checked on the bannock, it was soft and runny. She sighed. "Note to self," she murmured as she dusted some barley flour on it, "don't daydream while you're cookin'. Or don't cook while you're daydreamin'...shut yer gob, Lynder!"

Alynn hurriedly shoved the flour in the cupboard and set the table. Somehow—whether by an infallible internal clock or the smell of the simmering soup—Lukas knew it was time to eat. He came out of hiding and filled three mugs with water. But when he saw the spongy mess Alynn set at the center of the table, he looked a little skeptical.

"What was this supposed to be?" he asked, stealing a small bite. "It looks like an undercooked griddle cake."

Alynn sighed as she set a spoon at each plate. "I might have put in an extra egg, too much milk, I'm honestly not sure."

"It still tastes alright," Lukas assured. "What happened to yer hair?"

"Mum fixed it for me. Do you like it?"

Alynn's stomach twisted. She *had* to look nice. But when she looked up at Lukas, he was smiling at her. "Ye're beautiful, my dear."

After a hurried meal, Alynn let the others clean up as she left on Humility. They both knew the way well, and ten minutes of gentle trotting brought them to their destination.

Hiding behind brush and trees, the meadow was hard to find for anyone who didn't know the way. It was a gentle oval, like a trencher carpeted with heather and fringed with tall grasses. And at the edge of the trencher stood Drostan, watching her arrival with a contagious smile in his shining eyes.

"Every day, Lynder," he said, wrapping his arms around her as soon as she dismounted. "I don't know how you do it, but every day, you look more beautiful than the last."

"Thank you, love."

"I truly mean it."

Alynn felt her face grow red. She kissed Drostan's cheek, then lost herself in his embrace. She loved his arms around her, the silence surrounding them, the wind and the heather and the last shuttling rays of the sun.

Humility's ticklish breath whooshed against Alynn's neck, and she laughed. Drostan shooed her away. "I thought it was Aunt Cait's job to keep an eye on us," he teased as he tethered her to a tree. "Ignore her. How's life treating you?"

"Just grand." Alynn smiled, walking hand in hand with Drostan to the heathery middle of the meadow. "And have you calmed down at all about givin' your speech?"

"I decided I had other things to be nervous about."

"Such as...."

"Why, there's to be a feast, after Father is elected chief." Drostan took her hand and began to hum. "Do you remember the first song we ever danced to, when Father and I set up a celebration for the wrong St. Maura's feast day?"

Alynn smiled. "Of course I remember. They won't sing it at the feast, since Mum wrote it."

"I'll never forget the look on Aunt Cait's face when I took you by the hand—and spun you around—"

"Just like the song said," Alynn remembered. She held hands with Drostan and started dancing, softly and gently, picking up speed along with the song—

"The wind has tales of lovers true,
But none as good as me and you,
A peasant's lass, a lonely lad,
And joy like no one's ever had.

Though kept apart by sea and land,
My heart will reach to take your hand,
For Shannon has seen lovers true,
But none so sweet as me and you.

In my dreams I hear your voice,
I see your smile, and I rejoice,
For oceans know of lovers true,
But none so grand as me and you."

By now, Alynn and Drostan were flying, feet pounding and skirts twirling and hair flying in the wind. When he picked her up and spun her around, her heart soared. Gently, their spinning slowed, their eyes locked on one another's, the only sound in the stillness that of their breathing.

Drostan's eyes peered into hers, beautiful, deep, enchanting. His arms were warm around her; his smile calmed and excited her all at once.

"You, my love, are the finest lady in all of Orkney...I can only thank God that you found something special in me. I don't want to go one step further through life without you, Alynn. So please...may I ask your mother for your hand in marriage?"

Alynn's heart skipped a beat. She had to be dreaming. But no—the air around her, Drostan's hands in hers, the joy she felt, all of it was real. Drostan's eyes were wide and hopeful, almost anxious, waiting for a response.

"Please do!"

Drostan grinned. His embrace lifted her off her feet, and they were laughing and kissing and lost in each other's arms. All this warmth, this love, it was hers now. She might not have deserved it, but she wouldn't trade it for the world.

"How," she asked. "could the future chief of St. Anne's Cleft love a peasant girl like me?"

"The same way a beautiful young woman of God can love a twit of a shipwright like me." Drostan grinned. "Let's go tell your mother."

Drostan helped Alynn onto Humility before he leapt onto his own mare, and they set off at a gallop for the monastery. Alynn smiled the whole way home. She and Drostan, getting married! She'd thought about it often, daydreamed of taking evening walks together and watching their children play on the hearth—but now! She could hardly believe that everything was coming true. She looked back at Drostan, his eyes twinkling as he caught her gaze, and laughed aloud.

The ride home seemed to pass in a flash. Alynn jumped off Humility and unsaddled her faster than she'd ever unsaddled a horse before. Drostan simply tied his mare Thrymja to a post and grabbed Alynn by the hand, and they took off sprinting across the yard.

"Mum!" Alynn called as soon as Drostan slammed the door behind them.

Caitriona jumped. She nearly dropped her sewing and leapt from her chair, and even Lukas looked up from his Bible reading. "Faith, Alynn, what happened?" Caitriona demanded.

Lukas eyed them disdainfully. "Why are ye standing so close together?"

Alynn took half a step away from Drostan, but never let go of his hand. Drostan trembled with nervous excitement. "Aunt Cait," he announced, "I'd like permission to marry your daughter."

"Finally!" Caitriona's eyes were alight as she took them both in her arms and kissed them. "Och, Lynder, I'm so happy for you!"

"Congratulations, both of ye," Lukas said as soon as Alynn and Drostan had been released from Caitriona's grasp. He hugged Alynn but didn't know whether to hug Drostan or shake his hand. He ended up doing both.

"I just want to make one thing clear," Caitriona said, rubbing her sleeve over her eyes. "There's been certain— boundaries, if ye will—in place during yer courtship. Ye do know that they're to remain in place until ye're married, correct?"

"Of course," Drostan said. "My only concern is that we won't know how to properly kiss in front of everyone during the ceremony."

"Ye kiss all the time," Lukas said, a bit uncomfortably.

"Those aren't real kisses," Caitriona said. "You've seen the sort they're talkin' about—remember Sigmund and Brynhilde's wedding?"

"Och, that—why do people *do* that?"

"I'll explain later. Now! Drostan, pull up a seat, 'tis a good deal of plannin' that weddings take. Will the ceremony be here or at Samkoma?"

"Here, won't it?" Alynn asked. Samkoma was the feasting-hall, not nearly the proper place for a wedding.

"We'll have to have the feast at Samkoma," Drostan said. "There will be too many people to feed here, at least comfortably."

"And you'll perform the ceremony, won't you, Lukas?" Alynn asked.

Lukas smiled. "I'd be honored."

Alynn smiled back and took Drostan's hand. "Mum, could I borrow one of yer dresses?"

"I'll take care of the dress," Caitriona promised. "What about rings?"

"You can have one," Drostan told Alynn.

"You don't want a ring?" she asked.

He shrugged. "I've other rings. We could repurpose one."

"You might reconsider," Caitriona advised. "Alynn won't be able to go to every meetin' of Althing, not once ye have children. You'll want something to remind you of her. Trust me."

Caitriona glanced down at her own wedding band. Alynn's father Rowan had made it, mixing whatever scrap metals he had until the alloy looked like gold, and engraving half of a Celtic knot into it. The other half graced his own ring, the ring he'd carried to his grave on the ocean floor.

A short pang of grief for her father hurt Alynn's heart, but she was quick to blink past it. "Will I walk down the aisle alone?" she asked, her voice small. She squeezed Drostan's hand and wished she could bury herself in one of his wonderfully warm hugs.

"Of course you won't," Caitriona declared, almost before the last word had left Alynn's mouth. "I'll be with you."

Drostan rested his hand on Alynn's shoulder. He was one of the few people who knew just how much she hated to feel alone. And his strong arm around her, his gentle hand caressing her hair, was just one of his ways of saying "I love you."

June 11, A.D. 966—

O, joyous day, for Alynn is betrothed! I understand nothing of what is going on, all the talk of gowns and rings and bride-prices, but I know that Alynn is euphoric. Drostan seems to be in another world; Caitriona is ecstatic. Even at this late hour, I hear her stirrings in her cell. Perhaps no one can sleep tonight. Or perhaps we shall, and Alynn shall dream of the day of her marriage, and Caitriona of all the sewing she must do. And I shall see in my own dreams my daughter Alynn, saddling Humility and riding away from me, ready to make her own happy home.

My selfishness hampers the joy I feel for her. I shall miss her dearly. I know that Caitriona will remain, but she was not the one at my side during the Battle of Faith. She did not crawl to me, ignoring her own injuries, when all was said and done and she did not want me to suffer alone. She was not the one I fished out of the icy waters on a September morning long ago, the one who broke the silence of a thirty-nine-year isolation.

I shall miss Alynn's morning hugs and evening prayers. I shall miss the talks we have, the stories she tells and the ones she so attentively listens to. Everything about her, her smile, her laugh, the way she trips and falls and looks up with laughing eyes—all except for her cooking, I shall remember fondly, and long for the days I had her so close.

But for a while, I suppose, I still have her. I will memorize her laugh and her smile and the feel of her delicate arms around me. I have tried many times to capture her likeness with ink and pen, but the resulting fiend resembles the few illustrations Brother Hamish drew in the Psaltery. Perhaps I could convince Caitriona to make a sketch of her, for she is doubtless better than I.

I am glad for Caitriona's presence in more than one way. Being a parent is difficult enough, but navigating a young one's romance? Of this, I am ignorant. All I know is how my father whispered to me, after he caught me staring at Everhild during our last trip to Durness, "Look past her body and into her heart. She won't be bonnie forever."

I pray that Alynn and Drostan see each other's hearts. I pray their love is based on Christ, and in His love, rather than on mere emotion. And as time passes, as eyes dim and hair fades and the physical body declines into the cage I find myself locked into, may their affection for one another remain steadfast.

—L. McCamden

FIVE

Clashing. Panting. The pounding of feet in the snow as we shuffle around, trying to dodge each other's blades. Each blow I parry sends vibrations down my arm. My opponent's blade is sharp, but not too sharp, so that a well-aimed thrust would take off my arm. I imagine what that would feel like. I imagine what death is like.

But I will not die. I find an opening and take it.

The snow turns red, and a terrifying stench fills the air. 'Tis raw meat, an animal being butchered. Except that it isn't an animal, 'tis a man. 'Tis a man with blond hair and blue eyes, with freckles on his forehead and a small scar on his chin. His vacant eyes stare into space, his mouth open and gasping for air.

I stare at him. He calls out for me to either end his suffering or bind his wounds, but I do nothing. I stand, my dripping sword in hand, and I watch the life drain out of his eyes. I watch his chest as it stops breathing, his skin as it turns as white.

When I turn my gaze, I see a child. A child with blond hair and blue eyes, dressed in rags that hang from sharp shoulders. A face pinched with hunger. Hands bleeding from working too hard, blue toes sticking out of shoes that are falling apart.

"You killed my Da."

I say nothing. The world closes in on me. I see people—ragged and starving people, women and children with one message.

"You killed my husband."

"You killed Uncle Harald."

"I want Da back."

"Can we eat something besides wild greens?"

I press my eyes shut, but they're still there. *"I'll make it stop,"* I promise.

"How? You can hardly take care of yourself."

"My children are hungry. Get them something to eat."

"I miss Uncle Hakon's bedtime stories."

I see names with the faces. Dagny Volundottir. Her fatherless children Eyvind and Kelda and Sindri. I see Geirhild Karsadottir with Jofrid and Kenna and Steinmar and Meili. I see fatherless children, wives without husbands, broken hearts and hopeless lives.

A sudden blow knocks me off my feet. I fall hard on the blood-soaked snow, eye to eye with the dead man. I force myself to look away, and I see Konar the Mad, blood dripping from the helmet that covers his face, his evil grin dyed to an ethereal dark blue. His single eye burns holes into my soul.

His foot presses into my chest. I can't move. I can't breathe.

"You went berserk on the battlefield," he growls in his demon's voice. *"That means you and I have something in common..."*

I want to run. I want to sink into the earth and stay there, to hide in the snow so that Konar will not find me again. I try to scream, but my voice sounds far away.

"We're both monsters," he says. *"We have killed, and we'll kill again—"*

I scream again. My voice is louder, but still distant.

"Watch their face as the blade goes in, but watch the wound as the blade comes out. There's nothing better than watching a man turn inside out."

I scream again. And again. And my voice grows louder and louder until it fills the air and buzzes in my ears, and now I'm the one who's dying.

Alynn woke up with a shriek. Something was wrapped around her legs—she couldn't move. Her hand flew out to grab something. Anything. The floor. The edge of her bed. Her heart was hammering so hard her chest hurt, and she couldn't breathe. Her head spun, her stomach turned sour. She screamed into the darkness and took a rasping breath. White clouds were creeping into the edges of her vision.

Suddenly, an apparition flew through the door. A voice called her name, and arms grabbed her. Alynn tried to lash out.

"Stop it, dear heart," the voice said. "It was just a dream, you're safe."

Alynn opened her mouth to scream, but instead she drew in a ragged breath. She realized she was crying. "Please don't hurt me, I'll make things right again—"

"Alynn, you're safe. You're alright. I'll never hurt you."

Alynn recognized the voice. "Mum, I'm sorry—"

She drew in another breath, a gasp as if she'd been held underwater. Caitriona took Alynn into her arms. "Lord, give my daughter peace," she prayed. "Make these nightmares stop."

"They won't stop. I earned them." A rush of shame swept over her, and a wave of fear came right behind it. She started shaking, not with a simple trembling but with terror, with convulsions so strong she couldn't have stood if she'd tried.

"You didn't earn them. Don't talk like that," Caitriona said. "Breathe slowly. You're alright."

"I did earn them! Everything I did—I'm just—Mum, I'm so sorry—"

"Alynn...you did nothin' wrong. You were defendin' yerself. I'd have done the same thing, anyone would have. I love you. I'm glad you're safe."

"I'm sorry I woke you."

"I'm glad you did." Caitriona kissed her daughter's forehead, untangling the blankets from her legs. "You fell out of bed. Did you hurt yourself?"

"I'm...grand. Pure grand." Alynn tried to swallow the lump

in her throat and blink back her tears. "You can go back to bed, Mum. I'm sorry."

"You're not sorry," Caitriona insisted. "Do you want some fresh air? Or perchance 'tis a warm glass of milk you need."

"It isn't." Alynn closed her eyes, burying her head in Caitriona's shoulder, trying to make her heart stop pounding so hard. "I am so sorry...."

"Whisht, child. You're not sorry. You're beautiful, kind, compassionate—and that's why yer guilt hurts so much." She held Alynn closer to her and kissed the top of her head. "I love you. What do you need from me?"

Alynn drew another shaking breath, relieved that it came more easily. Suddenly, she was filled with something hot and livid—something she could only describe as hatred. She hated her nightmares. She hated the Norse raid on St. Anne's Monastery. She hated the memories, the bloodshed, the breaking apart of families. And she hated herself for being a part of all this.

"Go back to bed, Mum," Alynn said.

"Let me stay until you stop shakin'."

Alynn pressed her eyes shut. She grabbed her blankets and clamored back up onto her bed, curled into a ball and facing the wall. "Good night."

Caitriona tried to wipe the tears off Alynn's face, but Alynn pulled away. "I'm grand, now leave me alone," she said.

"'Tis not yer fault, Lynder," Caitriona said again, as she kissed her daughter's head and left the room. "I love you."

As Alynn lay in bed, digging her fingernails into her arm until she bled, she hardly heard her mother's words. Everything *was* her fault, and she hated herself for it.

She never went back to sleep. Fear held her captive, and the steady beating of rain on the roof seemed to laugh at her. When she was able to see the faintest bit of light come through the chapel windows, Alynn decided to light a lamp and start carding wool.

Everything was fine until Alynn accidentally knocked the

lamp into the basket of wool. By some miracle, nothing caught fire, but all the whale oil had spilled. Alynn sat defeatedly on the edge of her bed, burying her head in her singed hands.

She heard the door open, and a gentle footfall sounded on the creaking wooden floor. "Are you doing better, Lynder?" Caitriona's voice asked.

"Don't even bother sayin' 'good morning,'" Alynn sighed. "Lukas hasn't started the morning service, and I've already managed to ruin a basket of wool."

"What it needs is a good washing, nothin' more," Caitriona said. "I'm going to the village this morning, and I'd appreciate yer help with breakfast."

"But 'tis rainin'. At least wait until it clears this afternoon. You can't go now."

"I can't, can I?" Caitriona shut the door as she left, and Alynn sighed.

"Mum, you've gone daft," she muttered, halfheartedly making her bed. The door opened again, just long enough for Caitriona to give her a scolding glare, and Alynn wanted to go back to bed.

The rest of Alynn's morning was equally difficult. She tried reading Matthew's Gospel while making stirabout, only to have a spoonful of half-cooked oats smudging out the Beatitudes. She dropped the bowls, spilled the milk, and tripped over the threshold while coming inside with a bucket of water. By the time breakfast was ready, Alynn wished she could jump in the well and never come back up again. As it was, Lukas found her hiding in an empty cell, burying her face in her frock.

"Would it be considered insensitive to ask if breakfast is ready?" Lukas asked.

"Go on and eat," Alynn said. "I'm not hungry."

"Are ye feeling alright?"

"In my current state of luck, I'd choke on my stirabout and die." Alynn raised her head to look at him. "Are people clumsy in heaven?"

"Come, now, and eat yer breakfast," Lukas ordered. He

pulled Alynn to her feet and scanned her head to toe. Her dress was wet, her hair bedraggled, and there was a large spot of oatmeal on her frock. Alynn ignored the strange combination of compassion and amusement on Lukas's face as she brushed past him on her way out the door.

Cautiously, Alynn tried to change her luck by filling the bowls of stirabout and bringing them to the table without spilling them. Her face turned red as she saw Lukas eyeing the Gospel that was open to the fifth chapter. "And what happened here?"

"That was my fault," Alynn said, setting two bowls at the table and filling a third. "I hope you remember if Jesus blessed the peacemakers before He blessed the meek and what it is He promised the pure in heart, because you might have to rewrite that part."

"Alynn...." Lukas's voice trailed off as he desperately tried to salvage the soaked pages. "No more books in the kitchen. It bled through the pages, there's three hours' work repairing this...och, more's the pity. At least it's not vellum."

Alynn set the last bowl on the table and grabbed three spoons from the cupboard. "I'm sorry."

"It's alright, I've done worse," Lukas said, giving Alynn half a hug as he took three mugs from the cupboard. "Where's yer mother? I've not seen her all morning."

Alynn's answer was interrupted by a knock at the front door. She tossed the spoons on the table and ran to answer it, but Caitriona flew down the stairs and beat her to it. "Faith, lad, what are you doing out in this rain? Come inside," Caitriona scolded. She stepped aside to allow a tall figure's entrance, and Alynn recognized Drostan even before he pulled down the hood on his sealskin jacket. Quickly, Alynn stepped into his arms for a hug.

"Rough morning?" Drostan asked.

"I'd a nightmare last night."

Drostan held her tighter, and for the first time that day, Alynn smiled. "You haven't had one in a while, have you?" he asked.

"Not since the beginning of Lent."

"You're alright now," he whispered to her, before turning to Caitriona and Lukas. "Rothgeir's fishing boat went down in Treacherous Landing last night, and I'm here with a few men to repair it. Might we put our horses in your stable?"

"Of course," Lukas said.

"Thank you." Drostan turned again to Alynn, kissing her forehead and playing with her hair. "Dreams can frighten even the strongest men, Lynder. But they can't hurt you. You're safe here, you know that."

"I do." Alynn looked up at him, his hair tousled and wet where it had refused to stay contained by his hood. "You're wonderful. Have you eaten breakfast?"

"If I say yes, will you still give me something?" Drostan asked. Alynn laughed, and Caitriona turned towards the kitchen. "I can't stay, though. Rothgeir's with us."

Alynn groaned. Rothgeir was one of the most ill-tempered Norsemen on St. Anne's Cleft. He always found something to complain about. If it was raining, he'd curse the rain; if it were sunny, he'd curse the heat; and God forbid it snow. But he was the island's best fisherman, and so everyone put up with him.

"Can you come by for chapel?" Alynn asked.

"I'll try to." Drostan kissed Alynn's forehead again, took the piece of cheese that Caitriona offered him, and bid them farewell.

After breakfast and the usual round of chores, Alynn was instructed to go walk Patience. As far as Alynn was concerned, the whole thing was an exercise in futility.

Patience, really, was anything but patient. She whinnied and stamped her little hoof while Alynn was getting the halter ready, even though Humility nickered for her to be still. Patience only tossed her head, as if she were ignoring her mother's orders.

"Be still, dear heart," Alynn encouraged. "If you're gentle, I'll get you something good to eat, alright?"

Patience pranced. She'd just eaten breakfast, thank you, and wasn't the least bit hungry.

Alynn smiled and stroked her gently, then tried to get the halter over her head. "Good lass, Patience, I'll just slip this on you—nothin' to be feared of—faith, calm down!" Patience bucked, squealing loud enough to draw the attention of even the unconcerned hogs. Alynn's heart quickly tripped over itself. Even though Patience was less than half the size of Humility, her hooves were sharp. Alynn jumped out of their way just in time.

Finally, the filly calmed down, and Alynn slipped the halter over Patience's head. "I've seen birds less flighty that you, wee gomey. Is that so bad, now?"

Patience tossed her head, as if to say "Fine, but I still hate you."

Alynn smiled and tried to lead Patience out of her stall, but Rothgeir's blood-bay stallion—a massive animal with his owner's personality—stood in their way. Alynn tried to smile at the animal and prayed that Patience wouldn't spark a riot. "If you don't mind, I'll just be leavin'—"

The stallion reared, and Patience all but dragged Alynn out the stable door. Alynn let her. Neither of them felt like being tramped.

All through Alynn's training session with Patience, anxiety nagged the back of her heart. She knew it was from her nightmare. They were coming less frequently now, two and a half years after the Norse raid of St. Anne's Monastery that had nearly killed both her and Lukas. But they were still intense, and sometimes a restless fear would plant its feet within her and refuse to move until the next dreamless night.

It wasn't always fear—sometimes it was tinged with anger, or with the venom of self-loathing. But it always made Alynn even clumsier than usual. After she put Patience back in her stall, she managed to drop her spindle on Cara the cat and nearly slice her fingernail off with her nalbinding needle. By noon, Alynn was wishing she'd pretended to be sick and stayed in bed that morning.

Alynn was about to ask Lukas when he was going to start chapel when the front door opened. Four figures burst in, talking and arguing amongst themselves and shutting the door against wind-driven rain.

"For Thor's sake, boy, you should have knocked louder," grumbled Rothgeir, who was immediately recognized by his surly demeanor. He wrung water out of his blond beard and scowled. "Or let a man do it."

"I *would* have knocked louder, had you given me the opportunity," Drostan said. He took off his hood and kissed Alynn on the cheek. "Forgive our intrusion, milady. Did we miss chapel?"

"Ye didn't," Alynn smiled, hugging Drostan. He was dripping wet and smelled of salt. "I'm surprised Rothgeir came with."

"I'm not about to sit out in the rain," Rothgeir said. "Blasted weather. It's cold in here. Where's your firewood?"

Alynn didn't say anything, but she exchanged a glance with Drostan as Rothgeir loaded more wood on the fireplace.

Lukas came down the stairs, his Bible under his arm. "Welcome," he said, shaking hands with Drostan and the two other men with him. "You're free to join us in the chapel or warm yourselves at the hearth. Whatever ye wish."

"Many thanks," said the other two Norsemen at the same time. They were brothers named Folkvard and Havard, one tall and one short, but both with rounded stomachs and unruly beards. They continued their quarrel as they walked towards the chapel, their voices ringing through the stone hallways.

"When will you learn to bring the right nails?" Havard demanded.

"Nails are nails!"

"We're fixing a ship, you twit, not hanging shields on a wall! Och, and congratulations on your betrothal, Alynn."

Alynn sighed and smiled as she followed them into the chapel.

For most of his services, as well as the prayers he offered up throughout the day, Lukas would chant in Latin. When others were with him, he quickly translated then into Gaelic. Today, though, they sang a hymn that Caitriona had written:

We preach Christ Jesus crucified,
And yet alive again.
He sits at Father God's right hand,
And seeks to save all men.

Alynn squeezed Drostan's hand and harmonized with Caitriona as they sang. Drostan's voice was strong and sweet, and Alynn sang like a lark, but Folkvard and Havard sounded like frogs during mating season. Alynn smiled at them. They sang with honest hearts, and God didn't care if their voices belonged in a bog and not a church.

After the hymn, Lukas recited three Psalms from memory and opened his Bible. "It's a blessing to see so many faces," he said.

"I can't say the same," Rothgeir scoffed from his seat in the far back. "Blasted Christians."

"Shut up, will you?" Havard snapped. Rothgeir rested his feet on the back of the bench in front of him and scowled, but said nothing.

"Apologies, Lukas," Folkvard said. "Carry on."

Lukas shook his head as he found the right verse. His lesson on speaking the truth in love was wonderful, or it would have been if Rothgeir hadn't been constantly interrupting to complain about something.

"Love this, love that. Is it the only thing you talk about?" he demanded, letting a few curses slip out as he continued his rant. "Love doesn't catch fish, it doesn't build ships, and it certainly doesn't win wars. You're weak to think otherwise."

Alynn tried to ignore him. She wondered if she could cut out his tongue and make it look like an accident.

"On the contrary, I've found that it takes a good deal of

strength to love others," Lukas said. "Which is easier, patience or impatience? Humility or arrogance? Love or hatred?"

"What does it matter?" Rothgeir asked. "You Christians are entirely backwards. You say your God loved everyone, and He died for it. It's daft. It's weakness, I say."

"And accordin' to yer own stories, how many of yer gods will die at the end of the world?" Caitriona demanded.

"They'll die honorably in battle," Rothgeir said.

"What do yer gods do but fight each other?" Alynn snapped. "And if they can't survive a simple sword fight, they're not the sort of gods I'd like to follow."

Rothgeir swore again. "What do you know about it, you stinking mackerel?"

"Will you shut up, man?" Havard snapped. "Let the priest finish his lesson."

Lukas had been standing patiently at his lectern, reading his Bible and completely tuning out Rothgeir's complaints. "What did I miss?"

"Say what you will," Rothgeir said, standing up. "You're taking too long. I'm leaving."

"Good riddance," Caitriona mumbled.

"If it hadn't been for your complaining, Rothgeir, we'd be dismissed by now," Drostan said. Alynn relaxed with a grateful sigh as he put his arm around her. "I think you'll have to clean the bench. His feet were on it," he whispered to her.

Alynn couldn't stifle a giggle. "I will—with a rag attached to a ten-foot pole!"

Lukas shut his Bible. "I know ye're short on time, gentlemen, so if everyone will stand, we'll end wi' the *Kyrie Eleison*." Alynn stood, and Lukas prayed, and larks and frogs alike sang the closing hymn. Drostan never moved his arm. Alynn wished he never would. This moment, with affection and worship keeping her fear so far from her, was heaven on earth.

"I've got to get back to work," Drostan said. He kissed Alynn's forehead. "Will I see you on Friday for sword fighting lessons as usual, milady?"

Alynn smiled. "You will."

She walked to the door with Drostan, blushed as he kissed her hand good-bye, and stood by the opened door watching him leave. The rain was falling harder now. Drops splattered onto the hem of Alynn's frock after they collided with the stone floor, and a flash of lightning illuminated the sky. Alynn glanced once more at Drostan and prayed for his safety as she shut the door.

The rain kept increasing throughout the afternoon, from a steady downpour to a relentless outburst to the kind of storm that made children hide under their bedclothes. Caitriona jumped at every roar of thunder, and even Lukas seemed agitated as he ground leaves and chaff into pulp to make paper with.

Alynn was hopelessly hapless, stepping on cats' tails and tripping over chairs and getting her hair tangled in the yarn she spun. She was glad when Caitriona asked her to check the stable for eggs. It meant she was going to make dinner, and dinner meant tomorrow was on its way. Tomorrow could always be better than today.

The rain was pounding relentlessly as Alynn ran to the stable. Poor Patience was squealing and jumping in her stall, frightened by the noises and flashes of light. Honor and Humility were somehow calm. But there was one other horse in the stable—a huge, blood-bay stallion that Rothgeir was trying to saddle.

Alynn jumped when she saw them. "What the devil—"

"Blasted horse," Rothgeir muttered, finally cinching the girth. "He's acting up. We're leaving before the storm gets worse."

"Ye could have spent the night here," Alynn said.

Rothgeir tightened his horse's bit. "I don't know why we didn't. Drostan was in such a hurry to get home, he didn't even notice the ship on the horizon."

"A ship?" Alynn asked. "Rothgeir, what ship?"

"I don't know, girl," Rothgeir snapped. "It looked like one of ours, but only a—" he threw in a Norse word Alynn had been careful not to learn— "stinking mackerel would be out in *this* weather. She was getting pitched about fierce good—perchance even foundering. Couldn't tell."

"Founderin'—what's that mean?"

"Landlubber," Rothgeir muttered as he mounted his stallion. "They're sinking."

Alynn forgot the eggs as she ran back to the monastery. "Mum! A ship!" she cried the moment the door flew open. "I'll be back!"

"Lynder, what are you—"

Alynn quickly hugged her mother. "Fix extra food. Some of the sailors might be wounded, Lukas, do you have splints and bandages?"

Lukas looked up like a confused child. "*Quae infernum?*" he asked, his Latin thoughts running to quickly to be translated.

Alynn didn't offer an explanation. She ran out the back door again, saddled Humility, and started off for the southern shore at a gallop.

The rain fell in sheets, and the sea foamed like the mouth of a mad wolf. Between the thunder and the pounding of rain on the ocean, Alynn could hardly hear herself think. She left Humility tied at the edge of the woods and scanned the sea. She saw a ship—a beautiful ship, probably a Knarr—riding dangerously low in the water. Alynn guessed it had hit a rock; this part of the southern shore wasn't called Treacherous Landing for nothing.

Rothgeir's fishing boat was repaired and rocking in safe harbor, but Alynn couldn't handle it by herself. Her eyes lighted on a landing boat. Quickly, she towed it to the edge of the pier, leapt into it, and started rowing.

Alynn didn't know what she was looking for. Heads in the water, maybe, Driftwood with survivors clinging to it. The only thing she could see was the ship, a solid speck on the shifting horizon. She forced herself to concentrate on the oars, and on shifting her weight to offset the waves. If she lost her train of thought, she knew she'd be swept up in a train of fear and horrid memories.

Suddenly, the landing boat listed to one side—and it didn't lurch back. Something had grabbed it. Alynn looked behind her to see a hand and an arm, clinging desperately to the landing boat. She grabbed the arm and pulled with all her strength. Finally, the hand and arm were followed by a blond head, then a chest, then the body of a sailor. He knelt in the bottom of the landing boat and coughed, then looked up at Alynn. He shouted something. Alynn couldn't hear him over the storm.

"I can't hear you, sir!" she shouted.

The sailor yelled a reply, probably something along the lines of "What?" that made Alynn smile. She let the sailor take an oar and help her row back to the pier.

As soon as the sailor was safely ashore, Alynn leaned next to his ear and shouted, "How many men fell overboard?"

"I don't know," the sailor shouted back. "I was the first. There's probably more." His voice was caught up in the wind and rain, but Alynn understood enough. She climbed back into the landing boat and shoved off again.

Already, her arms were beginning to ache and tire from rowing. The waves pushed her in every direction, threatening to knock the little craft to pieces. But Alynn pressed her eyes shut for a moment and took a breath. She knew the fury of the waves. They'd claimed her father's life. She wouldn't let them claim anyone else, not if she could help it.

Ten yards from shore, she glimpsed another figure. She shouted to him, although she knew it wouldn't do any good, but the sailor saw the landing boat and swam for it with a surprising strength. She grasped the sailor's hand and pulled as hard as she could, just as a wave caught the landing boat and crashed it into the sailor's chest. Water swallowed the sailor, and Alynn was nearly pulled into the waves with him. But he was strong and righted things before the next wave came.

With a powerful heave, the sailor dragged himself into the landing boat. Alynn stared at him—sandy hair, sea-hardened skin, a faded black captain's coat. She gasped.

"Captain McMahon!" she cried, hugging him. The man stiffened with surprise. The storm's roar had dimmed, but barely enough to make her voice audible.

"How do ye know?" he demanded.

Alynn laughed. "Tarin—where's Tarin?"

Captain McMahon's eyes widened. "Tarin *McNeil?*"

"Aye, Tarin McNeil!"

"He's safe! St. Mark's Church at Skerray!"

Alynn smiled. Adrenaline kept her from feeling the relief and joy and wonder she'd anticipated, but she could feel later. She let Captain McMahon take an oar and threw her focus into rowing. Into surviving.

As they neared the pier, Alynn noticed a pained look on Captain McMahon's face. Perhaps he was tired. But when she noticed the blood soaking through his shirt, she quickly took the oars from him.

"There's one more man," Captain McMahon said above the storm's roar as he climbed onto the pier. He winced again and clutched at his chest. "Let O'Quinlan get him."

Alynn took one look at the sailor she'd already rescued, white and weak as adrenaline left his system, and shoved off one last time.

A roar of thunder threatened to send fear knocking into Alynn's heart. She was already drenched with rain, and both fresh and salt water were pooling in the bottom of the landing boat. Her arms ached; sharp pains shot up her back as she struggled against the waves. She kept fighting. She had to find the third man.

She scanned the ocean, looking for a head or a hand sticking above the water. Once again, she glanced at the water collecting in the bottom of the boat. She didn't have time to bail it out. Or could she afford not to? She looked up again and saw a head, struggling valiantly to stay above water. A hand appeared, stretching, searching. Alynn dropped the oars in the oarlocks and reached out. The hand caught hers.

Alynn gripped the edge of the landing boat and pulled. The sailor caught hold of her arm, dragging himself to safety with whatever strength he had left. As soon as he was in the landing boat, he lay weakly in the puddle and choked up water.

"I've got three men. Is that all?" Alynn shouted at him. The sailor was coughing too hard to answer, but he nodded. Alynn sighed gratefully as she started rowing back.

Alynn's tired arms strained against the oars, and her shoulders knitted together into one massive cramp. She looked at the shore and wondered if she'd made any progress towards it. *Lord, help me,* she prayed.

Suddenly, a wave taller than a rearing horse swept over the landing boat. Fear gripped Alynn's heart as the craft overturned. Head over heels, she fell into the water. She panicked. Memories of her own shipwreck crowded out her concentration, the cold water and the desperate cry of her lungs for air pushing into her consciousness until it was all she could feel. She thrashed in the water.

A hand grabbed her, pulling her onto the overturned landing boat. Alynn gasped for air and coughed, rubbing salt out of her eyes as soon as she was able to. The first thing she saw was a person in front of her. It wasn't the third sailor, nor was it Captain McMahon or Sailor O'Quinlan, and it disappeared in a flash of light almost as soon as Alynn noticed it. Her fear was gone, replaced with the indescribable peace that only comes after a particularly moving worship service or a long prayer. Another flash of light appeared beside her, and suddenly the third sailor was clinging weakly to the landing boat.

Alynn had seen angels before, and she grinned at the privilege of being able to see them again.

She felt her feet touch bottom, and she was next to the pier. While Sailor O'Quinlan helped the third sailor onto dry land, Alynn pulled the landing boat ashore. Her legs felt as weak and wobbly as whale fat.

Just as she finished tying off the landing boat, someone grabbed her shoulders and spun her around. Alynn shrieked and grabbed the hands that held her, but she stopped. It was the third sailor, a tall and wiry man with a very familiar, very long braided mustache. But what paralyzed Alynn was his eyes. They were a clear blue—not lonely or sharp, as Alynn wanted to think they used to be—but full of amazement, wonder, and love.

Alynn tried to find her tongue, but the sailor found his first. His voice brought back a flood of memories as he looked deep into her turquoise eyes, gently brushing the wet hair from her face.

"Alynn?"

SIX

Alynn's head spun. She was going crazy—she was seeing things—surely she was mistaken. But he was real, and he was in front of her, staring at her with more love and compassion than she'd ever seen in him before.

"You're dead," Alynn breathed. "I watched you—"

The man's hands grew gentler as they caressed Alynn's face. "I'm right here, Lynder," he said, wiping the tears that mixed with rainwater on her face. "And I won't let anything happen to you again."

Carefully, Alynn reached out one trembling hand and brushed some hair off the man's forehead. She was looking for a thin, white scar on the left side of his forehead, where he'd been hit with the broad side of a sword seven years earlier.

She drew back her hand quickly. It was there.

The color drained from Alynn's face as she called the name she'd thought she'd never say again: "Father?"

The strong arms of Alynn's father, Rowan McNeil, encircled her, clutching her to his chest as if she were the only thing in the world that mattered. He was smiling, and for the first time Alynn could remember, he meant it. "Alynn, I missed you...."

Alynn drew a shaking breath. She trembled, and her head

spun. This was Rowan? How was he here? He wasn't a ghost. She could touch him, feel his breath when he kissed her. Truly, was it him? It was, it had to be him—he had the same eyes, the same hands, the same comforting heartbeat. Not even the salt and the rain could wash away the scent of coal fire that always hung around him.

He was shaking—was he cold? Alynn wrapped her arms more tightly around him before she realized Rowan was crying. It had to be Rowan; she'd never met another man who would cry in his daughter's presence.

"Da—"

"I've got you, Lynder. You're safe. I'm right here."

"You drowned," Alynn said, forcing herself half an arm's length away so she could look at him. "I watched you, Father. You let go of the driftwood...and...and you...."

Rowan shook his head. "I had a rope. I tried to pull you back with me—I couldn't hold on. I'm sorry—"

"Don't. 'Tis alright."

"I love you, Alynn."

"I love you too, Father."

For a while, they stood crying silently, arms wrapped around each other. Rowan kissed Alynn's forehead, whispering grateful prayers. Alynn was almost numb. She tried to breathe—to wrap her head around the fact that her father *wasn't* dead, and that he *hadn't* drowned, and that he was *here*—here with her, and she was in heaven. Rowan's embrace was the last thing she'd ever thought she'd feel, yet what she'd give anything to experience. It was everything she remembered.

Rowan wrapped his plaid around Alynn and pinned it. The wool was warm even though it was wet, and the fringed edge clung to Alynn's neck. She realized she was trembling. "Let's get you out of the rain. Where's yer home?" Rowan asked.

"At a monastery," were the only words Alynn could find to say.

"And you're well—they've been takin' care of you? Were you hurt when the landing boat flipped?" He felt her arms for broken bones, but the worst they met with were bruises and sore muscles.

"I'm grand, Father. But you—you were choking. Are you alright?"

"I've never been better."

Rowan kept his arm tightly around Alynn as she began to lead him to the edge of the woods. Instead of finding Humility tethered, they found Honor hitched to the hay wagon. Turning back to the ocean, Alynn saw Lukas giving blankets and a bottle of small ale to Captain McMahon and Sailor O'Quinlan. It made sense that they would stay and help the ship ashore.

Lukas returned to the wagon, glancing at the wet and bedraggled figures he saw before him. "You're Rowan McNeil?" he asked.

"I am, sir."

Lukas looked at Alynn, and his face softened when he saw her joy. "We're glad you're alright. Climb aboard, let's get ye home."

Rowan made sure Alynn was settled in the hay wagon before he sat next to her, covering them both with a blanket that had been left behind. "You're shiverin'," he said.

"I'm just tired."

"Then rest, Alynn. I've got you."

Alynn burrowed deeper into her father's arms. The wagon started for home with a jerk, and Humility trotted alongside them. Alynn didn't notice any of it. She was safe, warm, loved in her father's embrace. Nothing could touch her here.

She grew relaxed, but she also grew excited. By the time the wagon was rattling through the monastery's yard, Alynn thought her face would crack from ginning. Wouldn't Caitriona be surprised? As soon as the wagon stopped, Alynn took Rowan by the hand and flew across the yard with him.

"Mum!" she cried the moment the back door opened. "Mum, Father's alive—I was wrong, he's alive, he's *here!*"

Caitriona took a dripping-wet Alynn into her arms. "Child, what on earth—"

"Caitriona!"

She looked up and saw Rowan, his hair streaming past his shoulders in drowning locks and plaits, the ends of his braided mustache lying limp on his threadbare tunic. His eyes were wide and his mouth agape as he took a few spellbound steps towards her.

Caitriona stepped away from him, backing into her chair. She drew a shaking breath. "Rowan, I'm sorry—I didn't want for any of it to happen—I hated him, I hated every moment I spent with him—"

"I missed you, Cait."

Eyes glistening, Rowan hurried to take Caitriona into his arms, her willowy frame trembling as she buried her face in his shoulder. Rowan held her like a long-lost treasure, squeezing her hair and thanking God and letting tears slip past the eyelids he'd pressed shut.

"I've got you back, Cait," he whispered. "Och, thank God...I've got you back, Caitriona. I'll never let you go again."

Alynn smiled and blinked tears from her eyes. For seven years, her parents had been apart—each praying for the chance to see the other again, neither believing that it would ever happen. And now, they were two angels raised from the dead for each other, with tears of joy washing away the divide that once stood between them.

Alynn felt a hand on her shoulder. It was Lukas, soaked but smiling, and she hugged him. When he stiffened, she didn't notice. "Ye're certain that's yer father?" he asked.

"Of course I'm certain. Why wouldn't I be?"

"I thought ye'd look more like him."

"Our hair's the same color," Alynn said. "And Mum always said I have his ears. Tarin takes after him more than I do."

Lukas looked from Alynn to Rowan again and found the resemblance he was searching for. "I see it now," he said. "I'm happy fer ye, my dear."

"Thank you, Lukas."

Alynn turned her attention back to her parents. Rowan

cupped Caitriona's jaw in his hand, his thumb drying her tears and caressing the soft freckles most people never noticed. "Where's the man who took you?" he asked. "I'll take care of him."

"He's dead, Rowan."

"Thank God."

Caitriona held out an arm toward Alynn, and she lost no time in running over. "You won't guess who killed him."

"You did."

"Lynder did."

"You?" Rowan's eyes widened, and he kissed Alynn's forehead, drawing her into his and Caitriona's arms. "You killed a Viking?"

"I did."

"And you're alive? Did he hurt you?"

"Not badly."

"I'm so proud of you."

It was too wonderful for words—here, with both Rowan and Caitriona, this side of heaven, for the first time in seven years. Alynn smiled. She wondered if heaven could hold any more love than what was contained in this familial embrace.

Before long, the three of them were sitting on the floor next to the fireplace. Alynn leaned sleepily against her father's chest, feeling his hand tousling her hair, hearing his heartbeat. Alynn smiled, letting blessed memories run over her like water from a spring. She'd add this moment to the list of them. If she could only think of the last time she'd seen Rowan's eyes with so much love in them...

Laughter had never felt so good before. Sure, we'd had wee jigs like this since I was little, but this was the first one since Britta was born.

Britta was sleeping, all snug in the shawl that held her close to Mum's chest. It left Mum's hands free for playing her flute. Between the flute and

Father's timpan and me and Tarin dancing about, it was a wonder Britta could sleep at all. But there wasn't a noise that came from her, not a stir from her wee, soft form.

Tarin and I had been dancing forever. We were smiling so hard it hurt and laughing until we could scarce breathe. Tarin was just three, so he was mostly jumping up and down and letting me spin him in circles. But Aunt Sorcha had taught me a couple of dance steps. I loved to leap from one foot to the other and kick the air. I did it over and over again.

Eventually, Tarin stopped. He crawled into Mum's lap, peeked at Britta, and curled into a wee ball of freckles and red hair. "G'night, Mum," he prattled. "G'night, Da. G'night, Alynn. G'night, Bitta."

I smiled and yawned. I climbed into Father's lap, and he set his timpan on the ground to make room for me. "If you're sleepy, why don't you go on to bed?" Father asked me.

"Can you play a quiet song?" I asked.

Father made room for both me and the timpan in his lap. His arm wrapped around me so he could touch the bow to the timpan's three strings, and soft music filled the air. It was like an angel singing a lullaby.

I don't remember falling asleep, but I must have, because I woke up lying on my bedroll. Father was sitting beside me, tucking me under the quilt. There was something in the way he looked at me that made me smile. I'd never seen him look at me that way. This was the way he looked at Mum and Britta when they were resting together in the big bed. This was the way he looked at Tarin when he was falling asleep in his lap.

"Da," I asked, "do you love me?"

Father smiled. "Of course I love you, dear heart. And no matter what happens, no matter how far apart life takes us, I'll always love you." Then he kissed my forehead, and I fell back to sleep.

That was the last time we ever danced as a family. Mum was kidnapped a few weeks later, and Father didn't have the heart to play his timpan for a long time afterwards. Even when he did, it didn't sound the same without Mum's flute. Tarin and I didn't feel much like dancing, either.

'Tis too late to go back and change things. 'Tis too late to ask for another dance. But it isn't too late to fall asleep in Father's arms one last time.

Lukas watched the reunion at the hearth from the kitchen table, sipping his soup straight from the bowl since no one would bother correcting him. Alynn was asleep. She was peaceful, joyful, a gentle smile on her face. She did look like her father—their now-dry hair was identical in color, as far as Lukas's imperfect vision was concerned. If Rowan fell asleep, he could get a closer look at their faces without making a fool of himself.

Rowan, though, was probably too full of joy to sleep. He drowsily turned his attention from Caitriona, asleep or at least resting on his shoulder, to his daughter.

"Who found them?" Rowan asked.

Lukas gave a start and nearly spilled his soup before he looked up at Rowan, trying not to stare at the braided mustache that fell to his chest. "I did—well, rather the Lord directed me to Alynn, and Caitriona found us." He took a sip of his tea and winced. As usual, he'd steeped it far too long.

"Where was Caitriona?" Rowan asked.

"At the Norse village, on the northern shore." Lukas glanced at his mug. "Her tea is so much better than mine. Do ye know that she makes good tea?"

Rowan smiled—of course he knew Caitriona's tea was wonderful. He probably knew everything about Caitriona. He kissed Alynn's forehead again and said, "Thank you for takin' care of my girls."

"It's been an honor," Lukas said. "Especially to watch Alynn. She's meant the world to me since the day I found her, but I don't know how to raise her. I've tried my best, and Caitriona's done her part well. She's getting married. We'll see how she turns out."

Rowan paid a bit more attention. "Married? To who?"

"To a lad named Drostan Leifson," Lukas said. "He's a hardworking, good Christian lad, red hair, a shipwright by trade and noble by blood. He's destined to be chief of the Norse someday. He's won my approval, but Caitriona knows him better than I do."

Rowan looked at Alynn, her head resting peacefully on his shoulder. Even to Lukas, she looked more like a child than a maiden awaiting her wedding.

Lukas stood and placed his mug in his empty bowl instead of the washbasin. He half-smiled at his mistake and decided to leave the dishes for morning. "I'm going to bed. There are several empty cells, upstairs and down. Take yer pick of them."

"Where do the girls sleep?"

"Upstairs, in the main hallway. Not *in*—near. Blast it."

Chuckling, Rowan shook Alynn's shoulder to wake her. She seemed not to notice. Caitriona, though, stirred and sat up, rubbing sleep out of her eyes. "She's not going to wake up," she murmured.

"She's not grown out of that yet?" Rowan asked.

Lukas tossed the rest of his tea into the pig's bucket. "A glass of water will work, usually."

"No need." Rowan lifted Alynn, still damp and wrapped in his cloak, into his arms. She hardly stirred, only subconsciously putting her arms around her father's neck. Rowan smiled and watched her sleep with love in his eyes. "We're blessed, Cait," he said in a gentle voice. "We are so, very blessed."

The next morning, Alynn awoke nearly too sore to move. Her back, her arms, her shoulders—everything hurt, and she groaned as she sat up. She stretched until she could move freely again.

She ran her fingers through her matted hair, wondering why she thought today was special for some reason, and why sleepy sunlight was creeping through the crack under her door and no one had woken her up. When she saw the familiar green and blue plaid lying in her lap, though, she remembered that her father was there.

Without noticing her dress drying at the foot of her bed, Alynn threw off her covers and ran to the cell next door. Caitriona was putting on her frock, and Rowan was tying his boots. Alynn smiled and leapt onto the bed next to him.

"There's my Lynder," Rowan grinned, hugging her. "You slept well?"

Alynn smiled. "I did. And you?"

"Mum and I did so much talkin' last night, I don't know if we slept at all, at all," Rowan said. He kissed Alynn's head. "No matter. I've got my girls back."

"Here's yer plaid, Father."

"Many thanks," Rowan said as he draped his plaid over his left arm. He fastened it over his right shoulder with a finely-crafted pin, evidence of his skill as a blacksmith. "Is it true, Alynn, what Mum says—that in two short years you've fought a battle, learned to read, met a man, and pledged to marry him?"

Alynn leaned contentedly against Rowan. "I can't read all that well."

"I'm still proud of you."

Alynn smiled and whispered "Thanks," just as Lukas stepped into view. His hand was raised, as if he was prepared to knock on the door that was already flung wide open.

Lukas quickly tucked his hands into his sleeves in propriety. "Good morning, all. I was wondering—och, goodness—" He quickly turned his back to the room, and Alynn knew it was because she was still in her undershift. "I was wondering if ye'd join me fer the Divine Office of Prime. It would be a good chance to express yer gratitude to the Lord fer finding one another."

"We'll be right down," Rowan nodded as he finished tying his boots. "Thank you, Father."

"Call me Lukas, please."

"Run and dress, Lynder," Caitriona said. Alynn nodded and dressed quickly before joining her parents and Lukas in the chapel. Lukas was in his place at the lectern, chanting Latin hymns and Psalms from memory. Rowan and Caitriona were praying silently together at the front row of benches. Alynn sat next to Rowan, and the three of them held hands.

"Lord, we thank You for gettin' us here safely," Rowan said. "All of us, Lord. Thank You that we've found each other again." He paused, squeezing Caitriona and Alynn's hands, and his voice cracked as if he had a lump in his throat. "Thank You."

"Thank You that Father's alive," Alynn interjected.

"And thank You for protectin' Alynn while she rescued him," Caitriona said.

Rowan prayed again. Alynn was content to listen to the sound of her father's voice and to agree in spirit with his prayers, only voicing her own during moments of silence. Finally, the sleepy sunlight seeping through the stained-glass windows became the full light of another day. Rowan said a final "amen" and drew Alynn and Caitriona in for a hug.

"I've never thought I'd hold ye both again, this side of heaven," he smiled. "Thank You, Lord."

Alynn peeked past her father's shoulder to see Lukas, waiting patiently and rather awkwardly for a chance to enter their conversation. "Would ye like me to see to breakfast, Caitriona?" he asked.

"Whisht, I'm making griddle cakes," Caitriona tisked. "Lynder, come and help."

Alynn did all she could in the kitchen, setting three places at the table before laughing at herself and setting a fourth. Rowan tried to help, but he ended up stealing griddle cake batter until Lukas suggested he come and help feed the livestock. A plate of griddle cakes sat steaming on the table by the time they returned, and Caitriona had even placed flowers from the linden tree next to each plate.

"Now," said Caitriona, after everyone was seated and the prayers had been said, "there are some stories that need to be told. What happened, Rowan? How are you...?"

Rowan's eyes twinkled as he took another bite of his griddle cakes. "Still alive?" he asked.

"Even I'm curious," Lukas said as he cautiously sipped his steaming tea.

Rowan smiled. "As soon as Alynn fell overboard, I grabbed a rope and tied it to the mast. Then, I jumped off with the rope around my waist swam over to her, and gave her a piece of driftwood. But the rope wasn't long enough. It dragged me back towards the ship. I don't know how long I swam around in that water lookin' for her, but by the time someone hauled me back into the ship I was afraid she was gone forever. So I grabbed Tarin, took him into the tent we'd made on deck, and we cried."

Rowan paused and squeezed Alynn's hand. "When we got to port in Skerray, I could hardly think straight. We stayed at the church for a while—St. Mark's—and everyone there took care of us. Such grand people, they were. Eventually, I took over for the blacksmith who'd passed away. I rented a house, and every spare penny I put away, in hopes I'd be able to find you again, Lynder."

Alynn blinked. "Did you ever move?"

"Never."

"Never?"

"Not once."

Alynn opened her mouth to speak, but nothing came out. Part of her was glad that Rowan had finally learned to settle down, and part of her wondered why he'd taken so long. Finally, she whispered, "Please keep going."

Rowan smiled. "Tarin made friends with all the sailors. He'd ask them to look for you on their journeys. I wish ye could have seen his face when Tamlane said he'd found you. He's never smiled harder. I left him in the hands of our landlady, and of the church, for fear another storm would come up. And then—I found my Caitriona, too." Rowan squeezed his wife's hand and raised it to his lips; she blushed, and he glanced at his daughter. "Now, Alynn, I'd like to hear yer story. What happened after yer shipwreck? How'd you come here?"

"Lukas tells that story better than I do," Alynn said. "I was panned out for part of it."

Lukas looked up when he heard his name and quickly swallowed the last of his third griddle cake. "What am I—"

Alynn smiled. "The story of how you found me. Can you tell it?"

"Aye, it's one of my favorites." Lukas wiped his mouth on his sleeve. "It all began on a frightfully stormy morning, two Septembers ago. The Lord woke me afore sunrise and told me, 'Get on yer horse and ride north.'

"'But Lord,' said I, 'the Norsemen live to the north. They'll kill me.' But the Holy Spirit kept urging me, so I put on my cloak and followed His leading. I rode through the woods, then I tied my horse to a tree and continued on foot. I walked straight towards the village, right past it, until I could see the ocean.

"Then, the Lord said to me, 'Walk out on that pier.' I was frightened nigh to death, but I did, and I saw a girl on a piece of driftwood, floating in the ocean. So I fished her out, woke her up—we had a wee scuffle wi' the Norse, but God helped us out of it—I brought her back here, and she's brightened my life ever since."

Alynn glanced at Rowan to see that his eyes were shining. "Thank you for takin' care of my daughter," he said to Lukas. "I don't know what would have happened if you hadn't listened to the voice of God. He truly speaks to you?"

"Daily." Lukas helped himself to another griddle cake. "And I'm glad, or I'd have gone mad thirty years ago."

If Rowan was curious, the only sign he gave was the raising of his eyebrows. "Now, I've two other things I'd like explained. Alynn, you fought in a war?"

"I did," Alynn said.

"The Norsemen tried to raid the monastery two years ago," Caitriona explained.

"God protected us, and He's used it in remarkable ways,"

Lukas said. "We have a ministry to the Norse that we'd have never had afore."

Alynn felt herself smile. "We were outnumbered fifty to one, but God made the Norsemen fight themselves. It was grand. There's metal clangin' everywhere, this wonderful rush of energy—I was frightened, but I felt so strong afterwards. I can teach you how to sword fight, Father, if you'd like."

"I'll have to think about it," Rowan said, squeezing Alynn's hand. His griddle cakes lay forgotten on his plate. "I can hardly imagine you holdin' a sword, let alone usin' it. 'Tis such a gentle person you are. You're—alright, though, aren't you? You weren't wounded?"

Alynn touched her shoulder involuntarily. "Just a scratch."

"She nigh bled out, frightened me half to death," Caitriona corrected.

"Aye, but she kept fighting," Lukas said. "She killed the man who had kidnapped Caitriona. I believe she saved you quite a bit of legal trouble, Rowan."

Rowan smiled and fondled Caitriona's hand. "Now, I can take both of ye with me," he said.

"To where?" Alynn asked.

"Skerray. Or perchance we could try our luck in Limerick again. You'd like livin' close to yer family, wouldn't you, Cait?" Rowan grinned. For once in his life, his eyes held an almost boyish excitement. Alynn hardly recognized him.

Caitriona smiled. "I'd enjoy that. I don't know that Alynn would, with her gettin' married and all."

Alynn's griddle cakes turned to rocks in her stomach. To know that Rowan and Tarin and Caitriona were alive, but never see them again? Or to leave Drostan? Which was worse?

"'Tis alright, Alynn," Rowan promised. "Don't worry about it right now. We'll be stayin' here for a while."

For however brief a time, Alynn was relieved. "Thank you, Father. I'll try and—"

A sudden knock at the front door interrupted her. Lukas opened it, and Alynn smiled when she saw Drostan. She stood and flew to him.

"Alynn! Good news!" he called, taking Alynn into his arms. "Your captain friend's here!"

"I know," Alynn smiled. "You'll never guess who's with him."

"Tarin?"

"Not quite."

Drostan looked at Alynn, then at Caitriona and Rowan, and then at Alynn again. "He looks like a relative of yours. Is he your uncle?"

"He's my father."

Drostan's arms squeezed tighter around Alynn. She laughed—halfway with the joy of being able to say the word "father," and halfway with the thrill of being hugged by Drostan. "Alynn, that's wonderful," he said. Then, he leaned close to her ear and whispered, "I'm happy for you."

Suddenly, Alynn heard Rowan clear his throat and felt his hand on her shoulder. He tried to separate her and Drostan by a few inches—or a few miles, even. But Alynn only took half a step. "Who is this?" Rowan demanded.

"Father, this is Drostan—we're gettin' married."

A strange looked crossed over Drostan's face and stayed there, probably for longer than he'd have liked it to. He seemed afraid and sheepish and out-of-place all at once. He ran a hand through his hair before giving Rowan a firm handshake.

"I've heard quite a bit about you, Tristan," Rowan said.

"Drostan—and it's a pleasure to meet you, sir," Drostan said. "And quite a privilege to know your daughter. She's the finest young lady on St. Anne's Cleft."

"I don't doubt it," Rowan said.

Alynn blushed. "It was me or Maggie or Valgerd Rothgeirdottir, and either way, you'd have ended up with the worst in-laws this side of Dover."

Drostan gave a teasing scowl with half a smile tucked in it. "Stop that."

"Well, if you'd like to come inside, Drostan, I'd like to speak with you," Rowan said.

"It would be my pleasure, sir, but at the moment the *Darting Swallow* is sinking in Treacherous Landing, and I'd best get over there," Drostan said. He seemed almost ashamed for his forwardness, like a mouse who had just given orders to a wolf. He glanced at Alynn for moral support, but she was too busy reveling in the joy of having both parents and her betrothed in the same room to even notice. "Some other time, perchance?"

"Sure, the ship," Rowan sighed. "I signed on as a crewmate. I should be down there helpin'. Do you know how she's doing?"

"I'm not certain," Drostan admitted. "It looked like there was one man aboard, and he was signaling for help like mad. Folkvard, Havard, and Rothgeir are there helping."

"Rothgeir?" Alynn sighed.

Drostan shook his head. "He knows his way around ships, that's certain, even if he is a perfect twit about it. We'd welcome your help, Mr. Rowan."

"I'll be glad to," Rowan said.

"Finish yer breakfast, will you?" Caitriona asked.

"I'm full. That was the best meal I've had in years," Rowan said. He kissed Caitriona, but couldn't find it within himself to take more than two steps away from her. "Would you care to come with, love? It'll be a thrill for Tamlane to see you again."

"Can I come, too?" Alynn asked.

"That would be grand. It's a mile's walk, or you're welcome to bring your horses. I've got to go before Rothgeir tosses someone overboard." He took Alynn by the hand to lead her out the door, but she let herself slip out of his grasp.

"If you don't mind, I'd rather walk with Father," she said. "'Tis been two years."

"Of course."

Alynn smiled. Drostan led the way to the southern shore while Caitriona, Rowan, and Alynn walked behind, talking and laughing as they went. It took them twenty minutes to get to the beach, and all the while, Drostan didn't say a word.

As soon as she saw the *Darting Swallow*, Alynn realized it was in a bad condition. She usually rode high in the water. Now, there were only inches separating the top of the ship from the ocean. Havard was using his cupped hands to bail out water, and Rothgeir was sitting on a barrel so he could steer the ship without getting himself wet. Rowan walked out to Captain McMahon and Sailor O'Quinlan, who were standing anxiously on the beach.

Alynn couldn't hear the few words they exchanged, but both men looked stunned when they saw Caitriona. Captain McMahon swore in his surprise and exclaimed loudly enough for Alynn to hear, "Are ye sure, man?"

Rowan laughed. "Could anyone forget a face that beautiful?" Alynn looked up at her mother to see her blush.

Captain McMahon was quick to walk up and grin at them both. "Of course it's ye, Caitriona. Finest lass to walk the Emerald Isle!"

Caitriona smiled. "'Tis grand to see you again too, Tamlane. You haven't changed much."

"I'm glad ye're alright—don't hug me, I'll soil yer dress," Captain McMahon said, keeping Caitriona an arm's length away. He looked at Alynn and grinned. "Begad, ye look like yer mum! How's our brave guardian angel this morning? Sore?"

"Everywhere," Alynn laughed. Captain McMahon laughed too, and for the first time in Alynn's memory, his face betrayed a twinge of pain. "Are you hurt?"

Captain McMahon pulled on his bloodstained tunic. "I got keelhauled by the lifeboat last night. It's scrapes and bruises. Nothing serious."

"You were what?" Caitriona asked.

"It wasn't my fault!" Alynn said.

"It's a small price to pay fer my life," Captain McMahon said. "I'm glad Rowan's found ye both. I've got to make sure the ship comes in."

He left to speak with Drostan, Rowan, and Sailor O'Quinlan for a moment. Alynn watched the ship creep into the harbor. Someone gave a shout, and, grabbing the ropes tossed to them, the men on the pier carefully towed the ship inland.

Someone slipped. Alynn looked up and saw that it was Rowan. Her heart stopped for a moment, but it resumed when Rowan stood, laughing it off. He rubbed his head where he struck it on the pier, and Alynn's heart stopped once again when she saw blood smeared on his hair.

SEVEN

Alynn froze. Her heart pounded, her head spun. She watched blood turn Rowan's hair from a sunbeam-blonde to the matted red of an autumn leaf. Caitriona hadn't noticed, and she put a hand on her shoulder. "Are you alright, Alynn?" she asked.

When Caitriona touched her shoulder, Alynn found her feet. She ran to Rowan, pulled him off the pier, and put her arms around him. "Da...not again, please don't—"

"What are you doing, Alynn?"

"You hurt yerself. Let's get back to the monastery, Lukas is a fierce good doctor, you'll be alright—"

"Lynder—"

Caitriona flew up. "What happened? Are you—?" She saw a drop of blood fall from a strand of Rowan's hair, and her eyes grew wide. "Rowan...."

"Cait, 'tis nothin'."

"What happened?" Caitriona demanded. She searched Rowan's scalp for the source of the blood, and he winced when she found it. Alynn flinched.

"'Tis just a scratch," Rowan said.

"How? What happened?"

"I was shipwrecked, Cait. I probably banged my head on

somethin' last night, and it started bleedin' again when I slipped. 'Tis fine, truly."

"Bloodwort," Caitriona ordered, and Alynn handed her the pouch she kept tied to her belt. Caitriona emptied it and pressed its leafy contents to Rowan's wound with a doctor's firmness and a mother's concern. "You'll need stitches."

"Don't frighten Alynn like that," Rowan said. He tried to glance her way, but Caitriona kept his head still, so instead he motioned for her to come to him. Alynn took his hand, and they both smiled—one with nerves, and one with comfort.

"Is everything alright?" Drostan asked. He gave his tablet-woven belt to Caitriona. "Here's for a bandage."

"Thank you, heart."

"You're making too much of a fuss over nothing," scoffed Rothgeir as he sauntered up. "Cursed, stinking Irish mackerels!"

Alynn's eyes snapped. "If you had the heart of a pig or the brain of a troll, you'd be concerned, too."

Rothgeir sniffed. "I don't give a—"

"Rothgeir, do everyone a favor and head back to the village," Drostan interrupted. "You've done your job."

"Aren't I getting paid for this?" Rothgeir demanded.

Drostan sighed and took a copper coin from the pouch tied around his waist. "Here."

"Halfpence? That's it?"

"I'll give you some steel if there's another word of complaint out of you." Drostan was firm, and Rothgeir grumbled as he left.

"Ye won't need Rowan to do anything else, now that the ship's at bay, will ye?" Caitriona asked. She seemed polite, yet worried.

"Och, away wi' ye," Captain McMahon said.

"You might have Lukas look at your chest, Captain," Drostan suggested. "I'll start work on the ship right away."

"Shouldn't someone fetch Alva?" Caitriona asked.

"She's not dead yet?" Folkvard asked, before Havard told

him to shut up.

Rowan tried to charm Caitriona out of her worries by drawing her close to his side. "If she's ill, perhaps we should leave her be,"

"Alva's old, not ill," Drostan said. "She's the island's doctor. Rather eccentric, but she knows what she's doing. Folkvard, Havard, can one of you see if she's available?"

"We would," said Havard, "if we knew where she lived."

Drostan sighed. "You've *never* had to fetch Alva?"

Folkvard shook his head. "Aunt Bertha won't let us."

"Fie." Drostan glanced at the clouded sky, trying to think. "I'll fetch Alva. You two, stay with the ship. See if you can't pull her farther onto the beach, survey the damage, and salvage what ropes and sails you can, but don't touch her otherwise until my return." Drostan took Alynn's hand and led her back to the monastery. "Let's see if we can't get everyone taken care of."

Alynn was glad Drostan was fetching Alva, but she missed him. She wished his comforting voice would soothe the knots out of her stomach. She hated watching her father lying still in bed, hearing the occasional gasp of pain when Caitriona's needle went too deep. When the two of them were left alone in the room, Alynn sat on the edge of Rowan's bed and squeezed his hand.

"You're not worried, are you?" Rowan asked.

"I am," Alynn said. "So is Mum."

"You know there's nothin' wrong with me."

Alynn managed to smile. "You were bleedin' a lot."

"Head wounds do that. They look worse than they really are. It didn't even hurt until Mum put bloodwort on it."

Lukas came in the room. "Yer captain friend is doing well," he said.

"What happened to him?" Rowan asked, sitting up.

"Och, scrapes and bruises. He's blessed that nothing's broken. Rowan, I'd like to keep an eye on ye fer a bit, make sure yer head's right on the inside. Ye haven't been dizzy or nauseous recently, have ye?"

"I've not, sir."

"Good." Lukas glanced at Alynn and smiled. "I know females tend to worry too much, but it's a small price to pay fer their compassion."

"I agree," Rowan said, running his fingers through Alynn's hair. "I'm a blessed man."

Lukas half-smiled and took a key from his belt. "Alynn, would ye fetch us some bandages? We'll get Drostan his belt back."

"I will, sir," Alynn nodded. She kissed Rowan's forehead and left for the armory. On her way back, with her arms full of bandages, she heard a knock at the door. But when she opened it, there was no one there.

"Hello?"

"Down here."

Either Alynn had grown or Alva had shrunk since their last meeting, and the fact that Alva hadn't climbed the last stair yet compounded the height difference. The woman of cures was shorter than most twelve-year-olds, slightly built, so that she looked more like a fairy or half-elf than a full-blooded human. Her coif and plait were the same creamy wool-white, her clothes somber shades of red and green, her face covered in the soft wrinkles that come with age. She smiled, and Alynn smiled back.

"Sorry," Alynn said.

"It happens more often than you think," Alva assured, her voice rasping yet kind. She mounted the last stair with the help of a cane and stood at her full height, a head shorter than Alynn. "I congratulate you, my dear, on finding your father. I assure you, he'll mend well, just as you did after the Battle of Faith."

"Thank you, Alva." Alynn tried to shut the door behind them, but something black darted into the monastery just before she could. It coiled around Alva's cane, oozing upwards, finally crawling up her back and onto her shoulder. It was then that Alynn realized what it was: a snake.

She jumped backwards, giving an involuntary screech that she tried to muffle with her hand. If she'd had her sword, she would have hacked it to bits. Alva simply chuckled. "This is Vorthmathir. Give her a kiss, Vorthmathir. Show her how gentle you are."

The asp stretched out until its undead amber eyes were staring directly into Alynn's soul, her every thought and feeling bare before him. Alynn could hear her heart beating, feel it pulsing through her chest. She was shaking and wanted to run, but she couldn't feel her feet. "Stop," she breathed the moment she found her tongue, while the hellish creature was a mere six inches from her. "Please stop."

"Vorthmathir, come here and give *me* a kiss," Alva said, and the monster turned around and licked his mistress's lips. His duty finished, Vorthmathir slid down Alva's chest and wrapped around her waist like a belt. There he stayed, warm and secure, his tongue occasionally flickering to taste the air around him.

Finally, Alynn could take a breath. "*Why* did you name a *snake*?"

"He eats my mice."

"Get a cat."

"I've tried, child. They make me ill." Her nose was already running from the many cats that prowled the monastery. "Might I see your father, and his friend the captain?"

"Can—can you leave yer pet outside?"

"But I held his egg as it hatched. We've never been apart." Alva's eyes, kind and grey, looked up at her like a pleading puppy's. "You won't separate us now, will you?"

Sighing, Alynn led the way to the cell Rowan had been placed in. She was glad to hear Drostan's voice greet Alva in the hallway and feel his arm slip around her waist. "Can you get rid of the snake?" she whispered.

Drostan mimicked her Irish lilt. "The *sneyk*? 'Tis just a *sneyk*, a *sneyk* won't hurt you—"

"Drostan, you—"

Behind them, Alva's laugh got caught in her throat and came out as a coughing fit. Alynn was able to catch her laughter, but Drostan wasn't. It was a merry group that threatened the solemnity of the sickroom as Drostan held open the door for the ladyfolk.

"What took you so long?" Caitriona scolded as she snatched a bandage from Alynn's arms. "Hold still, Rowan. Don't let me make it too tight."

"Cait, I don't—"

"Don't argue with me," Caitriona scolded, "just wear the bandage, at least for a few days."

Rowan sighed. "Lynder, ask the doctor to check on Tamlane. I'm grand now."

"I'll get to him in a moment," Alva promised. "I'd like to meet the father of Alynn the Dauntless."

Caitriona gave a relieved smile, but Rowan leaned back, closed his eyes, and resigned himself to his fate. Alva studied Rowan for a moment, as if she'd expected a different person. True, Rowan didn't meet the traditional criteria for a blacksmith—he was thin and gangly, not unlike a beanpole with long hair. If Alva had envisioned him as a warrior, she was met with a peasant. He'd been nondescript enough in Ireland, but was a novelty to the Norse.

"How could anyone find a wound on your head?" she asked. "When your wife was taken, you vowed you'd never let another woman cut your hair, didn't you?"

Rowan chuckled. "All men in Ireland wear their hair long. You'd love to meet the governor of Limerick City. I mistook him for a woman the first time I met him."

Alva shook her head with the disdain only elderly people have for the younger generation, sliding his hair back to examine his wound. "You've taken good care of it, Caitriona.

Beautiful stitches. Bandage it for a few days, and take care in combing it, and he'll mend fine. I doubt you've had internal damage, sir, but have you been dizzy, or sick to your stomach?"

"I've not."

"Good, very good." Alva's claws ruffled through Rowan's hair, looking for further scratches, before re-wrapping the bandage around his head. "Have you been called a stinking Irish mackerel yet?"

"I have."

"Good."

A thousand curses lit on Alynn's tongue, but a single stare from Vorthmathir silenced all of them. So instead, she turned to Drostan and whispered, "Is she kin to Rothgeir?"

Drostan shook his head. "If she is, no one admits it. It's been said that she's a half-elf. I think it shows. What is she, four foot nine?"

Alynn glanced at Alva. "I think she looks more like a banshee."

"In appearances, I agree. But she's a blasted immortal. She treated Elder Steingrim for chicken pox when he was a child."

"Truly?"

"Children!" Caitriona scolded. She took the salve Alva handed her, with instructions for its use and an offer of more if it was needed.

"It shouldn't get infected, but if it does, come get me," Alva said. "But then again, I'm sure your man of God knows all about such things as well—come get me anyway. You can't learn healing through books."

Despite Alva's reservations, Alynn knew that Lukas was the best doctor on St. Anne's Cleft under the age of sixty, and she was proud of that.

It wasn't until Alva turned to see Captain McMahon that Caitriona and Rowan noticed the snake wrapped around her waist. Vorthmathir stuck his tongue out at them, as if bidding them a grotesque farewell, and stared into everyone's souls until Alva disappeared around the corner.

Rowan's eyes widened. "Was that a dragon?"

"It was a snake," Alynn corrected. St. Patrick had driven the snakes from Ireland, so it was no wonder Rowan had never seen one. Alynn hadn't seen one until she'd come to St. Anne's Cleft, either.

"Oh." Rowan leaned against the wall, a bit disappointed. "'Tis close to a dragon, isn't it?"

"I've wondered that," Drostan said. Dragon or not, Alynn was glad it was gone.

"You have faith in the woman, despite her eccentricity?" Rowan asked.

With a nod, Drostan began to unbuckle the straps that held his vambrace on his right arm. "When I was a lad of five," he said with a wince, "I tripped and fell into our fireplace. My father insists I'd have died had Alva not tended to me." The vambrace came off and revealed an arm wrinkled with burn scars. "Truth be told, it's a miracle I have all my fingers."

Rowan eyed the scars carefully. "'Tis a miracle you still have yer arm. Does it still hurt?"

"Not much, if I keep it covered."

"I see." Rowan adjusted the bandage on his head. "While you're here, Drostan, do you mind if I have a word with you?"

Drostan fidgeted. "Of course, sir—but I will have to leave—eventually—to make sure no one's drowned anyone else back at Treacherous Landing...."

"I understand." Rowan was silent for a moment, eyeing Drostan with a gaze as sharp as icicles, or a sword glinting blue in the sunlight. He stood to his full height, took Alynn by the shoulder, and made her take three steps away from him. His glare returned to Drostan, and he said sternly, "She is not yours. You will not touch her, nor hold her, nor be alone in a room with her, until I give word. Do you understand me?"

Drostan nodded, but Alynn saw the unassuming way he wiped his hands on his trousers. "I understand, sir."

"Good." No part of Rowan betrayed any sense of approval. "'Tis many good things about you that my wife has told me.

But until I can judge yer character for myself, consider yer betrothal suspended."

Drostan's mouth opened, and a single angry spark flashed in his eyes. His fists clenched. For a moment, Alynn thought he would strike Rowan, and wondered which of them would win in a fight. Then, as she finally comprehended Rowan's words, she felt her own rush of emotions. But it wasn't quite anger—it was loss. She felt small and alone, desolate like a lost lamb on a hillside. She looked at Drostan just in time to see the color drain from his own face. He looked at Alynn, and each felt as if the other was slowly fading from existence.

A strange and out-of-place determination came into Drostan's eyes, and he turned to Rowan again. "Let me hold her once more," he said.

"You'll hold her again, unless you're not the man Caitriona's made you out to be," Rowan said. "Go on."

Before Rowan's words had time to settle in Alynn's mind, Drostan's arms were around her so tightly she could hardly breathe. Alynn listened to the rhythm of his frightened heart "I love you," she whispered.

"I love you too, Lynder," Drostan whispered back, "and I'll get you back. I promise."

He kissed her head, and she kissed his cheek, and he pressed her golden head to his heart. Just as Alynn was beginning to feel safe, as if things were going to be alright again, Drostan squeezed her tighter and let go.

Drostan looked at Rowan, a look somewhere between fear and anger in his eyes, and he left the room. Alynn wished with all her might that she could follow him. As soon as she heard the front door shut, she knew she was free to speak. She glared at Rowan, but she couldn't find any words.

"I'm simply trying to protect you, dear heart," Rowan said. His face had gone from steely determination to soft understanding in a matter of moments, and Alynn wondered which one of them was a mask. "I want a good Christian man for you, raised in the church and not among pagan thieves. I know you understand—"

Fuming, Alynn left the room. A good man? A Christian man? Drostan was a better man than Rowan! But Rowan wouldn't see it that way. He'd always see Drostan as a Norseman—a raiding, pillaging Viking at that. Once he found out that he was the nephew of the man who'd kidnapped Caitriona and started this whole debacle, Rowan would have nothing but contempt for him. Alynn went into the backyard and slammed the door shut behind her.

A gentle rain had begun to fall, calming and cooling her emotions. She inhaled it. It graced her hair with dripping jewels and dampened her dress until it clung to her narrow shoulders. She breathed in the wonderful fresh scent of the rain. She could pretend she was a child back in Limerick again, but pretending never solved anything.

Just a few hours ago, she'd had the whole world. And now, all she had was a gentle rain.

June Something, A.D. 966—

Forgive my lack of a date. I'm exhausted, but my mind will not let me sleep until I process my emotions.

Alynn's father, Rowan, has returned as if from the dead. I rejoice with Alynn and Caitriona at their reunion, and yet Rowan is such a strange character that I have too many questions to ask, but none of the social graces to ask them with. He looks strange. I've never seen hair like his, except for in depictions of Christ in illuminated Gospels. He has devoted a lifetime to growing out his mustache, but he shaves his beard. Curious.

It seems that every McNeil I meet is more emotionally scarred than the last. In Rowan I sense fear. It is not a common apprehension, but the fear of loss, as if he believes his family is soon to be snatched from his hands. Along with this fear is despair. I pity Rowan. Aye, he feels joy at his reunion with his family, but he seems unaccustomed to positive emotion.

He is a decent man at any rate, hardworking, loyal to his family. I know there is greatness within him, and I intend to help him unlock it. But not now, of course—give him a few days to settle in with his family, and I can later ask to chat with him over tea. Caitriona's tea, of course. Mine is awful.

There, I've written. Now, devil mend it, let me sleep.

—L. McCamden

EIGHT

Alynn awoke the next morning to the thin, grey light of a trembling morning sun trying to break through clouds. Raindrops pattered on the roof, and a lonely wind whistled through the belfry. Alynn lay still for a moment. She remembered the joy of Rowan's return, then the pain of having Drostan wrenched so rudely from her, then the guilt she'd felt for walking away from her father. By the time she'd recalled the stony silence between them at the dinner table, Alynn wished she could roll over and go back to sleep.

But today was a new day, and perhaps it would be a better day. Perhaps she and Rowan could apologize to each other and pretend yesterday never happened. Alynn bounced out of bed and dressed quickly. Before she opened her parents' door, though, she stopped to listen.

"Rowan, you needn't be quite so gentle."

"If I go any faster, I'll either break the comb or rip yer hair out."

"You won't, love. Trust me. It'll take all day otherwise."

"'Tis a good thing I have all day."

Alynn knocked.

"Not now," Rowan said.

Crestfallen, Alynn took the slightest step backwards.

"Never mind," she said. "It...'tis nothin' important."

Something needed to be cleaned. Alynn wasn't sure what. She'd spill the barley flour if she had to, she just needed something to scrub. But first, there was the morning stirabout to tend to.

Alynn had the eggs gathered and breakfast on the table by the time Lukas finished with his morning devotions. "Ye've been productive this morning," Lukas noted as he stole a fresh bilberry from the table.

"Busy day." Alynn set four mugs of milk on the table. "When's the last time we washed the chapel floor?"

"It isn't dirty. Don't bother washing it."

"Sabbath's in two days, tomorrow's laundry day...."

"Alynn, take some time to spend wi' yer father." Lukas gently took the spoon with which Alynn was stirring the stirabout. "No one cares what the floors look like."

"Father would rather spend time with Mum than with me. I'll get some work done today, and perchance tomorrow we'll do somethin' together."

"Are ye alright with that?"

"I haven't much choice." Alynn made herself smile, then left to set bowls on the table, mentally reciting her list of chores. *Weed the garden, sweep and dust, card some wool, I've a reading lesson most likely. And today's Friday—I've sword fighting lessons with Drostan after chapel. Can't forget that.*

Would Rowan let her go? He would, Alynn decided, if he didn't know. He'd be so busy catching up with Caitriona that he probably wouldn't notice her slip out anyway.

Alynn drew a bucket of water for the washbasin, and when she came back, Lukas was having a cross between a discussion and an argument with Rowan and Caitriona.

"Two points of consideration," Lukas was saying. "One, could it wait until after breakfast; and two, will ye make me wear my cuculla like ye did fer Sigmund's wedding? Because we all know that didn't end well."

"You needn't dress up," Caitriona said. She wasn't wearing

her kerchief. Her golden hair cascaded past her shoulders and nearly to her knees. Even Rowan's mustache was freshly brushed and braided, and his plaid was draped regally over his left arm. "It isn't truly a wedding."

"So does it matter how many witnesses there are?" Lukas asked.

"It isn't the ceremony they're supposed to witness," Caitriona corrected, rather quietly.

Rowan held up a hand in mock surrender. "As long as Norse law will recognize a Christian wedding."

"We have an agreement." Lukas tucked his hands into his sleeves. "We gather together to reunite Caitriona and Rowan McNeil in holy matrimony. Caitriona, will ye take Rowan as yer husband?"

"I will."

"And Rowan, ye'll take Caitriona as yer wife?"

"With all my heart."

"Then ye're married again. If we could eat breakfast afore I die, I'd appreciate it."

Caitriona and Rowan kissed each other. Lukas, as uncomfortable as an eight-year-old at a wedding, turned to the fireplace and stirred the stirabout. Alynn took four bowls from the cupboard and held them as Lukas filled them. "Did you have a nightmare last night?" she asked.

Lukas drew a deep breath, and Alynn noticed the twinge of pain in his eyes. "Nay, I was working with Patience yesterday. We ran into some difficulties, and now everything hurts."

Sympathy tugged at Alynn's heart. "She didn't kick you, did she? Are you alright?"

"It's nothing time and some willow tea can't cure, my dear," Lukas said. "And breakfast will help. Here's fer ye and yer parents."

Alynn opened her mouth to protest, but she quickly shut it. She watched as Lukas scraped the sides of the pot, trying to get as much stirabout as he could, yet she knew that he'd come up half a bowl short. She'd intended that half bowl of stirabout for herself. The oats that would have gone into it were safely tucked away in a bag, ready to give to Dagny and Geirhild and their children.

Lukas looked up at Alynn to see her balancing three steaming bowls in her arms, her eyes open uncommonly wide. "You can have some of mine," she said softly.

He half-smiled. "It'll do me nay harm. I've gained eight pounds on yer mother's cooking as is."

Alynn made herself smile and sat down to eat. It was a joy to watch her parents, seated across from her, talking and smiling and laughing and holding hands like a courting couple. And there were the little things about Rowan that Alynn had forgotten—the way milk stuck in his mustache, how he always kept his right elbow on the table. And there was the way his eyes crinkled when he smiled, which Alynn had never noticed before. Had he ever smiled so hard before? He certainly didn't have laugh-lines like Leif did.

Alynn looked at her bowl and realized it was completely empty. And for once, she didn't have to convince herself that she was full.

By the time Alynn had washed the dishes, Lukas had disappeared, Rowan was fixing a bent metal spatula, and Caitriona was watching him with an almost spellbound fascination. Alynn carefully gathered up the food she'd saved for the widows Dagny and Geirhild—a small sack of oats, a lump of butter, and some cheese, along with a halfpenny she'd found in the chapel—and tied them all in a cloth bundle. Finally, she put on a hood and rode to the village.

The trip to the village usually took twenty minutes at a decent pace and ten at a gallop, now that a new path had been made through the forest for the convenience of churchgoers. But Humility went slowly because of the rain, and at least half an hour passed by the time Alynn entered the village. The sound of hammers rung out everywhere, like the pealing of bells at a wedding.

After stabling Humility at Leif and Drostan's house, Alynn

quickly completed her errand. She tried not to cast so much as a glance over her shoulder when she heard the door to the widows' house open, and a little girl's squeal as she found the offering—either Kelda or Kenna, one of the six-year-old cousins everyone mistook for twins. Or maybe both of them, from the chatter of voices that quickly ensued. Alynn smiled, stuffed her empty sack into her sleeve, and left to find the source of the hammering.

The sounds led her to the very edge of the village, where the town faded out into the pasture where all the villagers' livestock grazed. There was not a single goat, lamb, or horse to be found in the pasture; rather, it was full of men putting up A-frame tents.

Alynn wandered for a bit before she found Drostan, straddled atop a tentframe so he could secure it with wooden pegs. His hammer rang out louder than any other in the field, and he smiled when he saw Alynn. "Good morning, milady! I was just thinking of you," he called as he slid to the ground. He took her hand, still smiling, and motioned towards the many tents. "We're setting up for Althing."

"Ye're makin' grand progress," Alynn said. The rain was gentle now, so she pulled down her hood of undyed wool and freed her hair from it. If Drostan noticed, he pretended not to.

"We've barely started. There's so many people coming— chiefs, chiefs' wives, landowners, artisans, skalds. Every freeman in Orkney is welcome, not that all of them will come. We can only house four or five hundred men. Ask Lukas to spend the week up here. He'll have some brilliant opportunities to witness to people. Perchance we'll see a few miracles."

"Miracles are up to God, not Lukas." Alynn picked up her skirts and trotted to keep up with Drostan's long strides. He noticed and slowed down for her. "Will there be a smithy?"

"Of course. What does your father specialize in?"

"You'll have to ask him that. I know he's fierce good at makin' cloak pins and horseshoes."

Drostan shrugged. "They're the same shape. Makes sense.

He's welcome to make and sell them here."

"He'll be glad to hear that."

By then, Alynn and Drostan had reached the edge of the sea of tents. It was quieter here; Alynn could hear herself think, and she could see the quiet malaise that was tugging somewhere at Drostan's mind. She smiled compassionately. "What's wrong?"

"About what your father said the other day—is there anything I can do, or say, or keep from doing, that would make him like me?"

A pin pricked at Alynn's heart, and that terrible feeling of distance crept between her and Drostan. "I don't know, love. Father...you'll have to earn his trust afore you can earn his favor. If you ask Erik to flirt with me at Mass on Sabbath, then swoop in and save me—"

"No."

"'Tis the only thing I can come up with."

"And it would probably work. But I'm not putting you in that situation."

Alynn sighed. Would it be worth it to ask Erik herself? No—to be honest, she didn't want to be in that situation either.

The rain, which had been lightening, grew suddenly fiercer. Drostan drew Alynn's hood over her head and tucked her hair back into it. "Care to stay at my house until the rain lets up?" he asked.

Alynn smiled. "I won't melt. I'll watch you work, so long as I won't distract you. I can't have you mistakin' yer thumb for a peg."

"I know the difference." Drostan's arm rested on her narrow shoulders as he led her back to the tents. Alynn realized how wet her dress was, but she didn't care. She felt safe. "I'd put you to work, but...."

Alynn laughed. She was dangerous enough without a hammer; she'd probably crush her hand or put someone's eye out. "If you think of anything I can do to help, let me know. I have to stay until Humility's rested."

"You're welcome to stay longer. You can wait out the rain if you want to, or leave before it gets worse. Take Thrymja, and we'll trade out at sword fighting lessons." Drostan took his hammer again and helped attach a canvas sail to the wooden tentframe. He kept a caring eye on Alynn. "Are you getting along with your father? I mean—I'm glad you're here, I'm just—surprised you're not spending time with him."

"He's with Mum," Alynn said, trying to sound comfortable with the fact. She couldn't tell if she was jealous of the attention Caitriona was getting, or guilty for not making more of an effort to spend time with Rowan, or wary of letting Rowan too close to her again. She didn't have a reason to be, unless she didn't want to go through the pain of losing him again.

"To a man, there's nothing more wonderful than spending time with the lady you love." Alynn felt her ears grow red. "Give him time, Lynder, he'll come around to you eventually. He's probably missing you right now."

"He stopped missing me the moment he set foot on St. Anne's Cleft, and he won't start again unless I die before he does."

"That's not true." Drostan set his hammer aside, giving Alynn the sideways glance and the compassionate smile that always made her melt. "Go see him. Take Thrymja."

Alynn smiled. Thrymja had a broader back than Humility and was not nearly as friendly, but she was well-loved by her owner, and it was an honor to be offered her use. "You're sure?"

"Of course. I'm getting the better end of the deal, anyway."

Alynn embraced Drostan, kissing his cheek. "Thank you, love. You can keep Humility until Sabbath if you're too busy for sword fighting lessons."

"I'm never too busy for you." Drostan kissed her forehead. "I'll see you after chapel. Now go spend time with your father."

By the time Alynn returned to St. Anne's Monastery, butterflies were flitting around inside of her. But were they excited to see Rowan or nervous? Did she have a valid reason to be nervous? She stabled Thrymja and half-walked, half-ran to the monastery.

"Da!" she called.

Her voice echoed throughout the stone hallways. No one answered.

"Da?"

The hearth was empty, the smoldering fireplace the only sign of life. Alynn stirred the embers and added more wood until a tiny flame appeared, then she left to see if Rowan was in the chapel.

"Father?"

The chapel was derelict. Lukas hadn't even left his Bible on the lectern. Frustrated, Alynn ran upstairs. Her parents weren't in their cell, or hers, and Lukas wasn't in his. *Figures,* Alynn thought. *I suppose even Drostan is wrong on occasion. But where the devil could they be?*

Alynn tromped downstairs. The library was locked, and the scriptorium where Lukas could occasionally be found writing was empty. Finally, Alynn found Lukas outside, hoeing the barley fields.

Lukas saw her approach and stopped working. "Where'd ye run off to?" he asked. "Yer father was asking fer ye."

Of course he was, Alynn scoffed to herself. "Where is he?"

"He took yer mother to visit yer captain friend."

Alynn sighed. "I'm not surprised. Ask him to give you a hand in the fields this afternoon. You oughtn't be doing all of this yerself."

"Noah finished the ark when he was six hundred and twenty. I ought to be able to handle the barley and oats," Lukas said. "Go on inside afore ye catch yer death of cold."

Sighing, Alynn turned back to the monastery, but she drew a bucket of water before she went inside. Was everything Rowan's fault for not waiting for her, or her own for leaving in the first place? Why did she have to insist on giving away food? It probably didn't help Dagny and Geirhild much, and there definitely wasn't much in it for her. Alynn took out her frustrations on the chapel floor, scrubbing it on her hands and knees. Her hair dangled in disorderly locks across her face, and she kept tossing it over her shoulder only for it to fall back on the other side.

She had half the floor finished when she heard the chapel door open. Through her filter of hair, she thought she saw Rowan. He knelt in front of her, looking unusually happy and rather amused. "Somewhere in here," he said, clearing the hair out of Alynn's face, "I've a daughter...there she is."

Rowan was smiling at her, and he meant it.

Alynn hugged Rowan, soapy fingers and all. His arms around her were heaven, as comfortable as a warm blanket on a winter's evening. She could fall asleep here.

"I missed you," she said.

"I missed you too, heart. Where'd you run off to?"

"I was runnin' errands."

"Ah." Rowan kissed the top of her head and pressed water out of her hair with a gently powerful hand. "Might I come with, next time?"

"Perchance. How's yer head doing?"

"I haven't given it a thought all morning," Rowan said. Indeed, most of his bandage was covered by his sun-colored hair. "Now, suppose you show me around? I'm lost in such a large building."

Alynn smiled. "Of course."

She led Rowan through the downstairs—the armory, the scriptorium, and the weaving-room. She climbed the ladder to the belfry and showed him St. Barnabas, the bell. All the while, she held his hand, and she felt his loving gaze on her.

When they were finally upstairs, Alynn showed Rowan her room. Instead of looking at the notebook on her bedside table or the wool she was carding, Rowan turned to the sword that was mounted on the wall above her bed. "It feels like yesterday you were showin' me the first pair of mittens you made. I can't imagine you fightin' off Vikings."

Alynn drew her sword from the wonderful sheath Drostan had given her. Seeing the blade shine in the dim light of her bedroom always made her heart beat faster. "Does this help?" she asked.

Rowan smiled, taking the sword from her and inspecting it carefully. "Lovely weapon—a bit too sharp, but I'm glad it's served you well. You've killed quite a few people with this, haven't you?"

Alynn was silent. Carefully, she took her sword from Rowan, sheathed it, and set it on its pegs.

"You don't talk about it, do you?"

"I don't."

Something came over Rowan's face—it couldn't be concern, could it? —and he drew her into a hug. "I'm sorry," he said gently.

"Don't be sorry for me. 'Tis Lukas who got the worst of it, broken ribs at his age. He can't get in or out of a chair without groanin', yet he tends the barley and the oats singlehandedly, maintains the building, and preaches Mass every Sabbath, with never a word of complaint."

"He sounds like a good man."

"In all the churches I've been to, I've yet to meet a better pastor. You'll like him, Father. He taught me to believe in salvation by grace through faith."

"Praise God." Rowan sat on the edge of Alynn's bed, and she sat next to him. "I'm proud of you, dear heart. It takes courage to believe what most consider foolish."

"'Tis easy to believe here. No one believes in salvation by works, and we're certainly not punished for thinkin' differently. Lukas doesn't keep to the Psalms when he teaches—and he taught me to read, so I can see for myself what the Bible says."

Rowan smiled. "That's grand. Tarin's learned to read, too."

"How is Tarin?"

"He's pure grand. Runs around, skins his knees, helps out around the house. He tries to cook, sometimes, but all he can make is stirabout and terrible, *terrible* vegetable soup. But he's a good lad, gold-hearted. Right as I was leavin', he told me, 'Da, if you find Lynder, tell her I love her and miss her, and give her a great big hug.'"

Alynn wanted to cry as Rowan gave her Tarin's hug. She tried to see his green eyes and his freckles and the gap between his front teeth, and she half-remembered, half-imagined the feel of his twig arms around her. "Can you tell me more about him?" she asked.

Rowan's eyes shone. He told about Tarin and his friend Connor running off to hunt frogs in the moor without telling anyone first, and half the town of Skerray went out looking for them. He told about playing his timpan for a wedding party, and how the landlady's cat watched mice drink its milk without so much as lifting its tail. When he had run out of stories, Alynn began to tell her own—how she had learned to sword fight, how Humility tried to teach Patience to like carrots, and the time she tried taking a bath in the heated Norse pools, but her clothes blew away and she had to chase them in a borrowed undershift.

All the while, the rain danced cozily on the roof, and Alynn relished the warmth of Rowan's hand over hers, and somehow they crept closer to one another until their shoulders were touching. When all the words had been spoken, Alynn wrapped her arms around her father and remained there in a still, happy silence.

When Alynn looked up, she saw Caitriona smiling at them from the doorway. "Is it time for chapel?" Alynnshe asked.

"It was an hour ago that chapel ended," Caitriona said. "Lukas said not to disturb ye, as if I would."

"Drostan!" Alynn muttered, leaping to her feet and strapping her sword belt around her waist. "I hope he hasn't left yet—"

"What's the matter?" Rowan asked.

"Sword fightin' lessons, every Friday after chapel—" Alynn grabbed Rowan's hand and pulled him out the door with her.

Alynn tossed a blanket and Drostan's saddle over Thrymja's

back and had moved onto bridling her by the time Rowan had made heads and tails of Honor's saddle. Alynn tightened the girth for him and fastened the straps of Honor's bridle. "Follow close," she told Rowan. "But not too close."

"How do I know if I'm too close?"

Alynn took Thrymja's reins to lead her out of the stable and nodded towards Honor. "He'll know."

It seemed to take an eternity for Rowan to climb awkwardly on Honor's back. He sat too rigid in the saddle, and Honor snorted as he followed Thrymja past the yard, through the forest, and over a stream to the meadow. The distance between them lengthened, but Alynn tried not to care. She hoped Drostan hadn't given up and left.

A sigh of relief escaped her when she saw Drostan and Humility, followed quickly by guilt and worry. Drostan stood leaning against a tree, arms crossed with a knife and a half-whittled peg in his hands, his dripping hair lying in streams on his stolid face. "Kind of you to come, milady."

Alynn leapt off Thrymja. "I'm fierce sorry—"

"Don't worry." His voice was flat, and if his heart held forgiveness, his eyes didn't show it.

Alynn took a deep breath, and her voice came out softer than she wanted it to. "I was talkin' with Father."

"Grand. I'm glad for you." He didn't mean it. His eyes were fierce, his tone brusque.

"Please don't talk like that. You're the one who told me to go talk to him."

"I know. I should have figured you'd go off and forget about me, forgive my naivety."

"I told you I'm sorry, now quit being a gomey about it."

"Being a—Lynder, I have better things to do with an hour than spend it whittling pegs in the pouring rain. Althing is three days away. I have responsibilities, people depend on me, and I still haven't memorized my blasted speech!"

Alynn flinched as Drostan raised his voice. Glaring, he snatched Thrymja's reins from her white hand, mounted her quickly, and nodded curtly to Rowan as he left.

Alynn watched him canter away with her mouth agape. She wanted to shout after him and apologize again—as if that would make a difference—or do something to prove her sincerity. Something to assure him that she didn't value him or his time lightly. But something that felt like a dagger pierced her chest with sadness and guilt, and her tongue felt paralyzed.

Humility shot her an arrogant glance. "You shouldn't have made him angry," she seemed to say. "He has a nice stable with lots of carrots. I like him."

"He shouldn't have left you like that," Rowan said. He had stumbled out of the saddle to place a hand on Alynn's shoulder. "What did he say to you?"

"He's right," Alynn somehow muttered through the lump that stiffened her throat. "He's the chief's son. He has things to do."

"Is it some time alone that you need?"

No. She needed a hug, and someone to talk to, and the encouraging words that Rowan had always excelled at offering. He could turn the most dismal of circumstances into a garden of hope. Even if he spoke lies, they were beautiful lies, and Alynn believed them with all her heart.

But when she turned to Rowan, he already had the wrong foot in Honor's stirrup, and he chuckled as he fixed his mistake.

"Father, come back, please!"

Either Rowan didn't hear, or he pretended not to as he trotted off.

What was that? Alynn demanded to herself. Why hadn't Rowan offered to stay? He didn't need to charm her with his beautiful lies. All she needed him to do was sit and listen, and who could she talk to now? Humility?

Angrily, Alynn punched an oak tree and reveled in the pain. This was her fault, wasn't it? *She* had forgotten about sword fighting practice, *she* had spent all afternoon talking to Rowan, *she* had let him leave. And now what could she do about it?

Nothing. Absolutely nothing.

Alynn punched the oak again, this time with her left hand. Scratches and lines of blood covered her fist, but she didn't care. She deserved it. Finally, too depressed to scold herself and too tired to pace, she sat in the wet grass and let tears slip silently down her face. For the first time in a long time, she felt frighteningly, utterly alone.

Like not even God was there.

Time passed; Alynn didn't know how much of it. But the rain began to fall more steadily, and when she heard a low rumble of thunder, she decided to return home. She put Humility in the stable and crept through the back door. She didn't know why she wanted to slip in unnoticed. Would Caitriona scold her for staying out for so long? She had chores to do. But when she heard Rowan and Caitriona talking at the hearth, Alynn stopped behind the corner of the kitchen wall, listening to their conversation and the sound of her dress dripping onto the stone floor.

"Cait, I thought she'd be better off—"

"Of course you did," Caitriona snapped. Alynn glanced around the corner to see her mother pacing in front of the fireplace, and she hid again quickly. "Rowan, no matter what you think, we're not better off without you. Our daughter has been without her father for long enough. She doesn't need you leavin' her alone when what she wants you to do is listen."

"Caitriona, I didn't know that. I'm sorry." Rowan sounded more contrite over upsetting his wife than abandoning his daughter. Alynn was unsurprised.

Caitriona sighed. "I know you meant well. I'm just worried. I'm going to look for her."

"You needn't. She's alright." There was a moment of silence, but Rowan broke it, his voice primed for a story. "The winter after you were taken, Alynn took Tarin to watch some men ice fishin'. A snowstorm blew in. I was at work when it happened, didn't know a thing about it. Alynn took Tarin through the storm and straight to the smithy, all on her own.

At ten years old! She's fine, Cait. She's fine."

"Sure, I'm fine," Alynn said aloud before she could stop herself. Rowan and Caitriona both looked up at her, and Alynn was too upset to stop talking. "Tarin's wee fingers were frost-nipped, my nose hurt for a week. I was frightened, Tarin was frightened, we could have gotten lost and died that day. But sure, we've always been grand by ourselves, just pure grand."

Caitriona flew to Alynn and hugged her, ignoring her sopping dress. "Lynder, you daren't stay away that long again, you had me worried sick!"

"I'm sorry, Mum."

"I'm sorry too, Alynn," Rowan's voice said. Alynn felt his hand on her shoulder, then his strong embrace around her. "I didn't know you don't like being alone."

"You're like that, I know. 'Tis not yer fault."

A rough hand wiped the rainwater from her face. There was silence, a deep and thoughtful silence, but a short one. "My fault or not, I don't want that to happen again. You know you can always talk to me."

Alynn didn't know that, but she didn't say anything.

"I know I haven't always been there for you, but—look at me, Alynn—I want to change that. Is that alright?"

Alynn so desperately wanted to believe what Rowan was saying. He seemed to mean it. His voice, his eyes, everything about him was sincere, but it seemed too good to be true. But then she realized that, if Rowan had been willing to give up his life for her, he wouldn't mind giving her a few spare moments.

Nodding, Alynn said the only thing she could find to say: "Thank you."

NINE

I've watched a cat play with a mouse. It bats it around and lets it go and catches it again and lets it think it can escape. But its fate is sealed. No matter how safe the mouse thinks it is, the cat is there, watching it. And that's how Konar's treating me.

When his sword hits mine, my parries are scarce enough to keep his blade from striking me. Sparks fly. Our swords are dull and dented from crashing into one another. My heart pounds loud enough for me to hear it—for him to hear it—and he knows I'm afraid.

I'm just a wee mouse to him.

He isn't even trying. 'Tis evil, that gleam in his eye is. He's enjoying himself. He grins with his unnatural teeth every time he strikes another blow. I back up. I throw every bit of me into blocking his blows, keeping myself safe, but death strikes again and again, mere inches from me.

Then I'm on the ground. 'Tis Konar's foot that's pressing into my chest, driving me into the ground, straight into my grave. I can't breathe. I need air. My mouth is gaped open, but my throat is stiff and my chest is made of rock. The world goes dark, but Konar's face remains, hideous, leering, one eye sliced out and replaced by a soulless, bleeding socket.

"Enjoy the afterlife," he snarls. "Heaven has no place for murderers like us."

He raises his sword, and with what little breath I have, I scream.

Darkness. Terror. Pain. Konar's foot was on her chest, pressing her very life out of her. Screams echoed around her, as if hell was opening and greeting her with a chorus of the slain. Her hand flew out, and it landed painfully on her wall.

The door opened, and footsteps flew towards her. Something grabbed her. Alynn blindly threw a punch, but her fist didn't connect with anything. Her breath stung her throat as she reached for a sword that wasn't there.

"What's wrong? Are you ill?"

A tremor seized her until her insides were scrambled like eggs. Nausea tormented her stomach, and her chest was so tight she couldn't draw a breath. Fear tore at her like a mad wolf, biting, mauling, snarling. She was helpless to get away from it. She reached out for whatever had grabbed her. If it was good, it would help her; if it was going to hurt her, she would die faster.

"You're alright, Alynn," the voice said, in a worried tone that seemed to know it was lying. Strong arms scooped Alynn up like a toddler, and she screamed again when she was lifted out of bed. She grabbed at whatever was holding her, unwilling to add her fear of falling to her panic. "We'll take care of you."

Alynn's captor paused, then kicked open a door with force enough to slam it against the wall with a jarring crash. A sleepy voice muttered, "What the devil—"

"Wake up, she's dyin'."

Alynn was laid down again, and hands kept touching her. She tried to brush them away. "Did she come get ye, or did ye hear her wake up?" Lukas's familiar voice asked.

"She was screamin', you didn't hear her?" A hand grabbed hers. "Stay with me, Lynder. Keep fightin'."

"Get a light, will ye?" The hand let go, but it was replaced by Lukas's gentle touch on the forehead, then two fingers in her neck. She tried to lash out, but a hand stopped her. "Steady, my dear. It's just me. No one's hurt ye, ye're home, ye're safe. I speak peace over ye, dear one, in Jesus' name...God's perfect peace, which surpasses understanding. God's perfect love, which casts out fear. There ye go, breathe easy now...there ye go...we've got ye, Alynn. Ye're safe."

Alynn realized she was breathing too quickly; she filled her lungs and let the air seep out of them slowly. She could see Lukas's figure faintly in the darkness as it bent over her caringly, one hand grasping hers and the other smoothing her hair. The frantic snapping of flint against steel sounded beside her. Sparks like fireflies rose gloriously before dying, tiny banners of smoke remembering their places.

Alynn inhaled once again. Her head was clearing, her heartbeat calming. She still trembled, but mildly, as if she was shivering even though she wasn't truly cold. "Thank you, Lukas," she breathed.

Finally, a candle was lit. Rowan held it up, hair unkempt and eyes wide with terror. "What happened?" he demanded.

"She had a nightmare." Lukas kept his healing hand on Alynn's arm, and she knew he was praying for her in spirit. "She's had them on and off since the Battle of Faith."

Rowan didn't seem to accept the explanation, as if Lukas had misdiagnosed consumption as a common cold. But he knelt next to the bed and kissed Alynn, taking her hand again. "You're alright now?" he asked. "You're sure you're not sick? Does anything hurt?"

"Don't worry. I'm grand now. I'm always grand when Lukas prays for me." Blinking, Alynn realized how heavy her eyes were. "May I go back to sleep?"

"Of course," Rowan said softly. He glanced at Lukas. "Is she alright?"

"Aye, she's fine." Lukas patted Alynn's shoulder. "Let's get ye back to yer own bed, my dear. Goodnight."

"Thank you, Lukas."

"Ye're quite welcome."

Somehow, Alynn found her feet. Rowan kept his arm

around her and guided her out of the room. Caitriona was in the doorway, Rowan's plaid wrapped around her, and she gave Alynn a hug and a kiss before she continued to bed.

"I love you, dear heart," Caitriona whispered. "I'm proud of you for calmin' down."

"Goodnight, Mum."

"Goodnight, Lynder."

Alynn's bed had never been more comfortable. Nestling into the hollow her body had formed in the straw mattress, she snuggled into the blankets that Rowan pulled up to her chin. "Thank you, Da," she murmured.

Rowan gave her a brushy kiss on the forehead. "Sleep well, dear heart."

Snug in her nest of straw and blankets, with Lukas's prayer and Rowan's presence, Alynn slept as soundly as a cat on a hearth.

For all the peace she'd felt after Lukas had prayed for her, Alynn woke up jittery. She was used to being exceptionally clumsy after her nightmares; usually, she accepted it. But this morning, she took a deep breath and rallied her senses around her. She wouldn't break anything. She wouldn't hurt anyone. She would be peaceful, self-assured, with the grace of a stream or a soaring hawk.

Her self-assurance dwindled when she snapped two tines off her wooden comb while brushing her hair. What power did she have over her haplessness, anyway? She ought to just stay in bed and make the world safer for everyone else. Regardless, she donned her good pink dress, made sure the hem was too short to trip over, and left to help Caitriona with the Sabbath preparations.

Caitriona, resplendent in a gown of robin's-egg blue with sleeves like angels' wings, was fluttering around the kitchen. She tended to Eucharist bread and breakfast bannocks all at once and muttered to herself about which songs to sing during worship. "Alynn, didn't we sing 'Come Thou Fount' last week?" she asked.

"We did."

"Blast it."

"We can do it again. There's always 'Alone with None but Thee, My God,'" Alynn suggested. "And nigh everyone knows 'Christus Resurgens,' even if it is Latin."

"That's an Easter song. How about 'Christ Be Beside Me'?"

Alynn smiled, stirring the stirabout. "Grand."

The back door opened, and Rowan came inside with a bucket of water. He stopped when he saw Caitriona and stared at her, eyes aglow. Caitriona glanced up at him. "Why aren't you wearin' yer bandage?" she demanded.

"'Tis yer soft hand and tender heart that work miracles on knitting wounds. And you're exceptionally beautiful today."

Caitriona smiled, but her gaze followed him across the kitchen. "You just don't want to look daft during Mass."

"Maybe."

"When the last guest leaves, the bandage goes on. Go fix yerself up for service."

"Fair enough, love." As her parents kissed, Alynn turned her attention to filling the teakettle and heating it in the embers of the fireplace. She felt a hand on her own shoulder, and Rowan's voice asked, "Are you doing better after last night?"

"I am." Alynn turned into the embrace Rowan offered. "Sorry if I frightened you. The first time I had a nightmare like that, I think Mum was more frightened than I was."

Rowan squeezed her tighter and kissed her head. "How often does that happen?"

"Every two months or so in the good times, twice or thrice a week in the bad. I've been doing well for quite a while, though. 'Tis nothin' for you to worry about."

"Well," Rowan said, taking her chin in his hands, "I'm yer da, and I'm going to worry, and as soon as church is over, I'd like to have a more thorough conversation. I just want to make sure you're alright, my heart."

Was anyone ever truly alright? And if not, what could be done? Rowan could offer a prayer, but so many other people were already praying for her that it probably wouldn't do much good. "I'm grand," Alynn promised. "Go take care of yer head. What kind of tea would you like with breakfast?"

"It doesn't matter."

Alynn sighed and mentally ran over the list of teas everyone in the monastery enjoyed. "Mum, do we have any linden dried?" she asked as Lukas came inside with a pail of fresh milk. "Lukas, is linden tea alright?"

"Aye."

"Fresh linden makes better tea," Caitriona said, picking up her skirts so the dew wouldn't muss them as she left. Alynn opened her mouth to call out after her and ask if the bannocks needed to be turned, but she heard the door open and shut before she could gather words. She reached for the metal spatula that rested against the griddle, but it had spent too long baking in the heat of the fire. It was as hot as Satan's pitchfork. Immediately, Alynn dropped it with a cry of "Devil mend it!"

Lukas sighed, checking the sacramental bread. "Did ye burn yerself?"

"I did. Where's the closest butter?"

"Butter?"

Alynn knew her hand was going to blister if she didn't care for it soon. "Aye, butter. What else do you put on burns?"

"Ye can't solve every problem wi' dairy products," Lukas said, taking the sack of barley flour from the pantry. "Stick yer hand in this."

"Does it work?"

Lukas gave a halfway twitch of a smile. "Better than what the Greeks recommend. Leave it until it stops hurting and call me when the meal's ready. I forgot to mark the Scriptures fer Mass."

Cautiously, Alynn buried her hand in the barley flour—both deliciously cool and uncomfortably coarse—and waited. Caitriona came inside with her bunch of linden flowers and gave Alynn a sideways glance. Alynn sighed. "Don't ask."

Caitriona took the bannocks from the griddle and set them

on the table to slice them. Rowan came downstairs, his hair combed and braided handsomely, and motioned for Alynn to be quiet. He approached Caitriona with a silent step and a gleaming eye.

Alynn sighed. *Father, whatever you're about to do, 'tis stupid.*

Rowan silently crept up behind Caitriona, laid his hands on her waist, and kissed her neck.

"Don't you dare!"

Her hand flew out. By some miracle, she dropped her knife, but her fist impacted the side of his face. Fiercely.

She ran. Like a child running from her drunken father, she ran. When Rowan reached for her hand, she pulled herself away, bashing her shoulder blade against the corner of the cupboard. She fell against the wall, a rag doll with its hair streaming about it.

For a moment, the loudest sound was that of Caitriona's panicked breathing. Rowan took a gentle step towards her, a hand outstretched as if he was approaching a wounded animal.

"Cait...."

Caitriona's eyes were wide with terror. "What did I do?"

"You're alright, Cait. I'm sorry. I didn't mean to hurt you."

"Rowan, I'm—I'm so sorry—I didn't mean to—"

"Whisht. 'Tis alright. You're fine." Rowan was on his knees now, taking Caitriona into his arms, stroking her gently. "What happened?"

Caitriona was shaking. "I'm sorry, I—I thought it was Konar—he'd do that so often, and then he'd—he'd take me, and—I'm sorry, I didn't want to hurt you, Rowan...."

"Whisht, you're alright now. 'Tis alright." Caitriona was crying now, and Rowan was holding her gently, stroking her hair, whispering his love to her. "I'm sorry I did that. I've never wanted to frighten you. 'Tis alright, Cait."

"Rowan," Caitriona breathed, her voice trembling, "I'm not the person you remember."

Rowan paused to collect his thoughts. "That's alright," he said gently. "You know what, I'm probably not the person you remember, either. We can start over, Caitriona. We'll get to know each other again." He held up his left hand, a band of scrap metal on his ring finger. "Do you know what this ring means?"

Caitriona fingered her own wedding band. "It means we're together."

"It means more than that. It means we're united, for better or for worse, in sickness and in health. It means that I love you, Aeryn Caitriona McNeil, and that nothing you can do— nothing that anyone else has done to you—can tear us apart."

Caitriona blushed, and Rowan brushed away her hair as he kissed her. He wiped her tears away, fondling her face, holding her close. When Alynn could finally see Caitriona's face again, she was smiling. "Thank you so much, Rowan. I love you."

"I love you too, Cait. I'm here for you. 'Tis alright."

Caitriona gingerly touched Rowan's cheek where she had hit him. "Did I hurt you?"

Rowan smiled. "Och, you can't hurt me, love. I'm grand. Is there anything I can do to help you?"

"You could fetch a leech," Caitriona ordered. "I won't have it turnin' black and blue during Mass."

"If you insist, milady."

"Just ask Lukas for one. He keeps them on his desk."

Alynn felt like she jerked herself out of a dream. She'd been standing there like a twit with her hand in a sack of barley flour, staring at her parents. She hurriedly dusted her hand off and followed Rowan as he walked past her. "She's done that to me afore," she said. "Does it hurt?"

"My heart, mostly," Rowan said. "She used to love it when I did that. What I want is to get my hands on the misbegotten brute who hurt her like that."

"He got what he deserved. A gash in the leg, a thump in the back—I probably broke a few bones through his chainmail, when I threw that axe at him. Then I took out his eye, Lukas put a knife in his neck, I kicked him between the legs and took his head with his own sword. He's the only person I'm proud of killing. And Drostan said he was sensitive to burns, so his current residence is fierce unbearable."

"What does Drostan know about the man who took Mum?" Rowan asked.

Alynn opened her mouth, shut it again, and quickly knocked on Lukas's doorframe, since his door was never shut completely. "Could you give us a hand?" she asked.

Lukas opened his door and set a notebook on his desk. "What's wrong?"

"Nothin'. Father found out what happens when Mum gets surprised in the kitchen."

Lukas eyed Rowan, focusing on the side of his face that was still red and smarting. "I'll place the leeches," he said.

"Leeches," Rowan muttered. "Och, the things we do for love. Let it bruise if it wants to. I don't give a fiddler's fart."

Lukas made a peculiar coughing sound as he turned with the leech jar in hand, and Alynn recognized it as the noise he made when he was tempted to laugh. "Is that a, em—common expression, where ye're from?" he asked.

"'Tis."

Lukas glanced at Alynn. "Ye've never used it."

Alynn felt her ears turn red. "I've never thought it something fit to say in church."

"That's never stopped anyone afore. I've got the leeches— I'll have to use that expression, now and again—thank ye, Rowan." With mirth in his eyes and a youthful spring in his motions, Lukas untied the cover of the leech jar, and Alynn ran to help Caitriona with breakfast.

Rowan ate his stirabout with two leeches and a look of discomfort on his face. Alynn could hardly stomach her food, so she sat next to Rowan to avoid the sight of the wretched creatures. Lukas handled them as if they were kittens. When breakfast was over, he peeled them off Rowan's face and let them suck on his own finger like infants.

"Alynn, will ye do us a favor?" he asked. "Put Eoban and Guinevere back wi' their friends. Just make certain ye tie the cover back on their jar, they've been known to escape."

At the mere sight of the hideous beasts, Alynn wanted to shriek and gag and run away all at once. "You named yer leeches," she breathed. "You don't bother namin' yer cats, but you name yer leeches, and I won't bother askin' why."

"I name all the good cats. My three favorites over the years have been named Theophilus. The other sensible ones who don't step in undried ink or habitually vomit on my pillow were given more common names." Lukas extended his hand to Alynn, who promptly ducked her head and left to wash dishes. She would rather muck stalls or clean out the chicken's coop.

"I won't touch those things."

"Don't make her," Rowan said, "not if she's wearin' her good dress."

With a glance to the heavens and a mutter about frivolity, Lukas left for his cell with Eoban and Guinevere still clinging to his finger. "Thank you," Alynn whispered to Rowan, embracing him. "Care for some soap?"

"Please." Rowan wiped a bit of blood off his face, but two welts remained, like mosquito bites that had been scratched until they bled. "Is he always eccentric?"

"'Tis the wrong word, eccentric is." Alynn took a dampened, soapy dishrag and gingerly wiped Rowan's face until he took it from her. "He was a hermit for thirty-nine years against his will. He's a bit short on social graces, but he's fierce better than he was two years ago."

Rowan rubbed his fingers over his face, as if he was making sure he'd removed the last trace of leech. "He's mostly avoided me so far."

"You've been preoccupied."

The back door burst open with a strength that Caitriona, who was gathering eggs, was incapable of. Into St. Anne's Monastery came Leif, neatly groomed and freshly bathed. Alynn flushed when she remembered that everyone had completely forgotten about Saturday baths in the turmoil of Rowan's return. And Lukas, if he had remembered, hadn't bothered to remind anyone. Typical.

Rowan set a firm grasp on Alynn's shoulder and stepped between her and Leif. "'Tis him. Get out the front door."

"Father—"

Her words never reached Rowan's ears. Rage emanated like an odor around him as he clenched his fist and raised it. Leif noticed, blocked the punch, and twisted Rowan's wrist behind his back.

"You're more like Alynn than I realized," he said.

"What did you do to my wife?"

Rowan struggled like a fish on a hook, and Alynn flew to his side. "It wasn't him, Father," she promised. "I killed that man. This one's good. Let him go."

"Don't think I've forgotten his face!"

Leif laughed placidly, a warm and hearty laugh that put most men at ease. Rowan seemed immune to it. "I'll look less like Konar when I trim my eyebrows. I meant to do that yesterday."

"Rowan." Caitriona sailed into the room, setting her angel's hands on her husband's shoulder. Leif released Rowan's hands, and Caitriona took them into her own before a further fight could ensue. "Look at me, Rowan. Leif is a good man. He's saved my life before. I wouldn't be here without him. He's as much a brother to me as Tamlane is to you. He's alright."

Rowan was given use of his hand back, and he popped his wrists as if preparing for a fistfight. "Leif, is it?"

"Aye, sir." Leif extended his hand, and Rowan shook it warily. "It's been a pleasure knowing your family. I'm glad you've returned."

Rowan never relaxed, and Alynn could understand why. Leif intimidated those who didn't know him—he was two inches taller than Rowan and fifty pounds heavier. Although his hair was auburn and his eyes were a warm hazel where Konar was flaming red and steely blue, their faces still bore a familial resemblance. Or at least Caitriona said so—Alynn had only seen Konar once without his helmet, and that memory was warped by time and imagination.

"Why do you look like him?" Rowan demanded. "The man who took my wife."

"He was, unfortunately, my brother, but you needn't worry. We're different as night and day, you've my word on that." Leif smiled as Drostan entered the room, Caitriona's forgotten basket of eggs in hand. "You've already met my son Drostan, I take it?"

"I have." Alynn shrank, knowing by Rowan's gaze that he was putting two and two together. Drostan was Konar's nephew. No matter how different they were, no matter how much they had clashed during Konar's violent lifetime, facts were still facts. Rowan would always keep Alynn as far away from Drostan as possible.

Alynn looked helplessly at Drostan, only to see another man with him. He was tall and looked to be Caitriona's age, with a frizzy blond beard and a steady gaze, richly clad in bright blues and reds. The tablet-woven trim on his collar spoke either of his wife's deftness with a loom or his ability to purchase the finest of clothing. And, as Alynn recognized the man, she realized that both were probable.

"Mr. Rowan, I'd like to introduce to you my somewhat-distant cousin, Chief Thorbjorn Farsight of Hrafney," Drostan said. "Thorbjorn, meet Rowan McNeil, father of the famed Alynn the Dauntless."

"A pleasure to meet you," Chief Thorbjorn said pleasantly, crushing Rowan with a handshake. "Especially on this side of heaven. I heard you were dead."

"Death and I are old friends. He still comes calling every once in a while." Rowan rubbed his hand; he probably wouldn't be using it anytime soon. "I just wish I could give him a cold shoulder of mutton, and he'd take the hint and stop."

Thorbjorn laughed. "You found a rare man, Lady Cait."

"I have," Caitriona smiled. "How are you gettin' on since last Althing, Thorbjorn?"

"I've been well. Kjallak's a big brother now. Kjartan, we've named him. He's...four months old now, I believe?" Thorbjorn beamed, his eyes alight. "I'm primarily here to get some sleep."

Caitriona smiled understandingly. "Is Svala well?"

"Aye. She probably needs sleep more than I do, but she manages, somehow. Mothers are magical like that." He gazed through the room as if he was searching for something. "Where is your priest? I'd like to speak with him."

How long did it take to put two leeches back in a jar? "I'll fetch him," Alynn volunteered, scampering towards the stairwell. She got perhaps halfway up before she heard footsteps behind her, and she turned to see Drostan hurriedly following her.

Something wasn't right. Drostan looked sick, paler than usual, with worry in his eyes. Alynn took him by the arms and searched him. He was afraid. She knew before she felt the sweat on his hands that he was afraid, but why? His face was drawn, as if he hadn't slept the night before, and he avoided eye contact.

"What's wrong?" she asked.

His gaze flitted up to meet hers for a moment. "The other night—I'm sorry, Lynder. I didn't mean to snap at you."

Alynn touched his face, as if to wipe away a tear that wasn't there. Finally, he looked up at her with his wonderful green eyes, alluring as a forest path, yet unwavering, as if not a breath of air stirred the oak's branches. He smiled at the forgiveness unspoken yet perfectly understood, but then the worry returned.

"I've no chance in Niflheim of earning your father's trust now, have I?"

"He just found out yer uncle kidnapped Mum."

Drostan swore mildly, then apologized for it. Alynn embraced him, wanting to laugh and cry all at once when she felt how rapidly Drostan's heart was beating.

"All's not lost, love," she promised, relaxing in Drostan's arms. "I'll find a way to come to you again."

"Last night, I realized—you'll have to choose. Eventually. Between going back to your family or starting your own. And as much as I want you to stay, I only pray you'll make the right decision. Even if that means I never see you again."

Alynn didn't want to think about that choice, but she knew she'd have to make it. She at least knew which way she leaned.

A hand grasped her shoulder and forced her away from Drostan. Alynn looked up to see Lukas, then looked down to see that his hands were wet with water from the leech's jar. She shrieked.

"Lukas, why!"

"Ye were standing too close together!"

"Go away! Wash yer hands!"

Lukas gave her a strange half-frustrated look before he left, wiping his hands on his scapular. "Chief Thorbjorn is here," Drostan called after him. "He asked to speak with you."

"Of course! Gladly!" Lukas wiped his hands a bit more vigorously. Alynn slipped her hand into Drostan's and left to greet visitors on the hearth.

June 18, A.D. 966—

It was a great blessing to meet the chief of Hrafney. He is a good man, hungry for God's word, and I know that his island is fertile ground. I was asked more questions today than I have since Christmas, and though I am now exhausted and weary of people, I have no regrets.

Althing starts tomorrow. I do not want to go. The crowds, the noises, the stench of so many people crowded together— the event has gotten less and less enjoyable as I've aged. But I bid a reluctant farewell to my books, and a hearty farewell to the cats (especially the one who defecated in my bed last night), and I leave despite my reluctance. I trust that God will provide the energy needed to interact with others, and possibly the will to enjoy it.

I have been observing Rowan, as I lack the boldness to initiate a conversation with him. I can see why Alynn is reserved around him. He loves Alynn, treats her kindly, and yet he spends very little time with her. His main focus is on rebuilding his relationship with Caitriona. Though a man familiar with romantic love would doubtless find no fault in him, I disapprove of his actions. After all, Caitriona loves those who love her daughter; perhaps the fastest way to a mother's heart is by loving her children. Let me at least lose Alynn to a decent man, rather than one who is blind to her!

O God, forgive my jealous heart! Who am I to judge Your servant?

—L. McCamden

TEN

"Caitriona, let's go!"

For lack of a hood, Rowan had folded his plaid so that his head was covered against the light rain falling outside. Caitriona wore a red hood to match her frock, but it fell over her back as she flitted throughout the monastery.

"I can't find my notebook!"

"It's right here on the table," Lukas called. He had tucked the skirt of his tunic into his leather belt in preparation for the horseback ride to the village and the first day of Althing. The edges of his braies were visible around his knees, but Alynn decided not to say anything. Lukas probably didn't care. Historically, he always said, monks had never cared much for modesty.

Finally, Caitriona pulled up her hood and took her notebook from the table. "Did everyone pack a change of clothes?" she asked. "There will be baths in the village, and everyone will be takin' one—includin' you, Lukas."

"Why?"

"I won't have it known that my household skipped baths on Saturday," Caitriona insisted. "They're pure grand, the baths are, and heated. You'll enjoy it. Who's takin' which horse?"

"I can take Alynn on Honor," Lukas offered. He poked the fireplaces just to make sure the embers wouldn't ignite while they were gone. "Are there any candles burning upstairs?"

"There aren't," Caitriona said, "I checked twice. We're ready to leave, then?"

Alynn couldn't think of anything else that needed to be done, so she pulled up her hood and left to saddle the horses.

She sat behind Lukas on the ride to the village, trying to maintain her balance without holding onto Lukas too tightly and throwing his off. They travelled slowly since the horses were heavily laden, but by the time they arrived at the northern shore of St. Anne's Cleft, the rain had stopped and the sun was beginning to shine. It was a perfect day for Althing.

In all her years of living in the bustling town of Limerick, Alynn had never seen so many people in one place. The Norse village and the nearby tented area looked like an anthill that had been poked with a stick, swarming with people and animals and the occasional hand-pulled cart. In the distance, one voice rose above the others—that would be the Lawspeaker, opening Althing by reciting the Norse laws from memory.

When they arrived at Leif and Drostan's house, Alynn left Lukas to tend to Honor. She joined her parents, who were in the main room chatting with Valdis the hired girl.

Valdis smiled gently when she saw Alynn. "I'm glad you have your father back. Have you eaten breakfast?"

"I have," Alynn said.

Valdis handed her a warm loaf of bread. "Take this anyway. You're too skinny."

"Runs in the family," Rowan said.

Alynn sighed. Valdis's bread was so tough that it was impossible to eat it after it had cooled—it turned into a brick, fit only to be pecked at by chickens. Yet the Norse seemed so accustomed to it that the only feedback Valdis received was an occasional "good bread" or impressed nod. Alynn made herself smile and say "thank you." She'd be giving this away.

Lukas pulled his hood down and ran his hand over what

little hair he had left. "Ye will be demonstrating yer metalwork here, right, Rowan?"

"Of course," Rowan said. He needed a hammer and forge like some men needed ale; he wasn't himself when he wasn't able to work with his hands. Alynn could nearly feel the excitement radiating off him as they left for the smithy. As soon as they arrived, he looked at the hammers and tongs and punch-rods the same way a woman might eye a queen's wardrobe.

"Who's the village blacksmith?" he asked.

"There isn't one," Caitriona said. "Everyone tends to their own needs."

Rowan's eyes gleamed. He tugged on the bellows and made the forge glow, then tucked a thin copper rod in the flames. "How much does a good cloak pin sell for?"

"You won't get coin for it. A bag of barley flour, perchance, or a fox's skin." Caitriona smiled, putting a hand on Rowan's arm. "Should I leave you to yer business?"

Rowan nodded. "Keep an eye on Alynn."

Smiling, Caitriona took Alynn by the hand and left. "I've to find Leif and be a good hostess. You ought to be free to find Drostan."

Alynn smiled, but the inedible loaf of bread in her hand reminded her of some unfinished business. "Thank you, Mum," she said, slipping away towards a ramshackle house with walls less wattle than daub.

The house Dagny Volundottir and her sister-in-law Geirhild Karsadottir called home was unusually quiet, considering that seven children lived there. Today, a low table was set up in front of the door, and all sorts of wonderful things were set on it. Most of them were tablet woven—belts, headbands, and garment trims—but there were a few nalbound hats and mittens. Kenna had tied some yarn to a post and was tablet weaving a belt that was exceptionally good for a six-year-old, though not ready to be sold.

"Good morning, Kenna!" Alynn called in Norse. Despite

Caitriona's best efforts, Alynn spoke the language clumsily and uncomfortably. It seemed only by some miracle that she was able to get her point across, but she usually did. "What are you making?"

"A belt. Come and look at it!"

Alynn knelt next to Kenna and admired her handiwork. She said nothing of the uneven edges—she always had a hard time with them, too—and watched as Kenna wove a few rows. She seemed comfortable passing the wooden shuttle between the lines of thread, though she struggled a bit turning the cards that held them in place. "Very good," Alynn said. "Where is your mother?"

"Inside."

As if she was handing her a note in church, Alynn gave Kenna the bread Valdis had given her. A smile lit up the little girl's face. "Thank you."

Alynn knocked, and it was a while before the door opened. Dagny's coif was askew, and her flaxen hair was distraught under it, but she still managed to smile. "Could you watch Kenna for me?" she asked. She began speaking more rapidly and using Norse words Alynn hadn't learned yet. She understood the next few sentences as "I wouldn't...Althing, and with the Darsidians here, I don't want her to be alone. I've started...and...my dress, and I need to wash it out. I don't mean to...you."

Alynn smiled sympathetically. "I'll watch her," she promised. "How much do your belts cost?"

"Kenna knows. Thank you ever so much, Alynn."

"Not a bother."

Alynn was glad to stand outside by the low dining table and display Dagny's wares to passersby. With Kenna's help, she even sold a belt and a roll of trim. Finally, Dagny came out wearing an undyed frock rather than her normal yellow one. "Mother, someone gave us halfpence for a belt!" Kenna exclaimed, leaping up from her loom.

"That's wonderful," Dagny smiled. She lifted Kenna onto

her hip and smiled at Alynn. "Thank you so much."

"I had a good time," Alynn said. The streets were emptying now—everyone was headed for the tented area, where most of Althing would be taking place. Alynn guessed that the opening ceremony was about to start. She'd promised Drostan she'd be there for his speech, so she quickly hugged Dagny and Kenna and set out to navigate the sea of people.

Having never been to an Althing before, Alynn had no idea where the opening ceremony would take place. The Lawspeaker must have grown tired, for his voice no longer rose above the casual din of people. Alynn tried to follow the crowds, but she ended up following a throng of strangers to the docks to unload some last-minute supplies. She turned and ran back towards the tent-covered meadow until someone speaking caught her attention. It was Drostan.

"...And that all disputes may reach a respectable end. And to ask—invoke—the blessing of God, I ask the priest to lead us in prayer."

Alynn paled as Lukas began to pray. She'd missed Drostan's speech.

Worming her way through the crowd of people, Alynn finally reached the platform where Drostan had been speaking. He was shaking, his face as red as his hair, and his palms dripped with sweat.

"You did grand, love—"

"Where *were* you?"

Drostan's grip on her shoulder was firmer than usual. A forest fire sparked in his eyes.

"I'm sorry—I'm fierce sorry, I was—"

"You *promised* you'd be where I could see you. You help! Just by being there, you help me think, and where were you?"

"I was helpin'—"

"You should have seen the look on my father's face." Drostan breathed heavily, and for a split second, he reminded Alynn of Konar. But the second ended when Drostan turned white and opened his mouth to retch, but nothing came up.

Alynn put her arms around him and waited. Slowly, his arms encircled her—begrudgingly at first, but then he softened. He was still trembling, but at least he wasn't upset. Not as much.

"I'm never speaking in front of people again," Drostan said.

"'Tis a terrible place to learn how to give speeches, Althing is. There's far too many people. Ask Lukas if you can practice at Mass. I'm sure he'll let you."

"How? Mass is Mass, not a classroom, and I can't preach a sermon."

"Well, perchance you can pray, or read a Scripture passage. The churches in Ireland always had a separate person to read the Scripture verses. A lector, they called them."

The fire had gone out of Drostan's eyes, and now they were filled with sleep and ashes. He tried to smile, and Alynn's heart fluttered. He was so adorable when he was sleepy. "How much did you sleep last night?" she asked.

"Between today's speech and losing you, I didn't sleep at all."

"Whisht, love, I'm right here. And I won't go anywhere for a while, on my word. Let's get you home."

"I need to be out there," Drostan protested. "This is my island. I need to—"

Smiling, Alynn put her arm around him and led him to his house. "You need sleep."

The house was empty; Valdis must have left to enjoy the festivities. Drostan stretched out on the bench, and Alynn took off his books for him. Impulsively, she tickled his feet.

"Stop that!"

At least he was smiling. It might have been a tired smile, but it was still perfect. Alynn covered him with a blanket, and he kissed her forehead. "Thanks, Lynder-my-love."

Alynn stayed until he fell asleep, and then for a moment longer. *Precious, perfect Drostan,* Alynn thought, *I wouldn't leave you for the world.*

When Alynn was able to pull herself away from him, her first order of business was to find someone she knew. Her first stop was the blacksmith's shop. Rowan was busy haggling over a cloak pin with an overweight Norseman, and since Leif and Caitriona were doubtless occupied being host and hostess, Alynn left to scout out Lukas.

The tent-covered area was like any other marketplace, only busier. Merchants advertised their wares, bards told stories, and old friends laughed as they caught up with each other. Finally, Alynn found Lukas praying for a young man. She waited until he finished and shook hands with him before approaching him.

"Alynn," Lukas said with a child's excitement, "I just met the future pastor of Hrafney."

Alynn looked at the young man as he walked away—dark-haired, over six feet tall, built as solidly as an ox and probably about as strong, but with a certain air of boyish mischief that gave Alynn questions. "And he's...?"

"Brett Oddson, fifteen years auld."

"He's fifteen?"

"He's already working on a beard." Lukas glanced at the crowds a bit worriedly. "Stay wi' us fer a bit, if ye don't mind. I need someone to slap me if I say something stupid in Norse."

"You're better at it than you think," Alynn promised.

Lukas sighed. "Thank you, my dear, but every once in a while I'll get confused and switch to Hebrew halfway through a sentence. At least the Norse alphabet is straightforward. Do ye get the letters 'eth' and 'thorn' confused, though?"

"More often than I care to admit." Alynn followed Lukas as he began to walk, apparently towards nowhere in particular. Every ten feet, he would either find someone to pray for or be approached by an inquisitive convert. Eventually, though, their stroll led them to one of the few sections of the meadow not covered by tents. Instead, the grass was covered in cowhides on which men sparred.

"What is this?" Alynn asked, mostly to herself.

To her surprise, Lukas answered. "Most of them are trials by combat," he explained. "The man whose blood stains the cow's hide first is declared guilty. Most likely some of them are doing it fer fun. The two over there—see how there's no witnesses? That's a pleasure match, or else they're training."

Alynn watched the two men fight, their swords flashing in the sunlight. They moved quickly and skillfully, and it seemed that neither of them would win until the sunlight flashed more brilliantly, and suddenly, the older of the two was holding both swords. Rather than drawing blood from his opponent, he returned his sword and shook his hand.

"He fights well for an old man," Alynn said.

"He isn't around my age, is he? Can ye tell from here?"

"Not terribly well. He's around yer height and dirty blonde, going grey. Do you know him?"

Lukas didn't answer. Instead, he headed towards the swordsman and, when he met him, didn't speak. He simply half-smiled and raised his hand in greeting.

The swordsman laughed and gave Lukas a friendly clap on the back. He made some motions with his hands, which Lukas returned, and they both smiled again.

Lukas's smile turned guilty, and he spoke carefully in Norse. "Einar, my friend, ye have my apologies."

The swordsman's smile disappeared, and he shouted a few words in Norse that Alynn had been careful not to learn. "You...you can speak?"

"I don't speak Norse very well, so I'll apologize in advance for what I say wrong. I speak Latin and Gaelic best."

Einar nodded towards Alynn. "Is this your daughter?"

"My foster-daughter, Alynn the Dauntless. And I should tell you, my name is Lukas McCamden, not Magnus."

Einar looked surprised. "You're the ones who won the Battle of Faith two years ago?"

"Aye, we are."

Einar laughed. "Alynn, I taught this man everything he knows about combat—all without the benefit of language."

"I pretended to be deaf and dumb, to circumvent the language barrier," Lukas explained quickly in Gaelic. He nodded towards a dull practice sword. "Can you still fight, my friend?"

"I can! Of you, Lukas, I have my doubts. What was our count last Althing?"

"Fer the week? Thirty-nine to thirty-three, my favor." Lukas stepped onto the cowhide and stretched his arm. "I haven't practiced much this year, so go easy on me."

"Start again," Einar said. "It'll keep you young." And with that, he launched his attack.

Einar seemed as comfortable with a sword as Caitriona was with a nalbinding needle. He delivered each blow with the speed and strength of a champion racehorse. Lukas fought even faster, his blade flashing as if not metal but light itself came from his hand. Before long, Einar was on the defensive. They stayed on the cowhide, circling each other since they could move neither forwards nor backwards. Suddenly, the sparring stopped. Einar's tunic had a neat gash across the chest, and a single drop of blood had fallen on the cow's hide.

"Well done," he said, shaking Lukas's hand. He said more things in Norse that Alynn didn't understand—and neither, apparently, did Lukas—but a friendly clap on the back made translation unnecessary.

As long as he stayed with his friend, Lukas was taken care of. That left Alynn free to enjoy herself. She knew that the embroidered coifs she'd brought wouldn't trade for much, but she could use some kohl eyeliner. And how much were shoes? The boots Lukas had made her were functional, but they were old and worn, and Caitriona insisted she needed new ones.

And while she was there, she would explore—and there would be stories to hear. Not just from the bards, but also from the merchants and Viking raiders who had been far to the south. There might be a man who had seen Gaul or Spain, or even been to Rome. Some of the men had gone even farther and seen people called Blue Men, who had skin as dark as the sky at midnight. And Alynn, just for fun, would ask to see a merchant's silver dirham. Dirhams were from the Middle East,

Caitriona had told her—the land where Jesus and the Apostles lived. Wouldn't Lukas love to see one of them!

By midday, Alynn had spent at least an hour and a half wandering around trying to find the best deal on shoes. There were five different cobblers. One of them set his prices far too high, one set an unsettling smile at every girl who walked past him, and Alynn had spent so long staring at a third's that she was too embarrassed to go back. She was trying to figure out if trading two coifs for a particularly beautiful pair of shoes was worth it, or if she should just skip the whole thing and ask Rowan to make her a pair. He was handy with leather, wasn't he? And even if she were to buy the shoes, she wouldn't have enough left over for eyeliner. How much could she get him to negotiate down?

Alynn sighed, turned around to walk to the other vendor she was considering, and nearly ran straight into Drostan. His hair was disheveled from sleeping, and his eyes still looked tired, but he was smiling.

"How long have you been standin' there?" Alynn asked. She always thought Drostan looked adorable with his hair tousled, but it was rather unbecoming for a chief's son, so she ran her fingers through his ginger locks. But not too much, she told herself, or else he'd catch the eye of every girl at Althing. "Faith, you're a mess."

"Not long. Shoe shopping, are we?" Drostan eyed the cobbler's wares. "Not bad. Which tribe is he from?"

"Hrafney, I think—you're from Hrafney, aren't you, sir?"

With a fright, the cobbler looked up from the high boots he was piecing together. He stared awkwardly at Alynn, who still had her hand entangled in Drostan's hair, then nodded.

Drostan laughed. "Svan the Speechless, best cobbler on Hrafney. A pair of his shoes will last eight months. And he keeps good scales."

Alynn shook her head. The Norse could do many things, but making shoes was not one of them. Why, she'd had her shoes in Ireland until they pinched her feet, and then she'd saved them for Tarin. "How about the man down the way? His are cheaper."

"What's his name?"

"Tryggvi Stein...something."

"He's Darsidian. Never trust a Darsidian. Which pair do you like?"

"The light ones that fasten with bits of antler."

Drostan's eyes shone. "See if they fit."

Alynn beamed. She had her old boots off in a moment and was relishing in the luxury of a new pair of shoes. Drostan was right—the cobbler knew what he was doing, either that or Lukas was worse at making shoes than Alynn had realized.

Drostan squared his shoulders and looked at Svan the Speechless, producing a wealth of carved wooden objects from his satchel. "Well, Svan, what will you trade for the shoes?"

Svan checked to see which pair Alynn had chosen, then glanced at Drostan's handiwork. "Two combs, sir. My finest work."

Good Lord, the man spoke in a whisper! Drostan tried not to notice. "Two combs, aye? I'll give you one for them."

"But—"

"A comb and a spoon, then."

"Sir, I—"

"If you could speak a bit softer, please. I don't want to make a scene."

Svan glanced around nervously. "Two spoons."

Drostan handed him the desired objects. "Good doing business with you, sir," he said, with a gleam in his eye as he glanced at Alynn. She didn't realize until that moment how much she was glowing.

"Thank you, love," Alynn said, taking her old shoes in hand. Shoes with no cracks! She felt more like a noblewoman than a peasant. "I'll pay you back."

"Which coif would I look best in?" Drostan asked. He kissed her cheek. "Don't bother."

Alynn snuck her hand into Drostan's satchel and pulled out

a spoon. Anyone could carve a spoon, but Drostan's spoons had a dragon's head carved onto the handle. Despite his insistence that the dragon heads were only there to make his spoons worth more in a trade, Alynn knew he was designing figureheads for ships.

"You're amazin', you know that?" she asked.

"Not as much as you are." Drostan smiled, his eyes twinkling like a sea full of stars. "Even if you are a lousy pickpocket. Put that spoon back. I'll see if we can't trade it for something to eat."

Alynn smiled. "*Skyr*?"

"Nay, the Gythians are famous for making cheese. It's the only thing they're good at. We're bound to find some."

"Perfect."

Drostan ran a hand through his hair. "We've the afternoon to ourselves. Tomorrow morning, I'm afraid I've a meeting with the chiefs of the six other tribes. A mere formality, they have to vote on if we get a chief or not. I wish you could come."

"If it makes you feel better, I'll wait right nearby," Alynn said.

"You and everyone else," Drostan chuckled. "Let's find that cheese."

Meanwhile, the six chiefs had gathered early in a tent set apart from the others, with guards so that their conversations were free from eavesdroppers. Thorbjorn Farsight of Hrafney was there, glancing at the men around him. Chief Hrodolf of Darsidia sat scowling in the darkness of a corner, his son Nokkvi at his shoulder. They were cruel men, but Hrodolf was old, and Nokkvi given to mindless fighting when he was angry. Mindless fighting, of course, was easily overcome.

Chief Helgi of Gythia was his typical short, slight, shrew-faced self, and was that Veikir of Fjorderny? He was pale and gaunt, his tawny beard thin and patchy, but he was still alive. Oakvin of Sjondri was meticulously groomed, his hair lightened with lye and his eyes darkened with kohl. He wore high boots and pants so tight his feet must have been numb. The tent's flap opened to permit Chief Ebbe of Laugvik. Late, as usual, but he had few other faults, and Thorbjorn was glad to see him. Behind Ebbe came his brother Yngvar, the Lawspeaker.

"Will we give Diaparn a chief this year?" Ebbe asked.

"Will they sacrifice to the gods?" snarled Hrodolf of Darsidia.

"What difference does it make?" sighed Veikir of Fjorderny.

Yngvar the Lawspeaker lifted a drinking-horn to his lips. "Without a chief, they are less powerful at Althing," he rasped. He drank again and settled down in silence.

Oakvin twirled his mustache. "I'd like to keep it that way. Haven't you heard the tales from the South, how Christian chiefs and kings demand that their subjects conform to their beliefs? How they punish, even kill, those who refuse?"

"But would Leif do that?" Thorbjorn demanded. He rose to his feet and gazed at each man in turn. "Since boyhood, I have known this man. We are friends and brothers. I knew who he was before he left for Scotland, and I know who he is since he has returned a Christian. He is different, but different as old wine is from new. He is a better man, a peaceful man—"

"A coward," Nokkvi interrupted. "Not to mention your father's first cousin. Of course you'd vouch for him."

"Peace," Veikir said, "for your words invite vengeance."

"What is a coward, young man?" Thorbjorn asked. "One who values life, and in doing so avoids needless fights? Or one who runs from what is needful? And which is Leif? He serves a God Who died when it was needful, yet returned to life, and which of our gods can boast that? Whose God led His followers to peace and victory in the Battle of Faith?" Thorbjorn held up a rosary necklace. "I have tasted the new wine Leif has. I know its value. And I know the son of Idir is neither a zealot nor a coward, and I call for his installment as chief of St. Anne's Cleft."

Ebbe nodded. "Thorbjorn speaks wisdom. Let us elect Leif Idirson chief."

"Leif may have proved himself, but his God hasn't yet," Hrodolf interrupted. "You're a convert to this alien faith, Thorbjorn. You say your God can work miracles?"

Thorbjorn nodded. "I've seen them."

"Would He begrudge us a miracle now, to test His reality?" Hrodolf raised a silver arm-ring in plain view of the six chiefs. "Have Him turn this to gold."

Thorbjorn looked from Hrodolf to the arm ring and back again. "I'm in no place to ask Him."

"So your God *can* work miracles, He just...*won't*, at the moment. Well, perhaps we'll give Him another chance." Hrodolf spoke in low tones to his son, who smirked his agreement. "Chiefs of Althing, hear my proposal. I trust you'll find it agreeable."

The next day dawned bright and sunny, and Alynn practically skipped beside Drostan as they wound their way through the tent-pocked grass. It felt like a holiday. After a short meeting to see if Leif would officially become chief, Drostan would be returned to her, and they could spend the day sightseeing. Perhaps they could get more of the delicious Gythian cheese. Maybe they could sit and listen to a bard's stories or draw tales of faraway lands out of a well-travelled merchant.

"I'll be back, Lynder," Drostan promised, kissing her cheek. He disappeared inside the chief's meeting tent, and a while later Leif came along. He smiled at Alynn—an unusually anxious smile—before he too entered the tent.

A crowd of Diaparnans gathered around, eagerly awaiting the parliament's verdict. It was hardly five minutes before the tent flap opened, and the Lawspeaker led the procession of chiefs onto the plain. The Lawspeaker's voice was loud yet ragged as he announced, "It is the pleasure of the Chiefs of the Thirty-Sixth Althing to announce that the tribe of Diaparn will be entitled to a chief recognized by the Seven Tribes of Orkney."

Everyone cheered, and Alynn beamed. Finally, the island got the chief they deserved. Now for a formal vote—a pointless one, since Leif was the only viable candidate—and life would be normal again.

"However," continued the Lawspeaker, "due to his forceful conversion of the island to a foreign religion, Leif Idirson will be banned from the vote."

If the Lawspeaker said anything else, it was drowned out by murmurs and complaints. Alynn began to wish she hadn't eaten so much breakfast. Leif hadn't forcefully converted anyone! What was going on? Who else was eligible for the chieftainship? Leif's hand started to fly towards his hilt, but he quickly stopped himself. He instead looked at the Lawspeaker, and at the other chiefs, with a glare of angry questions.

"Therefore, the Chiefs of the Thirty-Sixth Althing declare a new heir to Konar the Mad—Drostan Leifson!"

ELEVEN

Alynn watched Drostan's face as the crowd slowly erupted into applause. At first, the words didn't quite sink in. But then his eyes grew wide, and his face grew pale, and for a moment, Alynn thought he was going to vomit or faint or laugh with the insanity of it all. But he took a deep breath and looked at Alynn. She forced herself to smile encouragingly. Just get him through this moment, get him out of the public eye. Surely there was some mistake. Everything would be fixed by noon.

"Will any eligible man join Drostan Leifson on the ballot for chieftain of St. Anne's Cleft?"

One man stepped forward. "I challenge Drostan Leifson for the chieftainship," he said. Alynn recognized him as Ormund, Sigmund's oldest brother. His wealth, age, and family history—his father Steingrim was an elder of the tribe and a former Lawspeaker—made him a formidable opponent in the vote. But he was a man of questionable morals and uncertain courage. No Christian or true soldier would vote for him.

"Men of St. Anne's Cleft, make your decisions!" the Lawspeaker announced. His voice cracked, and he took a swig from a drinking-horn at his belt. "The vote is tomorrow, at the first full light!"

The crowd began murmuring, and the Lawspeaker left,

followed by a chief who bore an uncanny resemblance to him. Brothers, probably—they had the exact same beard, just in different shades of dirty blonde. Leif ran after them. The young dark-haired man who was with the elderly Darsidian chief walked up to Drostan and thumped his back. Drostan looked sick.

"So, Diaparn's future chief can't even give a speech?" he asked. "I almost hope you win the election, just so I can watch you drag your pitiful island down to a level so low that the Gythians look down their noses at you."

"I thought Darsidia already operated in that capacity," Drostan said. He held out an arm to Alynn, and she came to him. Sweat dampened the edge of her sleeve as he squeezed her hand.

"Who is this?" the dark-haired man asked, directing his ice-blue gaze towards Alynn. "I'll introduce myself, milady, as Nokkvi Hrodolfson, the future chief of the greatest tribe in Orkney."

"So you intend to challenge Drostan in the vote tomorrow?" Alynn asked. Nokkvi scowled and swore at her.

Alynn balled her fists. "May a cat eat you, and may the devil eat the cat. I've never met a man daft enough to insult Alynn the Dauntless until today."

"Alynn the Dauntless?" Nokkvi glanced her over head to toe, as if appraising a trader's ware. "I had a fishbone of a man come up to me yesterday, looked a bit like you, said you had a brother in Scotland. Asked if he was in any danger—which, unfortunately, he is, as my Vikings are heading straight towards him."

Alynn took a deep breath, forcing her anger aside. "I've yet to hear you say somethin' that doesn't make me want to kill you."

"I was getting there, milady. From what we've last heard of our men, and taking my brother Norbert's terrible leadership skills into account, they'll reach Skerray in two weeks' time. Should we come in contact with your brother, we'll give him to you at a bargain price. Unless he dies in transit. You'll get the body free of charge."

"Och, 'tis indescribable gratitude I'm filled with, at that bit of good news," Alynn shot back.

"I'll give him to you myself, if he lives," Nokkvi said. "I'll be awaiting a more personal declaration of thanks."

At that, Drostan, who had been trying to butt into the conversation, gave full vent to his wrath. "Nokkvi, if you say one more word to her—"

"Temper, temper—"

Alynn grabbed Drostan's hand and led him away before a brawl broke out. "—you'll die a slow and painful death, do you hear me, sir?" At least his anger had driven his fear away.

As soon as they were out of earshot, Drostan put an arm around Alynn and held her tightly against his side, slowing his pace so she wouldn't trip. "Come and get me if he does anything else to you. Nokkvi is mostly words, won't fight unless his temper's up, but if he touches you, I'll give him a blood eagle."

"If he tries anythin', he's either fierce courageous or so incredibly daft he can't tell night from day. Now, how are you holdin' up?"

"The vote. Aye." Drostan drew a breath and ran a hand through his hair. "I don't know what to think. I'm afraid, I'm excited, I'm nervous—it's almost as bad as the day I asked you to marry me. I nigh wet my trousers right there in front of everyone. Part of me thinks I'm dreaming, would you mind slapping me?"

Alynn couldn't bring herself to slap him, so she stepped on his foot. He winced and took a strange hop away from her.

"I should have gotten you softer shoes," Drostan muttered. "No one sees me as a chief. They still think I'm the toddler Leif brought home with him from Scotland—and I might be an adult now, but I've no idea how life works, no clue how to lead, I'm constantly standing on a hole." He looked at Alynn, his precious eyes wide and hopeful, and a gust of wind from

149

the ocean ruffled his hair. "I'm not ready, but I want to be."

Silently, Alynn breathed a prayer—not for eloquence, but for wisdom, and for the right words to speak. "Drostan, you may not know how to be a leader. Neither do I. But I know one thing—you will learn. And I will be right there beside you, learnin' with you, and helpin' you every step of the way." She watched courage and hope grow in him, displacing fear, and his nerves turned to excitement. Suddenly, he cupped Alynn's jaw in one hand and kissed her forehead.

"Thank you," he said. "Let's find Father and see who's behind this mess."

Drostan marched confidently into the tent the Chiefs met in, and Alynn followed timidly. She didn't know if she was allowed to, but no one threw her out, so she figured she could stay. What had possessed everyone to deem Leif ineligible for the chieftainship? Why hadn't Chief Thorbjorn stopped it?

It was hardly a moment before Leif stormed in. "*What happened?*" he roared.

Helgi of Gythia jumped. "My good Sir Leif, we meant nothing against your—"

Leif ignored him and stopped two feet away from Chief Hrodolf of Darsidia. "On your feet, spawn of Jormungand! The blind can see who's behind this!"

Hrodolf reached out for Nokkvi's hand to steady him as he rose to his feet, but he was nowhere to be found—out in the woods or in a tavern, Alynn guessed, nursing his wounds after his insult contest. Leif grabbed Hrodolf's arm instead. The old man winced. "The fault lies with you, son of Idir, and we hold you accountable."

"What laws have I broken? Where is Yngvar?"

"He's drinking the pain out of his throat, and by the time he's through, he'll be of no use to us," the Lawspeaker's brother said. "Steingrim was Lawspeaker for many years. Let him assist us."

"I've already sent for him." There was a fire in Leif's eyes as he studied each chief in turn. He quickly passed over the whimpering worm that Gythia had for a chief—his opinion was of no importance—but his gaze lingered on Thorbjorn Farsight for a while. "I want the facts."

Thorbjorn stood and, for a while, held his peace. His brows were knitted in what seemed like concern. "I'm sorry, Leif. I tried to convince them otherwise, but they're right."

Elder Steingrim chose that moment to enter the tent. A stoop-shouldered man with a spear for a cane and a beard like washed and carded wool, Elder Steingrim was one of the few people on the island older than Lukas. "What are you addlepates babbling about?" he snapped, sitting on the low stool Thorbjorn Farsight had vacated. "Leif may be a fool, but he's a decent one, and to be honest, I'd prefer him over my own son Ormund to lead us."

"Leif declared Christianity to be the island's official religion without a formal vote," said the chief with tight trousers, eyeliner, and meticulously groomed facial hair.

"There was no need for a vote," Leif insisted. "After the Battle of Faith, everyone realized the Christian God was stronger than those of Asgard and Vanaheim, and there was not a single voice raised in opposition."

"But perhaps," croaked a sick-looking man in the corner, "a legitimate vote would have proved otherwise. Words spoken are one thing, words written are another, and it's no secret that emotions are heightened after a battle." The poor man coughed violently into a handkerchief.

"Four months passed between the battle and the change of laws!" Leif snapped. "Heightened emotions don't last that long."

"Peace," called Elder Steingrim. "What they say is true, Leif. I'm sorry. The laws are clear that any change of that magnitude requires a vote. A formal vote, be that the raising of hands or the casting of ballots. But as I recall, neither of those transpired when you sold us all to an alien faith."

"They could have overlooked it," Thorbjorn interjected. "Konar did worse, and they ignored all of it. Leif, they're doing this to test your God. If He doesn't help your son govern, and keep him from going mad as Konar did, He doesn't exist in their eyes." He turned again to the other chiefs and said, "I have no doubt that Drostan will excel in his place of leadership, but you had no right to force him into it."

Leif fumed. "Your faith or lack thereof should not depend on my son's performance. He's eighteen this month! Do you realize you've put an island at stake? What about the people who live here? The eight hundred and seventy-two people who live here, does their wellbeing mean nothing to you?"

"Peace, Leif," Elder Steingrim called. The sick man coughed again into a handkerchief.

"Don't tell me to—"

Leif checked his sentenced abruptly and scowled. His fists were clenched, his shoulders tense, and for a moment, Alynn thought he would fly into a fit of rage. Suddenly, Leif drew his sword, thrust it into the ground, and stormed out of the tent.

Alynn stuck by Drostan's side until the sun began to hide behind the woods to the west, when she left to help Caitriona and Valdis make dinner. She might not be a good cook, but at least she could follow orders. Caitriona put her to work cutting vegetables to put in the soup.

Rowan was the first of the menfolk to wander in. He kissed Caitriona and hugged Alynn, then asked what he could do to help. Caitriona was wary of letting him do anything—bad cooking ran in his side of the family—but she finally asked him to bring the table down from the loft.

Alynn waited until Rowan had brought the table and four low stools down from the loft before she spoke to him. "What did you sell your cloak pin for?" she asked.

"I got a pair of scissors and a wooden spoon for one of them, and a penny for the other."

Alynn looked up from her cutting board in surprise, then regretted it when she sliced her finger with the knife. "A coin?" she asked.

"What else would a penny be?"

A whole penny? Just for a copper cloak pin? He should have gotten two antler combs or a roll of well-made tablet woven trim. Not a whole penny. "How much copper did you put into it?" she asked.

Rowan thought. "Probably a bit more than a halfpenny's worth. Who did that copper belong to? I need to repay them."

"Father, the Norse aren't like the Irish. To them, coins don't matter. The metal does. If you got twice as much as the copper was worth—he knew it was copper, didn't he?"

"I think so."

Alynn turned to Caitriona. "Mum, Father just got a whole penny for a cloak pin!"

Caitriona looked up at Alynn, then at Rowan, then at the soup she was stirring. "That's grand, love! What did it look like?"

"It was a penannular with scrolled ends and a knot at the fold of the pin." Rowan set the last stool on the ground and looked up at Caitriona. "I had just enough time and just enough copper to make you something. I hope you like it." And with that, he took something small and copper from the folds of his plaid and placed it in Caitriona's hands. She gasped.

"'Tis beautiful."

"I wanted it fit for a queen."

Rowan took the pin back, fastened it on Caitriona's keyhole neckline, and kissed her. She blushed. "I don't have anythin' to give you back."

"I have you, Caitriona. What more could I want?"

Alynn quickly turned back to chopping vegetables. When she finished, Rowan and Caitriona were wrapped in each other's arms and kissing passionately. Alynn decided to leave them be.

Lukas chose an awkward time to walk in the door. He spoke half a syllable, stopped, and stared. As if she was protecting a five-year-old's innocence, Alynn took him by the arm and led him back outside. "Fetch some water, will you?" she asked.

"What were they doing?"

"What married people do. Try to ignore them. Did you enjoy yer day? It must have been grand catchin' up with yer old friend."

Lukas smiled. "Aye, it was. Would ye like to fight Einar?"

"Drostan might need a hand to steady him, with the vote tomorrow and all," Alynn said. "But I'll think about it. Thank you."

"Is dinner ready?"

"Nearly. If you could fetch us some water, we'd appreciate it."

"Of course." Lukas tucked his hands inside his sleeves. "I'll, em—knock, I suppose, afore I come in wi' it."

"Grand idea."

Alynn and Valdis set the table, and Caitriona joined them eventually. She was still glowing, and she kept glancing down at her new cloak pin. Alynn was only able to catch glimpses of it, but she knew it was beautiful. Everything her father made was beautiful.

Where were Leif and Drostan? They should have been home by now. How long should they wait before they ate without them?

Finally, just as Caitriona was setting the last bowl of soup on the table, Leif and Drostan came in with wet hair, damp clothes, and red faces. Drostan looked quite a bit like a lobster. Alynn felt a pang of irrational worry over him. "Are you sunburned?"

Drostan kissed her cheek, and Alynn kissed him back. "Nay, I took a sauna and a quick bath with Father. I hope we didn't keep the meal waiting."

"Not long," Alynn promised.

"He needs a haircut before tomorrow," Leif said, "and Cait, would you mind trimming my eyebrows?"

Lukas looked up from where he was stealing a bite of soup. "Did you say eyebrows?" he asked.

"Aye. I'm starting to look like a Viking raider."

Lukas stared at him. "Ye trim yer eyebrows?"

Leif shrugged. "Everyone does."

"I'd be glad to trim yer eyebrows, Leif," Caitriona interrupted. "Alynn, can you be trusted with a pair of scissors?"

Alynn turned to Drostan. "Do you trust me with a pair of scissors?"

"I'll trust you with far more than that," Drostan promised. He sat on one of the stools, and Alynn sat next to him, with Lukas beside her.

"Eyebrows," he muttered. "Of all the types of superfluous frippery in this world...eyebrows! Good Lord!" Lukas thought deeply for a moment, then turned to Alynn. "Yer mother isn't going to make me start trimming my eyebrows, is she?"

Alynn gave his dark brows half a glance. "You need to keep whatever hair you have left."

"Good point."

As soon as the meal was eaten and the dishes were washed, Alynn took Drostan into the fading daylight and began to cut his hair. She turned first to the nape of his neck, trimming the hair on it until it was a patch of ginger fuzz. She'd thought it was ridiculous at first, the way Norsemen shaved the napes of their necks. But it made it much easier to comb out nits, and when the rest of Drostan's hair was allowed to fall nearly to his shoulders, the shaved patch was hardly visible. Alynn brushed out the rest of his hair and trimmed it, then evened out his bangs. But not too much, so that if she made a mistake, Caitriona could easily fix it. Mistakes were easy to make when the wind was blowing.

As soon as Alynn finished with the scissors, Caitriona took them to trim Leif's eyebrows. Lukas watched with both disdain and curiosity.

"Have you bathed, like I asked you to?" Caitriona asked him.

"Not yet."

Caitriona sighed. "Bath or eyebrows. Yer choice."

Lukas pulled off his cowl and scapular. "May I leave these here?"

"Of course. Just leave yer tunic on until you get there. The Norse tend not to traipse to the baths and back in their undergarments."

Lukas had learned long ago that arguing with Caitriona was pointless. So, somewhat resignedly, he set off with a promise that he'd be back soon. *An unnecessary promise*, Alynn thought as she waited for Caitriona to inspect Drostan's haircut. *I've seen cats that are fonder of water than he is.*

"Mum," said Alynn as soon as Caitriona seemed to come to a stopping point, "how'd I do on Drostan's hair?"

Caitriona glanced over at them as she wiped off her tweezers. "'Tis still a bit long."

"But I did alright, didn't I?"

"Alynn, you're deft enough with scissors to—"

Leif flinched. "Ow!"

Caitriona wiped a bit of blood off Leif's forehead and sighed. "Stop second-guessin' yerself. You do a better job than you think." She looked over Drostan's hair, inspected the shaved patch, and finished trimming his bangs herself. When she finished, Drostan ran his hands through his hair until it was fluffy as a cat with a new winter coat. Alynn laughed at him.

"Be careful to stay clean for tomorrow," Leif said as Caitriona turned her attention back to his eyebrows. "Wear your good tunic. You can borrow my sword belt if you want to."

Drostan tried to tame down his hair a bit. "Thank you."

Alynn put a hand on his tense shoulder. "Don't be nervous. You'll do grand."

"Do you think I'll win?"

"There's hardly a contest," Leif said. "If Ormund wasn't a spineless, weaselly, pagan cheapskate who can't even manure a field without turning green in the face, we might have something to worry about."

"Of course, we've nothing to worry about," Drostan snapped. "I'm too young, with no experience leading others, no oratory skills—what do you think drove Uncle Konar mad?

He was nineteen when he became chief. I don't think he could handle it."

Leif sighed. "Uncle Konar went mad for a number of reasons, the least of which was power. If anything, it corrupted him, but I believe he was born mad, at least to a certain extent. When he was nine or so, he pulled the legs off a live frog for his own pleasure. But it wasn't until a few years ago that—Cait, do you need me to stop talking? Because I don't want everyone here to think I'm falling ill with smallpox."

With a bit more vigor than necessary, Caitriona plucked a few final hairs from Leif's brow and looked at Drostan's. "I had Valdis do mine on Saturday," Drostan admitted. "Sorry."

"All's well, dear heart." Caitriona snipped a few long hairs off Drostan's eyebrows, then glanced up at the setting sun. "Leif, do you know anyone who owns a three-stringed lyre?"

"I've a two-stringed one lying around somewhere. Would that work?"

"It might. Ask Rowan."

Alynn grinned. She grabbed Drostan's hand and, with the excitement of a child going to a Christmas party, dragged him back to the house. "I hope it works," she breathed. "Please, God, make it work!"

It took a bit of doing to find Leif's old lyre, and a bit more doing to find the small horsehair bow that went with it. But when Rowan saw the two together, his eyes lit up. "I haven't played in a few months," he said as he took the lyre in his lap. "And this doesn't have a drone string."

"Can you play it?" Alynn asked.

"Of course I can play it. It needs tuned first." Rowan plucked the first string, then turned the tuning peg until it sang at just the right pitch. He looked up at Alynn and her shining eyes and smiled. "What do you want to hear?"

"A reel," Alynn said.

Rowan thought as he tuned the second string. "The Timpan Reel, what else?" he asked himself. He drew the bow across the strings, and the lyre sang with a beauty that belonged in the choirs of heaven. Rowan played a scale, then tapped the time with his foot, and began a rollicking beat. It was as wild as the wind blowing through the sails of a ship, as joyous as a stag running after its mate.

Leif listened with wide eyes, as if he'd never heard a reel before. Or was he impressed with Rowan's skill? Drostan tapped his foot. He'd caught the magic the timpan held within it and wanted to dance.

Suddenly, Caitriona's flute sang out in perfect harmony, like a bird freed from a cage. Alynn gasped. For a moment, she was a child again in Limerick City, full of wonder and a summery joy that made her want to dance and sing and laugh all at once. She grabbed Drostan's hand.

"We're dancing?" he asked.

"Please?"

Drostan's eyes were merry for the first time that day. Alynn lifted her skirts so she wouldn't trip over them, and her feet began to fly. Drostan wasn't half bad at dancing reels either. Keeping clear of the fireplace in the middle of the room, they stepped forwards and backwards and leapt and spun circles until Alynn was breathless. It was a moment that she wanted to keep in a bottle, so she could look back on it and smile.

Then Lukas came home from his bath, and Alynn was snapped out of her wonderful moment with a very unwelcome bolt of fear.

"Lukas, what happened?" she demanded.

The music stopped. Caitriona squeaked her flute, and Rowan froze like a statue.

Lukas stopped in the doorway, dripping wet. His tunic and undershirt were draped over his arm, and his braies were damp with bathwater. But what surprised Alynn the most was his chest. She was used to the odd knobs and lumps that covered his rib cage, left over from fractures that had never knit right. She'd seen them a dozen times, but she'd never seen a purple bruise the size of a man's hand before.

With the awkwardness that was expected from any man

caught in his braies, Lukas said, "I forgot a towel. Pretend I'm not here."

"Who hit you?"

"Where?" Lukas looked himself over and saw his bruise. "Och, aye, it looks worse than it is. I bruise easily. Ye know that by now."

Leif moved a board that comprised one of the sleeping benches and took a towel from within it. "I've seen that bruise afore," he said. "Horse breaking accident?"

"Aye."

Caitriona's hand flew to her mouth. "Patience did that to you?"

Lukas dried off and slipped his undershift over his head. "We ought to have named her Longsuffering. It's mostly healed already."

I should have been working with her, Alynn thought.

Lukas got his clothes back on, and Rowan found another tune to play. It was happy, but it felt hollow, as if the third string was necessary for a proper performance. The song ended abruptly when one of the strings broke.

'Tis my fault he got hurt.

Drostan's arm was around her, and Rowan began telling the story of how he learned to play the timpan, but Alynn hardly heard or felt anything. She was glad when Rowan asked to pray for her, and she crawled into the bedcloset to undress. When she was sure she didn't need a sliver of light anymore, she pulled the door fully shut and locked it.

I wish I'd get hurt instead of Lukas for once.

Alynn didn't know what had woken her up. She just knew she was dying.

Why do you feel like you've been fighting? Who did you hurt?

She knew she hadn't hurt anyone. She'd probably just had more night terrors.

159

But what if you didn't? Why are you panting? Why does your fist hurt, like you've punched someone?

She had to get a light, see if she'd hurt anyone. Or it would help her calm down. She tried to reach for her bedside table, but she felt a wall. She tried to get out of bed. She was in a box, a coffin—she was trapped—

You hurt someone, and they buried you alive.

Alynn beat against the wall. Someone would hear and dig her up again. Hopefully! What if they didn't? Her breath became panicked.

"Mum? Lukas?"

She kept hitting the wall. Her punches produced a hollow sound, so perhaps she wasn't buried after all. Maybe she was laid out in the chapel. Why would they bother doing that? They'd probably just stuck her in the yard somewhere while they dug a grave. Would she go to heaven, if she didn't have a proper funeral?

"Help me!"

Her hands were beginning to hurt. She saw nothing in the darkness, not even her own fists and nails as she struck and clawed at her coffin. Her breathing echoed—she needed air— was someone in there with her? She struck behind her and hit nothing. Suddenly, she heard Drostan's voice.

"Alynn?"

"I can't breathe. Get me out."

"There's a lock. A simple latch. Can you pull it?"

Alynn groped about on the wall, but all she felt was plain wood. "I can't find it."

"It's right here." Drostan knocked on the wall, and Alynn moved left.

"I'm going to throw up."

"You're alright, love."

"I can't find it, I'm sorry—"

"Calm down, Alynn." Drostan's voice sounded farther away, but just for a moment. "I'll get you out, but you need to go to the far corner, alright? Get over by the pillow."

Alynn crawled back to where she'd started out and curled up in a trembling, gasping ball. "I've got the pillow."

"Good. Now cover your head with it."

Before Alynn could move, there was an earth-shattering crack. A faint light emanated from the open door, and Drostan's arms were around her, pulling her back into the land of the living. "I've got you," Drostan said gently. "I've got you, love. You're alright now."

"I can't breathe."

"Just be still. Everything's alright." Drostan sat down, still cradling Alynn in his arms. "Breathe in through your nose, out through your mouth, like you're blowing out a candle. I'm going to count, alright? Breathe in...two...three...four, now out ...two...three...four...five—slower this time. In...two...three... four. That's better. Now out...two...three...four...five...six... seven...eight. Good job."

With each breath, Alynn was wrapped in warmth and love and light. The embers of the fire were just bright enough to make Drostan's face visible. Alynn became aware of others around her. Leif stirred the fire. Caitriona wrapped Rowan's plaid around her, and Lukas was praying from his bed in a corner.

Why, *why* did she have to bother everyone? Waking Drostan was bad enough, but rousing a household made Alynn wish she'd truly been trapped in a coffin in the middle of the yard. "I'm sorry," she breathed, burying her face in Drostan's chest. "I didn't want to wake everyone. I'm sorry."

"I woke everyone when I got the axe out," Drostan said. "You didn't. But even if you did, I'd say you're worth more than a few minutes' lost sleep. And Valdis is still asleep, if it makes you feel any better."

It didn't. Why couldn't she take care of herself? Why hadn't she been able to find the latch? She'd had everything under control, if she'd just been able to find that blasted latch—what kind of twit wasn't able to open a simple latch?

Drostan helped clear her mind with a kiss to the forehead.

"Do you want to take a walk, or hear a story, or something?"

"You've a big day tomorrow. Go back to sleep."

"Assuming you're not going back in the closet, where are you going to sleep?"

"Don't worry about me."

Drostan smiled. "Lynder, there are times I can't sleep at all because I'm worried about you. I pray for you every night. And I always hate it when you come to me and tell me you've had another nightmare, because I wasn't there to help you fight it. I'm glad I was tonight."

Peace settled over Alynn. She knew how frustrating it was to try and help someone who didn't want to be helped. Maybe letting Drostan comfort her ended up blessing them both. She hugged him, then crawled in bed with her mother and lay awake until she was sure everyone else had returned to sleep.

TWELVE

The next morning, as a cool wind and patchwork clouds made the sun of no effect, Alynn stood in front of the platform where Drostan had first given his speech. She wore her pink Sabbath dress, with sleeves that hung in the Celtic fashion. She felt rather out-of-place among the Norse. Many of them wore their everyday outfits, only freshly cleaned. The women had donned extra jewelry or styled their hair more elaborately, and some might felt the occasion a good place to break in a new dress, but none of them wore hanging sleeves. Except for Caitriona, of course. She looked like a queen in her gown of emerald, but Alynn just felt like a street urchin mistaken for royalty and dressed for a parade.

Lukas stuck close to Alynn's side. Even he had been convinced to wear his good cowl and scapular for the occasion. They were the same as his everyday ones, just closer to the black they were supposed to be, and two years old instead of twenty. "Shouldn't you be with the others?" Alynn asked him.

Lukas tugged at his cowl. "Which others?"

"The Lawspeaker, the chiefs, everyone else who's about to be part of the ceremony?"

"The real ceremony comes at the feast on Sunday eve. That, I'm part of. This is just a vote." Lukas, still dissatisfied with the situation of his cowl, took it off and looked it over. "Is there a pin in here? It wasn't nearly so tight fer Sigmund's wedding."

"You'd just gotten over yer broken ribs then, you've filled out since."

Resignedly, Lukas donned his cowl again, and Alynn made sure the hood was centered in back. "Forgive me," he muttered, whether to Alynn or to God no one knew. But something was wrong with him, something more than a tight cowl. Did his bruise cause more pain than he let on? Was he ill? Something was hurting him, but the more Alynn stared at him, the more she realized he was probably pained in spirit, not in body.

"Is somethin' wrong?" she asked.

Lukas wanted to answer, but he couldn't get his words together. Alynn began to worry. "We don't—och, blast it. It's naught ye need to concern yerself with, my dear. Ye've enough to worry about, and it's not *yer* fault."

What went on in that haloed head of his? Alynn had learned long ago that his emotions were as tangled as an unraveled ball of yarn left for the cats to play with. She slipped her hand into his, and he squeezed it.

"I hope Drostan is alright," Alynn said. "He's probably fierce nervous."

"Have ye prayed fer him?" Lukas asked.

"I have."

"So have I."

Finally, the Lawspeaker came onto the platform, with the six Chiefs behind him. "The time has come for the vote!" he called, his voice still rough from Monday's recitation. "Will Drostan Leifson and all who challenge him come forward?"

Drostan stepped onto the stage. Whether he was frightened or confident Alynn couldn't tell, but she eagerly searched him for signs. Sweat was smeared on the side of his crimson tunic, but his gaze was steady as he surveyed the crowd. His eyes locked with hers for a moment, and his expression softened. Alynn smiled, hoping to comfort him, praying he wouldn't panic or freeze up or stumble over any words he spoke.

Ormund stood next to Drostan as his sole competitor. He too was richly dressed, and he stood on stage with the ease of a goat on a cliff. Drostan offered him a handshake, which he accepted. *Good job,* Alynn thought. Now, the public saw that Drostan was civil even to his enemies—unless he genuinely wanted Ormund to win, which Alynn wouldn't put past him.

"Will the heads of every family from St. Anne's Cleft come forward?"

The group separated into two. Some forty men, the patriarchs of all the families of St. Anne's Cleft, stood forward, while Alynn stepped back with the onlookers.

"Those who will for Drostan Leifson to assume the chieftainship, raise one hand and say 'aye.'"

A volley of hands went up, and a chorus of 'ayes' resounded. Lukas's hand was raised, and so was Elder Steingrim's. Ormund must be rather disappointed—if he noticed. He was too busy counting the hands that were raised, along with the Lawspeaker and the six Chiefs.

"I have twenty-nine," said Chief Thorbjorn of Hrafney.

"As do I," said the pale, sick man beside him.

The old chief with a thick grey beard scowled. "Twenty-eight."

"There are twenty-nine, Father," said the young dark-haired man behind him—Nokkvi, of course, the son of the Darsidian chief.

"Twenty-nine for Drostan?" the Lawspeaker repeated. "Those for Ormund Steingrimson, raise one hand and say 'aye.'"

Alynn was caught in that limbo between nerves and excitement as the remaining hands were counted. Murmurs of "Thirteen" and "Aye, I've thirteen as well" arose from the six Chiefs.

"Thirteen for Ormund?" the Lawspeaker asked. "The ayes have it. St. Anne's Cleft, behold your chieftain!"

The Lawspeaker took Drostan's hand and thrust it upward,

as if forcing Drostan to celebrate his victory. Drostan laughed. Whether he was relieved that he was about to step off the stage, or if he still believed the whole thing was a dream, or even if he was genuinely excited, Alynn couldn't tell. All she knew was that she wasn't nervous anymore. She was ecstatic for Drostan.

Drostan strode gallantly down the platform as soon as the fanfare subsided, and Alynn sought him out through the crowd of people trying to shake his hand and congratulate him. "I'm fierce proud of you, love," she said, kissing his clammy cheek. "You didn't look nervous at all, at all."

"Good," Drostan said quietly. "I'm glad I didn't eat much breakfast. It's torture, standing up there, a million eyes staring at you, waiting for you to misspeak or trip over your own feet. I'm glad the vote's over. Now comes the hard part."

"Don't think of it that way," Alynn said. "'Tis a mostly well-behaved island, isn't it?"

"There's more to it than criminal justice," Drostan said. "It's maintaining an army, keeping everyone fed—"

"A gift for you, sir," a voice interrupted. Alynn looked everywhere, then looked down to see Alva the doctor, holding a basket of vegetables in red, rash-covered hands. "From my own garden."

"Many thanks, Alva," Drostan said, handing the basket to Alynn. "We'll put these to good use."

Alva smiled. "To think that I have seen your uncle, your grandfather, and even your great-grandfather Horik lead our tribe, and now you are taking their place. I will pray you have the wisdom of Odin and the might of Thor!"

"I'll take all the prayers I can get," Drostan said. "Thank you again." Alva smiled and hugged Drostan, and for the first time, Alynn noticed the snake around her waist like a belt. Vorthmathir stuck his tongue out at her, and Alynn stuck out her tongue back at him.

"Take it one day at a time," Alynn advised Drostan when Alva had left. "Harder than others, some days will be, and there's naught you can do about that. Just remember: as time goes on, it gets easier."

Drostan listened as he shook a few more hands. "Thank you, love. I'm afraid I won't be seeing much of you until Althing's over."

Somehow, the chief of Gythia had weaseled his way through the crowd. "My good sir," he said, "what think you of an alliance between our two tribes?"

"What sort of alliance, Helgi?" Drostan asked.

"A marriage alliance between yourself and my daughter Ragnhild," he said, motioning to the girl beside him as if she was a goddess of beauty. Alynn's upset glare turned into a curious stare. The angels who placed her freckles must have been drunk, or else they had spilled a bowl of them all over her face.

Drostan glanced Ragnhild over with more pity than interest. "I suppose news of my betrothal to Alynn the Dauntless has been slow to reach your shores?" he asked, putting a supporting hand on Alynn's back.

"Oh—terribly slow, sir," the Gythian chief flustered. "You've my warmest congratulations. But—even as a concubine, my Ragnhild will not disappoint you, and she comes with a sizable dowry, as well as the loyalty of our island."

From the spark in Drostan's eyes, Alynn knew he wanted to say something along the lines of "I don't care for Ragnhild. Keep your dowry; I'm more worried about finding a cricket in my boot than I am about your army finding a boat seaworthy enough to come to our shores." But civility got the better of him. "Christianity doesn't allow for concubines."

Chief Helgi of Gythia was crestfallen. "The offer stands, sir, if you ever reconsider."

"Or rather, it will, until you find someone else to forge an alliance with. I believe Nokkvi Hrodolfson is hopelessly single, if you run out of other options." Drostan must have realized his tongue was getting out of hand. "Although I do pray things won't come to that."

With a grimace somewhere between fear and disgust, Chief

Helgi of Gythia took Ragnhild by the arm and led her away. "Good riddance," Drostan muttered. "Lynder, I'll be busy until sundown. Go enjoy yourself."

"You're certain?"

"One of us might as well have fun today."

With one last kiss on the cheek and a wish for good luck, Alynn left Drostan to his newfound responsibilities.

True to his word, Drostan was busy meeting with the six Chiefs for the rest of the day. Since her parents were busy and her friends had disappeared into the crowds, Alynn stuck close to Lukas. It was wonderful to watch him pray with someone. Some people were converted to Christianity; others received physical healing. When they left to tell their family what God had done, Lukas would pause for a moment, sometimes praying under his breath, other times simply listening, and then leave to find his next target.

As the sun drew close to the western horizon, Lukas turned abruptly for Leif and Drostan's house. "It is growing close to dinnertime, isn't it?" he asked.

Alynn sighed. "How are you hungry? You had two helpings of Gythian cheese!"

"Aye, the best cheese I've ever eaten. All that did was stir my appetite."

Alynn didn't argue. She needed to get home anyway, and help Caitriona and Valdis prepare the meal.

Drostan deserved a feast in honor of his newfound chieftainship. He would get one after the formal ceremony on the last day of Althing, but in the meantime, Caitriona had a lavish meal prepared. There was boiled fowl, beets, and mashed turnips with delicious hot bread. Leif had even opened a cask of mead for the occasion. Alynn wouldn't drink more than a mug; she hated the taste of it.

The food was kept warm until the men came home. Rowan was soaked in sweat and the odor of coal, Leif's shoulders drooped, and Drostan looked dazed. Alynn embraced him. If learning how to become chief was anything like learning how to read, there did not exist a word to describe how tired he was.

"How was yer day, love?" Alynn asked.

"I hate Althing." Drostan slumped onto a bench. "Thorbjorn Farsight is the only sane man in this whole mess. Ebbe isn't bad, but Yngvar, his brother the Lawspeaker? His voice gets old after the first hour or so. And then what's-his-name from Fjorderny is dying of consumption. He nigh coughs his lungs out every time the wind blows wrong on him."

"I won't get you started on Oakvin," Leif said.

"Oakvin Geirsteinson is the most vain and pompous man in Orkney. He brushes his hair every hour—you can keep time by it. And by Odin, they never stopped talking." He groaned. "My head hurts."

Caitriona handed him a drink. "Much better you'll feel after dinner."

Drostan did seem to enjoy his meal. Some of the light came back in his eyes as he ate two birds, two platefuls of turnips, and slice after slice of bread. And while he didn't have too much more to say about his day, he mentioned his run-in with Chief Helgi of Gythia and his freckled daughter Ragnhild.

"What a way to meet your spouse," Leif said. "You handled it well."

"I've a hard time believing they haven't heard of yer betrothal," Lukas said with his mouth full.

"As have I," Drostan agreed.

There was a short lull in the conversation, until Rowan spoke up. "Alynn, you're usin' yer left hand."

Alynn quickly took her spoon in her right hand. "Sorry."

"You're left-handed?" Rowan asked.

"She's actually both-handed," Lukas said. "I'm surprised ye've never noticed."

"I'm not," Alynn muttered under her breath.

Leif glanced from Alynn to Rowan and back again. "So, Rowan," he said, "how'd you meet Caitriona?"

"Now, there's a good tale." Rowan leaned back for a

moment, gathering his thoughts. "Twenty years ago it was, on a lovely summer's day, when a lonely lad wandered through the sheep fields outside Limerick City. A change of clothes and halfpence he had to his name, and his father's old timpan in a case of otterskin. When he was certain he was far away from the town, and that no one was there to hear him, he took his timpan from his case, he began to play.

"He played a moment, and then he stopped, for he thought he heard a song answer his own. He took his bundles and followed the noise, and he stumbled across a shepherdess playing her flute. With her lambs about her, and her staff in her arm, and her tresses fallin' to the ground she sat on, she looked like a queen." Rowan took Caitriona's hand and kissed it. "To this day, I'm not sure why she married the lad. But he's certainly glad she did."

Drostan set his hand over Alynn's. "The best day of your life, wasn't it?" he asked.

Rowan chewed his bread thoughtfully. "It was."

Leif chuckled. "It's a sight better than the day I met Drostan's mum."

"Tell us the story, Father," Drostan said. "Please?"

Leif gave a wistful smile, staring through space and into the past. "I was...eighteen, I think, on my first raid with Konar. The only raid I've ever been on, mind you. And it didn't go well. I was wounded in a fight, dragged myself into the woods, and passed out before I could tend to myself. I kept seeing this Valkyrie in front of me. She was a vision. She had the reddest hair I'd ever seen, the bluest eyes, and the most perfect, freckled nose—she was perfect. Elspeth McLain."

Leif's smile grew softer. "I don't know why she didn't see me as one of the monsters who'd torn her home apart. But she didn't, and she nursed me back to health, made her father give me a job, and all but dragged me to church every Sabbath. When the time was right, we were married, and Drostan came along a year later." Leif chuckled, then reached across the table to ruffle Drostan's hair. "He's lit up my world ever since."

"Where's Elspeth now?" Rowan asked.

"St. Philip's church in Port Ellyn. Under the bush of white roses, along with our son Teague. She died bringing him into the world."

"Oh." Rowan rounded up the mashed turnips on his plate. "I'm sorry."

"Thank you." Leif realized he'd left his spoon in midair and set it on his plate again. "Valdis, I'm sure you have stories to tell."

Valdis turned as red as the beets she quickly choked down. "I don't, sir," she said. "There was the time my brother pushed me into a pond back in Trondheim, and I was sick for a week afterwards, but it's hardly a story."

"Anything's a story if you tell it the right way," Rowan said. He nodded towards Drostan. "What about you, lad? Do you tell stories?"

"Not often," Leif said. "How about it, son? Impress us."

"I'm not sure—" Drostan wiped his mouth on his sleeve, then a smile crept into his eyes. "It was Epiphany, right after the Battle of Faith, and we invited Alynn, Aunt Cait, and Nora McKenzie and her brood up for dinner to celebrate. Alynn took Nora's wee boy Olvir out to the woods—he was probably four at this point—so he could find something to give his mum, and I went with them since it was dark.

"Alynn and Olvir made a nice wreath out of pine boughs, like a St. Lucia's crown, and just as we were about to leave, a gale came in. I knew we'd make ourselves sick trying to go home, so I led everyone to a sod playhouse I'd built as a lad, so we could wait out the storm there. Olvir got frightened, started crying, and Alynn—I don't know how she did it. She sung to him, she held him, she got him to fall asleep."

He set his enchanting gaze on her. "I saw her heart that day. Aye, she was cold, probably frightened, but she didn't give a thought to herself—only to a little boy she hardly knew. It was then I realized she wasn't like the girls I'd grown up with. She was so much better. And she still is."

171

Alynn stuck close to Drostan's side for the first few days of Althing, hoping that her presence would give him a bit of stability as he adjusted to his new office. It seemed to work. By the fifth day, Drostan seemed to be more comfortable, and Alynn allowed herself the freedom to wander off. She'd already seen most of what there was to see at Althing—wrestling competitions, ball games, and tug-of-war. Some of the more violent games, such as horse-fighting, Alynn stayed away from, but she joined in a few games of *tafl* and even won a round. But she ended up at the sparring-grounds, watching Einar brandish a dull sword.

"Halfpenny to fight Einar Shattersword!" he cried, as if he was peddling wares. "Draw blood and win a penny, plus your halfpenny back! Learn from the master!" His eyes lit up when he saw Alynn. "You there! Sif in the flesh! How well did my student teach you?"

"It was very well he taught me," Alynn said. "Nearly all he knows."

Einar tossed her a dull sword. "Let me see. Do you have a halfpenny?"

"I shan't need it."

Einar laughed, and a sizable crowd gathered. Einar Shattersword was a legend in his own right, and tales of the Battle of Faith had been spread throughout Orkney. Watching this sparring match would be like watching Thor and Tyr do battle. Alynn swung the sword to test its balance and readied herself. Lukas had taught her never to start a fight; she waited for Einar to throw the first blow.

His first thrust was a rapid diagonal that would have slit her shoulder to hip, had her own blade not flashed out in answer.

"Lovely weather we've been havin', isn't it?" Alynn asked as she parried a pair of deft blows. "Warmer than usual. The sun's been out more often than not. The wind's fierce. It comes from being near the shore, I know. I grew up on the River Shannon, and we didn't have nearly as much wind. Have you ever seen the River Shannon? 'Tis quite a sight. They say it poisons the air, but I never noticed it."

Einar scowled with determination. He threw two more blows, and Alynn parried both of them perfectly before setting Einar on the defensive. Up-swipe, down-swipe, thrust—she wrapped her blade around Einar's hilt and twisted.

Nothing happened.

One second, and then another, ticked by, and then Einar laughed. "Lukas taught you well," he said. "The battle's a draw! Well played!"

Alynn smiled and felt herself blush. "What should I do now?"

"Don't untangle the blades and stab your opponent—he'll have the chance to do the same," Einar suggested. "Rather, carefully separate the weapons, keep the flat of your blade against the edge of your opponent's, and thrust the pommel into his gut. Like so." Slowly, so Alynn could watch, Einar maneuvered his sword skillfully against Alynn's and brought the pommel between her ribs. "Crack the sternum if you can."

"Thank you," Alynn said.

"The key is to do it quickly, or risk getting your neck slashed. You try."

They locked swords again, and Alynn let the flat of her blade slide along the edge of Einar's until she was able to touch his stomach with the pommel. "Well done," Einar said. He lifted Alynn's hand into the air and grinned at the crowd. "Look well, men, at the girl Einar Shattersword couldn't beat!"

The crowd cheered. "Do you spar, milady?" a young man asked.

"Charge him halfpenny if you win, and give him a penny if you lose," Einar told her. "You'll win eight times out of ten."

"You're sure?"

"Don't be coy, you're attractive enough. It'll give my old bones a rest, Thor knows I need one. Go on."

Taking a breath to steady herself, Alynn motioned for the young man to join her. "Your name?" she asked.

"Brian."

"You're Irish?"

"On my mother's side."

Alynn smiled. "Give her greetings from Limerick City."

She beat Brian easily and won his halfpenny. She won two more sparring matches, then lost one, and then won five more. The fifth was close; Alynn only won because she forced her opponent off the cowhide they were fighting on. She had sense enough to take a break before she lost any money. She sat in the shade of the woods and drank small ale from her drinking-horn, rubbing life into her right arm.

A man approached her with a scrap of paper in his hand. Alynn would have asked him to leave, but she noticed that he wore a plaid over his tunic, and he spoke Gaelic with a High-land brogue when he addressed her. "So ye're Alynn the Dauntless, I take it?" he asked.

"I am."

"And ye've a brother in Skerray? A lad of nine or so, with red hair?"

Alynn leapt up. "How do you—"

"He asked me to give you this." The man handed her a scrap of paper, and Alynn read it three times:

To Alynn I hope your alrite I miss you and want to see you soon Da is looking for you at St. Anne Clef so find him and come home becas its not the same without you. Love Tarin.

Tarin's handwriting was remarkably similar to her own, just messier, and even the misspellings were endearing. Alynn's heart leapt wildly within her. Her arm was no longer sore; she was trembling with energy, with longing. She could hear Tarin's voice, feel the fluff of his hair and the embrace of his tiny arms around her. She wanted him.

She looked at the Scotsman. "When are you leavin' for Skerray?"

"This afternoon. We sold out of our wares early. Why?"

"Take me with you."

Alynn didn't tell anyone she was leaving. Rowan would tell her to be patient, they would all leave as a family, and he wasn't about to let her get on another ship without his supervision. Caitriona would agree with whatever he said. And Lukas, having never known what it was like to love a brother, would tell her to honor her parents. So she told Einar, who was stretching for his next sparring match, where she was going.

Einar shook his head. "Och, a sister's love. You'd get along splendidly with my cousin Thora. I'll tell Lukas where you've gone."

Alynn grinned her thanks and ran to follow the Scotsman to his ship.

She stayed well out of the way of the men who were loading the few supplies and belongings. When the Scotsman finally introduced her to the captain, Alynn tried to stand up straight and look intimidating. She wasn't sure how well it was working.

"Alynn the Dauntless, aye?" the captain asked, eyeing her head to toe and back again. "Ye don't seem like the sort of wench we normally take aboard."

"I'm a shieldmaiden," Alynn said, "and I offer ye protection on yer journey."

"Truly, now?" the captain laughed. "Protection from what? Sharks? Seasickness?"

"Vikings," Alynn said.

The captain scoffed, but the friendly Scotsman interrupted. "Sir, she's got a wee brother in Skerray. He misses her more than I knew a lad could miss his sister. He'd have come here himself if the church would have let him."

The captain noticed the coin purse at her belt. "We might be grateful fer yer protection, but ye'll still need to pay fer yer provisions. Fivepence, and we'll take ye."

Alynn only had threepence, and she'd rather not spend it all on transport. "I'll give you a penny and a half. I don't need bread. Only water."

"I won't see ye starve, lass. Threepence."

"Two."

"Welcome aboard."

Alynn handed the captain her money and stepped gingerly aboard the ship, realizing how much she hated the unpredictable shifting of gravity. She sat on an unused rowing bench and intended to move as little as possible.

It seemed as if an eternity passed by before they finally shoved off.

Alynn drew her arms tightly around her to ward off the sea wind, and she realized she didn't have a cloak. She didn't have a change of clothes or even a comb. But none of that mattered. Tarin would love her even if she was dirty and unkempt. Her stomach twisted with excitement and the boat's motion. She was on her way to Tarin.

Two days—she'd step off the dock and ask where the blacksmith lived—or if his son had been left in the church's care—and then she would run to him and scoop him up in her arms, hold him close, never let him go. She'd sit next to him as they ate dinner, listen to his stories, and fall asleep with her arms wrapped around him. She could feel the soft rising and falling of his chest as he breathed. Each raised freckle on his soft, sunburned cheek.

Something jabbed her arm, jarring her from the fairy's world.

She looked around in bewilderment before she noticed that a landing boat had come alongside the ship, powered by a familiar redhead with worry on his face.

"Drostan?"

He put his finger to his lips and nodded towards three men clustered by the mast. One of them was staring at her with something awful in his eyes—she felt like a hare caught in the gaze of a snake. "What do ye think she'd take to?" he asked the captain. "Charm? Wit? Or should I just ask her outright?"

"Halfpence says she won't even give ye a glimpse of her ankles," the captain said. He lowered his voice. "I don't care…just don't rough her up any. It'll raise suspicion when we land."

"It doesn't sit right," the kindly Scotsman said.

The first man scoffed. "Ye might be an honest man, Filib, but the rest of us aren't. Serves her right fer getting on a boat with strange men, don't ye think?"

Alynn looked at Drostan, then at the three men, and then at her sword. "I can take them," she said.

"What do you mean, you can take them? You're at their mercy, Alynn, and God knows what they'll do to you before you even touch solid ground."

"I'm armed."

"And outnumbered eleven to one."

Alynn sighed. "I've faced worse odds. I'm findin' Tarin."

"You've spent your life trying to avoid your mother's fate," Drostan said. "Captured by Vikings, taken advantage of. The sad thing is that Vikings aren't the only ones who mistreat fair maidens like yourself. I certainly don't trust the men on this ship to carry such a treasure as you without taking a bit for themselves. I'll never forget the fear, the shame, the disgust on your mother's face after Konar would force himself on her. That look should not be the first thing Tarin sees in you when you find him."

Alynn's voice caught in her throat, and Drostan's eyes softened. "Come, now. It won't be much longer. I promise. We'll find Tarin long before the Darsidians do. I'll do whatever it takes to keep you—both of you—safe."

Oh, why did he have to be so persuasive? Alynn sighed, and the captain finally caught eye of Drostan. He let out a colorful string of words.

"Not in the lady's presence," Drostan scolded, helping Alynn into the lifeboat. "Since she has no trustworthy escort, Alynn the Dauntless has decided to delay her quest. We'll see you fine gentlemen in Skerray. And if you'd be so kind as to refund the lady's fare of passage, Captain—thank you. Did he charge you three halfpennies, Alynn?"

"Twopence."

"Twopence? Captain, you seem to have miscounted—thank you, and some gallantry next time would be appreciated. Here, Lynder. Grab an oar, will you?" They waited until the ship cleared them, then turned the landing boat back towards shore and started rowing.

Alynn felt strangely numb. She rowed, but not as forcefully as Drostan did, so the boat kept veering left. She'd been so close. She'd been on her way to Tarin. And she'd lost her chance. No, she hadn't lost it—she'd given it up willingly. And for what? Some peace of mind? A few smooth words? Wrath boiled within her, but towards whom, she did not know.

Her anger found an object when Drostan helped her onto the pier. He'd talked her out of it, hadn't he? If he'd have minded his own business, she'd be out of sight of the island by now. A fit of rage passed over her, and she shoved Drostan into the ocean.

"You don't know what 'tis like!" she shouted as soon as his head surfaced. "There's less than two weeks until the Darsidians get to Skerray. I've got to get there before they do. Are you worried at all? You're not! Of course you're not! You don't know what it is to have a brother, Drostan, and you never will! I was so close to findin' Tarin, and you just *had* to interfere, you gawkin', addlepated eejit!"

"Help me up."

"I won't!" She stormed off, regretted her decision, and came back to find Drostan halfway onto the pier. She helped haul him the rest of the way up. "I'm sorry. I didn't mean it—most of it."

Drostan stood, dripping, and wrung the water out of his hair. "You meant all of it. But I'm alright with that. You'll find Tarin, I promise, and I want to help you find him. But even more than that, I want to keep you safe. Do you understand?"

"I'll understand better when Tarin's out of harm's way. Come, now, you'll catch yer death."

Alynn took his hand as they found their way through the crowds to his house. Drostan began shivering as the wind picked up, and Alynn turned abruptly and took him to the smithy. She'd warded off more than one bout of hypothermia by visiting Rowan at his work and reveling in the heat of the forge. But never for too long, because the stench of coal fires would hang in her clothes and hair for days.

The smithy was abuzz like the rest of the village. Various smiths and customers milled about discussing prices, raising their voices against the din of hammers and the constant roaring of the forge. But it was warm, and Alynn was glad to see Drostan relax.

Rowan was bent over a workbench, pressing a design into the pin of a penannular. No—the opening of the horseshoe-shaped ring was too small to allow the pin to pass through it. Pins of this type were popular with the nobility for their impracticality, and it would fetch a decent price. Alynn crept closer to see the design, and she realized Rowan was humming.

She hadn't heard him hum since Caitriona had been kidnapped. She'd forgotten he did it.

"You're happy," she said.

Rowan turned to her with a smile she didn't know he was capable of. "I've got everything a man could ask for," he said, pulling her into a sideways hug. "A wife, a job, two beautiful children. When you can do what you love with the people you love, life is perfect." He gave her a brushy kiss and noticed Drostan drying off by the forge. "What happened to him?"

"I pushed him off the pier," Alynn admitted.

"And what is it he did to you first?" Rowan demanded.

"I—" Drostan stopped and knitted his brows. "I don't know."

Rowan laughed—a genuine, joyful laugh that Alynn couldn't remember hearing before. "Och, the best of women have their moments. Get used to it, lad."

Drostan grinned, and Alynn wanted to frolic as she returned to the sparring grounds. She had precious few opportunities to earn coins; she'd make the most of this one.

June 22, A.D. 966—

Despite my apprehensions, Althing is turning out to be most enjoyable. Sparring with Einar was a highlight of the week, and introducing him to Alynn was even better. Why he and I are so close though we only see each other once every seven years, I know not. But we have spent many hours talking, and he is even more of a kindred spirit now that we can communicate with more than mere hand gestures and translations of Latin notes. I've even grown more comfortable speaking Norse through our conversations.

I was finally able to sit and talk with Rowan yesterday afternoon. Business was slow because of some horse-fight, and we chatted over a stein of ale from Fjorderny. Good Lord, the man's a mess. He has lost much, gained little, and refuses to let go of what is dead. He strikes me as type of person who, rather than resisting death, will invite it in for tea, enjoy a conversation with it, and offer to walk it home afterwards.

I'm glad I understand Rowan a bit better now, both through his own words and the Spirit's insight into them. He's a good man, and a better father than I gave him credit for. Why I'm investing so much into him, though, I know not. He'll be leaving shortly to restart his life with Caitriona, and I may never see them again.

—L. McCamden

THIRTEEN

Somehow, Lukas managed to reserve the speaking platform for an hour at noon on the last day of Althing. Alynn, sweaty from sparring with various soldiers from other islands, made sure she was there early. Lukas would be glad for her company, and besides, she was tired. Her opponents—sixteen or seventeen, she'd lost count after ten—had fought with vigor, and two of them could boast that they'd drawn blood from Alynn the Dauntless and won the penny reward she'd promised. Alynn was bleeding lightly from her hand and her chest, and she hoped Caitriona wouldn't notice.

When Alynn arrived at the speaking platform, she found Lukas praying. Rather, Alynn assumed he was praying. He was sitting on the edge of the platform, staring through the opened Bible on his lap. Alynn sat next to him and touched his arm, and he snapped out of his reverie. "Good to see ye, my dear," he said.

"You as well," Alynn smiled. "What are you teachin' on?"

Lukas took a deep breath and stared at the horizon. "I don't know yet."

"What do you mean, you don't know yet?"

"The Lord hasn't given me anything. He keeps telling me to 'do His work.' Preach? Teach? Heal? Blast it, I don't know!"

"You're afraid, aren't you?"

"Well—I'm not terrified of public speaking, not like Drostan is...it's more apprehension than anything else." Lukas looked up at the crowd that had been gathering. It was large. Everyone had heard of the Battle of Faith, and everyone was curious about the God Who had helped two people defeat an army of a hundred and eighteen. More than that, everyone wanted to see a miracle.

Lukas shut his Bible and handed it to Alynn. "Pray fer us."

Dear Lord, show Lukas what to do.

For a while, Lukas simply stood in front of the crowd staring at everyone, gathering words and getting his bearings. "You've all heard of me," he finally said in Norse. "You've all heard of Lukas McCamden, and of my foster-daughter Alynn the Dauntless. But more importantly, you've heard of my God. And that's why you're here today—to meet Him. I serve a God Who does more than protect His children in battle. Aye, He does far more than that. And I believe He's going to show off today."

The crowd murmured in curiosity, and excited anticipation welled up in Alynn. She couldn't wait to see what God would do.

Lukas scanned the crowd. "There's someone here with a broken arm that didn't knit right," he announced. "It might be more than one person. If you've broken an arm, and it didn't knit right, come forward. My God is going to heal you today."

Alynn held her breath. Two men forced their way to the front. Lukas stepped off the platform and began speaking softly to them; first in greeting, then in prayer. Suddenly, one of them gave a shout and looked at his arm. He kept running his hand over the bone, as if it had been crooked once but now was straight. The second only stared and stretched out both arms. Apparently, they hadn't been the same length before.

Thank You, Jesus, Alynn smiled.

Lukas laughed and embraced both the men, then leapt back up onto the platform. "Now, for this one, simply raise your hand, and I'll pray for you where you are. If you've arthritis in the joints—raise your hand, if ye're able—my God says you're healed. My God says that pain is gone, that mobility is restored—you're feeling it? Praise God...praise God."

Some ten or twenty hands were raised, and cries of surprise began ringing throughout the crowd. Alynn felt that her heart would burst. *Thank You, Lord.*

But God wasn't quite done yet. "God's saved the best for last," Lukas said. "There's someone here—several people— who have had something happen in their life. It might be the death of a loved one, or a difficult experience, or even a series of small things. But something's happened to you in your life, and you haven't been quite the same since then. You need peace, you need joy—if you know someone back home who needs healed, raise a hand for them—praise God."

Lukas paused for a moment, and something stirred inside Alynn. Everything Lukas had said resonated within her, as if he'd tailored this bit of the sermon just for her. She'd lost too many loved ones, life had knocked her down more times than she cared to remember, and every day, something small would come along and take another chip out of her will to live.

She was supposed to be Alynn the Dauntless, a warrior afraid of nothing. She was supposed to be the girl who lived at church, the pastor's foster-daughter, who loved God and lived right and never fell. She wasn't supposed to know what Lukas was talking about.

But the stirring grew stronger. She needed help.

Alynn burrowed her way into the crowd before she raised her hand.

"Look at how many hands are raised," Lukas said. "You're not alone."

Alynn peeked. At least a third of the crowd had raised their hands. She felt a strange, giddy comfort, knowing how common her condition was.

Lukas began to pray. At times he lapsed into Latin, or into another language Alynn didn't understand, but a gentle peace settled over the crowd. Alynn kept her hand strained upward until her elbow ached from being too straight and her hand tingled. She felt something growing inside her. It was too quiet to be excitement, too calm to be joy, and too energetic to be peace. But it was beautiful, and Alynn wished it would never leave.

Was this how normal people felt all the time? Alynn laughed. Had God completely erased the guilt she felt, or was this just a more-than-welcome respite from it? A glimpse of what life could be like if she ever shook it completely? Whatever it was, she wanted it.

Lukas finished praying, and everyone applauded. Apparently, she wasn't the only one feeling normal for the first time in months.

When the applause died down and Lukas bade everyone sit down for a sermon, Alynn sat near the edge of the crowd. In the corner of her eye, she saw a drably-dressed girl. It was Kenna. She smiled when she saw Alynn, but then she winced and put a hand on her stomach. Alynn went over to her.

"Do you want to hear Lukas teach?" she asked. "You can sit with me."

"My stomach hurts," Kenna said.

Kenna's face wasn't red, nor was her forehead warm when Alynn touched it. "Why does your stomach hurt?" Alynn asked.

"Because I'm hungry."

Alynn waited for her conscience to start tormenting her, but it didn't. Shouldn't she feel at least *slightly* bad for this poor girl? Oh, she'd deal with herself later. "I'll take you to get something to eat," she offered. "Come on."

"Can you pray for our Guardian Angel to come back?" Kenna asked. "We haven't seen him in a while."

How much did they depend on the food Alynn gave them? "I'll certainly pray," Alynn promised. "He'll come soon, I'm sure of it."

Kenna's face lifted, but then her eyes grew wide. "You hurt

yourself," she said, pointing to Alynn's chest.

"So I did," Alynn muttered. It wouldn't do for her to walk around with a slit on her dress. Lukas's message wouldn't be more than a simple sharing of the Gospel. She could afford to miss it. She'd go back to the house, find a needle and thread for her dress, and trade the rest of her embroidered coifs for some food.

It felt so good to serve out of love, rather than from a guilty conscience.

The Gythian cheesemakers were selling their wares at a discount, and Alynn had to wait five minutes in line to buy some. She only had three embroidered coifs left, but she gave all of them for as much cheese as she could carry. The vendor even gave her a sack to help—a small boon, considering how much she'd spent. She prayed the food would go a long way with Dagny, Geirhild, and their children. Were they truly in as much need as Kenna made out to be? What about all the money they'd made selling belts and trim?

With a quick glance to make sure no one was around, Alynn set her bundle on the doorstep, knocked loudly, and turned to leave.

Something hit her, knocking her off her feet. By some miracle, her head missed the wood pavement and landed with a soft yet painful thud in the dirt. Her shoulder was crushed, though. She wondered if she'd broken her collarbone.

"I've got her!" a child's voice said.

Alynn looked up to see a four-year-old sitting on her. "Meili?" she asked.

Suddenly, she was surrounded by six other children. Kelda and Kenna. Jofrid and Steinmar and Sindri. Finally, Eyvind came out of the house and stared at her, somewhat taken aback. "You're our Guardian Angel?" he asked.

Guilt knocked, and Alynn didn't know how to do anything other than answer the door and let it in. The old, familiar pain was back, but it felt less like a needle prick and more like a knife stab.

"Did I hurt you when I jumped on you?" Meili asked. "I didn't mean to. I'm sorry."

Alynn took him into her arms. "I'm grand," she promised, stroking his blond hair. "Did you hurt yourself?"

"My leg hit your bone."

So that was why her hip hurt. It would mend.

The door burst open with a flurry of temper. "Children, whatever you're doing—Alynn, what on earth!"

Alynn wanted to cry. She stood, helpless as Geirhild Karsadottir ripped Meili from her arms, grabbed her aching shoulder, and forced her in the house. "What are you doing here?" Geirhild snapped.

"I'm sorry—"

"Don't you dare touch my children again!"

"Don't yell at Alynn, Mother," Meili said. "She's our Guardian Angel!"

Geirhild's face was firm. "Go outside and play."

Meili shut the door behind him, and Alynn was left alone with the wife of the man she'd killed. Geirhild's eyes locked onto her like an archer's aim. "What were you doing to them?" she demanded.

Alynn drew a shaking breath. "I brought food."

"You don't think Dagny and I do a good enough job of it?"

"I'm sorry! I just want to help."

"Are you a toddler? Stop crying!" Geirhild's voice grew louder and sterner, and she spoke so vehemently that Alynn couldn't catch all the words she spoke. "You have done enough to my family. You have...us apart and broken our hearts. Our pride is all we have...and you're stealing it with every crumb you leave on our doorstep!"

"Geirhild!"

Dagny stood in the doorway with a basket of greens from the garden. She looked from Alynn to Geirhild and back again. "What is this?"

Please, God, Alynn prayed, *if Dagny's mad too, just let her kill me. Or You can kill me. Just let me get out of here.*

"She's the one who's been leaving us food," Geirhild said. "I was just asking her to stop."

"You're our Guardian Angel?" Dagny asked. She dropped her basket and embraced Alynn. "I shouldn't be surprised. Thank you."

Alynn didn't know what to do with herself. She strained to swallow against the lump in her throat. She wanted to cry and laugh and disappear all at once.

Och, get a hold of yourself, Lynder, stop crying!

"I'm sorry," she said softly. "I didn't mean to hurt you."

"Don't listen to Geirhild. She's Rothgeir's niece, if it explains anything." Dagny smiled. "You've brought my children hope, Alynn. They know that even in this dark world, someone cares for them. And no matter how small the portions, I appreciate the help. You needn't cry, dear. I'm not angry."

"I know what it is to lose a father," Alynn said. "I know what it is to go to bed hungry. I know how hard it is, and I can't live with myself, knowing you have to go through everything I did, because of me."

Why did her voice have to quiver like that? Why couldn't she stop crying? Couldn't she do anything right?

"My children may have lost their father, but in his place they have your God, and He takes better care of them than Harald and Hakon used to," Dagny promised. "They've never gone to bed hungry. They've always had clothes and shoes. And don't tell anyone, but Bjarki Sturlason has been seeing me, and the children might have a new father before the year's out."

The door flew open. "Aunt Geirhild, Meili's on the roof again!" Kenna cried. With a sigh, Geirhild left to fetch him off it, and Kenna laughed. "Alynn, he might listen to you better," she said before she ran out to watch.

Alynn waited until she was sure Kenna was out of earshot. "They don't know what happened, do they?" she asked. "Who killed Harald and Hakon?" She hated saying their names, as if she was killing them all over again.

"They know, all but the little ones. And they've forgiven you, as I have."

How could they forgive her? Dagny had to be lying. Eyvind probably knew, he was a bit standoffish towards her, but the others looked up to her. They couldn't know.

Dagny handed Alynn her handkerchief. "You know I've been selling my tablet weaving. Between it and the garden and Eyvind's goatherding, we're fairly well off. I'm sure there's people in worse need than we are. Tell Pastor Lukas that he can redirect his charity, aye?"

"He doesn't know about this." It hurt to say, but if Alynn was going to tell the truth, she was going to tell all of it.

"What do you mean? Isn't it the church that's been giving us food?"

"It was, for about a year," Alynn said. "But since then, it's just something I've been doing."

"And your mother and Lukas know about this?"

"They don't."

Dagny set a hand on Alynn's shoulder. "Your mother keeps house well, she'd notice if any food went missing. You've been eating less to make up for what you've given us, haven't you? It's why the cheese is always in small pieces, the bread always sliced. It's why you're so thin. Child, I can't tell if you're a fool or a saint, or a bit of both."

Something hurt in the very core of Alynn's being—maybe it was her pride. She pressed her eyes shut and held her breath until an urge to cry passed, then she wiped her eyes and swallowed against the lump in her throat. Dagny was a mother. Of course she'd have a sixth sense about these things.

"It's alright, Alynn. You don't have to do this anymore. We're getting along just fine, I promise."

"Don't tell my mother about this."

"I'll do what's best for all of us. Are you feeling better, now that everything's brought to light?"

Alynn couldn't exactly say that she was feeling worse, so she nodded. Almost over. Almost over. Now she could find

Drostan, or collect her thoughts in the woods, or take a long walk off a short pier. Or all three. Almost over.

"If we need help, I'll ask the church for it. And don't let Geirhild threaten you. I'll talk to her when you leave. She oughtn't yell at you like she did."

Alynn nodded again. "Thank you."

"I'll see you at the feast tonight, dear," Dagny said. She squeezed Alynn's hand and smiled. Alynn was quick to smile back and quicker to leave. Her steps were hurried on the wood sidewalk. Almost over. Almost over.

"Alynn?"

Devil mend it, what now? Alynn turned to see Eyvind, and she tried plaster a warmer smile on her face. She knew she was failing. "What do you need, Eyvind?"

"I just wanted to thank you for being our Guardian Angel."

Alynn took a measured breath. She wouldn't cry again, not here in front of Eyvind.

"Eyvind?" she asked.

"Aye, Alynn?"

She looked into his eyes. "You know I killed yer father, don't you?"

"I know." He said it calmly, almost nonchalantly. "He could tell you were a girl when he was fighting you, right? You weren't wearing a helmet or anything?"

"I was wearing a tunic, and my hair was coming out of the plait I'd put it in. But he saw my face. He knew I was a girl. Why do you ask?"

Eyvind blinked. "Father always told me not to hurt girls. I know you wouldn't have killed him if he hadn't hurt you first. So if he'd listened to himself, he'd still be here."

Alynn took Eyvind into her arms, just like she would Tarin, and held him tightly. "I'm sorry."

"I know you are. And it took a long time, but I forgive you."

She smiled so she wouldn't seem unfriendly, and then she hurried away. To where or to whom, she didn't know, but she ended up in Leif and Drostan's stable with Humility.

"What do I do now?" she asked, her fingers combing through Humility's midnight mane. She sat on the gate, which swung slightly backwards but didn't creak with her weight.

Humility gave her a gentle nudge with her soft nose, sending the gate swinging another few inches backwards. "You're fine," she seemed to say. "You're a better person than you think you are. You give me carrots, don't you?"

Alynn smiled. "I give you carrots, I do. Too many of them. You're getting fat."

"Then maybe you should eat more carrots."

A basket sat near the stall—Alva's basket, it seemed. It was full of root vegetables, mostly carrots and parsnips. When Alynn had mentioned to Caitriona the rash she'd seen on Alva's hands, she'd set the whole basket aside with a tisk. Whatever had caused Alva's rash might well be on the vegetables she'd picked, and she wasn't about to poison her family. So Alynn picked up one of the parsnips and took a bite. It tasted like dirt and the texture was woody, so she spat it out and offered the rest to Humility, who sniffed it but refused to eat it. So she threw it into the pig's stall, where she knew it would be put to good use.

"Carrots and parsnips aren't that different, you know," Alynn scolded Humility. "You might have tried it."

Humility gave a low and lecturing snort. "You have so much to learn about the finer points of food, don't you?" She poked Alynn in the ribs with her nose. "Look at you. I've eaten scarecrows that weigh more than you do."

Alynn sighed. "Shut yer gob, dear, or the Darsidians will be eating *you* at the feast tonight."

The feast tonight.

Drostan was going to be sworn in as chief. He was probably at Samkoma, the feasting-hall, right then, running through the ceremony. Alynn said a silent prayer for him. Should she be there to watch? Would he be calmer? No—it was just a rehearsal. He would be fine, and she shouldn't intrude.

Or at least she prayed he was fine.

Samkoma, the feasting-hall, was rather hidden in the woods. It was rarely used, but kept up nicely, and it had been scrubbed clean for the occasion. The red paint had even been redone, or at least touched up, judging by the pleasant stench of eggs and madder. Drostan tugged at his crimson tunic and adjusted his sword belt. Maybe if he looked his best, no one would realize how nervous he was.

Someone clapped him on the back and drew him into a playful sideways hug. It was Leif, of course, but Drostan brushed him off and adjusted his tunic again. "You'll wrinkle it," he said.

"No one sees wrinkles," Leif assured. "Are you excited?"

Drostan's stomach twisted. There were no butterflies—bats, maybe, or vultures, or something else harsh and indelicate. "I don't want to think about it."

"Well, you have to, or else this rehearsal won't do us much good."

"Leif! Drostan!" bellowed Elder Steingrim. "What are we waiting for?"

"Nothing," Leif said, clapping Drostan again on the shoulder and leaving for the speaking platform. "Assuming Lukas is here."

"I've sent for him. Let's get started."

Drostan paused, one foot on the speaking platform, and turned to glare at Steingrim. "He's rather important."

"And so is punctuality, now take center stage, and let's get on with it. Yngvar, you're prepared?"

The Lawspeaker nodded. He held a helmet and a sword—a large and heavy sword, useless to anyone who didn't have an ox's strength. Silver ornamented the crossguard and hilt, and a ruby was set into either side of the pommel. It was Konar's sword. The helmet was Konar's helmet, and Drostan prayed that neither of them came with insanity attached.

With Leif standing to the side—calmly and nobly, but with a twinkle in his eye—Yngvar held the sword out to Drostan. "Before these witnesses, I charge you, Drostan Leifson, to uphold the—"

"Sorry I'm late," Lukas apologized, hurrying through the huge doors of Samkoma with bread, wine, and olive oil.

"For Thor's sake, shut the door," Steingrim snapped. "You're letting in a draft." Sighing, Lukas rearranged his groceries and shut the door, nearly dropping the oil in the process.

"We would have lent you a satchel," Leif offered.

Drostan, glad to leave the speaking platform for any reason, leapt down to give Lukas an extra pair of hands. "Please don't make me take Eucharist," he begged quietly. "Nothing sits well on a nervous stomach."

"Don't fret, lad. How could the body and blood of Christ do anything but good fer ye?" Lukas gave a twitch of a smile and rested a comforting hand on his shoulder as they returned to the speaking platform. "Is there a small table I could use?"

"Of course," said Leif as he left to find it.

By the time the Eucharist was set up and everyone had returned to their proper positions, Elder Steingrim was leaning on his spear and staring into space. Whether he was asleep or dead or simply very bored, Drostan couldn't tell.

"Can we get through the rehearsal before I die?" Steingrim snapped.

Yngvar groaned and took Konar's sword again. "Before these witnesses, I charge you, Drostan Leifson, to uphold the laws of the Tribes of Orkney. I charge you to execute your duties with justice and equity, to look upon a man for his character rather than his possessions, and to put before your own needs those of your people. For power is given to them who earn it and will use it to serve, not to gain. Do you swear to honor the charge laid upon you?"

The sword was extended to him, and Drostan took it in both hands. "I swear."

Now, Yngvar took the helmet. "Before these witnesses, I charge you, Drostan Leifson, to conduct yourself in a manner worthy of your station. I charge you to aspire to wisdom, to live nobly, and to obey the laws you enforce. Do you swear to honor the charge laid upon you?"

The helmet was placed upon Drostan's head as he responded. "I swear."

Yngvar stepped back, and Lukas took his place. He held a small bowl of oil and dipped his finger in it, but he stopped and looked awkwardly at the helmet that covered Drostan's forehead, nose, and cheeks. He set the bowl down, removed the helmet, and anointed Drostan's forehead.

"That doesn't work," Steingrim muttered. "Yngvar, just hand him the helmet."

"But he's already holding the sword," Yngvar pointed out.

"If you can hold a sword and a helmet, so can he. Hang it off the blade by the nasal if need be."

"That would work, if the nasal wasn't connected to the faceplate," Leif said.

With the help of his spear, Steingrim climbed the speaking platform to glare at Drostan, Lukas, and Yngvar. "How is it that the smartest men in Orkney can't figure out how to hold two things at once?" He took the helmet off Drostan's head and balanced it on the sword. "By the gods, was that so difficult? Now do it again."

He handed the sword and helmet to Yngvar, who recited his lines again. How was his memory so perfect? How could anyone be so at ease on stage? Yngvar couldn't have been more comfortable if his head was resting in his wife's lap.

"And now," Steingrim said once everything had been rehearsed again, "Drostan, do you have something prepared?"

"Short and sweet, lad, so we can get on with the feast," Yngvar said.

Brevity was no issue. Drostan took a deep breath and stared at the far wall. There was a good-sized knothole in it. "I realize that I was no one's first choice for the chieftainship," he began.

"I may not—"

"Speak up!" Steingrim barked.

Drostan spoke louder. "I may not be the most experienced—or the wisest...but the God I serve—I serve a God Who—a God—"

"Get *on* with it!" Steingrim ordered, striking the butt of his spear on the ground in frustration. "It's a simple speech! What's wrong with you?"

"You've never been afraid to speak in front of people?" Drostan asked.

Steingrim growled. "No chief can be afraid of public speaking. In fact, no Norseman can be afraid of anything! We are warriors in the heat of battles. We are Vikings and traders who risk being lost at sea, and you're over here too frightened to say a few words on a stage! My gods! Do we blame you or your corrupted blood? No Norsewoman would have produced such a coward as you!"

"Steingrim, you will not speak of my son that way," Leif snapped. "And leave his mother out of this."

"It's not entirely her fault, now, is it?" Steingrim asked. "Try again, Drostan, and make it worth hearing this time."

Steingrim was glaring at Drostan angrily. Yngvar was bored, Lukas was pitying, and Leif was still fuming over Steingrim's gall. But if Drostan looked to the seats, he couldn't help but imagine them full of people. Full of frowning, muttering, disappointed people. How could he lead them, if he couldn't even give a speech?

His stomach lurched. Panic surrounded him like a swarm of bees. He was going to vomit—or faint—which was worse? And in front of Elder Steingrim!

Drostan thrust the sword into Yngvar's hands and threw the helmet to the ground. "Steingrim's right," he muttered, "it's not in my blood. I can't do this."

A strong hand grabbed his arm just before he stepped off the stage. He tried to shake it off, but the hand grasped more firmly. "If the Lord knew ye couldn't lead this island, ye wouldn't be in this position," Lukas said. "No one admires a man who quits. Get back up here and try again."

Drostan drew a fresh breath of air into his lungs. It settled his mind the same way tea settled an upset stomach. He returned to center stage and stumbled through his speech. Steingrim was never satisfied, but eventually he nodded his approval.

"Yngvar, well done. Lukas, not bad. Drostan...."

"You did well, son," Leif said. "And Steingrim, don't be in such a hurry to leave, you're helping us set up tables for the feast."

"But my back, Leif!"

Lukas shook his head and gave something that might be considered a chuckle. "Consider it penance fer insulting the Scots."

FOURTEEN

It wasn't long before every seat in Samkoma was full. Alynn was squished between Rowan and Caitriona, who kept talking over her. Finally, Alynn stood up and sat between Caitriona and Lukas. At least she had room to cross her arms now.

"Are ye ready fer Althing to be over?" Lukas asked. He didn't have to wear his tight cowl; rather, he wore a black robe called a cuculla over his tunic.

Alynn made sure she wasn't sitting on her hanging sleeves. "I'm ready to go home. But it was grand, seein' so many people. Did you get to meet some of the traders who'd been to the Holy Land?"

"Aye, but they didn't speak a word of Hebrew."

Alynn smiled. "Where's Drostan? I hope he's not nervous."

"He was during the rehearsal, though Elder Steingrim had a hand in that." Lukas cursed Steingrim mildly, and Alynn didn't bother scolding him.

"I hope he's alright," she said.

"Steingrim?"

"Drostan."

Alynn glanced around the room until she saw red hair and a scarlet tunic to match. She stood up. Drostan made eye contact, and what might have been a smile crossed his ashen face. But it didn't stay long. He wiped his hands on the sides of his tunic, already damp with sweat, and ran his fingers through his hair.

There was no time to say anything. Before Alynn could move to embrace him and rub the tension from his hands and shoulders, or whisper a word of encouragement, Yngvar the Lawspeaker motioned for Lukas to join them near the stage.

Alynn blew Drostan a kiss, and he nodded in return. Then, the ceremony started.

Yngvar mounted the speaking platform and said a few words in greeting. Alynn sat down, squeezing the tail of her sleeve. Was it possible to feel someone else's anxiety? Her gaze was fixed on Drostan as he took Konar's sword into his sweating hands.

You're alright, love, Alynn wanted to tell him. *Close yer eyes and take a breath. You don't look as nervous as you feel. I promise. 'Tis a grand job you're doing.*

Yngvar balanced Konar's helmet on the sword, then stepped back. Lukas anointed Drostan's forehead with oil, then gave him Eucharist. The helmet almost fell as Drostan drank from the cup Lukas held, but Lukas caught and restored it so quickly half the audience probably didn't notice. Drostan's face reddened, and Alynn wanted to take his embarrassment upon herself.

It was Leif who placed the helmet on Drostan's head. "My son," he prayed, "may the Lord bless you and your rule over this tribe. May He give you wisdom and justice. May He go before you in battle and protect you from uprising. May future generations know you as a leader strong and noble." Drostan bowed his helmeted head. If he'd had a beard, he would have looked exactly like Konar.

Finally, Drostan was alone at center stage. Every eye was on him, waiting breathlessly for him to give his first words as chief. Alynn saw Lukas praying silently and joined him.

"I mightn't have been anyone's first choice as chief—of this island," Drostan began. He stared at Alynn, and she wished he could read her mind and gather strength from the thoughts she had towards him. "I'm not the wisest—I'm not—I haven't much experience. I realize that. But I serve the God Who brought His followers through the Battle of Faith. Just as—He'll help me, just as He helped them. I—with His grace, will judge fairly, and use the gifts He's given me to rule this island."

He'd done it. Drostan had given a speech.

Yngvar thrust Drostan's hand into the air and cried, "St. Anne's Cleft, behold your chieftain!"

Clapping turned into cheering. Shrill whistles pierced the air, and Alynn leapt to her feet only to find that Caitriona had already beat her to it. Others followed until the entire room was standing, celebrating with such a beautiful cacophony that Alynn wondered if the angels could cheer any louder when a soul was saved.

Yngvar grinned. "Long live Chief Drostan of St. Anne's Cleft!"

"Long live Chief Drostan of St. Anne's Cleft! Long live the chief! Long live the chief!" And after a final shout, the noise of the crowd died down, and food was carried in for the feast.

The feast went by in a whirlwind. Alynn was tasked with carrying drinks, and she handed out far too many of them. The mead was more popular than quite a few of the food items, although the puffin was gone quickly. Drostan ate with the rest of the chiefs on a table set up on the speaking platform. Alynn gave him a single horn of mead and was glad that he had eaten at least a few bites of stockfish. She hardly had time to kiss his forehead and whisper her congratulations before she was called away.

A small scuffle broke out in a corner. Rothgeir, unsurprisingly, was in the middle of it, drunkenly yelling about the neglected sacrifice to the gods. Folkvard and Havard, with a bit more mead and a few lies, got him out the door where he wouldn't be able to bother anyone. The general din of the feast picked back up again, and everyone forgot it had happened in the first place.

Finally, Alynn was given her own plate of food—pork, greens, and *skyr* with a piece of bread hard enough to build a house with—and was allowed to sit with her family. She sat next to Lukas, who had pulled up his hood and sat staring sullenly into his half-empty stein of mead.

"You doin' alright?" Alynn asked.

"Too many people," Lukas said, taking another drink. Alynn looked past him at her parents. Rowan was as sober as a saint, but Caitriona wasn't all there.

"Come on, love, 'tis a party," she was saying, offering him the rest of her third stein of mead.

"Nothin' stronger than ale," Rowan insisted. He shot a sideways glance at Alynn, and something warm sparked inside her. But she didn't have much time to think about it, because a shrill whistle interrupted her thoughts.

"How was the feast?" a man cried, as everyone shouted their approval. Alynn recognized him as the man who oversaw the celebration—she didn't quite know his name. He had a spiky brown beard that reminded her of a hedgehog.

"And now for some entertainment!"

The crowd roared again, and Hedgehog-Beard grinned. "From the tribe of Darsidia comes a fearsome warrior, a berserker who killed his first man at the age of five with nothing more than his mother's nalbinding needle! I present Skarsgaard Bonecrusher, the fiercest warrior in Orkney!"

A brute stepped forward. He was a head taller than Drostan, and nearly twice as wide, but his bulk was comprised of bones and muscles and strength. Alynn had seen him around at Althing, especially at the sparring grounds, and she'd been careful to keep her distance.

"Skarsgaard has been given a dull sword, capable of little more than fracturing bones," announced Hedgehog-Beard. He held up a small purse. "He offers five silver dirhams to anyone who can best him in a fight. What brave soul dares accept his challenge?"

The crowd murmured. Even the drunk men had a healthy

sense of self-preservation. Finally, a thin voice piped up and said, "I'll fight him."

Alynn recognized the voice. It was Sigmund's.

She scanned the room until she saw him, standing near a corner, his wife Brynhilde tugging desperately at his arm, begging him to reconsider. Quite a few people laughed as Sigmund brought his heron's frame into full view. Tall, yes, but not quite as tall as Skarsgaard, and as thin as a man who had just come out of a long illness. Even a dull sword would do him plenty of damage. What if he should hurt his only remaining arm?

"You, lad?" Hedgehog-Beard asked. "Come forward. Tell us your name."

Sigmund tripped over a bench but never quite fell, just hobbled a bit on one leg until he righted himself. "Sigmund Steing—just Sigmund."

Alynn glanced up at Elder Steingrim, was was—or at least used to be—Sigmund's father. He sat uncaring at his honored place beside Drostan, finishing the last of his puffin.

"What do you do for a living?"

His voice was quiet, almost ashamed. "I'm a candlemaker."

"Well, then, Sigmund the Candlemaker, here's a dull sword. No harming bystanders, no use of shields of any type—I know, it's just to speed things up a bit—and drop your weapons when you hear my whistle." Sigmund took his sword and stood ready, slightly crouched. Alynn hoped brains could triumph over brawn. If so, he would be a decent match to Skarsgaard.

"Ready?"

Skarsgaard chuckled. He didn't bother crouching or readying his sword. One blow would toss this wisp of a man to the ground, never to rise again.

"Fight!"

Almost before Alynn had time to worry, Sigmund made a rapid attack and kicked Skarsgaard in the pit of the stomach. The crowd gasped, and Skarsgaard seemed a bit taken aback. "He kicked too high," Alynn mused.

"Nay, he kicked too low," Lukas said. "I think he's aiming fer the *plexus coeliacus*—right below the sternum. A good hit brings any man to his knees."

Kicking, generally, was considered unsportsmanlike, but Skarsgaard seemed to make an exception in Sigmund's case to make up for the size difference. He seemed a good soldier, Alynn noted, who had respect for his comrades. Or at least the ones whose fate was already sealed.

Skarsgaard aimed a few blows diagonally at Sigmund's chest, but all of them were parried. Sigmund, shaking with exertion, aimed another kick. It had no effect on Skarsgaard other than to make him angry. Sigmund was knocked to the ground with a grunt, his breath knocked out of him, and Hedgehog-Beard whistled shrilly.

Sigmund reached weakly for the sword he had dropped, but Skarsgaard mistook his actions. He must have thought that he was trying to rise and fight again, or else he wasn't as gallant a knight as Alynn thought him to be. He took his sword and seemed ready to strike Sigmund.

Alynn's vision narrowed. All she could see was Skarsgaard's sword, glinting in the torchlight. Before she could think or plan or even feel, she was out of her seat. She leapt over a neighboring table, snatched Sigmund's sword, and blocked Skarsgaard's blow just in time.

The crowd gasped. Rowan shouted one thing, and Drostan shouted something else, but Alynn didn't hear any of it. She glared at Skarsgaard.

"What sort of man kills the injured for entertainment?" Alynn snapped. "If you want a fight, I will give you one. Leave him be."

Skarsgaard laughed. "A fine lass you are, to protect your boyfriend like this."

"And a fine man you are, to attack my brother when he is wounded." Sigmund was breathing again, removed from the fray with Brynhilde's help. Alynn could focus her entire being on Skarsgaard and on her sword. Energy flowed like the river of life throughout her. She inhaled strength and exhaled power.

Hedgehog-Beard wasn't about to get in the way of a good brawl. "Ready?"

Rowan shouted something again, and Alynn once again ignored him. He had nothing to worry about.

"Fight!"

Skarsgaard aimed two good blows at Alynn's chest, but she blocked them and threw a thrust of her own. She contemplated kicking Skarsgaard just as Sigmund had tried, but her skirts weren't suited for it. So instead, she blocked another thrust, threw in two of her own, and locked her blade around Skarsgaard's hilt. A single flick of her wrists, and she'd be holding both swords. The honor of having defeated Skarsgaard, not to mention the five dirhams, would be hers.

But Skarsgaard had seen this trick before. His grip was tight. Their swords froze for a moment, their blades locked around one anothers' crossguards, and Alynn felt the slightest twinge of panic run through her. She was going to die, wasn't she?

Skarsgaard gave an unsettling smile. Alynn's mind raced. Hadn't Einar Shattersword taught her something?

Quickly and carefully, she swung her blade around and thrust the pommel into his gut. There was an audible grunt, then Skarsgaard relaxed his grasp and doubled over, letting Alynn yank the sword from his hand. Hedgehog-Beard whistled, and the crowd applauded.

"No one," she muttered, "threatens my friends, or underestimates the power my God gives me. Understood?"

Skarsgaard didn't answer. He would start breathing again soon. Probably.

Hedgehog-Beard gave Alynn the purse. "Five silver dirhams and the honor of having defeated Skarsgaard Bonecrusher are yours, milady," he said. "Well done."

The noise of the crowd grew louder, and Alynn regained her peripheral vision. The sudden burst of energy drained from her, leaving trembling and a pounding heart in its wake. She smiled at the crowd, accepted her winnings, and stumbled into the waiting arms of her family.

Caitriona seemed to have sobered up a bit. She gave Alynn a scolding glare, then kissed her, and Rowan took hold of her shoulders. "What the devil was that?" he demanded. Alynn didn't bother figuring out if he was upset or worried. "What were you thinkin'? You could have been killed!"

Alynn shivered. "God has a habit of protectin' me."

"Good Lord, Rowan, let her catch her breath," Lukas said. Alynn tried to sit but missed the bench, and she didn't object to Rowan's hands as they scooped her up like a toddler.

"You're alright?" he asked.

"I'm grand." Had she gone berserk, right there in front of everyone? No wonder she was so tired. And she'd gotten sweat all over her good dress, too! At least it hadn't ripped. Lukas gave her some small ale, and she sipped it gratefully. *Breathe, just breathe...there we go,* she told herself. She stopped shivering.

The musicians started playing. There were shrill flutes made from bones, and wooden flutes that sounded a bit like bagpipes, and flutes made from cow's horns that were gentle and soothing. There were lyres and panpipes and round *bodhran* drums, just like the drums Alynn had heard in Ireland. The music itself was more like a cacophony than anything else. Lukas detested it, Caitriona endured it, and Rowan winced at hearing it for the first time.

Sigmund had made his way through the crowd, little Matthew on his hip and Brynhilde solicitously at his elbow. "I just wanted to thank you," Sigmund said. He had caught his breath, and while his arm might be sore the next day, he wouldn't suffer any permanent harm. Alynn smiled and handed him the coin purse, five silver dirhams inside.

"I enjoy a good challenge now and again," she said. "Thank you for the excuse to fight."

Sigmund marveled at the purse and looked inside. "You earned this. Keep it," he said.

Alynn smiled. "I still owe you a left arm."

"And you repaid me with my life. I'd say we're even."

Sigmund left the purse on the table, but Alynn managed to sneak a single coin to Brynhilde. She had a fondness for beautiful things, and a dirham could be made into a ring or a necklace's pendant. She grinned her thanks as she left.

Alynn was glad to turn back to her small ale, and Rowan sat protectively next to her. She wasn't going to sword fight anyone else on his watch.

Hedgehog-Beard recruited a few men to clear away the tables and benches before announcing the first dance. "Chief Drostan, call your partner!"

Drostan stood, a bit shakily. "Alynn the Dauntless."

Everyone cheered, and the other chiefs went in a line claiming their partners. Oakvin of Thrandri had brought his wife, and Veikir of Fjorderny was coughing too hard to dance, but the other four chiefs chose whichever fair maiden had caught their fancy. Leif chose Nora McKenzie, and someone ran to fetch her from washing dishes in the kitchen. Thorbjorn Farsight called his sister, a lovely lissome creature not much older than Alynn, with hair that would have fallen to her feet had it not been tied in an elaborate knot. Alynn wished her hair would grow longer. It barely came to her waist.

As soon as the tables were cleared away, everyone joined hands in a circle and danced in a sideways fashion, as if they were playing ring-around-the-rosy. It was hardly dancing. But then the larger circle broke up into smaller ones, and soon Alynn and Drostan were by themselves, spinning in a ludicrous circle.

"What were you thinking, challenging Skarsgaard like that?" Drostan snapped.

"I couldn't help myself," Alynn said as she walked under Drostan's arm, and he ducked to walk under hers. "You've seen me go berserk before. I can't do much to stop it."

"So I'm expected to control my temper, but you have a license to ignore common sense—" Everyone changed partners, and Alynn found herself with a man from Fjorderny who seemed positively afraid of her. He was more than willing to give her back to Drostan when the time came. "Would you have done it for anyone besides Sigmund?"

"Of course I would have."

They danced faster now as the music's tempo increased, and everyone gave a shout. "Nay, you wouldn't have. You only go berserk for people you care about. And if you care for Sigmund more than me, go ahead, challenge Brynhilde for him."

"Drostan, you're—" Another set of hands grabbed her, and she was about to smack whoever had touched her until she realized they'd switched partners again. This time, her partner was intoxicated and a bit disoriented from spinning. She was glad to be back in Drostan's arms again, no matter how cold and uncaring they were. "You know I love you, don't you?"

"I thought I did."

Alynn stepped once again under Drostan's arm. "Nothing's changed! What you are is jealous, love."

"I'm not jealous!"

The rise of Drostan's voice was covered by another shout. The circles come together again until the room was filled with people, dizzy and laughing, joined hand in hand. But neither Alynn nor Drostan laughed. Instead, Drostan leaned close to her ear and whispered, "My house. Now."

He kept a tight grip on her arm as he led her through the crowd and out the door. Twilight was fading into night, but Alynn could still see the houses they passed, and even make out the vibrant red of Drostan's hair. But then they got to Drostan's house, and he kicked up the fire. Sparks flew everywhere, and in the new light was so bright that not even love could be blind.

"If I catch you fighting someone three times your size again, I'll break your sword," he snapped. "He could have killed you!"

"As I told Father, God has a habit of protectin' me." Alynn wrenched her wrist out of Drostan's grasp. "He did a grand job, I'd say."

"He would have protected Sigmund just as well, don't you think? Why do you throw yourself in harm's way for him, but

205

you don't even bother showing up to my speech?"

"I've apologized about the speech. You need to let it go."

"Do you realize how frightened I was up there? I thought you were the one person I could count on, but no, I can't even trust my own betrothed to show up when I need her most!"

Drostan's words struck Alynn like a drunkard's fist, and she flinched. He noticed. A bit of himself came back, and he turned quickly away from her. Should she speak? Should she set an arm on his shoulder, promise she'd never leave? Why *hadn't* she been there? She should have been; he'd asked a single, simple task of her, and she'd failed. She was such a miserable waste of space.

By the time Drostan had found more words to speak, Alynn was already halfway out the door, and she wouldn't bother coming back inside.

"Lynder!"

It wasn't Drostan's voice. It was Rowan's. "He had no right to shout at you like that," he said. "Do you want me to talk some sense into him?"

He placed a steady hand on her arm, but she brushed it away. "Don't pretend you care!" she snapped.

"Of course I care, my heart. I'm yer da."

She stopped and wheeled around to face him. "You say that. You've said a lot of things you've never meant. 'This is the last town,' you said. 'I'll be home in time for tea,' you said. 'I'll play with ye on Sabbath,' you said. And you never did! Twenty-three houses, a few months short of five years, and did any of those things happen? They didn't!"

Rowan was stern. "That doesn't mean I don't care."

"I got a job in Barrygone. Five days a week at a spinnery for six months, did you realize anythin' was different? You didn't. You didn't even know I had the job until we moved. Again. And what about Askeaton? Did you notice I didn't eat a bite of dinner until you found a job?"

Rowan started to interrupt, and Alynn would have let him. Even now, he was trying to find excuses. But he found nothing, so Alynn kept going.

"You never once fixed a meal. You never once patched anyone's clothes. You only hugged us when we were between houses. You didn't know I had pneumonia in Drumquin until I panned out at Mass. You didn't know I was both-handed until this week. You still don't know what color my eyes are!"

Rowan took Alynn's chin in his hand, but she pressed her eyelids shut. He could say blue. He could say green. If he really knew, he'd say they were a bit of both, or that they changed colors like the ocean. But what Rowan said was, "Don't be daft. You have the loveliest brown eyes I've ever seen."

Alynn looked up at Rowan until he realized his mistake. It was satisfying to watch shock, and perhaps a bit of sadness, rise into his face. But it was also devastating. Alynn couldn't bear to watch him suffer, nor stand to hear his insincere apology. She turned and ran. She didn't know where she was going. She just knew she needed to leave.

And, unsurprisingly, Rowan didn't do a thing to stop her.

It was fully dark by the time Alynn stopped running. She wasn't lost—well, she wasn't *quite* lost—but reason had interrupted her emotions. She couldn't go back to the monastery. A farm family was staying there to watch the animals, and Alynn wasn't about to explain why she had returned alone in the dead of night.

She could make an A-frame shelter. She'd watched Rowan make plenty of them when they were between houses in Ireland. Tarin had loved sleeping in them. He would run around trying to find the longest and straightest sticks and drag armfuls of pine boughs that were nearly as big as he was. Precious Tarin. Alynn prayed he would never need to make another shelter.

Making a decent shelter would take too long, and Alynn wasn't about to ruin her best dress, so she found some pine boughs to lie on. She wished now that she'd worn a plaid. It would have made a wonderful blanket. Instead, she spread her sleeves so that her face wouldn't be pricked by pine needles and settled down like a squirrel in her nest.

But she couldn't sleep. Drostan's words and her own guilt ran like rabbits through her mind. Drostan couldn't trust her. Surely he didn't mean it. Or maybe he did. Maybe she should just entrust herself to Rowan and move to Scotland or Limerick or wherever else he thought would make a good place to live. Or had his temper simply gotten the better of him, and he'd patch things up once he cooled down?

The ground shivered. It might have been an approaching horse, or a frightened deer. Alynn didn't care, just so long as it didn't notice her. But soon the shivering turned into the audible thudding of horse's hooves, and Alynn wondered what someone was doing out at this hour.

The horse slowed as it passed her and gave a nervous shake of its head. "Steady, lass," Lukas's gentle voice said. The horse stepped gingerly off the beaten path and whooshed a breath in Alynn's ear.

"Get up," it seemed to say. "You interrupted my perfectly good night's sleep."

Alynn groaned. Lukas dismounted and seemed to navigate more by touch than sight. "Alynn?"

"I'm here."

"What did we tell ye about running away?" Lukas felt around in the grass before Alynn placed her hand on his shoulder, and he hugged her quickly. "Thank God ye're safe. Let's get ye home."

Alynn stood and shivered as a breeze blew through her. She didn't want to go home, but she didn't want to argue, so she climbed obediently onto Humility's back. Lukas felt around for the reins and started Humility off at a decent trot. Humility didn't object. She was eager to get back in her warm stable.

It wasn't until they were nearing the village that Alynn spoke. "Why'd you bother comin' after me?" she asked.

"It wasn't a bother at all, my dear. No decent man can sleep when his daughter's lost." A single lantern was dying near Drostan's stable door. Caitriona must have set it out; Lukas would have never found the right longhouse in the dark.

The stable was warm and drowsy; the animals were dozing peacefully, and the hayloft looked even warmer and more inviting. "Can I sleep in here?" Alynn asked.

"Why?"

"I just want to be alone for a bit."

"At least tell yer mother goodnight. She's worried sick."

Lukas opened the door and kept a sheltering arm around her. They were met by firelight, and by a relieved gasp from Caitriona as she flew to Alynn and hugged her with the fierce tenderness of a hen hiding her chicks. "What did we tell you about runnin' off, Lynder? Stop it!"

"Don't bother worryin', Mum," Alynn muttered.

"Of course she's going to worry," Rowan said. "We were all worried."

"Sure you were." Alynn turned to the bedcloset, casting one more glance around the room before she shut the door. Valdis was putting her carding away, and Leif, who had been kept barely awake by the excitement of Alynn's disappearance, bid everyone a final goodnight. Drostan was still dressed and standing up, as if he'd wanted to talk to her but hadn't gotten the chance. He didn't try to smile at her. He just stared, then tried to speak, but nothing came out.

Alynn's gaze on him was steady. "Spit it out."

"I didn't mean what I said. I'm sorry."

"'Tis alright if you meant it. Don't lie on top of everything."

A strange look came over Drostan's face, but he offered her an embrace, and she accepted it. "No one's perfect, Lynder. And if you can forgive me for all the times I've broken your trust, I know I can forgive you as well."

"Thank you."

Drostan's voice was soft and low, as comforting as his arms around her. No one could stay mad at him for long. "Goodnight, my love."

FIFTEEN

Alynn was glad to be back at the monastery that morning, in her own cell, untangling her thoughts as she carded wool. Before the McNeils had left that morning, Dagny had talked to Caitriona, who she was in the process of relaying her new-found information to Rowan and Lukas. They'd know all about the way she'd skipped meals to provide for Dagny's and Geirhild's children. Whether or not Rowan would care was debatable.

A long walk off a short pier would make things a bit more bearable. But Tarin was out there, and if death was intent on separating them, he'd have to find another way to do it.

Alynn's hands slipped on the wool combs, and the sharp tine pierced her finger. It hurt a bit more than being pricked with a needle, and it bled more, too. Let it bleed. Her humors were probably out of balance, anyway.

Her fight with Drostan had been processed, at least mostly. But her rant to Rowan still haunted her. Who was she to snap at him like that? He was right. He'd risked his life for her. Of course he loved her! Was she being too sensitive? No—she was right. Rowan *had* ignored her. They could go weeks without exchanging more than a handful of sentences, let alone a decent hug. Or were all fathers like that? With whom did the fault lie?

Lukas knocked on the doorframe. Or at least, Alynn assumed it was Lukas. He was usually the only one who bothered knocking.

"Not now," she said.

"I've got something fer ye."

Sighing, Alynn opened the door to see Lukas holding two mugs of tea and a tiny white kitten. She took it from him and cuddled it to her chest. It mewed ever so gently, and she kissed its little forehead.

"Thank you," she said.

Lukas set the mugs of tea on her bedside table and sat on the edge of her bed. "I believe it's a male, if ye'd like to name it."

Such a beautiful white thing—she had a cousin back in Limerick with hair nearly that light. "Declan," she said. "Look at yer wee pink nose...aren't you a cute wee thing?" The kitten yawned, showing a tiny pink, toothless mouth.

Lukas half-smiled and tucked Alynn's hair behind her ear. "The farm children found a whole nest of them in the stable. He's less than a week auld."

"He's precious."

"Ye both are."

Alynn and Lukas sat quietly watching Declan until he fell asleep. Then, Lukas handed Alynn a mug of tea and said, "Can we talk about a few things?"

She knew that was coming. She should have been a bit more prepared. She sipped her steaming tea.

"We're just concerned about ye, my dear. I know what guilt is. I know what power it holds." He paused for a moment; did he mean for Alynn to start talking, or was he just collecting his thoughts? "I've never told anyone this—I trust you not to tell anyone, for my reputation's sake—but several years ago, I don't even think I was twenty yet, I came across a Norseman while I was hunting. Young, probably younger than I was. He started coming towards me. Now that I think about it, he probably just wanted to borrow an arrow, his own quiver was empty. I planted one arrow near his feet as a warning shot, but he picked it up, strung his bow, and came closer, talking in Norse—I panicked. And I killed him."

He stared through the wall, and Alynn sat frozen for a moment. Was there anything to say? Did God forgive murderers? Hadn't Moses killed a man and been forgiven?

"When I came to my senses, I was sick for a week. Couldn't believe what I'd done. I still can't imagine what hell I put his family through. It was hard enough—when I woke up after the Battle of Faith and ye weren't there, I started calling yer name. Yer mother came to me, said ye'd been wounded, and she started crying. Fer the worst half-minute of my life, I thought we'd lost ye."

Lukas squeezed Alynn's hand with a strong farmer's grip. She thought she heard a trembling in his voice, and it reminded her of the single time she'd seen him cry. It frightened her.

"I believe," he said, "that God's forgiven me of my actions that day. I've earnestly repented of them. After all, He forgave Moses, and David, and even Paul the Apostle, back when he was called Saul and persecuted the church. Do you agree wi' me there, that I'm forgiven?"

Alynn nodded.

"Why, then, do ye feel unworthy of forgiveness or love? Were yer actions worse than mine?"

"They weren't, but—"

"But what?"

Alynn's voice caught. "If God's forgiven me, why do I feel like this?"

Lukas paused for a moment. "God wants to tell ye something," he said. "Might I be His voice fer a while?"

"Please."

"He says, 'You call yourself a murderer, My daughter, but I call you by a different name. I call you beloved, forgiven, set apart. I do not see your sins, but the price My Son paid for them. You have repented, and you have trusted Me for your

212

salvation; in the same way, trust Me to wash your heart from these dead works. Just as I have forgiven you, you must also forgive yourself.'"

Alynn's spirit burned within her; she knew God loved her, but rarely did He voice His affections this loudly. His smile was always in the sunlight, in birdsong, in the kiss of a quick breeze or the aroma of flowers on a spring day. Alynn could see Him in a baby's laugh, an act of kindness, the autumn harvest, and sometimes in a quiet whisper when she was lying in bed waiting for sleep to come. But this? She was honored and humbled all at once.

"Thank you," she said.

"Do ye believe it?"

"I want to."

Lukas was silent for another moment, and he squeezed her hand again. "Talk to me," he said.

So she did. She started with Dagny and Geirhild. Everything she'd done, everything she'd wanted to do. Geirhild's reaction and Dagny's reassuring lies. And suddenly, she found herself talking about her argument with Drostan, how she wanted him to trust her, and how they'd roughly patched things up afterwards.

She talked about how she'd snapped at Rowan. She hadn't meant to. She knew that men didn't care about little details as much as women did—but still, shouldn't a father know these things about his child? Did he even care about her at all? He'd mostly ignored her in Ireland. She knew now it was because he had to work in order to provide a roof over their heads and a bit of food on the table. But was a hug every morning or a hand with the dishes once a week that much to ask for?

Lukas didn't interrupt. He kept his arm around her, listening intently, asking questions when her voice halted. When all had been said, he remained silent for a moment—praying, perhaps. Alynn felt a weight lift off her spirit. She felt exposed, like someone had seen her undressed, but she felt better.

"Dear child, don't ye think fer a moment that ye're alone in this," Lukas said when he was certain Alynn had finished. There was something strange in Lukas's voice, something trembling and livid and caring all at once, as if love had taken his box of emotions and dumped them onto the floor of his mind. "Yer parents, myself, Leif and Drostan, we're all here fer ye. Don't think ye deserve to feel this way."

Alynn pressed her eyes shut, and Lukas held her close. "What do I do now?" she asked.

"Ye lay everything down at the foot of the cross, just as ye did wi' yer worry fer Tarin. God wants to heal ye, my daughter. He wants ye to feel peace and joy. He doesn't want ye to worry about Dagny or Geirhild or their children or even what yer father said to ye. I'm sorry ye've had an argument wi' Drostan, but everyone fights. Ye've apologized to each other. Forgive him, forgive yerself, and let it go."

"Aye, sir."

"As fer what yer father did—on his behalf, I apologize. He oughtn't have neglected ye the way he did. But he's been through a lot in this life, and he pulled away from ye not in malice or ill-will, but in pain. Ye need to forgive him, dear."

"I'll try."

"Talk to him. It might help." Lukas found a tendril of a curl near Alynn's ear, pulled it straight, and watched it bounce back into place. "Might I pray fer ye?" he asked.

"Please, if you've time for it."

"I've always time fer ye, my heart." Lukas held Alynn even closer, rested a hand on her head, and began praying. He began in a strange language, then switched to Latin. But long before Alynn could understand what Lukas was saying, she felt a delicious peace wash over her, as refreshing as a fire on a winter evening, as needed as a drink after a summer day's work. It clothed the nakedness her spirit felt, but in a soft and wonderful robe instead of the rags she'd been accustomed to. Finally, with a half-chuckle acknowledging his mistake in choice of language, Lukas regained his use of the Gaelic tongue.

"Lord, we pray Ye'd give Alynn Yer peace which passes all understanding, that it might guard her heart and mind in Christ Jesus. We pray Yer joy over her, for the joy of the Lord is her strength. Show her Yer love—Yer vast and unfailing love. Neither I nor Rowan nor any other mortal man will be a perfect father, but Ye, Lord, are our perfect heavenly Father. Ye made the color of Alynn's eyes, Ye know the number of hairs on her head, and Ye love her so much Ye gave Yer only Son fer her. And fer Alynn, and fer the short time Ye've let us spend wi' her, we thank Ye, Lord. May she have every blessing, receive every promise Ye've given her, and have wisdom in the days ahead. In the name of Christ Jesus we pray, amen."

Beautiful, wonderful peace surrounded her, as if she'd opened the door after weeks of clouds and rain to see that the sun was shining and the air was warm. Lukas was in no hurry to leave. He sat with her for a quarter hour, bouncing her curls until they were too relaxed to be called curls anymore. Alynn didn't mind. The kitten sleeping in her hands began to stir, and she stroked it gently. He probably needed to get back to his mother.

"I'll take him," Lukas said. "Are ye doing better?"

Alynn smiled gently. "I am. Thank you, Lukas." She studied him as she placed Declan in his hands. He had been given the same peace she'd been, but he also seemed to have absorbed some of her sadness. "What was it you were worried about?"

"Pardon?"

"At the election, when you said that something was botherin' you, but it wasn't my fault—I've told you what's wrong with me. Now 'tis yer turn."

Lukas half-smiled and stroked the fuzz on the kitten's nose. "I was grieving, I suppose. I've known fer a while that we'd lose you to marriage, and I'd reconciled myself to that. But I'd always hoped that ye'd look back on me as yer father, and when Rowan showed up, I realized I wouldn't even have that...."

He paused for a moment, taking a measured breath as if his ribs were causing more pain than normal. But he soon steadied again. "I've seen that my fears were unfounded. Ye're much too loyal a person to forget me."

Alynn leapt off the bed and embraced Lukas as tightly as she dared. "How could I forget you? You've saved my life more than once. You've done a better job of raisin' me than my father did. I promise, you'll always hold a very special place in my heart."

Lukas held her tightly. For a moment, it was just the two of them again, alone against the world, but with a faith in God and a bond between them that would carry them through any trial life threw at them. Alynn remembered the day they'd stood hand in hand, staring at the door that separated them from an army. The feeling that they would live or die as one, however God saw fit.

And after that—Alynn remembered lying next to him, her arm stretched as far as her wounded shoulder would let her so she could clasp his hand. She remembered the joy in his eyes when she smiled at him, the way his pain disappeared when she spoke to him. She remembered the prayers they'd lifted up for each other's recovery. They had held hands through the valley of the shadow of death, and they emerged with their hearts just as entwined as their fingers.

"Alynn?"

"What is it?"

"I love ye, too."

Slowly, everyone settled back into the daily rhythm of work. Not that it was monotonous, of course. Alynn emerged from the root cellar while preparing Wednesday's dinner to find a pig staring at her. One of the paddock's fenceposts had broken, and everyone spent the evening chasing after livestock. Lukas and Rowan set out hewing a new fencepost as soon as breakfast was over the next morning, and Alynn decided to work with Patience so Lukas wouldn't have to.

Patience was skittish as usual, but she let Alynn lead her around on her halter. They avoided the graveyard—Alynn didn't know if horses could be scared of ghosts, but she didn't risk it—and threaded through the derelict buildings in the front yard. They had been cells once, since St. Anne's Monastery hadn't been built large enough to house all the monks who had once lived there. Many of these cells still had beds in them. They reminded Alynn of some of the houses she'd lived in.

Alynn led Patience around the front yard until she couldn't hear the thwacking of axes anymore. She figured it was safe to take Patience back to the stable. After some effort and a few poorly-received tugs on the lead rope, the filly finally turned back towards the monastery. Alynn was surprised at how far they'd walked. The clouds were threatening rain, and she wanted to get a few weeds out of the garden while the weather held. She walked faster.

With the fencepost repaired, Rowan and Lukas had returned to their normal chores. Alynn finally spotted Lukas out in the oat field, and Rowan filling a drinking-horn with well water. He stopped and looked up at her, setting the horn down as he came towards her.

"Can we talk?" he asked.

A thousand words ran through Alynn's mind, some of which would have made a sailor blush. But she'd tried running away, and it hadn't fixed anything. This time, she'd stand her ground. Accept responsibility and Rowan's apology, if he bothered offering one.

Alynn stood silently as Rowan approached, sheepishly tugging his hair as if it was coming out of its braid. "I take it you're still mad at me," he said.

"I am."

"I'd be mad at me, too, if I were you. I'm sorry."

"Thank you. I forgive you."

Alynn started off for the stables again, but Rowan stopped her. She tightened her grip on Patience's lead rope. "I was wonderin' if there was anything I could do to help make things right again," Rowan said.

"You could quit makin' me think you care before tossin' my heart into the street like dishwater."

"Come, now. You know I love you." He reached out a hand to her, but she shied away from him—and, sensing her apprehension, so did Patience.

There was hurt in Rowan's eyes. Alynn almost felt bad for him, but she forced herself to keep her distance. He knew how to elicit sympathy.

"You ignored me for almost five years, Father," Alynn said. "We can't grow close again overnight. Not because you say a few smooth words. And if you'd rather focus on getting to know Mum again, go ahead. I'll be leavin' soon anyway, marryin' Drostan, and you'll be free to love and ignore whoever you want."

"I won't ignore you anymore. I promise."

"Don't lie to—"

Alynn accidentally yanked on Patience's lead, and the filly bucked. Her sharp hooves pierced the air like tiny daggers, aimed straight for Rowan's face. Without thinking, Alynn dove forward and shoved him out of harm's way. Something hit her. She fell. A satisfying pain shot through her forearm.

Rowan grabbed Patience's bridle and tossed her to the ground, and when she tried to rise again, he stunned her with a blow to the head. Alynn sat up, grasping her arm. Her sleeve was torn, but only the slightest trickle of blood came out.

"Don't tell Mum," she said.

"Lynder—don't worry, you're alright." Rowan knelt beside her, feeling her arm to see if anything was broken. When nothing grated, he ripped her sleeve to inspect her wound. "Did she hurt you anywhere else?"

"She didn't. I get cut all the time, Father. Don't fret."

"Let me fret," Rowan said. "You shouldn't have done that."

"But I did, and you'd have done the same for me."

"Thank you."

"Not a bother."

Rowan set a comforting hand on Alynn's shoulder, and she let herself relax. Something nagged the inside of her until she said, "I shouldn't have run off the other night. I'm sorry."

"'Tis alright, Alynn. You learned that from me." Rowan sighed and gave a smile that had only a hint of happiness in it, like a bitter cup of tea sweetened with the slightest drop of honey. "I'm ashamed of myself, to be honest. Everything you said was true."

"You worked because you had to make ends meet. I realize that now. I oughtn't have been angry."

Rowan was silent for a moment. "That's half right. More than anything else, I think, I was afraid."

Before Alynn could ask what he was afraid of, Lukas's voice cut into her thoughts. His sleeves were rolled to his elbows and he was half-running, concern in his eyes. "What happened?" he demanded.

"Patience kicked her," Rowan said.

"That blasted—" Lukas switched to Latin for a bit, and Alynn was glad— "Are ye alright?"

He knelt beside her and felt her arm, wiping away the bit of blood that was there. Alynn flinched, and Rowan gave her his hand to squeeze. "It's not broken," Lukas said. "But ye might have bruised the bone, so don't be surprised if it hurts like the devil fer a few days. Wrapping it tightly might help. So might leeching it."

"I don't like leeches," Alynn said.

"But it would take down the—"

"I'll be fine, Lukas, thank you anyway."

Lukas sighed. "Just be gentle wi' it. Ye're young, ye'll mend."

Her arm wasn't the only thing that needed mending; her sleeve was a mess. Sighing, she accepted Rowan's arm to help her stand before the thumping of horse's hooves caught her attention. She recognized the rider before his horse; what was Drostan doing here on a Thursday?

"There she is," Drostan said, dismounting with a smile in

219

his eyes. "I've missed you, Lynder."

"I've missed you too, love," Alynn said. "What brings the chief of St. Anne's Cleft to visit his loyal subjects?"

"Lukas suggested I copy the Book of Proverbs into Norse, for my own benefit. Heaven knows I need some wisdom."

"Then I won't keep you," Alynn said.

"Please do." Drostan smiled, kissed her forehead, and went with Lukas into the monastery. "How long do you think it will take?"

"Two days if ye're diligent, lad—half an hour or so per chapter. There's some firewood fer ye to chop if ye get fidgety."

Alynn and Rowan followed them inside. As expected, Caitriona fussed over Alynn's wounded arm with all the overbearing love a mother can have. She put salve on it and wrapped it tightly and made some willow tea for the pain. Even though the garden was full of weeds, the chicken coop was filthy, and the milk would spoil if it wasn't churned, Alynn was told to mend her sleeve. After changing into her oat-colored spare dress and found a needle and thread.

Alynn prided herself in her mending skills—one of the few domestic arts she excelled at. She went ahead and darned one of Lukas's socks while she was at it. She was just about to find her carding when Caitriona beckoned her to the kitchen, bade her sit at the table, and placed a plate of *skyr* in front of her. "Snack time," she said.

"Mum, what are you—"

Caitriona sat across from her. "Neither of us are movin' until every bite's gone."

Alynn stared at the corner. "Is about what Dagny said?"

"'Tis because the *skyr*'s about to go bad, Lynder, of course 'tis because of what Dagny said." She took her daughter's hand and gave a worried smile. "It was a kind thing you were doing, dear heart. You just took it too far. Now, eat up."

Slowly, Alynn took one bite, and then another. She hadn't realized how hungry she'd been. Behind her, footsteps sounded, and the cupboard was opened. It was probably Lukas making tea. But instead of a friendly hand on the shoulder or ruffling of hair, Alynn was met with a vambraced hand stealing a spoonful of *skyr*.

"Get yer own!" Caitriona scolded.

Drostan gave a *skyr*-covered smile. "I never realized how hungry copywork makes you."

"What have you done so far?" Alynn asked.

Drostan helped himself to a plate of *skyr*. "I'm nearly done with the third chapter."

"Grand job," Alynn said with her mouth full.

"Rowan might be able to draw you a picture, if you'll leave him space," Caitriona said. "He studied with an illuminator when he was a lad."

Alynn hastily swallowed. "I didn't know that."

Caitriona smiled. "There ought to be a few pictures of you and Tarin in his timpan case."

"I might let him decorate a capital letter here or there, but I'd rather not waste space. Not that it's a waste, I mean—"

"Paper's precious, I know," Alynn said. "I'm done, Mum."

"Let me see yer plate." Caitriona eyed the trencher the way she would an embroidered work. "Well enough. Would it hurt yer arm to sweep?"

"But the garden—"

"I'll tend to the garden, my heart. Rest if it hurts." Caitriona kissed Alynn, took her plate, and left for the garden. Drostan finished his *skyr* with a bite twice as large as it needed to be, setting his plate in the washbasin with Alynn's.

"I'll be chopping wood," he said with his mouth full.

"Be careful," Alynn said.

"It's second nature by now," Drostan promised. He took his axe from its holder on his back, and soon a rhythmic thwacking rang throughout the woods and the doors open to let in light and fresh air. It was like music to Alynn as she washed the plates, then set about sweeping.

Sweeping might have been a simple task, but it was no small

one. There were too many hallways, too many cells, and the stairs were a nightmare. Alynn was always afraid she'd trip and fall headlong and land tangled in the broom, but she hadn't so far. And no matter how clean she thought the monastery was, there was always a decent pile of dust ready to be swept outside.

As Alynn was leaving the doorway, a motion caught her eye. It was the swish of a black tail, the bright flash of a horse's eye—was it a pooka? But pookas only came out at night, so it had to be a mortal horse, unless Norse pookas were exceptionally bold.

There was a tiny rider on the horse, modestly clad in dark reds and greens. It bid the horse lie down for ease of dismounting, and then Alynn recognized the rider as Alva.

"Lovely day, Alva!" she called. "Come in, and welcome!"

"Thank you, dear," Alva said. She had a satchel with her, and Vorthmathir was curled around her waist. Alynn shivered. "Is your father within? I'm here to take out his stitches."

"He's in the field. Should I send for him?"

"Please."

Alva sat at the hearth and accepted the glass of milk Alynn offered her. But before she could fetch Rowan, Drostan came inside.

"Why, Chief Drostan!" Alva exclaimed pleasantly. "What are you doing here?"

"I'm copying part of the Bible."

"You're too lively a lad to be cooped behind a desk," Alva said. "I'll make you some tea to help you focus. You have mint, don't you, dear?"

"Of course," Alynn said. Quickly, she helped Alva set a kettle to boiling, found the mint, and left the healer to her craft.

Rowan was helping Lukas in the fields, but he followed Alynn with a surprising lack of complaints. Finally, Alynn was able to ask him, "What was it you were afraid of?"

"Hmm?"

"You said you worked because you were afraid."

"Och, that." Rowan took Alynn's hand as he opened the door. "I was afraid I'd lose you. It hurts to grieve when life takes someone you love. I've realized now that it hurts worse to regret not lovin' them enough while you still had them."

And with that, Rowan resigned himself to his fate and sat at the hearth, where the light was best, as Alva took scissors and tweezers to his scalp. Alynn was tasked with holding his hair out of the way, and she did so dutifully, with a clear view of the operation. Alva's hands were surprisingly steady for a woman of her age. Not once did she clip Rowan's skin. The only payment she asked was for Rowan to fix her bracelet. Its cardinal feature, a ruby, had fallen out of its setting, and Rowan was only too happy to oblige her.

Before she left, Alva wished to see Drostan at his work, and so Alynn led her through the hallways to the scriptorium. Two windows and a candle gave the room ample light. Books, paper, ink, and the materials used to make them were lying on various shelves and desks. Drostan had just finished the fourth chapter of Proverbs. His hands were more used to sanding wood than forming letters, but his script was decently legible.

"Drink this the next time you find your mind wandering," Alva said, giving him the tea she'd brewed. She smiled and laid her cane aside to embrace him. "Good-bye, dear. I hope you don't need to see me for a while."

It must have been nice, growing up in a close-knit town and never moving. Alynn walked Alva to the door and watched as she mounted her dark horse, stuck her cane in the saddlebag, and cantered into the forest.

Alright. Where had she been before Alva came? Sweeping—had she gotten everything? The upstairs, the chapel, the hallways—but not the kitchen. Ten minutes' work, if she was thorough. She took the broom and swept up a decent pile of crumbs, dirt, and dead bugs. The kitchen had needed sweeping more than she'd thought it did.

When she swept it out the door, she heard her name called. At first, she thought it was Lukas or Rowan, but they were both in the field. So she turned to see Drostan, white and panting, leaning against a chair. He swallowed hard. "I don't mean to—interrupt, Lynder—but you're alright—aren't you?"

"I'm grand, love." Was it so hot in the scriptorium that Drostan should be sweating like that? And why were his legs shaking? "State of you, what's wrong?"

"I don't know—I'm nervous. I thought I'd be better—once I talked with you—but—"

He blanched, wincing as he staggered to the cupboard for a bowl and vomited into it. Alynn held his hair back until he was finished, then helped him into a chair and touched his forehead. It was cool and clammy, like a nervous man's, not warm like a sick one's. "You're not runnin' a fever. And you were hungry an hour ago."

Drostan shivered. His legs seemed to have a mind of their own, twitching like fish in a net. "I think Alva put—something—in that tea."

"The tea wouldn't have done anythin'," Alynn promised, getting Drostan a clean bowl. "I'll get Mum, and we'll set you up in a spare cell with a bowl and a blanket, right? How's that sound? Are you cold?"

"I'm not cold—I'm not hot—"

"You might be havin' a panic attack," Alynn suggested. "Breathe in...two...three...four, and breathe out...."

Drostan seemed to relax a bit with the deep breathing. But his legs never stopped shaking, and when he retched again, Alynn knew something was wrong. She ran to the back door, yelled for Caitriona, and returned to Drostan. She knew she wouldn't want to be left alone, had she been in Drostan's situation.

Caitriona took a single glance at Drostan and flew to him, examining him with a mother's tenderness. "Are you runnin' a fever? When did this start?"

"No fever...and five minutes ago, if that." Drostan's agitation only increased. "It's Alva's tea, I'm telling you. I was fine before I drank it...and it wasn't ten minutes afterwards...*this* happened...."

"Alva's tea?" Caitriona went to the empty teakettle resting near the stove and held it to her nose. "Was this clean when you used it?"

"Of course it was." Alynn tested the scent for herself. It was mostly mint, but she caught a whiff of something she thought was mouse urine. What did Alva use mouse urine for?

Loud footfalls interrupted everyone's thoughts. Leif appeared, striding purposefully through the kitchen. "Where's Drostan?" he demanded.

Drostan stood on shaking legs like a newborn foal. "I'm right here—"

"Sit down, son. What happened?"

Drostan rubbed his legs. "I don't know. More importantly... how did you know?"

"Parents get premonitions," Caitriona explained. She went white as she realized what that meant. "What do I do?"

"Stay with him," Leif ordered. "How did he get like this?"

"Alva's tea didn't...sit right with me." Drostan pressed his eyes shut and swore in Norse, then vomited again.

Laying a hand on his son's shoulder, Leif began praying in Norse. Alynn couldn't catch most of the words he spoke, but she agreed in spirit, and Caitriona added her "amen" when he finished. Drostan looked a bit more at ease now, but his legs refused to quiet themselves.

Alva might not have had anything to do with it. It might have been an accident or an allergy. But Alynn couldn't sit idly by and watch Drostan shake like that, not when the famed woman of cures might have answers.

When Leif announced he was going to find Alva, Alynn went with him.

SIXTEEN

The ride to Alva's house was long and silent. Leif was praying too hard to say anything, and Alynn knew better than to interrupt his stillness. She tried praying, but her mind kept wandering back to Drostan. The way his legs shook. The fear in his eyes, the pain that he felt. What else could have caused it but Alva's tea? He was perfectly healthy, and one of the strongest men on St. Anne's Cleft.

It wasn't until a tear meandered to her lips that she realized she was crying.

Leif dismounted when they saw Alva's black stallion tied to a fence. Alynn followed suit, but Humility was interested in the stallion. She tried to start walking towards him before Alynn had gotten her foot out of the stirrup, but Leif set a steadying hand on her shoulder before she fell.

"Thanks," Alynn said.

Leif made himself smile. "How are you holding up?"

"I'm grand."

"He'll be alright," Leif said to himself as much as to Alynn. "He's strong, he's young. He'll be fine."

Of course. Drostan would be fine. Why did it feel like a lie to think that? But he would be fine! But he might not be! Leif realized she was crying and drew her into a sideways hug. "Go back to him if you need to."

She wiped her eyes and took a breath, tethering Humility well away from Alva's stallion. She let Leif open the gate for her, but refused to advance much farther towards Alva's house until he was by her side.

Alva's house was derelict. It was built partially into the ground, made of sod that badly needed to be replaced. The yard was strewn with dead leaves and twigs, and a trio of goats grazed near the woods. A raven had built its nest near the chimney. It cawed eerily. Alynn took an unconscious step closer to Leif and made sure she could grab his sword if she needed to. She wished she'd brought her own.

Leif knocked on the door. "Alva, you're needed!"

The only answer was from a single cry from the raven. Leif knocked harder and called her name louder, and he was finally content to kick down her door. The wood of the doorframe was rotted and gave way readily.

Mice and rats ran screaming into the dark corners of the room. The fireplace was dying, and the pot over it hadn't been washed thoroughly in months. On the table sat a model ship. It was white—candle wax, but what were those scales on the sides? They were opaque, the size of fingernails—and the shape of fingernails—oh, dear—

"A model of Naglfar," Leif said. "It's made of the nails of all the patients she's lost."

Alynn shuddered. All that, and Alva wasn't inside.

Leif went to the bedcloset and, finding it locked, easily wrenched the door off its hinges. He threw out the mildewed rags that Alva considered bedclothes and made something squeak.

"Get me a firebrand," Leif said, disappearing into the bedcloset. "If I'm not back in ten minutes, run for help and a shovel."

Alynn looked to see that Leif had found a trapdoor, and that he was manipulating his body to fit into the tunnel it led to. "I'm comin' with you," she said, getting the brightest stick from the fire.

"You're staying right here," Leif said, giving her a warning glare. He finally squeezed his midsection through the opening, leaving only his shoulders and arms to awkwardly maneuver into the hole. "Your mother would kill me if anything happened to you."

But once he had gotten down the hole with the firebrand, there was nothing he could do to stop Alynn from following him.

Her thin frame slipped easily past the trapdoor. It led to a tunnel, too narrow for comfort, that Leif was crawling through on his hands and knees. Alynn could get through by stooping. She was glad when the ceiling rose and she was able to stand straight in what looked like a root cellar.

Indeed it was a root cellar. Most of it, rather than being taken up by food, was filled with drying herbs. Alynn recognized chickweed, wormwood, and plantain. Three of the walls held a torch each. There was hardly light to see by.

Suddenly, she *felt* something. Cold, clammy scales on her ankles. It tickled like caterpillar's feet, grating as it slid up her legs, up to her knees—

Alynn shrieked. A snake. There was a snake on her—cold—slimy—venomous—

"Stop screaming, you'll scare it," Leif said. "Don't move."

"I can't move!"

"*Silence!*"

The voice was harsh and rasping. It seemed to come from everywhere at once. It made Alynn stop screaming, even as Vorthmathir climbed to her waist and settled with a threatening tightness around it. At least he'd stopped moving. Leif stepped closer to Alynn and set a protecting hand on her shoulder

"Alva, show yourself," Leif demanded. "Where are you?"

"Where am I?" A walking stick emerged from the shadows, knocking one of the torches off its sconce. It flared for a moment, then died.

Leif's voice was steady. "Alva, your chief needs you."

"Of *course*, sir. Anything for the *chief*." The torch on the opposite wall fell, and the darkness intensified. The room was lit only by two circles of light: one by Leif and Alynn, and the other on the far wall.

Suddenly, Leif grabbed Vorthmathir by the back of his head. He hissed, squirming frantically and spewing venom from his fangs. Leif held him in the torchlight; it gleamed in his undead eyes.

"Show yourself, or I kill the snake," Leif ordered. "Now."

The torch on the far wall moved, and Alva's face appeared in its circle of light. She smiled knowingly. "Is something wrong?"

"What did you give Drostan?" Alynn demanded. She would have drawn her sword if she'd thought to bring it with.

"What did I give Drostan?" Alva repeated. "A tea, to help him focus on his work. A lad so lively isn't meant to be caged in a scriptorium."

"What did you put in it?" Leif said. "Nightshade? Yew?"

"Mint, dear. Nothing more." Alva scratched her hands. It was hard to tell in the torchlight...but were they redder than usual?

Alynn felt her eyes fade into tunnel vision. With a berserker's cry, she ran to Alva, wrenched the torch from her hands, and examined her more closely. Her hands and wrists were stained with the pink of dried rose petals, pockmarked with a few small blisters.

"You wicked hag! May the devil make splinters of yer legs and a ladder of yer spine!" Alynn gripped the firebrand. She was going to bash Alva's head in with it. Leif grabbed her arm just in time.

"Contain yourself."

"Look at her hands!"

Leif knelt and examined the rash for himself. "What does this mean?"

"She used Devil's Bread!"

Slowly, the realization of what Devil's Bread was, and the powers it held, sunk into Leif's mind. He stood and paced into the shadows. The shrill, metallic shriek of a drawn sword called from them.

Without thinking, Alynn gave a cry of, "'*Mín er hefndin, ég mun endurgjalda, segir Drottinn*'!" She didn't know where it came from; some of the words she'd never heard before. But they seemed to have a profound effect on Leif. He paused, trembling, then sheathed his sword and struck Alva across the face.

"Alva Thoralddottir, you're under arrest for attempted murder." He bound her wrists with his belt, paying no heed to her squirming. "What cures do you know?"

"There are no cures for hemlock," Alva said, still reeling from Leif's blow. "If there were, I'd have had Vorthmathir bite him." At the mention of his name, the viper slithered up Alva's walking stick and settled around her waist, as if giving her a consoling embrace.

"What possessed you do to this?" Alynn demanded.

Alva gave an unsettling smile. "You simple creature. You weren't here during Konar's reign. You don't know the misery we put up with, twenty-six years of it, at the hands of a mad chieftain. He was born pure, and nineteen when his father died. It's a sad thing, watching power and fame go to the head of such a young man. You can't blame me, now, can you, for wanting the next twenty-six years to be a bit more peaceful? With a sane chief, not another young and corruptible one, not a repeat of history?"

"You don't know him!" Alynn cried. "He's nothin' like his uncle! He's more sane than you are!" And with that, she found the door to the outside world and ran through it.

Clouds were gathering, and the wind was chill. Alynn was numb. She couldn't feel anything, not yet, and for the moment, she was glad of it. She waited until Leif emerged from the root cellar with Alva. He seemed numb, too. But grief gathered in his eyes, and pain contorted his face until he bowed his great head and began to weep.

Alynn took a step backwards. Watching Leif weep was like watching a castle's wall falling. It wasn't right. She wanted to beg him to stop.

"Uncle Leif—"

He took her into his arms and prayed. It was nothing eloquent. It was a cry from the depths of a father's broken heart, a mix of Norse and Gaelic and groans that uttered what words could not, but doubtless God understood him.

Taking a few breaths to compose himself, Leif took Alynn by the shoulder and Alva by the arm and began a solemn procession back to the monastery.

Alynn's heart stayed in its numbed state until she saw Drostan again. He was resting by the fireplace, his hair tied back and a bowl by his feet, while Lukas read the Psalms aloud and Caitriona spun wool nearby. She looked up and smiled at Alynn, but her smile quickly turned worried. "Lynder, what's wrong?"

"Caitriona—" Leif's voice shook strangely— "I believe Alva has something to tell everyone."

For a moment, all was silent. Alva studied the floor, an evil smile on her face. Vorthmathir slid down from her waist and warmed himself in front of the fire. Caitriona's face grew anxious, as if it was her own son who was ill.

"Oh, don't worry, Lady Cait," she said. "It might hurt you to watch him die, but it's nothing compared with standing helpless as he goes mad with power, as his uncle did."

"There's nothin' you can—"

"Fool! You think that I'd try to save him, even if I could? There is no hope for those poisoned with hemlock! I wish I'd let him die when his father brought him to me thirteen years ago, his arm burnt to a crisp!"

Her eyes flashed like Vorthmathir's; her tongue seemed almost forked. She seemed to take pleasure in watching Drostan hear of his fate. His wide eyes looked from Alva to his father, then to Lukas, and finally to Alynn, and held out an arm to her. It was then that Alynn's numb heart shattered, and she buried her face in his chest and let her tears fall.

"I'll...I'll be fine," he stammered. His voice was raw, and his words sounded forced, as if he had a hard time getting them out. "Don't...cry, Lynder-my-Love."

"He'll be alright," Lukas promised. "The Lord's been working miracles since the beginning of time. He does them still. Everyone, start praying. Caitriona, wash the kettle, we'll see if a purging won't do him good."

"I'd hope his stomach's empty by now," Caitriona said.

"I've nay doubt it is, but there's more to purging than emetics. I'll see what Galen has to say."

Alynn prayed as well as she could, and Caitriona kissed Drostan's forehead before washing the kettle. She could hear her praying from the kitchen. Lukas disappeared into the library, then into the armory where he kept his medicinal herbs. Soon, a tea was brewing. When all was set, they gathered around Drostan, and Lukas began.

"Mark sixteen, verses seventeen and eighteen say, 'And these signs will accompany those who believe: In my name they will drive out demons; they will speak in new tongues; they will pick up snakes with their hands; and when they drink deadly poison, it will not hurt them at all; they will place their hands on sick people, and they will get well.'"

He placed his hand on Drostan's head, and the others followed. "Dear Lord, we thank Ye fer Drostan Leifson. Thank Ye that we don't have to ask what Yer will is; we know Ye want to heal him. And so we pray just that, fer Yer healing to be manifest in him. We plead the blood of Yer precious Son, Jesus Christ, over Drostan this day, and we thank Ye that by Yer wounds, he is healed."

Caitriona was next. "Lord God...Drostan's life isn't finished yet. He has so many people to help. He has an island to lead, a family to love. Och, Lord, don't take him from us yet...."

"Please—please, God, help Drostan get better...."

"Lord, You know my son. You know he doesn't deserve

what's happened to him. I pray that You'd take this suffering from him, that You'd heal him...."

Leif's voice trailed off, and Caitriona led the "amen." Even Drostan chimed in weakly. A divine peace had settled over the room. It was the sense that God was there, that no matter what happened, everything was going to be alright. It was like a mother's touch on a feverish face, but a thousand times more beautiful.

"Your God won't be able to help you," Alva said from the corner. She had freed her wrists from her fetters and came towards them. "He won't survive the night."

Five retorts shot from ready lips at the same instant, so that it was impossible to tell who said what. But it was Alynn, who was trying her best not to fly into a berserker's frenzy and kill her on the spot, who faced her and walked slowly towards her, like a wolf stalking its prey.

"Don't you dare tell me what my God can and can't do. I serve the God Who parted the Red Sea. I serve the God Who's raised the dead. The same God Who gave me and Lukas the victory in the Battle of Faith is going to give Drostan victory over this poison. And no devil in hell, yourself included, will be able to stop Him!"

Alynn took another step, but her foot landed on something that squirmed. A snake. Alynn had stepped on Vorthmathir.

A hand grabbed her, pulling her away from the darting viper. She tumbled onto the floor and watched as Vorthmathir extended the full three feet of his body, fangs dripping with venom, jaws agape. He locked his jaw on the first thing he touched.

Alva's wrist.

Alva screamed. Vorthmathir kept biting again and again—chewing, almost—and injecting deadly venom, not noticing he had missed his target. Dark blood streamed down his body and fell in droplets on the floor. Alva shook her arm, but Vorthmathir stayed latched on like a leech.

It was Leif who finally grabbed Vorthmathir by the back of

the head and threw him onto the floor. Alva began to gasp for breath, and she kicked at the snake as it tried to slither up her leg. "Shame on you...vile serpent...curse you!" She took another rasping breath, squeezing her wrist to stem the bleeding, and glanced up at those around her. "You fools, help me!"

"*Medicus, cura te ipsum,*" Lukas muttered, probably louder than he'd intended to, as he tied a dishrag around Alva's bony wrist. "Are you afraid to die?"

Alva snarled. "What do you care?"

"I care because God's forgiven worse people than ye. And if ye'll earnestly repent, God will still receive ye. If ye survive, ye'll find yerself in service to a wonderful Master, and if ye die, ye'll find yerself in glory."

"I live and die for the glory of Odin, young man," Alva snapped. Her voice grew harsher through pain and anger. "I trust in whatever fate he has for me."

"I know what fate my God has fer me, and fer all who follow Him," Lukas said. "The path ye're on leads to nowhere good, Alva. Please. Turn from it."

Alva glared at him, and a trickle of blood fell from her nose. "Never."

Lukas lowered his gaze and tucked his hands into his sleeves. "Send fer me if ye change yer mind. Sit down until the bleeding stops." Alva needed no second invitation as she sat, still gasping, still fuming.

Alynn nearly jumped when she felt arms wrap around her, but relaxed when she realized they were Drostan's. "Are you hurt?" he whispered.

"I'm grand, love." Alynn trembled as adrenaline left her system. "You just saved my life."

"You're welcome." He tried to stand, but stumbled. "I can't feel my feet."

Alynn helped him up and was surprised at how unsteady he was. "They're probably just asleep," she said. Drostan shook his head, and panic flashed in his eyes. He was trembling.

"Come, love. We'll get you a bed, and Lukas will get some medicine, and you'll wake up tomorrow morning and be fine."

Drostan stumbled like a drunken man as Alynn helped him to the nearest cell. It had been the abbot's cell, and as such was the warmest and most comfortable. Drostan settled into the feather tick and rubbed his feet.

"It's not working," he muttered. "I can't feel it."

"Here's the medicine, dear," Caitriona said, handing him a mug of tea. "Drink it up, and Lynder, keep him comfortable."

There was nothing Alynn could do but let the purging run its course. It seemed that anything that could come out of a person was forced out of him at an alarming rate. Alynn kept her attention to the waist up, wiping sweat and snot and vomit off Drostan's face. An unpleasant odor behind her let her know that the diuretic and laxative effects of Lukas's tea were potent as well.

Everyone pitched in to help. Leif hefted the filled chamber pots outside for Caitriona to clean, and Rowan had been called from the fields to fetch water. Lukas was hiding in the library, trying to see what Galen and Hippocrates had to say about poisons.

Slowly, the purging ran its course. Drostan was able to keep a sip of water down. Caitriona changed the bedclothes. The chamber pot was changed less frequently, and when Drostan fell into a somewhat-peaceful sleep, Alynn let herself step outside. She was surprised at how late it had gotten.

By nightfall, Drostan was awake, but barely, his body completely empty. He seemed a mere shell of himself as he lay weak and listless. In a raw voice he rasped, "Lynder...do me a favor."

"What do you need?"

"If anything happens...to me...don't do what Father did." His fingers were as forceless as butterfly wings as he took her hand. "Find someone else to love...get married...have children...."

"Don't talk like that," Alynn said, her own voice shaking.

"You'll be fine. You'll be fine!"

"Don't cry." He wrapped an arm around her, and she embraced him as best as she could. "Shh...God works everything out. Be strong...take care of yourself...I'd love to see your children, Lynder. Strong...noble, like you...."

"Don't, Drostan—"

"You can move...back to Limerick," Drostan said. "All your family there...they'd love to have you...you, and Tarin, and your parents...you'd be a family again—"

"Stop it!" Alynn almost shouted. She buried her face in Drostan's chest, tears falling freely. "Stop it, love! You're my family! I need you here, Drostan. I need you."

"I know." His voice was hardly more than a whisper, and his hand rested gently on her head. "I'll be fine, most likely...I just...wanted you to know...just in case."

She looked up at him, hoping to find a glimmer of strength in his eyes. Instead she saw him gazing back at her with the same love he'd gazed at her with so many times before. It had been there the first time they danced together, the first time they held hands, the first time he kissed her cheek and called her "love."

Drostan had something to fight for and a warrior's spirit in him. No tea, no sword, no sickness could take him easily. Alynn would be his faithful shieldmaiden beside him, strong in his weakness. And with the same God Who had won the Battle of Faith in league with them, what was there to be afraid of?

June 28, A.D. 966—

O, Lord, have mercy! The world spins. Drostan is poisoned, Alynn is injured, Alva lies dying in a downstairs cell. How to begin expressing my feelings, I know not, for everything is tangled like the brambles of an unkempt forest.

Drostan's purging was the most recent of events to transpire. Never have I purged an individual, and never do I hope to again. Blood, sweat, urine—those things I can deal with. Not vomit. I was retching when everyone else thought I was studying, and I'm about to make myself sick again, so I'd best speak of something else.

Watching that snake bite Alva was sickening as well. I found the vermin under our kitchen table and severed its head. Alva refuses salvation, yet still I pray for her. Perhaps there is nothing I can do—an uncomfortable fact. Though God will forgive her, I'd rather not spend eternity with my son-in-law's assassin.

Speaking of Drostan, we finally got him quiet, and his body is retaining fluids well enough now. He is asleep, and Alynn is watching him. If I wake in the night, I shall relieve her. I have faith for his recovery—God's fished me out of sorrier states—but fear still knocks on the others' minds. Leif is especially distraught; understandably so. And whether or not Drostan has faith for his own recovery will prove paramount.

My stomach still hurts. Perhaps the sun will bring healing when it rises.

—L. McCamden

SEVENTEEN

Alynn sat with Drostan throughout the night. By the light of a single candle, she carded wool until her arms ached and her hands were stiff, and then she simply sat back and closed her eyes. She wouldn't sleep...she'd start carding again, in just a moment....

A faint cry caught her worry. It wasn't Drostan—had she imagined it? She thought she heard it again.

Drostan stirred. "What was that?" he slurred, as if his tongue was numb.

"You heard it too?"

"Go...Alva."

Hesitant to leave Drostan, Alynn took her candle and went to the cell next door, where Alva had been placed for the night. Immediately, she regretted her decision. Half of Alva's face was pallid, and the other half was puffed and black as death— bruised from where Leif had struck her. Blood trickled from her nose and ears, and her hand was swollen to nearly twice its size.

"Alva?"

A gentle stirring was the only response. Alva's head was tilted back and her mouth was open wide, but even with her entire effort thrown into breathing, her lips were turning blue.

"Are you afraid?" Alynn asked.

Alva gasped in another breath. Her voice was gentle, nearly inaudible. "I hear Death walking up behind me," she breathed. "Don't let it take me...."

"Jesus will take you," Alynn promised. "Only let Him, Alva. He loves you."

Alva began to shake. At first, Alynn assumed she was cold, but then her body began to seize uncontrollably. Alynn jumped back, heart hammering, pulling back her candle so that all she could see was a shadow thrashing about. Alva was murmuring—whispering to herself, to Odin, to God, to someone or something—and then, as suddenly as the seizure had started, it ended.

Alynn called Alva's name, then slowly, cautiously, pressed an ear to her chest. There was no beating, only a deathly stillness.

A bowl—a bedpan—there was a pitcher of water nearby, and Alynn hovered over it, breathing deeply, until the urge to vomit left her. She left the corpse on the bed, clutched the candle in a trembling hand, and shook Drostan out of his half-sleep.

"What do you do with a body?" she asked.

Drostan groaned drowsily. "Make it look like an accident."

"Alva's dead. The snake—it killed her—"

Drostan sat up against the wall and extended an arm to Alynn. She curled next to him gratefully, shivering with fear and the chill of the night. "Are you feelin' better?" she asked.

"My stomach doesn't hurt anymore, but I still can't feel my feet." He spoke like a young child, unintelligible except to those who knew him well. Alynn lay her head on his chest so she could hear his heartbeat—so comforting, after Alva's stillness—and closed her eyes. She was warm and comfortable, her head moving with the rising and falling of Drostan's chest as he breathed, the wonderful beating of his heart....

Suddenly, it was morning, and Rowan was watching them.

Alynn tumbled out of bed, her hair in ruins, rather ashamed of herself. She shouldn't have fallen asleep—she should have been in a chair—she should have asked someone to take her place. "Nothin' happened, I'll swear on a relic," she promised, brushing her skirts out.

"I'll take yer word for it," Rowan said. His arms were crossed, his right ankle on his left knee. "Drostan's made it through the night, I see."

"He has. We thought nothin' less of him." She stretched. There was a crick in her neck, a catch in her back, and pins and needles running through her legs. She needed to remember never to sleep like that again. "Alva's dead."

"We know. Leif's hitchin' up the hay wagon to take her back to the village. He'll explain everythin', give her a decent funeral, not that she deserves one...." He stood up and gave Alynn a rather awkward embrace. "Don't worry, my heart."

Alynn pressed her eyes shut and squeezed as tightly as she dared—she didn't have to be afraid of breaking him, like she was with Lukas. "Thank you, Father."

"Mum's makin' stirabout. Are you hungry?"

"I'm not."

"You're eatin' anyway. I'll bring some in here." He indicated for her to take his chair as he left, and Alynn accepted his offer gratefully.

Drostan was breathing easily. He had stopped salivating, his legs were no longer trembling, and he seemed perfectly well. But he was still asleep—well, Alynn probably would be too, if she'd spent the previous day retching her guts out. He would wake soon enough. Where had she put her carding?

Drostan stirred—Alynn's carding could wait. She waited until he opened his eyes and smiled faintly at her.

"Did we get our miracle, love?" she asked.

He didn't answer. For a moment, Alynn wondered what was happening until she realized he was trying to speak—his mouth was moving, and a few grunts and mumbles came out, but no words. Drostan's eyes grew wide with panic, and he threw off his blankets.

"Mum!" Alynn shouted. "Lukas, help!"

Drostan had thrashed his way out of bed, but he fell when he tried to stand. Alynn caught him, barely.

A few eternal seconds ticked by before Lukas strode hurriedly through the door, followed closely by Caitriona and Rowan. "I've got him," Lukas said, throwing aside the book he'd brought with him. "Steady, lad. Steady...there we go. Try to keep yer heart rate down." He got Drostan settled in bed again, but instead of covering him with a blanket, he took off his socks and pinched his toe. "Can ye feel that, lad?"

Drostan tried to answer, but he shook his head instead.

Lukas moved upward, pinching right above his ankle. "Tell me when ye feel something." He got all the way up to Drostan's knees before he felt anything, and Alynn's stomach began to twist with worry.

"What does that mean?" Caitriona asked.

"Well, hemlock, or Devil's Bread, whichever ye call it, was used by the Greeks to execute prisoners," Lukas explained. "We know from the account of Socrates' death that Drostan will lose sensation from the feet up, and if it gets to his heart—which it won't, I'm sure—em—he'll die."

Alynn should have felt something. Grief, perhaps. Anger. Maybe fear. But instead, there was nothing. There was only a hollow feeling, a mind devoid of thought, and eyes that blinked and stared at nothing.

To everyone's surprise, Rowan sat on the edge of Drostan's bed. "We have a sayin' back in Ireland," he said. "You've only two things to worry about—either you're healthy, or you're sick. If you're healthy, you've nothin' to worry about, but you're obviously sick, so you've two things to worry about. Either you'll recover, or you'll pass on. If you recover, you've nothin' to worry about. But if you die, you've two things to worry about—you go up, or you go down. And you're goin' up, Drostan. So you've nothin' to worry about."

Drostan tried to thank him, but only ended up reminding himself of his muteness. So instead he smiled, and Rowan ruffled his hair.

Silently, Caitriona went to Drostan's bedside and kissed him, speaking encouragingly to him in the gentle tone she had used on all her children when they had been ill. Lukas gave a twitch of a half-smile. "Bear up fer him, my dear," he told Alynn as he left the room. "Stay wi' him. Pray fer him. And don't be afraid."

"I don't know how to pray."

Lukas motioned towards the book he'd dropped on his way in. "Start there."

Alynn picked up the leather-bound book. It was a Psalter. She was a slow reader, but she could pray earnestly, and she knew God blessed every earnest effort. She opened the Psalter, admired Lukas's handwriting for a moment, and started with Psalm One. She took a few minutes to read it to herself; it didn't sound like a prayer. She'd have to change the wording a bit. Or would God understand what she meant even if she didn't?

Before she could make up her mind, Leif came in, walking at a speed most people jogged at, and Drostan tried to sit up. Leif forced him down again. "Keep still—don't hurt yourself, son, I know you're sore. You're alright. Do you need a drink?" He took his drinking-horn from his belt and offered Drostan the small ale it contained. He drank it gratefully.

Leif glanced up at the others, a fear in his face that didn't belong there. "If you could give us a moment—I need to talk to him."

"Of course," Caitriona said. She shooed Alynn and Rowan out the door, gave Drostan one more kiss on the forehead, and shut the door so that father and son could enjoy what might be their last few moments together.

Alynn met daylight and the warmth from the hearth, but something seemed different about it. The light was thinner, the fire weaker. The air held a chill that did not come from the wind or the past night's darkness. She sensed that the sunlight was just as bright and the fireplace just as cheery as it was on any other day; her mind was the dark place.

Drostan was always able to pull back the curtains inside her, help her see the beauty in things. Just a glimpse of his carefree smile would lighten her mood, and his embrace would lift her spirits so that she'd forget what saddened her in the first place. But Drostan was dying.

A pang of sadness went through Alynn, and she blinked. Her eyes were wet.

"God, be with him."

Life, somehow, would keep going while Drostan was on his sickbed. So Alynn took out her emotions at the dash churn, then took a breath and focused on regulating her violent strokes before she ruined the butter. She could feel later, when all this was over. Right now, she needed to work.

Her arm hurt like the devil, just like Lukas said it might.

Rowan offered a hand, and Alynn accepted it. She went outside and let a gentle rain wash away her fears, replacing it with a quiet determination to be strong and immovable, the rock Drostan needed to stand on as he was buffeted by the storm of life.

When Leif finally emerged from the sickroom, Alynn entered with all the things that might lift Drostan's spirits: a *tafl* board, a mug of his favorite tea, and a carefully combed and neatly styled head of hair. Drostan's eyes lit up when he saw her. It was a dim light, but it was noticeable, and it lifted Alynn's spirits. They played four rounds of *tafl*, then Lukas recited some Psalms while rubbing a salve onto Alynn's deeply-bruised arm.

Caitriona, with a hopeful smile in her eyes, gave Alynn a dress and instructed her to take in the waist. It wasn't Caitriona's dress—at any rate, Alynn had never seen Caitriona wearing it—but it was made of silk as red as a holly berry, and smoother than anything Alynn had felt before. It shone in the candlelight and caught on Alynn's callouses as she touched it. She hoped she wouldn't ruin the dress. She wondered why she'd been given it in the first place. She needed busy work, not important work. Drostan's every breath distracted her, and she found herself picking out as many stitches as she put in.

When she finally finished one side of the dress, she set her hand over Drostan's. He made no move to acknowledge her touch, so she called his name gently. He neither stirred nor opened his eyes. A pang of panic shot through Alynn before she realized that he was only asleep.

She looked up at Rowan, who was slowly and carefully sharpening Caitriona's kitchen knives. He'd sharpened every other blade in the monastery except for the penknives, which Lukas always kept perfectly honed.

"Father?"

Rowan laid aside his knife and grindstone. "What is it, my heart?"

"Have you ever watched someone die?"

"I have." Rowan folded his hands, his eyes staring through space and into the past. "More than once."

"Are they always frightened, like Alva was?"

"It depends. The thought of dyin' might frighten them, but when the time comes...."

For a moment, he was his old self again, caught in a purgatory of haunting memories. But he took a breath and, voice shaking, made himself speak. "I should have told you a long time ago, about my family...I was thirteen when the typhoid hit our town. The church turned into a hospital, and they put me in the same bed as my wee brother Padraig. He was...cryin', screamin'. All the wee prayers an eight-year-old can give to heaven, he tried to say them in Latin, thinking God would hear them better.

"One day, when neither of us were panned out, Padraig looked at me, he smiled, and— 'Rowan,' he says to me, 'you don't have to be afraid. 'Tis like gettin' a hug from Jesus, dyin' is.' And then he shivered—his eyes went still—" Rowan stopped and took a breath. "He was smilin' when they took him out to bury him."

"I'm sorry."

"Thank you."

Rowan stared through the quilt on Drostan's bed. "But of the three people I've watched die—Padraig, then Libby, then yer sister Louisa—none of them felt fear as they died. Only love."

Alynn was silent. She squeezed Drostan's hand, wondering if he could feel it, wondering if he would die peacefully as Padraig had. She'd never heard Rowan talk about his family before. Frankly, she'd never known he'd had siblings.

"Who was Libby?"

"Libby was the only one the typhoid spared me. I had her five years more, then consumption took her. She was perfect—the sweetest soul you'd ever meet. I can't wait to see her in heaven someday."

"Why didn't you ever tell us about her?"

Rowan shrugged. "I used to talk about her too much. So I tried to overcompensate, forget about her, and that hurt even worse. I've been trying to find balance."

Silence reigned for a moment. Drostan stirred in his sleep, and Alynn touched him to make sure he was still warm and breathing. The blanket had fallen from his right shoulder. Gently, so as not to wake him, she fixed it.

"If I say somethin'," Rowan said, staring spellbound into the corner, "that makes me sound like a complete fool, will you still listen, and try to understand?"

"Of course."

He gave a grateful sigh and took a moment to compose his thoughts. "You and Libby have so many things in common that sometimes I'll get ye mixed up. She was loyal, caring, and thrifty, with a wee bit of stubbornness mixed in, just like you. And the other night—I don't know what my mind did—it was the way you stood up to me, I think, because Libby would do that every once in a while. 'Tis no excuse—I know you have blue eyes—but hers were brown."

"I suppose I overreacted the other night," Alynn admitted.

"I don't think you did." Rowan's gentle gaze rested on her, humble and apologetic. "You were right. I was so focused on makin' ends meet that I forgot about why I was tryin' to make them meet in the first place. 'Tis hard enough raisin' Tarin now that he's ten, I can't imagine you, at nine years old, tryin' to keep house and take care of a three-year-old. I'm sorry I made you do that. But 'tis fierce proud of you I am, for doing what you did."

"Thank you," they said at the same time, and smiled at their mistake. Alynn squeezed Drostan's hand again, more with delight than with worry. She couldn't remember the last time she'd had an honest conversation with her father. It was beautiful.

Alynn was not aware of the passing of time. The candle burned down, and she lit another one; one bucket of water was emptied, and Rowan left to fetch another one. Valdis came to visit Drostan but, finding him asleep, tucked a blanket around him. "It was his mother's plaid," she explained. It was a lovely plaid—dark cream and fawn-brown and two shades of blue, well-loved and well-cared-for. "Poor lad, I'd like to spit on the wretch that did this to him!"

Alynn remembered the sight of Alva convulsing on the bed, wallowing in her own blood, and shuddered.

"She came to the house before she came here yesterday," Valdis continued. "Said she had some rare mead for Drostan, and I told her—I said he was here, and that he didn't drink mead often, he was a good, respectable lad—och, she'd have found one way or another, the old dark-elf. It wasn't time to take your father's stitches out, dear. They should have stayed in until Sabbath, or at least washing-day. Good excuse on her end, I'll give."

Valdis sat with Alynn while Rowan ventured outside for a bit, and while Rowan was gone, Drostan woke up. He noticed the plaid wrapped around him, recognized it, and took it off.

"Are you too warm, love?" Alynn asked.

Drostan shook his head. He tried to fold the plaid neatly, but his hands refused to cooperate.

"You think 'tis too special to be used, don't you?" Alynn

asked.

Drostan nodded and pointed with his stiff fingers to the chamber pot beside the bed, and then again to the plaid.

"You don't want to soil it if you're sick again."

Valdis smiled and came close to the bed. "Don't worry, Master Drostan. Mothers don't mind getting their clothes dirty. And it won't be the first time you've soiled it."

Convinced, Drostan settled back into bed and let Alynn tuck him in. He drank the water Alynn offered him and mumbled his thanks. "Should I tell the others that he's awake?" Valdis asked.

"Please."

Alynn combed her fingers through Drostan's hair, hoping to make him feel a bit more dignified. His eyes, though still bleary with sleep, were brighter. More hopeful. Alynn smiled at them. Drostan pressed his face into the plaid and inhaled disappointedly.

"I know," Alynn said. "It doesn't smell like her anymore. We kept Mum's spare plaid for years after she was taken. It helped—kept her close."

Drostan looked up at Alynn, his eyes shining gently. "I won't be seeing my mother for a few years yet," he seemed to say, setting a hand over Alynn's. Her heart melted. She hardly noticed when Lukas came in and began examining Drostan, pinching his legs until he elicited a response. The paralysis had come nearly to his waist.

"Do ye mind if we hold chapel in here, lad?" Lukas asked. Alynn noticed he had brought the Gospels with him. Caitriona, Rowan, and Valdis had joined them.

Caitriona began to sing "Come Thou Fount," one of Drostan's favorite hymns, and the others joined in. Even Drostan mumbled along as best as he could, like an infant trying to learn how to talk. The sight of him trying his absolute best made Caitriona cry, and even Lukas's eyes went soft.

As soon as the song was over, they all sat—Lukas and Caitriona in chairs, Rowan on the floor, Alynn and Valdis on the edge of Drostan's bed. "I've heard everyone reassuring themselves today," Lukas said, opening his Gospel. "We tell ourselves that Drostan is young and strong, and as such, he'll recover. These thoughts help us take courage and find peace. But suppose we fix our minds not on how strong Drostan is, but on how strong God is. To help us take faith, I'd like to read a few Scripture passages.

"The first is the forty-first Psalm, verses one through three—" he began from memory— "'Blessed is he who has regard for the weak; the Lord delivers him in times of trouble. The Lord will protect him and preserve his life; he will bless him in the land and not surrender him to the desire of his foes. The Lord will sustain him on his sickbed and restore him from his bed of illness.'

"Matthew four, twenty-three and twenty-four. 'Jesus went throughout Galilee, teaching in their synagogues, preaching the good news of the kingdom, and healing every disease and sickness among the people. News about him spread all over Syria, and people brought to him all who were ill with various diseases, those suffering severe pain, the demon-possessed, those having seizures, and the paralyzed, and he healed them.'

"John nine, one through seven. 'As he went along, he saw a man blind from birth. His disciples asked him, "Rabbi, who sinned, this man or his parents, that he was born blind?" "'Neither this man nor his parents sinned," said Jesus, "but this happened so that the work of God might be displayed in his life...." Having said this, he spit on the ground, made some mud with the saliva, and put it on the man's eyes. "Go," he told him, "wash in the Pool of Siloam"...So the man went and washed, and came home seeing.'

Lukas kept on reading stories of paralyzed men being healed, the blind seeing, the deaf hearing, and even the dead raised to life. For half an hour he read, then they took turns laying hands on Drostan and praying for him.

When the prayers were finished, Alynn opened her eyes expecting a miracle. It might be a small thing—his tongue might be loosed—or he might be perfectly healed and whole. But instead, he was as limp and as mute as ever, and the blankets were wet.

"Never fret," Lukas said. "I figured ye'd be incontinent, once the paralysis reached yer waist. Some of the older men who once lived here had contrived an apparatus to mend the issue. I'll see if I can't reproduce it."

"I can make one," Caitriona said.

Lukas looked at her strangely. "How do you—"

"I've had four babies, I know how diapers work. Alynn, fetch some clean blankets."

Alynn kissed Drostan's cheek, which was red with embarrassment, and took Lukas out the door with her. "We've prayed for him," she said once they'd reached the hearth and she knew Drostan wouldn't be able to hear. "We've stood in faith, and why isn't he well? Why isn't God doing anythin'?"

Lukas answered with a strange harshness in his voice. "Why did the prophet Elisha die of illness? Why have yer parents buried half their children? Why was my father killed before my eyes?" Alynn was nearly frightened of him before she saw grief mixed with the anger in his eyes. "I don't know!"

His fists clenched around the back of a chair. Carefully, Alynn rested her hand on his shoulder; he sighed and looked to heaven. "All I know," he said, "is that God will work this fer our good."

Strangely comforted, Alynn resumed her post at Drostan's bedside. *Tafl* no longer interested him; Alynn tried to keep his spirits up by reading aloud or having a one-sided conversation. It didn't go as well as she hoped.

People kept knocking on the doorframe. Caitriona was there to see if anyone wanted a snack or a drink; Lukas would stop now and again to see if Drostan's paralysis had spread. The numbness seemed to have stopped around his waist, and Alynn prayed it wouldn't rise any higher. Rowan—oh, God bless Rowan, he was fetching water and telling stories and, from some reservoir Alynn didn't know he had within him, was spreading genuine cheerfulness.

When Lukas came in to check on Drostan's paralysis again, he finally had a bit of good news. "Drostan, yer father's letting us keep Alva's horse," he said. "Have ye seen it? Magnificent black stallion from Hrafney, seven years old. She had some unpronounceable Norse name fer it, so I'm thinking we should rename it."

Drostan nodded, then looked to Alynn for suggestions.

"Faith."

He shook his head.

"You're right, that's more of a girl's name. What's another word like it?"

"Trust," Lukas said. "Hope, Surety—"

A knock sounded that was too heavy-handed to belong to either Rowan or Caitriona. Alynn looked up to see Captain McMahon, and she smiled at him.

"Captain, what's another word fer 'faith'?" she asked.

Lukas snapped his fingers. "I've got it. Reliance."

Drostan nodded his approval, and everyone's eyes turned to Captain McMahon. He had removed his hat out of respect for the sickroom, and he nodded respectfully at Drostan, but there was a singular twinkle in his eye. "Well, sir, it seems that yer crew can't get on right without ye," he said. "A few strakes needed replaced, and they said it would take until next week for a permanent repair. Under the circumstances, I asked for a temporary fix...ye've nay doubt, though, that what they've done will last until we get to Scotland?"

"The ship's fixed?" Alynn asked.

"There's a few minor leaks, but she sails well enough," Captain McMahon said. "We're just loading on a few supplies, and we'll be ready to leave within an hour. I was just wondering if ye'd like to come with, Alynn. Give us a hand wi' yer brother and all."

"Ye needn't fear fer Drostan if ye choose to go," Lukas said. "We'll take fine care of him."

Alynn had guessed that the ship might be fixed before

Drostan recovered, and she'd already settled on a course of action.

"Captain," she said. "I've trusted God to care for Tarin since the day I lost him. And now—now I'm trustin' you to get to Skerray before Darsidia does. I'm trustin' you to get Tarin here in one piece. I know you won't let me down."

Captain McMahon smiled. "I'll guard him wi' my life, Alynn. Ye've my word."

"You can't sword fight, can you?"

"Nay, but I've been in a few barfights in my younger days. Give me a dagger, and I'll clear a room."

Alynn wanted to say that a dagger couldn't stop a horde of armed Vikings, but she stopped herself and trusted God to do His part. "So long as you keep Tarin out of danger. And would you mind givin' him somethin' for me?"

"Not at all!"

Alynn ran into the scriptorium and carefully tore a piece of paper out of a book. *Dear Tarin,* she wrote, *I'm fierce glad you're alright. I miss you more than you'll ever know, but I'm needed where I am for a few days. Listen to Captain McMahon; he'll bring you to me. I can't wait to see you. All my love, Alynn.*

She hurried back and slipped the scrap to Captain McMahon, who tucked it safely in the sealskin pouch he wore like a necklace, tucked into his shirt. "The church at Skerray?" he asked, as if repeating a question Lukas had asked him. "Benedictine, not well attended."

"I mean the building itself. Is it comparable to this one?"

"It's a good bit smaller. Why?"

"Is there a belfry?"

"Of course."

"Stairs or a ladder fer entrance?"

"I've never noticed. What are ye getting at, Brother Lukas?"

"Should the Vikings arrive while ye're there," Lukas said, "hide Tarin in the belfry. If there's a ladder, pull it up after him; if there's stairs, block them as well as ye can. Whatever ye do, stay up there wi' him until the danger's passed, and kill anyone who gets through yer defenses."

"Well then!" Captain McMahon said. "Not a bad plan ye've come up with, Brother."

"It was my fallback, in case sword fighting training didn't go as well as we hoped." Lukas glanced at Alynn with a smile in his eyes. "Fortunately, Alynn's a fast learner. Ye've seen her fight, haven't ye, Tamlane?"

"Aye, I did, at the feast the other day. I'll admit I didn't believe the stories at first, about her killing people and all, but now—" Captain McMahon chuckled nervously— "I've a healthy respect fer her now."

"Do you have time to tell us a story before you leave?" Alynn asked. "For Drostan. I can't think of any more."

Captain McMahon leaned against the wall, thinking. "It was October of '59," he said, "and a man offered me twice the normal fare to take him to Tromso in Norway. So, naturally, I agreed. But I didn't realize how far north Tromso was, nor how cold it was. It was so cold that ghosts couldn't haunt an inhabited house, fer if they entered one, they'd be too busy warming up by the fire to do anything else...."

For twenty minutes, Captain McMahon spoke of faraway places, of treasures and kings and the first and only time he agreed to carry a shipment of bear cubs to Iceland. Alynn listened intently, but even more wonderful than the captain's stories was the light in Drostan's eyes. An occupied mind and active spirit, Lukas had told her once, is the best distraction from an infirm body.

Captain McMahon left reluctantly, but not before hugging Alynn good-bye and ruffling Drostan's red hair for good luck. Alynn was comforted to know that Tarin would know at least one person—probably two, if Rowan went—and quickly prayed for safe travels.

Lukas had given Drostan a Gospel to read. With her patient busy, Alynn left to see what chores Caitriona had left her. To her surprise, she found Rowan at the hearth, grinding barley at the hand mill.

"Father?"

Rowan looked up. "Am I doing this right?"

"What are you doin' here?"

"I wanted to stay within earshot, in case you needed anythin'." He inspected the flour and, finding it too coarse, ground it again. "I'll never look at griddle cakes the same way. This is harder than you make it out to be."

"Not that—why aren't you going to find Tarin with Captain McMahon?"

"What good would it do? Tamlane can fight off Vikings better than I can. He knows where to find us. He knows where Tarin is. We've been brothers in all but blood since First Communion. If you can trust him, so can I."

"But yer things—"

"I asked him to bring my timpan. Everything else is replaceable." Content with the texture of his flour, Rowan emptied the hand mill into a sack and looked up at Alynn. "I realize now, Alynn, that I wasn't a good father to you or Tarin. I know 'tis too late now, but...with the few days I have with you, I want to make things right between us. And I'll start by sayin' that I'm sorry, that I love you, and that I'm not leavin' you again. Not when you need me as much as you do now."

A small part of Alynn's mind said not to trust him; he'd let her down so many times, he'd surely do it again. But that part of her was silenced. Rowan wasn't lying this time; his tone, his eyes, the way he held out an arm to offer an embrace, every part of him was genuine. He was a fallible man, and they both knew it. The difference now was that he was willing to admit and face his mistakes, to do hard things if he was called to.

"Da?"

"What is it, Lynder?"

Alynn accepted Rowan's embrace. It wasn't absentminded, not hurried like she was used to—it was the earnest attention and affection she'd spent her life longing for, and it had been worth the wait. "I forgive you. And I love you, too."

EIGHTEEN

"Lynder."

It was her father's voice trying to wake her, but Alynn tried to ignore it. Was something wrong? She didn't want to wake up just to hear bad news. Or was it time for her to start her chores?

"Someone wants to see you, dear heart."

One of the cats, probably. They were forever coming into her room and sleeping on top of her. Blasted cats. Such twits. Except for Cara. Cara was nice.

"Come on."

Alynn groaned. Her shoulder hurt. She'd been sleeping on the floor; of course her shoulder hurt. She let Rowan help her to her feet and rubbed sleep out of her eyes as he guided her three steps through a dark room. Her leg bumped into something—a bed. Drostan's bed.

She remembered now that Leif had come to the monastery yesterday afternoon and, at midnight, had relieved her of her vigil. How long had she slept? Five hours? What time was it, anyway? She didn't care. It didn't matter. She wouldn't be able to focus on anything. She needed to go back to sleep.

Drostan was awake. Smiling, he reached out to her, and she sank onto the bed beside him. It was so much softer than the stone floor. "Do you mind if I go back to sleep?" Alynn asked.

"Go on, love."

Alynn sighed her thanks before an epiphany struck her. "You can talk," she said.

"Aye, I can talk now. Go back to sleep."

"But you can talk!"

There were other voices in the room—not that they mattered—Caitriona's and Leif's voices laughing and crying and thanking God, and Lukas's interjecting praise. Alynn laughed. She'd never be able to sleep now.

"I'm getting better," Drostan said. His voice was soft, but it was still a voice, and Alynn understood him easily. "Just like you prayed."

"And nothing hurts? Can you feel yer feet?"

Alynn sat up, and Drostan followed suit; he still used his hands, but his waist moved more freely. Alynn hoped it meant that the paralysis was wearing off. "I don't know yet."

Leif had seen the procedure done often enough to mimic it. He took off the blanket that covered his son's feet and touched them. Drostan closed his eyes to focus, and for a moment, Alynn held her breath with him.

"Anything?" Leif asked.

Drostan was about to shake his head and say no, he couldn't feel his feet quite yet, but then he started laughing—the most beautiful sound Alynn had ever heard. "Stop!" he cried. "That tickles!"

Alynn laughed. Thank God. Oh, thank God. Drostan was going to be alright.

In a moment, Caitriona had her arms around both of them. She kissed them and smiled and thanked God for her son, her son was alright again. Leif had yet to move from the foot of the bed but stood head bowed, shoulders trembling, a diamond tear tumbling onto the blankets.

"You're hungry, aren't you?" Caitriona asked, standing and drying her eyes. "What do you want for breakfast?"

"Do you have any eggs?"

"Two or three of them?"

"Two's grand, I won't have you overworking your chickens."

With one last kiss for each of her children, Caitriona left to prepare breakfast. Drostan cupped Alynn's jaw in one hand, his thumb caressing her windblown cheek. "Thank you," he said. "Your prayers, your time. Sitting up with me all night. I appreciate it, and I'll never forget all you've done for me."

"You'd have done it all for me."

"I pray I'll never have to." He kissed the four freckles on her nose and made her blush; she buried herself in his chest and smiled. He was alright. Her world was alright. The battle was over, and the spoils were theirs to share.

Caitriona made five-minute eggs for everyone; how there were enough to go around was anyone's guess. But between the eggs and the bannocks left over from yesterday and the warm tea with milk, there was a holiday feast. In fact, it felt like Christmas, with everyone gathered to share a meal in the cramped cell together, their bread in their laps and their eggs in their hands. No one minded the touching shoulders or the bumping elbows or even the lack of a table. It was the merriest meal Alynn had ever partaken in.

Leif was quick to leave for the village and spread the news of Drostan's recovery. As expected, Lukas and Rowan also disappeared after breakfast. They were probably going to the fields—Rowan didn't know his way around agriculture, and Lukas was probably taking delight in teaching him. To Alynn's surprise, they both reappeared with a new pair of crutches.

"It was a team effort," Lukas said.

"It was a competition," Rowan corrected. "I enjoyed it."

Alynn paid them no heed. Drostan was on his own two feet, a bit unsteady, but strong enough to keep his balance. Grinning, he took one small step, then another, then stumbled. Alynn caught him.

"Don't let me squish you," he warned, trying to find his balance again. Rowan helped set him aright. "Thank you, sir."

"Take it easy." Rowan stood beside him, ready to catch him should he falter again. Drostan knit his brows in determination and set off again. His gait was still uneven, and his stride short, but he was walking, and Alynn couldn't have been prouder of him. He walked out into the hallway and stopped.

"Are you alright?" Alynn asked.

"I'm out of that room," Drostan said. "I'm out of that blasted room, and I couldn't be more grateful." He leaned against the wall and drew a breath. "I want to go outside one of these days. But my legs feel like they're asleep. I'm surprised I got this far."

"But you did, love. I know God didn't bring you this far just so you could totter around like an old man for the rest of yer life. You'll get better. He'll keep healin' you. You just have to keep believin'."

Drostan thought for a moment, then laughed. "I suppose I could work on impersonating Elder Steingrim." He hunched over and took two small steps, transforming his voice into that of an old man. "Oh, Thor, my back hurts. Do I blame myself or my corrupted blood? No Norsewoman would have produced a complainer such as me."

They laughed together, and Alynn stuck close by Drostan's side as he returned to bed. Today would be a good day.

Drostan rose repeatedly throughout the morning to fight his way through his room. He fell twice. The first time, Alynn helped him up; the second, she was spinning yarn and he had crawled into a chair by the time she could free her hands. But each step seemed to strengthen him, and at noon, he was able to make it to the scriptorium. But when he picked up his book, he found it nearly halfway finished.

Drostan froze for a moment, then ran a gentle finger over the runic script. "Isn't this Lukas's handwriting?" he asked.

"It can't be," Alynn said, "unless he knows Norse better than we think we do." She picked up the book and rifled through the pages; ten chapters were written in Lukas's hand. It was all in Norse except for a single Gaelic note in the margin, right next to where the handwriting changed. "To make up for lost time, in faith that you'll finish what you started," Alynn read. "L. McCamden with C. McNeil."

Drostan flipped through the pages, reading verses here and there, smiling at the places Lukas had gotten 'eth' and 'thorn' mixed up. "I'm blessed to have such a family as yours, Lynder. No one could ask for better."

"I can thank them for you, if—"

"Nonsense, I'm doing that myself." Drostan tried to rise from his chair, but Alynn kept him down.

"Rest for a half hour first, get a chapter done," she said. "They'll keep, love. Should I stay in here with you?"

"You'll commandeer my attention." He kissed her cheek and picked up his pen. "There's circles under your eyes. Go take a nap."

"I can't sleep in the middle of a workday."

"Then go out into the paddock, find a comfortable knoll to sit on, and start counting the sheep. No one will blame you." Alynn laughed.

Never had a day of chores seemed so delightful. The carding, the spinning, the baking of next week's bread and tomorrow's Eucharist, everything was infused with hope. Drostan was a frequent visitor in the kitchen, stealing food and kneading dough and offering a kiss on the cheek. He seemed to rely less and less on his crutches. Finally, at dinner, he appeared at the table with nothing besides a hand on Lukas's shoulder to steady him.

Dinner was nothing special. It was soup and bread and small ale with tea afterward, but it felt like a feast. Drostan's presence would have made wild greens and tree bark feel like Christmas dinner. Leif arrived halfway through, and the merriment only increased.

Leif had brought with him a three-stringed lyre, and Rowan tuned it after dinner. He played the reels and jigs Alynn had grown up with, plus a few more he'd learned in Scotland, and everyone sang along. Caitriona pulled Alynn out of her chair and danced with her while Drostan watched with shining eyes. When Caitriona was out of breath and Rowan was running out of songs to play, the lyre's melody changed. It was calmer now, like a glassy starlit sea, and under its spell Lukas fell asleep.

They were blessed. They were so very, very blessed.

When Rowan finished his song and laid the lyre aside, the look in his eyes said he was remembering a story. He glanced at Lukas, asleep in his chair, and chuckled. "My father before me played the timpan," he said. "I'd two younger siblings, and whenever one of them were out of sorts for lack of sleep, Da would play for them. Send them right to sleep, it would. He'd play for Mum and my big sister Maeve when they were ill. It did everyone good."

Lukas woke up with a start. "I wasn't sleeping," he insisted.

"You snored twice," Alynn said.

"Och, if ye say so."

Leif chuckled. "I've some good news from the village," he said. "The Karve we've been working on—the *Eagle's Flight*—she'll be ready to sail in a few days. If the *Darting Swallow* needs its repairs finished in Scotland, which I'm sure it will, it might be in everyone's best interests to sail there and get Tarin out of harm's way as soon as possible."

Alynn gasped. "Truly?"

Leif smiled. "Aye, truly. And Drostan needs some experience at the helm of a ship if he's to be chief. I'd say he'd be happy to take you."

"Honored," Drostan said, eyes shining. For the first time, Alynn was genuinely glad she hadn't left with the Scottish merchant.

But at the same time, something wasn't quite right.

Words knocked around inside her, trying to come out. She just didn't know what order to put them in. She arranged them and changed them and was wondering if they were worth saying at all when Caitriona said, "Faith, child, what's on yer mind?"

"I was just—" Alynn took a deep breath and, before she

could change her mind, said, "I'm not movin' again."

"What do you mean?" Rowan asked.

"I'm goin' with to get Tarin, but then I'm comin' back. Ye can go back to Scotland, or Limerick City, or wherever else strikes yer fancy. What you said, Father, when we left Ireland, was that family is home. You and Mum and Tarin—ye'll always be my family. And I'll always love ye. But my home—my family—'tis here with Drostan now. I'm stayin'."

With everything within her, she knew she was making the right decision. She looked at Drostan; his eyes were glowing. He stood, scooped Alynn out of her chair, and embraced her. "Thank you," he whispered. "You're the best thing that's ever happened to me." The light of the hearth danced in his hair, and his eyes shone. He held Alynn tightly in his strong grip, as if nothing could break them apart.

Slowly, Caitriona's and Rowan's bickering voices became audible. "We can't just—"

"Cait—"

"Don't 'Cait' me—"

"Aeryn Caitriona McNeil. He's a decent lad, he'll treat her right. You oughtn't worry so."

"I'm not worried, I'm just—"

"'Tis alright, Mum," Alynn promised. She squeezed Drostan and turned to Caitriona. There were contagious tears in her eyes as she embraced Alynn and kissed her. Alynn's own voice shook as she said, "I'll come visit."

"I'll miss you, dear heart."

"I'll miss you too, Mum."

Rowan put a hand on her shoulder, giving one of the forced smiles she'd come to expect from him, but this one seemed sadder. His eyes said that he wanted to say everything—he loved her, he'd miss her, he'd never forget her—but there were no words strong enough for what he felt. Then he kissed her, wrapping his arms around both her and Caitriona. "Ye've my blessing," he said. "Be sure to visit us, though. And we'll come up every so often, see how ye're gettin' along. Give a hand with the children, if you're alright wi—"

Lukas's chair scraped chillingly against the stone floor as he stood. "Rowan, I've a proposition fer ye," he announced.

It was rather unlike Lukas to interrupt, so he commanded everyone's full attention. He was aware of it. He looked at all the eyes staring at him and blinked. "I...I've never enjoyed living alone," he said. "Now that I know what a family's like, I can't see how I managed without one. I've grown fond of Caitriona, Rowan's a decent man, and if Tarin's anything like his sister, he'll come to take up a significant portion of my heart. I could use a hand in the fields anyway. So if ye'd like to stay—the three of ye—ye're welcome to."

Alynn was out of her parents' arms in an instant, bounding across the hearth and hugging Lukas too hard. "Thank you, Lukas, thank you so much—"

"Gentle—"

"Sorry. Thank you."

Caitriona laughed. "Can we stay, Rowan? Please?"

"You want to stay?" Rowan asked.

"Of course I want to stay. The village needs a decent blacksmith, and Lukas needs help in the fields, and you'll want to be close to Alynn's children, won't you?"

"Fair play to you, love. We're staying." Rowan nodded respectfully at Lukas. "Thank you, sir. We appreciate it. Truly."

Alynn laughed. Imagine! Her whole family under one roof! Could all of heaven contain more love than a family gathered together? Tarin was all that was missing, and he would be there soon enough. In the meantime, Alynn would simply rejoice in having Drostan whole again.

Eyes. Wide eyes, hungry eyes, surround me. Each pair has a message. Sad eyes tell me, "You killed my da." Empty eyes tell me, "We don't have enough to eat." Angry eyes don't need words; they just scowl, and I press my eyes shut to block them out.

Then the voices start. "I miss Father." "I'm cold. My tunic's worn."
"Mother, I don't want any more wild greens. Can I have bread?"

And then I see myself as the one in charge of them, just as I'd been in
charge of Tarin. I'd always hated it when he talked to me like that. When
his tunic went threadbare, when his trousers were too short but not too
wide, when he'd noticed I hadn't eaten anything so he could have a few
more bites of food. But there's seven of them. I had a hard time caring for
one, just a single sweet child who minded well, and now there's seven.

"Stop it," I say aloud.

"Never," the voices say.

"Jesus." Faith rises within me, and I stand tall, summoning it, feeding
off it like a fire. "Jesus, show me what 'tis really like."

Something warm touches me, and I open my eyes. The dreariness melts
away, and there's a fire, there's soup, there's laughter and playing and love.
Dagny holds Meili, blocking out the other noises, smiling as he falls asleep
in her arms. Geirhild measures out yarn for tablet weaving, complaining
about how busy she is but admitting that the money's nice. She's gotten a
chicken for her last roll of trim, and it simmers in the soup pot, making a
sumptuous dinner.

When everyone sits down to eat, Steinmar says, "I wish Father was
here. He always liked seeing us happy."

"Me too," Kelda says. "But we're getting a new father, aren't we,
Mother?"

Dagny blushes and tells her daughter to hush, she'll find out in due
time, but the spark in her eyes says yes.

It isn't as bad as I think it is. There's still joy, there's still provision,
there's still love. I smile, and then my dream changes. I don't remember
the new dream so well—I think there's dancing fish involved, or something
else that normally only dwells in dreams, but nothing frightening.

All the while, that touch of warmth never leaves me. I know,
somewhere deep inside, that nightmares don't have a hold on my
anymore. And I couldn't be more grateful.

The next day was Sabbath. The church was full of both

Christians and those who clung to their old faith, and Alynn wondered if she would have to put chairs in the upstairs hallway again. Drostan hid upstairs the entire time, pacing and muttering to himself. It was nearly time for service before Alynn had the chance to ask him what was wrong.

"We all agree I should say a few things to everyone, and I'm just trying to figure out what to say." Drostan took a deep breath, then flashed a smile. "I'm not as nervous this time."

"How can you be?" Alynn asked. "God was with you in yer sickroom, He'll be with you on that stage."

"I know—well, most of me knows."

"Is there anything I can do to help?"

"You're grand, Lynder. When does service start?"

"Five minutes."

"Alright." He put an arm around her—not, thank God, because he needed help walking, but simply so he could keep her close—and they went straight into the chapel together. They sat together until the bell rang, when Rowan took his place beside them and Caitriona joined Nora McKenzie on stage to lead worship.

Lukas took his place behind the lectern as always, but instead of praying over the worship service, he gazed at the crowd with a gleam in his eye. "I'm certain ye've all heard of the miracle that's taken place here," he said. "But all the same, I'd like to invite Chief Drostan onstage to give his testimony. If ye would, sir—"

Drostan leapt onto the stage as nimbly as a cat, accepting and returning Lukas's hearty clap on the back. The congregation stood, cheering and clapping at the sight of their leader restored to them. Drostan looked bewildered for a moment, but he smiled.

"Good morning!" he said when the cheering died down, only to raise the clamor up again. When silence finally overtook the crowd, Drostan stood silently, measuring his breathing. He was nervous.

Lord, give him peace, Alynn prayed.

"Well," he said. "I'm sure that, by now, everyone knows that Alva tried to poison me. She was worried that I'd go mad as my uncle did—I can assure you all that I won't—but she gave me hemlock. Devil's bread. It was the strangest feeling, knowing I might die, but not fearing it. If I feared anything, it was that I'd leave you here without a chief and bereave my family. I wouldn't be standing here today if it weren't for your prayers.

"So I thank all of you who prayed for me. I thank my father for overseeing the village in my absence. I thank Alynn, Aunt Cait, Lukas, and Rowan for tending to me and keeping my spirits up. But above all, I thank God. The same God Who protected His children in the Battle of Faith has saved my life, and I charge you, men and women of St. Anne's Cleft, to trust Him, for He has proven Himself faithful."

The crowd clapped again, and Drostan surrendered the stage to Caitriona and Nora. Everyone was in high spirits, singing loudly and proudly and ignoring the ones who couldn't keep in key. When the three hymns were sung and Lukas returned to his place behind the lectern, everyone waited in quiet expectation of an excellent sermon. At first, there was only silence. Lukas seemed to be praying; Alynn wondered if he'd been able to prepare anything.

"We've all prayed a lot of things in the past few days," Lukas finally said, preaching in Norse as he always did. "I've prayed, primarily, for Drostan's recovery and a divine peace upon him and the rest of us. I've prayed for wisdom in helping him. I lost Galen's *Method of Medicine* and prayed to find it again! But the one thing I haven't prayed, the one sentence I haven't said this week, is 'God, if You will fer Drostan to recover, please bring about his healing.'

"And why not? Why did we not suppose, even for a moment, that God sent this calamity, or that He wanted to take Drostan from this earth? Why did we know that God willed to heal him? And how do we know that God wills good for all his children—for you farmers, when your crops are failing? For you parents, when your children are ill? When everything seems to be going wrong at once, how do we know God's not behind it, and more than that, He wants to bring healing to the situation?"

Lukas held up his Bible. "All the miracles we've seen—all the stories I have to tell you—trust them if you will, but the real proof's in here."

NINETEEN

Three days later, Alynn was standing in the bow of the *Eagle's Flight,* peering into the mist. "I can see it!" she cried. "'Tis Scotland! I can see Scotland!"

"This isn't another seagull, is it?" Drostan teased. He put one hand on her waist and held a spyglass with his other. "Good eyes, Lynder! Land ho, gentlemen! Hard to starboard!"

If the ship hadn't been lurching on every toss of the ocean's waves, Alynn would have leapt for joy. "I can't wait to see Tarin again," she breathed for the tenth time that day.

"I know," Rowan said. "Now get back to the tent before I lash you to the mast. I won't have you fallin' overboard again."

"A swim would be refreshing in this weather," Drostan said. "Rowan, could you give us a full mainsail?"

"Aye, Cap'n." Rowan tugged a rope, sending the mainsail billowing in the strong wind.

Alynn picked her way among fishnets and rowing benches and sat in a small sailcloth tent below what Drostan called the poop deck. "Are you excited, Mum?" Alynn asked Caitriona, who had hardly left the tent since Rowan had made it the first hour into their voyage.

Caitriona laughed nervously. "I'm excited, I'm afraid, I'm impatient. It'll hurt if he doesn't recognize me—or if I don't recognize him—why'd Da leave him alone? The lad's ten years old."

"I know one thing for certain," Alynn said. "Tarin is going to love you."

An hour later, the *Eagle's Flight* finally came to port. The dock seemed to sway under Alynn's legs when she stepped on it. Her stomach churned with anticipation.

Drostan left Folkvard and Havard to dock the ship. "Where do we go?" he asked Rowan.

"I'll take Caitriona to the house we've been renting," Rowan said. "Ye two check the church. He's there quite often, but I'll come collect ye if he's not. Sound good?"

"Aye, sir." Drostan took Alynn's hand and headed towards the church. It was a good bit smaller than St. Anne's Monastery, certainly not taken care of as well, but it was the teaching inside that mattered. Drostan opened the door, and Alynn's heart skipped a beat as she stepped inside.

"Tarin?"

The building contained only one room, and that room contained only one candle. But between it and the six dirty windows that lined two of the walls, there was enough light to see by. Alynn's eyes adjusted to the dim light and saw, in the front row of pews, the red-haired head of a little boy.

Alynn took one more step into the room. "Tarin?"

The head turned around to reveal a familiar freckled face, square like her own. His eyes lit up when he saw her. "Lynder! You're back!"

Tarin's face grew blurry through the tears of joy that crept into Alynn's eyes. He flew into her welcoming arms, and she scooped him up like a toddler. "Och, Tarin...och, thank God, I've missed you!"

"I missed you too, Alynn. I knew you were out there! I knew Da would find you!"

"He did." Alynn held Tarin even closer. He buried his face in the hollow of her shoulder, just as he'd done since he was a baby, and she kissed him. "And I knew I'd find you."

Neither of them said anything for a moment. Silence wove their hearts together so that they could pick up where they had left off, yet they seemed closer than they had ever been before. When Tarin got heavy—had he grown five inches or six?—Alynn sat in a pew, Tarin on her lap, and she thanked God for him.

Drostan knelt next to them, and Tarin looked up at him. "You're the one who's marryin' Lynder, right?" he asked.

Drostan smiled. "I am. My name's Drostan."

"You'd better be nice to her, because I've a slingshot, and Connor says I'm the best shot in Skerray!"

Drostan chuckled. "I wouldn't hurt her for anything, Tarin. You've my word on that."

"Good." Tarin snuggled into Alynn's arms again, before the door flew open and a furious fireball ran down the aisle, golden hair streaming behind it.

"Tarin!"

Whether Tarin recognized his mother's voice or merely his own name didn't matter. He looked up at Caitriona, who had stopped running and knelt by the pew. Her eyes were round. For the first time, Alynn realized how similar they were to Tarin's.

"Did Captain McMahon tell you about Mum?" Alynn asked him quietly.

Tarin studied Caitriona for a moment. "Is this Mum?"

Caitriona nodded. "Tarin—can I give you a hug?"

Tarin stood and accepted Caitriona's embrace. Caitriona held him as if he was going to melt away, kissing him and pressing her eyes shut so she wouldn't cry. "I missed you," she whispered. "I never stopped lovin' you, Tarin." She wiped her eyes and took a deep breath. "Thank God you're alright."

Tarin had grown serious, as if he was thinking. "Aren't you the one who scolded the big red-headed girl because she kept pullin' on my hair?"

Caitriona laughed. "You remember that?"

"I do. It was you, wasn't it?"

"It was me, dear heart. You remember me."

Tarin looked over Caitriona's shoulder to see Rowan, and he smiled at him. "Thank you for findin' Mum and Lynder."

Rowan laughed. He drew everyone into a group hug, kissed them, and said, "I'm so glad we're all together again."

"Alynn, are you stayin' with us?" Tarin asked. "With yer gettin' married, I mean? I don't want you to leave again."

"Well, Tarin," Rowan said, "what do you say we move one last time? So we can be with Alynn. Would you like that?"

A grin lit up Tarin's face, and he jumped into Alynn's arms. He knocked her off-balance, and sent her tumbling to the ground, laughing and smiling and thanking God. With Tarin in her arms and Drostan's steady hands helping them up, Alynn was in heaven.

Tarin's first order of business was to show Alynn off to all his friends. She was presented first to the priest, Father Malcolm, who spoke in monotone and had a hairy mole near his nose. He seemed pleasant, yet unexceptional enough to decrease church attendance singlehandedly. Then there was Hamish and his sister Mairead, the stuck-up children of the dock owner. The boys had exchanged their fair share of black eyes, but neither of them seemed worse for it. But Tarin's best friend was Connor Sullivan, whose widowed mother Shona owned the house Rowan was renting.

Shona reacted to Alynn and Caitriona's presence the same way the all the other people of Skerray had. Her curious stare turned into a surprised smile, and she wished the McNeils hearty congratulations on their reunion. But while the other townspeople treated them with a cool civility, Shona's excitement was genuine. She grinned and hugged everyone and offered to make dinner since Tarin had gone through most of the food Rowan had left for him.

"Yer son's a dear, Caitriona," she said as she mixed dough for bannocks. "The whole town will miss him. Father Malcom wanted him to be the next priest, he's smart enough fer it. He's reading already."

"I kept the note you gave to Captain McMahon," Tarin told Alynn. "'Tis under my pillow."

"And I kept the note you gave to me," Alynn said. "'Tis under my cot."

"You've got yer own cot?"

"I do. And you'll have yer own cot once you come back to the monastery with us. You'll have a cell all to yerself, just like a monk."

"But I can come visit you in yer cell, right, Alynn?"

"Of course."

Tarin grinned and hugged Alynn. He'd hugged her so many times she's lost count, but they were making up for lost time. She couldn't get too many. Caitriona smiled as if her heart would burst. "Could I have a hug, too?" she asked.

Tarin gave Caitriona a hug, then stood on a kitchen chair so he could see her face better. "You don't have freckles," he noted sadly.

"I do have freckles. They're just hard to see. Look closer."

Tarin leaned closer, and he grinned when he noticed the faint flecks on Caitriona's cheeks that were invisible to most people in most lights. "I don't think they count."

"You don't! Then where did you get yers from?"

"The angels."

"The angels? Aye, I'll take that. You got yer green eyes from me, though. And what else?"

Shona found a small hand mirror and handed it to Caitriona. "This'll help. What do ye see, Tarin?"

Tarin looked carefully. The familial resemblance between him and Caitriona was there, just not easily put into words. He smiled, then she smiled, and Tarin's eyes lit up. "I smile like you," he said.

"You do."

Tarin noticed Caitriona's arm slip from his shoulder down his arm. "'Tis another hug you want, isn't it?"

Caitriona laughed, and Tarin disappeared for a moment into her embrace. Alynn couldn't bear to be left out. She wrapped her arms around Tarin and Caitriona, and Tarin squirmed with something less than joy. "Ye're squishin' me," he said, his voice muffled. Alynn and Caitriona backed up and apologized in unison, then everyone laughed.

"Set the table, dear hearts," Caitriona said, tending the bannocks while Shona chopped onions to fry with the salmon.

"I can chop onions," Alynn said.

"We can't have too many cooks in the kitchen," Shona said. "Asides, someone needs to keep Tarin out from underfoot."

Tarin grinned. Once the table was set, he hugged Alynn and refused to let go. "I really missed you," he said.

"I missed you, too."

"And that's really Mum? Not just someone we're friends with, like Captain McMahon, right?"

"Have you ever," Alynn asked, sitting on the dirt floor next to the hearth, "seen anyone who loves you the way she does?"

Tarin snuggled next to her. "Sometimes you did."

"When?"

"A lot of times. Remember that one time when we didn't get to go campin' because that nice lady let us stay at her house? And I went campin' all by myself and you and Da couldn't find me and nigh had a fit over it?"

"Och, I remember. And it was rainin' hard."

"It always rained. It still does. Here, too."

"It doesn't always rain," Alynn said, cradling Tarin close to her. "Every once in a while, we can see God smilin' at us. Like right now."

Tarin smiled. For all he'd grown, he was still little—little to her, anyway. Little enough to disappear when he buried himself in her arms. They sat for a time in silence until Drostan came into the house, then Connor with the fresh salmon, and Tarin wouldn't allow himself to be seen cuddling his sister. He instead jumped up, ran to Connor, and said, "Come, I know she's got stories to tell us."

Alynn laughed, and Drostan offered to tell the story of the day they'd first met. Both boys listened eagerly—more because swords were involved than anything else—and no one noticed when Rowan came inside. Drostan finished his story just as the salmon finished frying, and no family in Skerray had a merrier meal.

But the best was yet to come. As soon as Alynn finished washing the dishes, the McNeils and Drostan left for their own house. It felt more like a rented room at an inn than a true home; even Tarin said so. Alynn knew she could fix that. She put a kettle on for tea and turned the quilt around on the big bed so that everyone could see the patch on it. She'd made the patch herself; it was a lovely white diamond on a sea of blue, and it glowed gently, like a sail in the moonlight.

Rowan took his otterskin timpan case and found some pictures in it. There was Alynn as a toddler, holding her sister Louisa before the scarlet fever took her; there was Caitriona holding Alynn and a wee baby Tarin as tenderly as a mother could. Then there were two pictures of young girls—one of them, after close inspection and a few wrong guesses, was Caitriona before she and Rowan had married. And the second was Libby, who did look surprisingly like Alynn.

"Is she in heaven now?" Tarin asked when he saw Libby's picture.

"She is. I'm sure that she and my mum are watchin' over Louisa and Britta, tryin' to make sure they don't turn out quick-tempered and hard-headed like my big sister Maeve. And every once in a while, my da and my brother Padraig take them fishin'. Och, there must be grand fishin' in heaven."

Rowan smiled, a bit sadly, but the sadness disappeared as he took his timpan and drew his bow across the strings. The instrument sang like only an Irish timpan could. "Tarin, pick us a song."

"Play 'Drowsy Maggie,' Da."

Rowan put his fingers against the strings and made them sing; Caitriona joined in with her flute. Alynn took Tarin by the hand and said, "Do you remember the dance, Tarin?"

"What dance?"

"Come! Do it with me."

Alynn picked up her skirts so Tarin could see her feet, and she narrated her steps. "Back twice, forward twice, spin around—"

Tarin stumbled into his father's lap, and the music stopped. "I can't do it," Tarin giggled.

"Sure you can," Drostan said. "We'll show you. May I, Lynder?"

Alynn smiled, and Rowan and Caitriona started the song again. Drostan knew the steps, when to go backwards and forwards, when to spin around. Tarin watched, and when he was ready, he took Drostan's place and did his best. Alynn couldn't have been prouder of him.

The music and the dancing and the laughter lasted well into the night. It was fully dark when Rowan ran out of songs to play. Alynn's face was red from dancing, and she realized how tired she was. Tarin was already half-asleep, leaning against Caitriona's chair, smiling as her fingers played with his hair.

"Girls, take the bed," Rowan said, setting his timpan in its case. "Drostan, when are we sailin' out?"

"Around noon tomorrow, if you can manage to get packed by then. Is it alright if we make a stop before going home?"

"'Tis yer ship. So long as we're on dry land when the storms hit in September, we're grand." Rowan prayed for Alynn and Tarin, then kissed Caitriona goodnight. Alynn and Caitriona settled down on the big bed, while Rowan and Drostan made pallets on the floor.

Tarin started out on the floor, but just as Alynn was drifting off to sleep, she felt a little hand on her arm, then a knee in her side and a foot on her back. "You're sleepin' with us tonight, Tarin?" she asked.

"If 'tis alright."

"Of course 'tis alright—just this once."

Tarin nestled against her, warm and sleepy, and Alynn's heart was full as she drifted off to sleep.

She slept for perhaps an hour or two before the tolling of

church bells woke her. At first, she thought it was Prime, and that it was time for her to wake up and start her chores. Maybe Tarin would help her. But then Alynn heard shouting, the slamming of doors, and she leapt to her feet. She grabbed her sword.

"Alynn!"

She looked back to see Tarin's wide eyes staring at her. Rowan stood at the door, a metalworking hammer in his hand. Caitriona had stirred up the fire, and now she sat praying at the kitchen table. "Father, get back," Alynn ordered.

Rowan turned to her. "Go back to bed."

"You can't fight a sword with a hammer. If anyone comes through that door, you're going to die. You'll leave us alone again, Mum a widow. You don't want that."

"I'm not about to let my daughter—"

The door burst open, and a naked sword glinted in the firelight, poised to bite into Rowan's neck. Eyes locked on the threat, Alynn parried the blow in one swipe and sent the attacker's head rolling in another. Energy coursed through her. No one threatened a berserker's family and lived to tell the tale.

Rowan's eyes were wide. "You just—"

Ignoring him, Alynn leapt over the corpse and into the raid. The Darsidians were everywhere, but they hadn't done anything. Not one home was on fire. Not one woman was screaming. Everyone was fighting back. If Alynn hadn't been in a berserker's trance, she would have thanked God she'd found Tarin when she did.

There was a cry down the road; Shona the landlady was widowed, and her son Connor wasn't nearly old enough to protect her. Alynn flew down the street, ignoring the rain, ignoring everything but the power that flooded her. Shona's door was open. Alynn ran the intruder through before anyone could say anything.

"Get me yer fireplace poker," she said.

Trembling, Shona obliged, and Alynn pinned the dead man to the exterior wall. Hopefully, he'd deter anyone else from bothering the Sullivans.

An idea struck Alynn, and she ran back to the rented house and grabbed the Viking's severed head. She couldn't bring herself to cradle it the way Saint Cuthbert held the head of Saint Oswald, so she held it by the hair like a lantern and set off for the pier. A few men stared at her. Let them stare. It wasn't every day one saw a girl in a bloodstained nightshift who carried a sword in her right hand and a severed head in her left.

Finally, she found her mark. Dark hair, green eyes, richly dressed—this man was Norbert, son of Hrodolf chief of Darsidia, the younger and gentler brother of the insolent Nokkvi. Drostan was talking to him, shouting from a distance to lessen the risk of combat. Alynn didn't care. She walked straight up to Norbert, put the severed head inches from his face, and pressed her sword against the back of his neck.

"Gather your men, Norbert," she hissed. "Leave in peace or die in pain. Your choice."

Norbert opened his mouth, and for a while, nothing came out of it. Alynn pushed her sword tighter against his neck. Drostan called her name. She blocked out his voice.

"Stop," Norbert breathed. "I'd gather the men if I could. But they're relentless, driven, greedy. I'm a child in their eyes. They won't listen to me."

"Then give them reason to."

Norbert nodded, almost imperceptibly. "I might need your help."

"We'll both help you," Drostan said. Hurriedly, he pulled Alynn away from Norbert and directed her back towards the fray. "Alynn, don't kill anyone else."

"You don't know how going berserk works, do you?"

"You're still in charge of yourself. Remember that. Don't kill anyone unless you have to, alright?"

Alynn took a deep breath. The Darsidians were still there. People were still in danger. Her heart was still beating like a drum, her limbs still trembling with energy. It exhilarated her.

Norbert blew a horn, and some of the men made their way

back to the ships. True to his word, though, a good dozen refused to stop fighting. Alynn drew an empowering breath. "Norbert."

"What?"

Once again, she stretched forth the severed head. "Take this."

"Milady—"

"Grab it by the hair, blast it, and tell people that if they don't listen to you, 'tis their head next. Now go." Trembling, Norbert obliged, and Alynn spotted two Vikings looting the smithy. "Och, don't ye dare, men. Don't ye dare touch my father's work." Drostan drew his sword and ran after her.

Both Vikings felt a blade at their necks a moment later. "Didn't ye hear yer leader's horn?" Alynn snapped. "Drop what ye've taken. Leave in peace or die in pain."

"I'd rather die than surrender," one of the men scowled.

"Would you die at the hands of a woman?"

Drostan put a small scratch on his captive's neck. "Alynn the Dauntless takes no quarter, lads. You'd be wise to heed her."

The men left for their ship, and Norbert joined them with the rest of the stragglers. He'd long since discarded the severed head, but he still looked sick. Shivering, Alynn glanced around the village to make certain everything was peaceful. Had the rain picked up, or was she just now noticing it?

"It's alright now, Alynn." Drostan took off his tunic and slipped it over her head; she was quick to drop her sword to put her arms through the sleeves. It was warm, and it smelled nice. "They've left. They won't come back. And your family's safe. That's the important thing."

Alynn hoped with everything within her that her family was alright. She wouldn't be sure until she saw for herself. Gathering what was left of her energy, she picked up her sword and ran back to the house.

It was warm inside. Tarin was there, running to hug her, calling her name. Everyone was talking. "Lynder, what were you doing out there?" "What happened?" "Is that blood? Are you hurt?" "Give her some space, now, let her catch her breath."

"Ye're alright?" Alynn asked. The warrior beat of her heart collapsed into a frightened patter, as rapid as the steps of a child running to his parents' bed after a nightmare. "Ye're alright, all of ye?"

"Da threw up because he saw a dead person," Tarin said. "And you're cold. But we're alright besides that."

Alynn was more than cold. She was dizzy and trembling and a fog was coming over her mind. "I'm tired," she said. "Let's go back to sleep."

"Can I have my tunic back?" Drostan asked.

"You can't. It smells nice."

Caitriona laughed. "You're the only one who thinks that, dear heart. Does anyone want tea while the fire's going?"

Alynn declined shakily as she returned to the bed, her hand on Tarin's steady shoulder. The next thing she knew, Caitriona was washing the breakfast dishes while Drostan helped Rowan and Tarin pack their few belongings. Alynn hardly had time to dress and eat the bowl of stirabout kept warm for her before they left for the *Eagle's Flight*, sent off with the blessings of Father Malcolm and a crowd of grateful villagers.

Instead of going north, Drostan had the ship skirt the coast to the east. It took Alynn a while to realize that the mainland wasn't getting any smaller. "So where exactly are we goin'?" she asked Drostan, who had been standing nervously on the prow for an hour and a half.

"Meet—visit—I don't know if anyone's still alive, and even if they are, they won't recognize me—"

"Who?"

"The McLains. My mother's family. I thought that, at least, we could stop by her grave, say a prayer—why am I nervous?"

"You've every right to be," Alynn said, taking his hand. "More than likely, someone's still there for you. And I've no doubt they'll love you."

Drostan chuckled. "They have every reason not to."

"Don't say that! What did you ever do to them?"

"They'll see my father in me."

"They'll see yer mother in you, love. How couldn't they love the one piece of Elspeth McLain that's still on this earth?"

"I suppose you're right." Drostan drew his spyglass to his eye and wiped his hands on his trousers. "Rowan, Havard, haul wind. Folkvard, bring us starboard."

"Towards the port, sir?"

"Starboard. Right. Towards land."

"But the port—the dock—"

Drostan sighed and took the tiller. "You build ships, Folkvard, why am I surprised you can't sail them? Alynn, would you mind coming to shore with me?"

"Can I come?" Tarin begged.

Drostan smiled. "I need you to help your father keep Folkvard and Havard in line, alright? If they start fighting, you've my permission to throw them overboard."

"Yay!"

With a deep breath, Drostan ran his hand through his hair and turned the tiller. The ship was soon in port, and Drostan found the dockmaster—a man in his twenties with hair every bit as red as his own. "I'm not sure if we'll be here overnight," he said. "It depends on how much of my kin is still alive."

"Who's yer kin?"

"Elspeth McLain, died in 951. She's at the church? St. Philip's?"

"Should be. McLain's a common name around here, but I'll see if anyone knows her. The church is up the hill to yer right, the cemetery's around back. I'll take yer fee tomorrow morn."

"But if we leave afore—"

"Then I'll not have lost anything."

"Thank you, sir." Drostan took Alynn's hand and found the right path to the church. Alynn found herself trotting to keep up with him. "Help me look," he said.

"Suppose there's no names?"

"There's a white rosebush. At least there was."

There were quite a few bushes growing in the cemetery. Alynn scanned all of them—pink roses, red roses, no flowers at all. Finally, she found it.

"Drostan," she called after pausing to gaze for a while. "She's here."

Drostan hurried over and knelt at the gravestone, dusting it off, finding nothing written on it. "Hello, Mother," he stammered. "I...it's been a while. Fifteen years, I guess, since I've seen you last. I had to see you while we were still in Scotland...just so say hello, I suppose...and tell you I'm getting married. This is Alynn. She's the kindest heart on St. Anne's Cleft. You'd have loved her, Mother."

He drew a breath, laying a hand on the gravestone. "And Teague! Well—that's what Mother wanted to call you. Father would have named you Idir, but he wouldn't have settled for anything other than Teague after what happened. I keep thinking you'd have loved playing with Tarin, but you'd be Alynn's age now. If you'd lived, I'd have asked you to be chief instead of me. Father's doing fine. He misses you both, probably more than I do...of course he does. I never knew you...."

Alynn knelt and put her arm around Drostan when his voice trailed off. She wanted so badly to say something to comfort him, but none of her words seemed right. "I wish I could have known you," Drostan said. "I wish I remembered you. I wish I knew what you looked like, what your voice sounded like...what it's like to have a mum and a wee brother."

"They're in heaven, love," Alynn promised. "You'll see them again someday."

"I know Teague is—but Mother—"

"She loved Jesus, didn't she?" She smiled, hoping she was comforting him. "What did yer father tell us? No one could love Jesus the way she did and not get to heaven."

"Lynder?"

"What?"

"Do me a favor—put a braid in my hair, just a wee one."

Alynn did as she was instructed, and Drostan took his dagger and cut it off. He tucked it under the roots of the rosebush. "I know it's too late to ask you to remember me, but I want you to know that I'll always remember you. Both of you. Mother—Teague—I love you. It was nice to see you both."

He stood, helping Alynn to her feet, and drew her into his arms. "Thank you," he said. "I didn't want to do this alone."

Alynn was about to tell him that he'd never be alone again so long as she could help it, but the gate to the cemetery squeaked open before she could say anything. Rather, a gate that was accustomed to squeaking was thrown wildly open, and it released a noise more akin to a shrill scream. The dockmaster was there, along with an older, slightly rounder, and weather-worn man who was apparently his father.

"Drostan?" the older man asked.

"Aye, sir?"

"God be praised—I'm Elspeth's brother, yer Uncle Paul."

Drostan laughed. He hugged Paul, then the younger man, his cousin Alistair. "Och, the last time I saw ye, ye still slept in diapers," Paul said. "Look at ye, yer da's build, yer mum's hair—how have ye been faring? How's yer da?"

"I've been alright. Father's alive and well, never remarried."

Paul smiled. "Och, aye. We figured as much. It's hard to love a woman the way yer da loved Speth and move on. And that uncle of yers, the one we heard stories about—"

Drostan nodded towards Alynn. "She did everyone a favor and killed him a while back. That's Alynn McNeil, we're getting married."

Paul's eyes lit up. "Welcome to the family, Alynn! Come—spend the night. We'll catch up over dinner. Yer Aunt Aggie's made partan bree and blaeberry pie."

"Partan bree?" Alynn asked.

"Crab soup, lass. And plenty of stockfish to go with it. Do ye still eat stockfish, Drostan?"

"Aye, it's one of my favorites. Alynn's parents and her wee

brother are with us. Would they—"

"The more the merrier!" Paul said. "And tell yer da to come with next time. We miss him. Now! We'll have yer Uncle Micheal and Aunt Gormlaith come up with their brood, and yer Aunt Mairi and Uncle Pat with theirs—ye've fourteen cousins, three second cousins, a few fourth cousins thrice removed—"

"Do they count?" Drostan asked.

"Hardly, but they're still McLains. Come! Alynn, get yer family! We'll have a feast!"

A feast it was, with three aunts and three uncles and too many cousins to keep track of, and the most delicious crab soup Alynn had ever tasted. While Drostan declined Paul's offer to stay another day—he had his village to return to—he sat up until dawn with them, laughing, talking, and getting the recipe for partan bree.

"I know it won't be the same when you make it," he told Alynn as he handed her the recipe written on a piece of birchbark. "And I'm alright with that. Just practice once or twice afore you inflict your attempt on the rest of us, aye?"

Alynn smiled and shook her head. "You're going to sleep the moment we're on a set course."

"Aye, Cap'n Lynder." He kissed her cheek and took the tiller. "Now! Let's go home!"

TWENTY

"Ow!"

"Sorry—"

"Quit pullin' so!"

"We would, if you'd quit movin'—"

"Aunt Ruari—ow!"

Caitriona smiled compassionately and kissed Alynn's head. "Ruari, be a bit gentler."

Captain McMahon had sent word of the wedding to Alynn's family in Limerick, and Caitriona's mother, youngest brother, and two of her sisters had come for the event. Everyone else sent their love and said they would have come with, but someone had to stay home and watch the children—and it took everyone's help to raise Alynn's twenty-one cousins, with two more on the way.

Alynn's grandmother was the great Maura Quaid. Few other women in Limerick could say they'd borne fourteen children and raised ten of them into adulthood. She was everything Alynn remembered—soft hands, sweet smiles, wise words, and a sharp tongue. Aunt Sorcha was a taller and thinner version of her mother, but Aunt Ruari was round with red curls and a harsh hand as she brushed and styled Alynn's hair.

Uncle Oisin was nineteen, but he looked seventeen and

acted fourteen. No one expected much of the youngest of ten children, and Oisin was in no hurry to impress anyone. He sat in a corner, eating an apple, grinning at Alynn. "So what will that make Drostan?" he asked, his voice deepened beyond Alynn's recognition. "My nephew-in-law?"

"A better man than you," Sorcha teased.

"How many braids?" Ruari asked.

"Seven small ones—three up, four down, and don't forget to leave plenty hangin' loose in the back," Caitriona said.

Maura smiled. "Och, won't she be a vision! The angels in heaven will envy her."

Ruari tugged on Alynn's hair too harshly, and she winced. "Ow!"

"Ruari," Caitriona said, "isn't there somethin' else you can do?"

She turned and saw Tarin sitting on Alynn's bed. His eyes grew wide, and he fled from the room before anything else could be said. Everyone laughed. "'Tis alright, Tarin," Alynn called after him. "Come back."

Reluctantly, Tarin came back into the room and sat on the floor at Alynn's feet. "Don't let her get to me," he whispered.

"I won't, dear heart."

Eight hands made quick work of Alynn's hair, and then Caitriona took her place in the hairstyling chair. Her hair was done much more simply—in four braids, three piled on her head and a fourth trailing down to her knees. With her hair thus arranged and her Norse frock exchanged for a cream-colored gown with hanging sleeves and a plaid of darkest green, she looked like a queen.

Alynn stood and shook out her skirts, and footsteps sounded in the doorway. It was Leif, smiling, eyes alight. "And I thought your mother looked beautiful in that dress."

Alynn blushed, but Caitriona chased him out. "Faith, Leif! Where do you need to be right now? Go!" Alynn laughed, her fingers caressing the crimson silk of her gown. It had an ivory center, golden lacing, and hanging sleeves, yet she didn't feel out-of-place in it. She felt beautiful.

Rowan stepped into the room, his hair curled by the women's wishes. It suited neither his face nor his personality, but his everyday clothes, freshly cleaned and regally draped, suited both. "Are you ready, Alynn?"

"I think so."

"Don't be nervous," Ruari said.

"You've nothin' to be nervous about," Maura said.

Sorcha smiled. "You've found a good, Godly man, Lynder. He'll care for you well."

"You'll have cute babies," Oisin said, his mouth full of apple. "Just make sure the last one doesn't turn out like me."

Rowan raised an eyebrow at him. "Oisin, I was hopin' you'd have changed a bit since I'd last seen you."

Oisin pretended to be offended and stroked the red moss on his upper lip. "I'm a man now! I've got a mustache!"

Rowan laughed. Oisin turned red, and Caitriona shooed him out the door. "Och, make yerself useful, Oisin. Go save some seats for everyone." He stood up, kissed his sister's cheek, and nearly ran into Leif as he left for the chapel.

"I'm leaving," Leif promised. "But here's this."

Into Caitriona's hands he set something made of gold—or gilded, at least—set with rubies and clear crystals. Alynn had heard of Norse wedding crowns. The poorer brides wore wreaths of flowers on their heads, and Alynn would have loved wearing roses and violets. But she certainly wasn't going to object to the elaborate diadem as Caitriona placed it among her braids.

"I wore that crown once," she said. "It was one of the worst days of my life. But I pray that today's one of the best days of yers, my dear heart." Eyes glistening, she kissed her and smiled. "I'll always love you. And so long as I draw breath, I'm here for you."

Rowan blinked. He was thinking, trying to find words of his own, as he set a rough hand on her silk-clad shoulder. "You've found a rare man," he said. "He's been through a lot since I've met him, and he's kept his head through all of it. He still loves God, still loves you. I apologize for comin' between ye."

"Thank you."

Carefully, as if he was worried about ruining her appearance, Rowan embraced her and kissed her cheek. "Come on," he said. "Everyone's ready."

Alynn carefully descended the stairs and found herself standing in front of the chapel's double doors, arm in arm with Rowan, her stomach churning with excitement. The aisle was sprinkled with flower petals thanks to Kyrri, who was standing next to Maggie on the right side of Lukas's lectern. Nora McKenzie played the songs of heaven on her harp. Lukas stood behind his lectern, looking proudly at Alynn. And to his right stood Drostan, handsomely dressed in the same outfit he wore to his election feast, wiping his sweating hands on his trousers.

Alynn took a deep breath and stepped onto the flower-carpeted aisle. Her heart was still pounding with excitement, and the fact that she was being stared at by an audience even larger than regularly came to Mass didn't help. But as every step she took brought her closer to Drostan, and every moment closer to being his wife, she slowly calmed down.

Rowan squeezed Alynn's hand as he gave her to Drostan. "I love you," he whispered. "Ye've my blessings."

Alynn hugged her father and kissed his cheek. "I love you too," she whispered back. But as Rowan sat next to Caitriona, she couldn't have felt happier as she faced Drostan in front of the lectern.

"We are gathered here today in the presence of God an' these witnesses to join Drostan Johann Leifson and Alynn Maura McNeil in holy matrimony," Lukas began. "The family was founded back in Genesis, where it is said in chapter two, verse twenty-four, 'For this reason a man will leave his father and mother and be united to his wife, and they will become one flesh.' Therefore, it is my great pleasure...."

Alynn started tuning out. She had never seen Drostan

gazing at her with such a sparkle in his eyes, or felt his fingers intertwine with hers so lovingly. She smiled.

"First Corinthians chapter thirteen tells us what true love is," Lukas continued. "It says, 'If I speak in the tongues of men and of angels, but have not love, I am only a resounding gong or a clanging cymbal. If I have the gift of prophecy and can fathom all mysteries and all knowledge, and if I have a faith that can move mountains, but have not love, I am nothing. If I give all I possess to the poor and surrender my body to the flames, but have not love, I gain nothing.'"

Lukas took a red cord, made for the occasion, and loosely tied Alynn's hand to Drostan's. His voice continued, strong and sweet and melodic.

"'Love is patient, love is kind. It does not envy, it does not boast, it is not proud. It is not rude, it is not self-seeking, it is not easily angered, it keeps no record of wrongs. Love does not delight in evil but rejoices with the truth. It always protects, always trusts, always hopes, always perseveres. Love never fails....

"'And now these three remain: faith, hope and love. But the greatest of these is love.'"

Maggie handed Alynn her sword, and Drostan was given his. They exchanged weapons carefully—Alynn had dropped Drostan's during the practice ceremony, as it was a bit heavier than her own—but this time, everything went well. Then Lukas handed them each a ring.

Alynn's head spun. Drostan had agreed to wear a ring.

"I give you my sword as a sign of my protection," Drostan told her. "And I give you this ring as a sign of my love. I swear to you that no matter what comes, neither trial nor plague nor famine will take my love away from you. Alynn the Dauntless, you are the best thing that's ever happened to me. Nothing but death will take you from my arms."

He set the ring on the crossguard of the sword she held. It nearly slid off, but he caught it, and placed it more carefully the second time. It stayed.

Alynn realized it was her turn to speak. Her mouth was so dry the words had a hard time coming out, but they came nevertheless. "I give you my sword, though I can wield it; I give you this ring, though you will have no need of it, for by my actions I will remind you daily of my love for you. I give you respect, for you deserve it; I give you my trust, for you have earned it. And the sun will shine brighter upon us both, for between you and God, I lack nothing."

She placed the ring on Drostan's crossguard and gazed into his eyes. He was proud of her.

Lukas took their swords. "Hurry and kiss each other," he said, quietly so the audience couldn't hear. "Afore I cry in front of everyone."

Gazing into Alynn's sparkling eyes, Drostan slipped one hand behind her head and his other around her waist. Slowly, they stepped closer and pressed their lips together. Warmth and love and belonging surrounded them; they parted for breath and kissed again. It was only when they parted a second time that they realized everyone was cheering for them.

"Long live Chief Drostan and Lady Alynn!"

Drostan laughed. He slipped his ring on Alynn's finger, and she put her ring on his. Alynn looked at the crowd; Rowan and Caitriona and all her kin were crying, and Leif didn't look too far from tears himself, but sweet Tarin was smiling. As all Irish brides did, Alynn turned and kissed Lukas on the cheek before she sailed down the aisle, her hand still tied to Drostan's.

Humility and Thrymja were saddled and waiting outside, ready to take them to the wedding feast at Samkoma. The love-knot slipped off their wrists; Alynn would treasure it forever. Drostan helped Alynn into the saddle, and they took off, nearly racing, laughing with exhilaration.

This is home, Alynn thought as she caught a glimpse of Drostan's eyes smiling at her. She'd done it. She'd grown up, she'd found love, she was ready to start a family of her own. It would be hard. She knew that. But it would be worth it. What was that song Caitriona had written after her own wedding?

It seems the wind blows colder now,
The clouds obscure the light,
But to you my vows I've made,
And for your love I'll fight.

We'll make a sun to shine on us,
We'll dance in light so grand,
We'll laugh and smile and pray and sing,
With you I'll always stand.

August 3, A.D. 966—

So! All this fuss and bother over dresses and feasts and hair and flowers has finally paid off. As of the twenty-sixth of July, Alynn is married, the ceremony was beautiful, and I miss her. She returned on Sabbath for Mass, and I trust she and Drostan will attend faithfully. But I've never seen her happier, and I cannot help but rejoice with her.

Though Alynn is gone, I still have her family. Rowan's wounded heart is healing splendidly, and Tarin is a dear. He is every bit as sweet as his sister and highly intelligent. He's already picked up quite a few words of Norse. Brett Oddson, whom I met at Althing, will be arriving from Hrafney before the summer's out. I shall offer to train Tarin along with him for the pastorate.

For Caitriona, though, I have my worries. She hasn't been herself since Alynn's wedding—she falls asleep easily, and her eating habits have changed. Rowan is treating her gently. I feel he knows something Tarin and I do not. Her kinswomen, too, were whispering amongst themselves, saying how there were already seven Mauras and five Donnells in the family so they should pick a creative name, and how they're certain everything will go well, and how they're happy for her. I suppose that, if anything of significance is happening, Tarin and I will be notified eventually.

Caitriona's mother is a remarkable woman—I see now why the name Maura Quaid is famous in Limerick. She assured me that, though I no longer operate in the capacity of father towards Alynn, I can consider myself her grandfather. She also gave me her opinion that grandparenting is much more enjoyable than parenting, and I shall take her word for it. After ten children and twenty-three grandchildren, she should know.

While Tarin is doubtlessly the brightest blessing God has given me lately, I must note that one of the kittens born during Althing is turning out exceptionally friendly. He's a lovely silver color, forever rubbing against my legs and hiding in my sleeves.

In fact, he's currently asleep on my shoulder. I confer upon him the title of Theophilus the Fourth, long may he live.

I'm alone now. The McNeils are seeing Caitriona's family safely to the ship and might not return until after dinner, unless Alynn invites them to spend the night. Though I still dislike being alone, I take solace in the fact that my family will return soon.

Lord, I thank You for settling me in a home as the happy father of children. I pray Your blessings on my sons and daughters, and upon all the little ones to come. May we keep the unity of the Spirit in the bond of peace, loving each other as You love us.

My family—what a beautiful pair of words!

—L. McCamden

AUTHOR'S NOTE

I can pinpoint the exact moment I got the idea for most of my books. For *Where the Clouds Catch Fire,* it was the moment I watched a music video. The very first book I ever wrote—one no one will ever read—was based on the imaginary friends I grew up with. But this book is different. There wasn't a moment of inspiration. It just seemed like the next logical step in telling Alynn's story.

As I did with the first book, I stopped myself midway through the drafting process and said, "Wait a minute. I haven't thrown any Christian things in here." So I picked a topic that was near and dear to my own heart: God's faithfulness.

I've seen God work in my own life. I prayed for friends; He gave me some. I had anxiety for five years; He healed me. I know that the God Who loves me enough to send His Son to die for me, Who was with me through every panic attack, Who gave me a job and a passion and a family, won't stand to watch me suffer. Not with poverty. Not with sickness. Not with fear.

Paul asks us what can separate us from Christ's love. Hardships? No; even death brings us victory. Rainclouds don't mean the sun's stopped shining. Bad things don't mean God isn't there. It's our job to trust Him, even when it's raining.

Well, I have an associate degree to earn and a few more books to write, so I'll see you, God willing, in the third book of the Clouds Aflame series.

Blessings,

M.J. Piazza

ABOUT THE AUTHOR

Micalah Elise Janelle Piazza grew up surrounded by books in northern Illinois. Her flexible schedule as a homeschooler afforded her plenty of time to read and write, and she began work on her first novel at the age of ten. She is currently a full-time college student and after-school tutor, playing piano on her church's worship team and crocheting in her spare time. She lives in Texas with her parents, sister, and dog. You can contact her at m.j.piazzaauthor@gmail.com, or on her official website, www.cloudsaflame.com.

Made in the
USA
Middletown, DE